A Sydnee Marcola Adventure

AGU: BORDER PATROL

CLIDEPP REQUITAL

Book 2

BY

THOMAS DEPRIMA

Vinnia Publishing - U.S.A.

AGU:™

Clidepp Requital

AGU:™ Border Patrol – Book 2

Copyright ©2014 by Thomas J. DePrima

ISBN-13: **978-1-61931-025-4**

ISBN-10: **1619310252**

Cover art by: Martin J. Cannon

1st Edition
Amazon Distribution

Appendices containing political and technical data highly pertinent to this series are included at the back of this book.

To contact the author, or see information about his other novels, visit:

http://www.deprima.com

Kudos to my cover artist, Martin Cannon, for the incredible
cover image he created for this book.

This AGU:™ Border Patrol series includes:

Citizen X
Clidepp Requital

The AGU:™ series:

A Galaxy Unknown
Valor at Vauzlee
The Clones of Mawcett
Trader Vyx
Milor!
Castle Vroman
Against All Odds
Return to Dakistee
Retreat And Adapt

The AGU:™ SCI series:

The Star Brotherhood

When The Spirit... series:

When The Spirit Moves You
When The Spirit Calls

Colton James novels:

A World Without Secrets
Vengeance Is Personal

Table of Contents

Chapter One
~ May 12th, 2285 ~

"X, we've just received a message from the *Glassama*," his Chief of Staff reported during their daily morning meeting. "They were attacked as they were about to finish off the Spacc warship."

"What?" the Supreme Rebel Leader, screamed. "We told that idiot NOT to attack the Spacc ship."

"He claims the Spaccs targeted his FTL envelope generator as he was about to depart the area. He then saw it as his duty to destroy the Spacc ship. But during the engagement, our freighter attacked the *Abissto* with the torpedoes we had secreted inside ordinary freight containers. The *Furmmara* was then destroyed when the *Abissto* returned fire."

"Great Lullelian, it's a nightmare! Why did our freighter attack one of our own warships?"

"The *Abissto* was attacking the *Glassama*."

X groaned. "Do I have to drag every morsel from you? Why was the *Abissto* attacking the *Glassama*?"

"We don't yet know who was in command of the *Abissto*. The *Furmmara* hadn't visited it yet. As far as we knew, the *Abissto* was still in orbit above Diabolisto, and the oxygen generation system was not operational."

"Then someone must have fixed it if it was able to attack the *Glassama*."

"It had to be Space Command. They had refused border entry to all Clidepp military vessels, so it couldn't have been anyone else."

"Damn all Spaccs."

"What do you wish to do?"

"Do?" X continued in a loud voice. "What *can* we do? That operation has now ended, and ended badly. I assume the Spaccs have picked up our people on Diabolisto?"

"Unknown, but they must have. We've received no reports from them in months, and not a single query message has been answered since we first learned that Spaccs were in the vicinity. They must either be in Spacc custody— or dead."

"We'll have to assume the worst. It's time to proceed with the next step, and I've just made a decision about the target. The Spaccs will regret sticking their noses in our business once they see grief-stricken Terran families on their nightly news. Instead of the Clidepp embassy on Earth, our new target will be the GA Trade Conference."

"X, no! I mean, are you sure about this? It was one thing to attack a Clidepp diplomatic ship in GA space, but to destroy a GA political event and perhaps kill hundreds or thousands of GA citizens? I think you might be going too far."

"And what has the GA Senate done to stop the spilling of innocent blood in the Clidepp nation? Nothing. They talk about freedom and peace and then say what's happening in our nation is none of their affair. Well, we're going to make it their affair. It's becoming clear that we can't defeat the Clidepp military on our own. At best we can just drag out this civil war for annuals until everyone is so tired of war that one side or the other capitulates. We must do whatever's necess-ary to involve the GA in this war, and then let *them* defeat the Clidepp military."

"Whenever someone has attacked the GA, Admiral Jenetta Carver has been called in to defeat the attackers. Then she absorbs the other nation into the GA. We'll lose our indepen-dence if that happens. We'll just become Region Four of the GA."

"Could the GA be a worse master than the Triumvirate? Does the GA torture innocent citizens and send them to death camps? No! Being absorbed by the GA might be infinitely better than the existence our people have now."

"Do you really want us to be part of the GA?"

"No, not really. What I want is for the GA to take on the Triumvirate and squeeze their heads until the blood flows freely from their eyes and ears. Then we'll offer to step in and take over the reins of power. If we handle this properly, the GA will be happy to back away rather than getting involved in yet another nation's messy reconstruction."

"They won't let us take power if they learn we've killed their innocent citizens."

"That's the *only* way to get them involved, but we'll plant irrefutable evidence that the Triumvirate was behind the act."

"But why would the Triumvirate attack a GA trade event?"

"To make the GA believe we were actually responsible, and we'll even name the minister who was behind the attack."

"But if the GA thinks the Triumvirate is guilty, they'll want to deal with them directly. They won't want us involved."

"They will after we plant evidence that we're really responsible."

"But— but if they believe us to be responsible, they'll ally themselves with the Triumvirate and both will come after us."

"No, they won't. The Spacc Intelligence service is the best there is. They'll discover that the Triumvirate was guilty all along."

"How will they do that?"

"The evidence we'll plant pointing to our involvement will eventually take them to that conclusion."

"What? I'm confused. I don't understand."

"Don't worry. I know what I'm doing. I've been planning this for a very long time. I'll be leading the Spaccs around by their noses until they're worn out trying to figure out who was responsible. They'll be delighted to let us assume the reins of power for the new Society of Aligned Planets."

Having been out of touch with family and friends since first being marooned on Diabolisto meant that Sydnee had dozens of vidMails to view and answer once communications were restored. Damage resulting from the collision with the rebel-controlled *Glassama* during the attempted envelope-merge hadn't been repaired, but one of the rescue ships had loaned the *Perry* a portable communications system. However, so much had happened that she didn't know where to begin with her responses.

Sydnee feared telling her mother that she had almost been killed three times, but when the transport ship carrying the *Perry* reached Earth, that information could become public knowledge. A formal Board of Inquiry would be convened to investigate the envelope-merge accident, the attack on the rebel camp on Diabolisto, the loss of the three Marines during a later battle on Diabolisto, her deadly shootout with Colonel Suflagga, the near destruction of a freighter and loss of cargo, the space battle with rebels from a neighboring nation that resulted in the near complete loss of the *Perry,* and the total destruction of the two stolen Clidepp destroyers, the *Glassama* and the *Abissto*.

Almost as daunting a duty was that of replying to Katarina's vidMails that reported how Admiral Carver's Second Fleet had defeated the Uthlaro armada handily and annexed the former Uthlaro territory, now known as Region Three, thereby forever bringing the Tsgardi-Hudeerac-Uthlaro-Gondusan accord to an end. Her best friend had had a front row seat to the final conflict from the Auxiliary Command and Control Bridge aboard the battleship *Pholus,* and Katarina's excitement was obvious in her vidMails as she related the events in a play-by-play account of the battle. Her recounting of the event took several days because each vidMail ended suddenly when it reached the maximum allowable time limit for daily transmissions.

Then there was the vidMail from her brother. Sterling had stopped responding to Sydnee's vidMails years ago while she was still a student at the Northern Hemisphere Space Academy, so she was delighted to have received a vidMail from him now but a little frightened at the same time. Why did he choose to send a vidMail now? He couldn't know that she had been aboard the *Perry* because they hadn't spoken in all those years, and she had eventually stopped sending unanswered messages. She decided to respond to his vidMail last and chose not to even listen to his message until the others had been dealt with.

The oldest vidMails from her sister Sheree were as light as always, so Sydnee put those aside. The later vidMails showed Sheree's real concern for her sister's failure to respond, so she decided to answer those first and would touch upon the subjects of the earlier vidMails if she had time.

"Hi, sis," Sydnee began as she smiled and stared into the camera lens while she recorded the first vidMail. "I'm sorry I haven't been able to respond until now. The *Perry's* communication arrays were both damaged in a collision during an attempted interdiction stop. The people who hijacked the other ship tried a dumb maneuver that caused severe damage to both ships. We couldn't even communicate with Space Command HQ to report the problem. I'm fine, and no one aboard the *Perry* was seriously injured. Actually, I wasn't even aboard the ship when the accident occurred because I was on a mission to a nearby planet. I was ferrying a MAT full of Marines down to the surface when the *Perry* detected the hijacked ship entering and then immediately leaving planetary orbit. They took off in hot pursuit, and when the ship failed to stop for inspection, the *Perry* attempted to stop it forcefully.

"The hijackers were stopped, but only because their ship was too badly damaged to continue on. It took months for the engineers to repair enough of the damage so the ships could even maneuver again, and then there was a small battle when the hijacked ship tried to get away— again. Don't tell Mom about the reason for the damage because I know how she worries about me and my being in Space Command. But I have to tell you I've never felt more alive than during the past few months. I was really dreading this posting, but it's turned out to be so much more than I ever expected. I've made a number of wonderful new friends out here, and they're the kind of people who you can always trust to have your back in a fight. That last part is probably something else you shouldn't tell Mom.

"Because our ship was so badly damaged, we're going to be leaving here soon and returning to Earth aboard a transporter ship that will bring the *Perry* to the Mars shipyard for repair. The transporter is one of the new DS vessels, so I'll probably be home in a couple of months.

"I love you, and I'll see you soon.

"Sydnee Marcola, Lieutenant(jg), aboard the SC destroyer *Perry*. Message complete."

Sydnee took a deep breath and then immediately began composing a message to Katarina. "Computer, new message to Katarina Somulowski, Lieutenant(jg) aboard the SC battleship *Pholus* in Region Two. Begin message.

"Hi, Kat. I've just been viewing your vidMail segments about the great victory over the Uthlaro armada. The situation sounds like it was terribly exciting— and dangerous, so I'm glad you're safe and that it's over. The fight with the THUGs is bound to go down as the most difficult war in Space Command history and the best tactically coordinated and fought. It has to be wonderful to be in Admiral Carver's command, even if you're a low-level officer who normally spends most of her days training. Remember what they taught us at the Academy— all of the training will come in handy some day.

"We've had a little excitement out here, but it pales in comparison to what you've been through, so I'll tell you about it one day when you're bored silly again and want to view something other than a training manual.

"We're going to be headed to Earth soon aboard one of the new DS transporter ships because of severe damage sustained to the *Perry* during an envelope-merge attempt. It's possible the *Perry* might even be retired— *finally*. I have no idea where I'll be sent if that happens. Captain Lidden says he'll recommend me for transfer to a ship in a more forward area, but with the situation in Region Two resolved and things heating up along the Clidepp Border, I suppose it'd be difficult to find a more forward location than right here.

"Sorry to talk so fast, but because the demand for vidMail time is so high right now, I have to cut this short. Once we're on the transport I should be able to catch up.

"Be well and stay safe. I love you.

"Sydnee Marcola, Lieutenant(jg), aboard the SC destroyer *Perry*. Message complete."

Sydnee took another deep breath. She would have loved to tell Katarina about her own adventure, but she didn't want to spoil the moment for Kat. She would view all of Kat's vidMails and simply share in her best friend's excitement for now. Her own tales could wait.

The next vidMail would go to her mother, so she took several deep breaths to compose herself. Before she started the recording, she checked her face in the mirror to see if her expression looked bored enough.

"Computer, new message to Kathee Deleone, Park Central Towers, New York City, USNA, Earth. Begin message.

"Hi, Mom. Sorry I haven't vidMailed lately, but the communication equipment on the *Perry* hasn't been working in months. They just got it restored. We haven't even been able to contact Space Command.

"I'm fine and looking forward to seeing Earth again real soon. Our ship is returning to Mars for repair work, so I should be there in a couple of months.

"Nothing new to report here. Just the same old job. Katarina tells me the war in Region Two is over. That's great news. Now maybe we can have some peace for a while.

"My love to everybody.

"Sydnee Marcola, Lieutenant(jg), aboard the SC destroyer *Perry*. Message complete."

Sydnee breathed a sigh of relief once she'd gotten through the entire message to her mother. She always felt a tinge of guilt at perpetrating the deception, but she knew her mom would be pleased if she believed her daughter was bored and safe. Consequently, Sydnee always tried to make her mom believe there was no danger in her job.

She thought about viewing her brother's vidMail next, but decided to relax just a bit more after the mental strain of recording the first three vidMails, each with its special considerations.

As she lay back in her rack, she stared up at the overhead and wished she could be totally honest with everyone. It was a lot of work watching every word she'd spoken and then remembering how she'd handled every previous delicate conversation. She hadn't lied to anyone, although she had stretched the truth to the breaking point with her mom, but that was necessary to give her mom some peace of mind. Life had been so much simpler when she was just a cadet at NHSA.

Now that the comparatively *easy* vidMails had been taken care of, it was time to turn her attention to the one from Sterling. She got up from her bunk again and moved to her desk to hear what he had to say.

As Sterling's face appeared on the monitor, Sydnee couldn't help thinking how much older he appeared than the last time she'd seen his image. Of course, it had been seven years since he'd stopped replying to her messages, and Sterling had only been fifteen then— a boy. He was twenty-two now and a grown man. He even had a moustache. It look-ed good on him. Sydnee stopped thinking about everything but his words as he started to speak.

"Hi, sis. I'm sorry. I'm sorry. I'm so sorry. I feel like such a jerk. I was wrong to shut you out of my life. I was upset that you chose a life in the military, and that was very wrong of me. It's your life and you have to live it as you see fit. No one can tell you it isn't right to devote yourself to the service simply because dad was killed in the line of duty. I guess I just felt that, as a woman, you should want a home and family.

"I actually began to accept your choice years ago when I saw how proud you were during your graduation from

NHSA, but I had sort of painted myself into a corner and I didn't know how to get out gracefully. I should have just walked across the wet paint and confessed my sins, but it's easier said than done. I was just too proud to admit I was wrong. And I should have sat with mom, Sheree, and Curtis at the graduation, but I couldn't face them either, so I sat up in the stands.

"I want us to be close again, as we were growing up. I've missed my big sister and hope you can forgive me. If you reply to this message, I'll know we can make a fresh start. And if you can't forgive me, I'll kick myself every day for ruining what we once had.

"I love you, sis, and I hope to hear from you.

"Sterling Marcola, Bishop's Gate Towers, Cape Town, South Africa, Earth. Message complete."

Sydnee just stared at the screen as the image faded. Her first reaction was anger. *Sterling had attended my graduation at NHSA and never told anyone he was there?* she thought. *How could he do that?* But then she remembered how truly contrite he appeared over his earlier behavior. She would forgive him, of course. He was her brother, and she still loved him. And it sounded like he had suffered as much as she from the prolonged separation. She touched the record button and began speaking from her heart. She used up almost the entire time allotment and then quickly signed off. It was such a relief to have completed what she'd foreseen as a chore. In her signoff she told him she loved him and hoped he would message her again soon. Then she retired to her bunk again to think through the events of the day.

A chime in her left ear brought her up out of her reverie. She touched her Space Command ring and said, "Marcola," when the carrier was established.

"Marcola, this is the watch commander. Report to Commander Vernon Galeway in the A deck conference room."

"Right away, sir. Marcola out."

Sydnee hopped off her bunk and checked her appearance before hurrying to the door, which picked this time to malfunction. After an unsuccessful attempt to open the door manually, she used the flat of her fist to smack the bulkhead where the switch was located. The door slid open noiselessly.

"Lieutenant(jg) Marcola reporting to the Commander as ordered," Sydnee said as she braced to attention in front of a Commander standing in the conference room with a Lt. Commander.

"At ease, Lieutenant," Cmdr. Galeway said. Gesturing towards the Lt. Commander, he said, "This is my XO, Commander Helen Wheeler.

"When I learned of your amazing performance during the past few months, I told Captain Lidden I wished to meet you. He was good enough to arrange this meeting. He said he would approve a transfer off the *Perry* to a posting more consistent with your remarkable abilities and where you'd have a better path to promotion. Have you decided where you'd like to go?"

"Um, I haven't really thought about it, sir. I suppose a lot will depend on the outcome of the Inquiry Board hearings. I don't know if they'll agree with your assessment of my performance."

"You never know how an Inquiry Board will rule. They sometimes have issues of which we may be unaware, but after reading the reports filed by you and the supporting documentation from the people under your command, I personally believe Captain Lidden's assessment is accurate. You did save everyone aboard the *Perry*. If you hadn't convinced your fellow officers and the Marines to get that Clidepp destroyer operational to come here to assist the *Perry*, everyone aboard would most likely be dead. When I spoke to you following the *Missouri's* arrival here, I wasn't aware of your official rank. I only knew you were in command of a destroyer. I think I was even *more* impressed when I learned that a junior pilot had gotten a Marine platoon to follow her in battle."

"Um, I was the only officer there, sir. Lieutenant Kennedy had been killed."

"I realize that, but I'm still impressed. If they hadn't had confidence in your leadership, I doubt you could have gotten them to follow a ship's bridge officer into ground combat. I wish I had an open position on my ship. If I did, I'd try to convince you to transfer to the *Missouri*."

"Thank you, sir."

"Perhaps something will open up before it's time for you to make a decision."

"Yes, sir."

"Would a posting to the *Missouri* interest you?"

"Um, yes, sir."

"Okay, we'll have to see what happens in the days ahead. It was a pleasure meeting you, Lieutenant. That's all."

"Thank you, sir." Sydnee said as she braced to attention and turned to leave.

As the door closed behind Sydnee, Lt. Cmdr. Wheeler said, "She wasn't what I expected."

"What were you expecting, Helen?"

"More of a Type A personality, I suppose. She seemed almost— indecisive."

"I did sort of spring things on her. I'm sure she's concerned about the Board of Inquiry that will investigate her actions on the planet. Three Marines died, two in battle while under her command. And she did shoot and kill a former high-ranking officer in the Clidepp military, although he had joined the rebels and it was reportedly a case of self-defense."

Sydnee flopped onto her bed as soon as she was back in her quarters. The offer of a post aboard the *Missouri* had come as a complete surprise. But she had to remind herself that there was no open post available and that it was simply a question to determine her possible future interest. Her response was likewise noncommittal. Yes, she had an interest, but that didn't mean she would accept such a post. Scout-Destroyers only carried shuttles and maybe a tug but no fighters or MATs. That could always change, of course. Still, it was nice to receive the query from Commander Galeway. It showed that Captain Lidden's opinion of her actions was shared by others— others who didn't owe their lives to the appearance of the *Abissto* during the battle with the *Glassama*.

She was grateful beyond measure that she didn't have to make a decision today. There were far too many other considerations, and she might later regret a hasty decision.

The DS transport ship *Babbage* finally arrived at the battle site three weeks later to pick up the *Perry*. The gargantuan ship had been delayed, owing to a diversion to pick up the GSC Destroyer *Portland* before proceeding to the location of the *Perry*. The other Tritanium-sheathed warship had been performing interdiction duties much closer to Earth. Although pre-Dakinium, it wasn't nearly as ancient as the *Perry*. Until a permanent replacement for the *Perry*'s assigned sub-sectors was named, the *Portland* would patrol in its place.

The first three frame-sections of the *Babbage* constituted a bow unit that, when swung fully open, revealed a space large enough to accommodate five SC destroyers. Once the *Babbage* was open and the *Portland* had been freed from captivity in the enormous hold, tugs arrived to push the *Perry* into position. When it had been secured, the *Abissto*, the *Glassama*, and the freighter *Furmmara* were guided in and secured, as were the *Furmmara's* link sections too badly damaged during the battle to ever be used again. On command from Sydnee in her capacity as acting captain of the *Abissto*, the freighter's cargo section had been broken in half by torpedoes after the freighter first fired torpedoes at the *Abissto*. Although no torpedoes had struck the freighter itself, fires and control-systems damage resulting from the cargo section breakup had prevented it from continuing the fight. Following the engagement, the *Perry's* engineers had deemed the freighter undependable for use until significant repairs had been made.

The unloading and loading operation took several hours to complete, but when the nose of the *Babbage* closed, the hull again became an airtight hold, sans gravity. Kilometers of undamaged cargo containers from the *Furmmara* would remain behind at the battle site until a freighter dispatched from Simmons SCB arrived to collect them. Not being a DS ship, the SC freighter would require months to reach the battle site. Until then, the GSC Scout-Destroyer *Rhine* would provide security for the containers.

The *Perry's* batteries were fully charged and would be adequate to maintain the gravity deck plating throughout the ship for the entire voyage to Mars. Gravity at the entrance threshold was substantially reduced and then grew progressively stronger moving away from the hatchway until it reached a full g.

The crew was immediately assigned visitor's quarters in the *Babbage*, while rebel crewmembers rescued from the *Glassama* and *Furmmara* were assigned more basic accommodations in an empty hold, with suitable Marine guard around the clock.

Sydnee was ecstatic with her temporary quarters, but they weren't really anything special. They were just the standard-size billet assigned to any Lieutenant(jg) aboard ships constructed during the past fifteen years. But after the shoebox she had occupied aboard the ancient *Perry*, the visitor quarters seemed like a deluxe suite aboard a passenger liner.

With the battle site cleaned up, the *Babbage* and *Missouri* headed for Diabolisto. At Light-9790, it seemed as though they arrived before they left. As the two ships established their orbit path, Sydnee received a message via her CT.

In response to the single-word query, "Marcola," Sydnee touched her ring and said, "Marcola here."

"Marcola," she heard Commander Bryant say, "jump into your personal armor and hoof it down to the shuttle bay."

She didn't understand the reason, but the order was clear enough. She stripped down and stepped into the padded body suit, then slipped into her body armor. Bryant hadn't said anything about weapons, but she decided that since she'd been ordered to wear her personal armor, the situation might involve some danger. She strapped one knife to her left thigh and the other to her right calf, then strapped on her pistol belt and clipped her rifle to her chest plate ring. Grabbing her helmet, she hurried out the door on the run. She required two lifts and a transport car, but she finally arrived at the *Babbage's* shuttle bay.

"Loaded for bear again, I see," Lieutenant(jg) Jerry Weems said with a smile. It was the way he'd greeted her the first time they'd met and had become a standing joke between them. On her first interdiction, she hadn't known what to expect and had brought all of her issued weapons.

"If what I suspect is true, we might need them."

"And what is it you suspect?"

"I seriously doubt we're doing an interdiction, so we must be going down to Diabolisto to help round up the Clidepp rebels."

"Yeah, you're probably right. But why? We're not Marines. And I'm sure the *Babbage* has its own shuttle pilots among the bridge crew."

"We know the planet, and the *Babbage* pilots probably don't have any personal armor since they don't perform interdictions."

"What about the *Missouri*?"

"It's a scout destroyer with limited personnel, so the same basic reasons apply. No Marines, no interdiction pilots, no personal armor."

"I was *really* hoping to never see that miserable planet up close again."

"Maybe it will just be a quick drop and pickup."

"Not with my luck. And I'd feel better if we had the MAT. Think we can get the captain to open the hull so we can fly it out?"

"The way they wedged the Clidepp destroyers and the pieces of that freighter inside, I don't think we'd be able to get the MAT out without moving everything."

"Might be worth it if we have to ferry a couple of hundred prisoners up here. The shuttles are so small we'll have to make thirty trips."

"That doesn't sound so bad."

Weems laughed. "You'd probably like to make all sixty legs by yourself."

"I wouldn't mind. This might be the last opportunity to fly again for a couple of months."

"Ahhh. Three weeks of no flight duty and no bridge duty. It's going to be a relaxing cruise home."

"I'm going to really miss that Marine combat range. It was a great way to unwind."

"We'll get you a pair of magnetic shoes and you can do laps around the inside of the ship hold in full EVA gear."

Sydnee chuckled, then said, "Not the same thing as shooting at a combat target that could jump up from behind every window or from a hidden sniper platform in a jungle tree."

The doors to the shuttle bay opened then and two squads of Marines double-timed it into the bay. The last one in was Marine First Lieutenant Kelly MacDonald.

"This your gig, Kel?" Sydnee asked as the Marines lined up in front of the nearest shuttle.

"Nah, Major Burrows is taking an active role. He'll be here in a minute. He's leading the unit on the surface this time."

"Really? That's unusual."

"I think he wants to see the layout down there firsthand so he's prepared to answer questions at the board hearings. And he said something about getting some terrain shots from altitude."

"Why? I mean we have all the images from the helmet cameras and the surveillance cameras."

"The Major just wants to be fully prepared when it comes time to show the Board how miserable that mud-ball is and what we were up against. I understand he found the images of the two battles with Lampaxa Vorheridines so entrancing that he watched them over and over. And Sgt. Booth designed a new unit patch that shows the Lampaxa head. It looks more frightening than the real thing."

"Nothing is more frightening than the real thing," Weems said. "Since we got back, I've had several nightmares about those monsters."

When the shuttle mechanics entered the bay, it gave Sydnee and Weems a chance to perform their walk-around. The shuttles weren't very old and looked sound and well maintained. Then it was simply a matter of waiting around until Major Burrows arrived and gave them their orders.

Marine Captain Burrows, always referred to as Major Burrows because a ship can only have one captain, finally arrived three-quarters of an hour later. He called MacDonald, Weems and Sydnee aside and asked, "Marcola, how's your arm?"

"Um, my arm, sir?"

"I read that your shoulder was dislocated during the attack on the *Glassama*."

"Um, yes sir. My arm is fine now. I feel a twinge sometimes if I twist it the wrong way, but most of the time it feels a hundred percent."

"Any doubts about piloting a ship with an arm that isn't *quite* a hundred percent?"

"None, sir. The physical requirements for flying a shuttle aren't that demanding."

"How about flying a fighter?"

"Um, a fighter, sir?"

"Let me outline the mission. You and Weems will fly your shuttles down to the planet and surreptitiously land in a clearing a kilometer beyond where the three rebel fighters are parked. The location information has already been down-loaded into the navigation computer of both shuttles. After disabling your shuttles so they can't be commandeered during your absence, you'll deploy to the fighter clearing, disable one of the fighters and then take the other two. You'll each perform a single, low-level flyover of the rebel encampment to send the rebels scurrying for cover while my Marine fire teams surround the camp. When the rebels come out from cover and assemble to discuss the situation, we'll move in and take them prisoner.

"At least that's the plan," Burrows said. "We all know that no plan survives first contact with the enemy. We'll be in constant communication, and with this new armor, the only light weapons that can harm us are mortars, RPG's, and hand grenades. According to reports from Lt. Marcola, the rebels have few weapons left, but stay sharp!"

"Sir," Weems said, "I don't know how to fly a Clidepp fighter and Lt. Marcola might not either."

"That true, Marcola?" Burrows asked.

"Yes, sir." Sydnee said. "We're both experienced pilots, and I don't believe the injury to my arm will affect my flying ability at all, but the controls of those Clidepp fighters might be considerably different from the Marine fighters."

"But you flew that Clidepp tug you stole from the rebels to the *Perry*."

"Um, yes, sir. But a tug is considerably different than a fighter in maneuvering and flight characteristics. I was able to correlate the tug's controls with those of SC tugs I'd flown, and Lt. Weems had no trouble later flying that tug as well. Of course, we can't really know for sure until we see the cockpit of the fighters. If their ships are like ours, we might be able to work it out, but I don't know about performing a low-level flyover without a little practice."

"Well," Burrows said, "perhaps this is one of those instances where the plan falls apart even before we meet the enemy. I've been told you're the best pilot aboard the *Perry*, Marcola, so I'll make a decision about the flyover once we're down on the planet and you and Weems have had a chance to examine the fighter cockpits."

Chapter Two
~ June 2nd, 2285 ~

The shuttles approached low and slow, then flew at treetop level for the last twenty kilometers, using oh-gee engines for propulsion and maintaining altitude, and thrusters for attitude control. It was doubtful that the nearly silent approach would attract any attention, but the Marines in the passenger compartment had already sealed their armor and were ready to deploy the second the shuttles touched down. As the hatches were flung open, the Marines leapt out and secured the LZ while Sydnee and Weems powered down the systems and incapacitated the small ships in ways that could easily be undone, but only by someone who knew exactly which system interfaces had been disconnected.

As Weems and Sydnee exited their shuttle, they closed and locked the hatches so no one, or no wild creature, could get inside without leaving clear evidence of the attempt. Scouts had gone on ahead, reconnoitered the area, and ascertained the absence of sentries. Informed it was safe to continue, the entire group made their way stealthily to the clearing where the fighter craft were parked.

"The area appears to be clear," Burrows said on Com channel Two to Sydnee and Weems. "Take a look at the fighters. My people will spread out and watch for any enemy soldiers while you determine if you can fly those things. Pick the two best craft and disable the third."

"I think that'll be unnecessary, sir," Weems said. "Look at the furthest fighter. It looks like the engine is being overhauled. There are pieces all around the ship."

Burrows glanced towards the ship and used his right eye to select settings on the display menu inside his helmet that would lighten the image and zoom in. "That appears to be the case, Weems," he said after a few seconds. "Okay, check out the other two while I verify that third fighter isn't going anywhere soon."

Sydnee headed towards one fighter while Weems headed towards the other.

Opening the control pad cover on the side of the cockpit, Sydnee examined it for a second before pressing a button that the visual-translation assistant built into her helmet identified as 'hatch.' The cockpit cover slid back to give full access to the pilot and copilot seats.

She climbed into the cockpit and immediately began studying the flight controls and instrumentation. Her helmet translator was invaluable. All she had to do was focus her attention on any relevant symbols or text. The helmet then identified wherever she was looking and translated the Yolon to Amer. From that point on, the Amer translation immediately replaced the Yolon on the inside SimageWindow in her helmet whenever she focused on that text or symbol. But there were a few controls that weren't marked at all. She sincerely hoped they didn't activate the ejection seat. There *was* a button marked 'eject' with a spring-hinged cover over it to prevent it from being accidently depressed. Hopefully, that was the *only* control for ejection.

After just a few minutes, Sydnee believed she understood the controls well enough to take off— but controlled flight that allowed her to make a low-level pass over the rebel camp was another matter.

"Major Burrows?" Sydnee said on Com channel Two.

"Burrows."

"Major, I believe I can fly this ship."

"Well enough to make a low pass over the rebel camp?"

"I really won't know that until I get this ship in the air and see how responsive it is, and how well I can control it."

"Understood. Weems, how about you?"

"I believe I can get it in the air and fly it out of here, but I don't think I should try a low-level pass until I have some flight time in it. Lt. Marcola has had flight training in the FA-SF4 Marine Fighter that I haven't had yet, and I haven't had any fighter time at all since coming to the *Perry*, other than simulator time."

"Understood. Okay, Marcola, you'll do a few passes over the camp as low as you feel comfortable while Weems takes his ship up to three hundred feet and circles the camp. I'll leave two of our people here to watch your backs until you take off. There's no question that the third fighter is incapacitated. Give us thirty minutes to get into position near the rebels before you start the engines. Then take off when you feel comfortable with the controls. After you complete your mission, park your fighters in the clearing where we left the shuttles and stand by for new orders. Confirm."

"Confirmed," both pilots said.

The fighter roared over the rebel camp in what was, locally, the middle of the night. Everyone had been asleep and staggered out of their shelters, trying to comprehend what was happening.

Sydnee completed a three-sixty, coming in so low on the second pass that leaves on the ground rustled from the trailing vortices. The rebels dropped flat to the ground, sure the fighter was attempting to land in the camp clearing until it disappeared over the trees again. Weems, in the other fighter, completed wide, looping circles around the camp at three hundred feet above ground level. After Sydnee had completed several more ground-shaking passes, she headed for the clearing where the shuttles were parked. Weems broke off and followed.

"What's going on, Currulla?" one of the rebels shouted.

"Like I know," Currulla said testily.

"That looked like a Clidepp fighter," another said.

"Yeah," several more chimed in as they stood up.

Following Colonel Suflagga's death, military discipline had all but disappeared. Perimeter sentries were never posted at night, and recently they had even been lax with keeping campfires burning all night since they had never been bothered by creatures unless they entered a swamp. Besides, the fires only attracted more insects.

"Light the fires," Currulla said. "I think we're about to have visitors."

"You think our rescue ship is finally here?"

"Yes, but not one from our people."

"What do you mean?" someone asked.

"I think the Spaccs have finally come for us."

"Everybody grab your weapons," someone screamed.

"No!" Currulla screamed. "No weapons. Put your hands on your heads."

"You intend to surrender?" someone shouted.

"Would you rather spend the rest of your life on this miserable planet? It's a pretty good bet our own people aren't coming to get us, and I want off this mud-ball. If we resist, they might decide to leave us here. This is the GA, not the Clidepp Empire. That means there are no death camps here. A clean prison cell with clean clothes, hot food, and a peaceful nighttime without biting insects would be a thousand times better than this life."

Currulla punctuated his remarks by dropping the knife and scabbard he had in his belt to the ground and placing his hands on his head. A second later, one of the other rebels joined him. Like a ripple spreading out on a pond, the rebels dropped the meager weapons they had and put their hands on their heads.

"Well, I'll be damned," Burrows muttered to himself as he witnessed the spectacle of complete surrender before he had demanded it and even before he had announced the presence of his platoon among the trees that surrounded the camp clearing. On Com-Two, he said, "Lt. MacDonald, light up the area now that the fighters have left."

Several hover-flares streaked skyward from somewhere among the tree cover and held position over the camp area as they blossomed into a light that suddenly turned night into day. The rebels twitched in surprise, but all held their positions with their hands on their heads.

On Com-Two, Burrows said, "MacDonald, move your people towards the center of the camp and herd the rebels into a group away from their weapons."

"Everyone move in," Lt. MacDonald said on Com-One. "They appear to be surrendering, but watch them closely for any indication of treachery."

Two hundred three rebels remained from the original two hundred eighty-three that made it to the planet. Sixty-three had been killed in battle, and the rest had either been killed by the indigenous life forms while hunting for the Marines or foraging for food, or simply never returned after running from the battle scene. Since there was no place on the planet to run to, it could be assumed the latter had either died from wounds received in battle or been eaten by the local wildlife— perhaps both.

After each prisoner was thoroughly searched for weapons, their hands were secured and they were moved to a different part of the camp area to await transport. It took almost an hour to process the prisoners. They all appeared despondent and offered no resistance, but things like that could change in an instant, so the Marines didn't take any chances and treated them as they would any dangerous enemy combatants.

When the initial processing was complete, Burrows called for the shuttles to come to the camp area one at a time. The rebels had originally made their camp in a treed area, but they had moved to a large clearing after Currulla decided that all was lost and they should make their presence as obvious as possible to anyone coming down to the planet.

It took thirty-four trips to transport all of the rebels to the *Babbage* in the small shuttles. Once a group to be transferred was seated in the shuttle and the hatches closed, the misters and air-purification devices were turned on to kill all insects that had flown or crawled in while the hatch was open and clear the air of any pollens or pollutants.

Following the ninth run for each shuttle, Sydnee and Weems were relieved by the *Babbage's* own shuttle pilots but were transported back down to the planet to retrieve the two functional fighters. The third was destroyed by explosives so it couldn't be scavenged. The rebel camp was dismantled and the remaining military supplies were collected in a clearing and burned or destroyed by explosives.

Once aboard the *Babbage*, the rebels were processed by the ship's medical staff. All were covered in bug bites but otherwise were in fairly healthy condition. They'd had plentiful medical supplies and the planet had abundant food supplies for survival, if they didn't get killed trying to harvest it.

"I'm kinda glad that's over," Sydnee said to Weems as they left the shuttle bay after returning with the fighters. "I mean, it was fun making the flights to the planet and back, and having a chance to fly those Clidepp fighters, but I never want to set *foot* on that planet again."

"Not even to get a Lampaxa Vorheridine steak?"

Sydnee gave him look that made him chuckle before she said, "I thought I was going to be the consumed, not the consumer, when we tried to recover the MAT."

"Okay. So maybe that wouldn't be much of an incentive for revisiting Diabolisto," Weems said with a grin.

"I can't think of a single incentive to visit that planet, other than to save your life if your ship is running out of oxygen."

"That cave the Marines found wasn't too bad."

"Only because we had the insect-misting devices. Without those, we would have had to remain sealed in our armor the entire time."

"Yeah, it would have been pretty miserable if we'd had to do that." As they neared their quarters in the visitor area, Weems asked, "Hey, wanna grab some chow?"

"Thanks, but I think I'm more tired than I am hungry right now. All I really want is eight hours in the incredible bed in my assigned quarters. I had a gel-comfort mattress on the *Perry*, but in this bed I can actually spread my arms out."

"Okay. How about afterwards?"

"Um, okay. Say 1400?"

"It's a date."

"Um, okay. See you later."

As soon as she was in her quarters, Sydnee stripped off her body armor and jumped into the shower. As the hot spray struck her body and ran off in rivulets, she felt the tenseness in her muscles drain away like the water. She stayed there until she began to feel so sleepy that she feared she would fall asleep in the shower if she stayed much longer.

Slipping between the sheets on the gel-comfort bed was even better than jumping into the cockpit of an FA- SF4 fighter for a quick trip around the planet. Well, okay, maybe it wasn't quite that good, but it was about as close as she could come on this day. She glanced up at the chronometer to estimate how much time she could sleep and still be ready to have lunch at 1400, set a wakeup call with the computer, and then closed her eyes. There was no tossing or turning of which she was later aware. She was asleep in seconds.

Sydnee was awake and alert before the computer finished announcing the time in her wakeup call. Her sleep in the new bed had been restful, and she felt wonderful. She dressed quickly and spent several minutes pulling a brush through her hair. When she felt that her appearance was as perfect as possible without makeup, she sprayed just a hint of her favorite scent onto her hair.

As she stepped out of her quarters, she found Jerry Weems standing near the bulkhead opposite her door. His appearance there brought her up short. "Are you waiting for me?" she asked.

"Of course. We're having lunch together, aren't we?"

"Um, yes. I just didn't expect you to be waiting outside my door. I assumed we'd meet in the mess hall."

"I'm just a couple of corridors over, so I figured we'd walk to the mess hall together."

"Um, okay."

Weems stepped next to her and matched her stride as Sydnee turned and began walking down the brightly lit corridor. After a few paces he leaned in towards her and sniffed. "Great perfume," he said.

"Perfume?" Sydnee said coyly. "Probably my shampoo you smell."

"Well, then you use great shampoo."

"Thanks. I like it. It leaves my hair clean and shiny."

"I see that. You look great."

"Thank you. So do you. And you seem more buoyant. Is it because the mission here is over, or because we're headed home?"

"Maybe it's because of you."

"Wow, you *are* feeling buoyant."

Weems just smiled in response.

The officers' mess was similar to every other ship's mess hall. Gleaming chrome and glass food displays and counters allowed the officers to select whatever they wished from appetizers, salads, and fresh fruit. A mess attendant stood by to dish up whichever of the hot entrées or side dishes the officers selected and would even prepare a few items to order at every meal. Food synthesizers were available to anyone who cared to use them, but mostly they were just used to create sweet, zero-calorie desserts for people who were watching their weight.

Weems did most of the talking during lunch. It became obvious that a level of trust had evolved in his relationship with Sydnee to where he felt safe lifting at least part of the invisible cloak people maintain as societal armor to conceal their true feelings and personality. He talked about growing up in Calgary and developing an early interest in flying and outer space that had never slackened. Sydnee could relate to that completely. He was far from ready to say what had landed him on the *Perry*, but the lunch date began to establish a personal bond that could be strengthened over time.

―――――――――

"What now, great leader?" Colonel Suflagga's unofficial second-in-command said to Currulla as he squatted next to him on the deck of the hold where Currula's gravity-shielding cloth and bedding had been rolled out. Irritability was evident in his voice.

"What do you mean?" Currulla asked candidly.

"I mean, what's the plan now that we're inside the ship?"

"There's no plan. We're being held prisoner by Spaccs, in a hold inside a Spacc ship. What? Do you think we're going to take over the ship or something?"

"Why not?"

"This isn't the Clidepp military, and this isn't a ship sitting in a dockyard for repairs. Look around you. This prison is fully staffed with armed Space Marines. So just sit back, relax, enjoy the food, the beds, the absence of insects, and the first comfortable sleeping environment we've had in months."

"You may be content to be a model prisoner but not the rest of us. We never had a chance while we were stuck down on that miserable planet, but now that we're off, we intend to get back home. That means commandeering this ship."

"You're a fool, Klieppaso— just like Suflagga."

"Suflagga was a great commanding officer. Don't talk disrespectfully about him."

"We don't have a chance of taking over this ship. All you'll do is get yourself— and maybe a lot of others— killed."

"We've already done the hard part. We're *inside*."

"Getting locked inside a prison is no great accomplishment. The stupidest of people have been doing it successfully for eons."

"If you're afraid, we'll do it without you. Just keep acting like a model prisoner. It'll make the Spaccs think we've given up."

"I *have* given up. And what I'm most afraid of is that you'll get more of our people killed needlessly. Now leave me alone so I can get some sleep."

"Just stay out of the way when things start to happen, Currulla. If you don't, you'll be the first one to die."

Currulla scowled as Klieppaso stood up and walked towards where his own bedding was located. Currulla saw him shake his head towards several of the more militant members of the rebel band as he passed them. Klieppaso had been desperately trying to solidify his position as military commander ever since Suflagga had been killed; but there had been no need for a military commander, so there was little support for officially designating him as such. Being stuck on Diabolisto, nobody wanted a commander organizing daily drills and maneuvers. Whether this was just a power play or he really intended to try a takeover of the *Babbage* was anyone's guess at this point, but Currulla couldn't go against his people and warn the Spaccs. He didn't think the rebels who might be supporting Klieppaso had firmed up any plans yet, so he laid down and tried to sleep.

The *Babbage* left Diabolisto orbit within two hours of the Marines completing their work planet-side and transporting back to the ship. Nothing of the Clidepp military hardware remained on the planet—at least nothing still usable or salvageable. Within six months the vegetation would over-grow the rebel encampments, effectively erasing all obvious record of their stay on the planet. Dying vegetation would eventually cover the scrap on the ground, and in the annuals to come it would become buried in the subsurface layers.

Chapter Three
~ June 10th, 2285 ~

"Does everyone understand their assignment?" Klieppaso asked as he faced his five lieutenants. Each had been charged with carrying out a specific task in the upcoming operation. When all nodded, he asked, "Are your men ready?" Again all nodded. "Good. Let's take our positions. I'll give you the signal when it's time to move."

The *Babbage* had been underway to Earth from Diabolisto for seven days GST, and most of the rebels appeared happy to be aboard. And why wouldn't they be glad to be off a hot, humid mud-ball where insects feasted daily on their blood and the larger indigenous life forms were developing a taste for their flesh? The others seemed totally demoralized and sat in small groups most of the day. As a result, the attention of the Marine guards had grown the slightest bit lax. But when prisoners were being contained in one large common area instead of individual cells, there was no letting down of the guard.

Not being a warship, the *Babbage* didn't have a Marine contingent. And despite its enormous size, its ship's complement was small by any measure. So guarding the prisoners had fallen to the Marines from the *Perry*'s crew.

Klieppaso and his rebel supporters had been closely monitoring the guards' operating procedures and schedules since first being housed in the former hold. The Marine actions and reactions were rigid and predictable. Klieppaso believed that by interjecting chaos into a tense situation, he could use the guards' momentary confusion and indecision to advantage.

The Marines became aware of a problem when one of the prisoners used the intercom mounted on the bulkhead just inside the hold. "Help!" the rebel shouted, "One of our people is unable to breathe. He's dying."

The sergeant in charge of the detail immediately reported the problem to the *Babbage's* sickbay, then used the closed-circuit vid system installed in the hold when it was designated as a prison cell. A group of about ten Clidepp prisoners were gathered around one who was lying on the deck. They seemed to be trying some sort of resuscitation.

The four Marines in his squad had begun preparing themselves as soon as the call came. They knew some kind of action was called for, and they would be ready when the sergeant decided what that would be.

"Prisoner down— emergency procedure seven," Sgt. Davidson said. "We'll collect him and bring him back out here where the medics can work on him. Look sharp, people. Let's move in."

The squad entered the hold as soon as the sergeant entered the code to raise the door. They were armed only with stun batons and stun pistols.

The Marine who would remain at the door was the least experienced member of the detail. It was his job to stand in the entranceway outside the bay and shut the wide door after the detail passed back out with the ill prisoner or to shut it immediately if something went wrong.

The two hundred three rebels were spread out all over the hold as the four Marines entered. One of the Marines moved to the right, herding prisoners there towards the ship's hull at the rear of the hold. Another Marine did that on the left, while Sgt. Davidson and Lance Cpl. Lynch slowly moved towards the Clidepp rebel who was down, clearing a path by herding the rebels ahead of them towards the back of the hold. Everything seemed to be going smoothly, but the Marines never realized that the rebels closest to them were the smallest of the band.

The guard in the corridor who had responsibility for closing the door was concentrating so intently on what was happening with the prisoners inside the hold that he never realized the medical people responding to the emergency had arrived behind him. The doctor and two orderlies were past him before he could react. He followed to stop them, leaving his post unguarded. It was then that Klieppaso gave the signal to commence the operation.

All the prisoners that Klieppaso controlled rushed the Marines and medical personnel at once. They had orders to subdue but not harm the Spaccs. The armed Marines immediately began to stun rebels who closed on them, but the men behind them grabbed the stunned rebels and carried them forward, using them as shields. The rebels in front had known they were going to be stunned, but they also knew the effect wasn't fatal. To a man they had volunteered for the duty.

As the tsunami of rebels attacked, the Marines were overwhelmed. A few rebels using the rebels in front of them as shields were stunned, but the size of the rebel force was too great. In seconds, the Marines and the medical personnel who had responded to the emergency were stunned as rebels got control of the weapons. The Marine who had left his post was stunned within seconds of the others. The final count was eight Spaces down and thirty-six rebels down. All would recover in a few hours. The rebel who had been 'dying' climbed to his feet and smiled at his commander.

As the rebels had begun efforts to take control of the hold, the two Marines in the security office were watching on the closed circuit vid system. Alerted to a possible problem when the sergeant notified the sickbay, they immediately swung into action. The first thing they did was have Engineering lock down the area. All bulkhead doors in that frame-section were closed and locked, preventing access to other corridors. All control gates in the ventilator systems were closed down so that escape through a ventilator shaft was impossible, and the hatches on the access tunnels that allowed emergency travel between decks were locked. The lift doors in that frame-section and deck were also locked, and lifts would no longer even stop at that level. Lastly, all monitors in the area were disconnected from the ship-wide net so they couldn't be used to secure information about the layout of the ship or information about the forces being assembled to retake that deck and frame-section. Other than shutting down the information net, it was essentially the same procedure that would be followed in the event of a fire, except neither the Alonn gas nor the fire suppression foam systems had activated.

The area where the prisoner hold was located was now isolated from the rest of the ship, although all sensors and the vid cameras in the hold and corridors continued to operate. The air supply was limited to what presently existed in the hold and corridor. Engineering could unlock and release any of the hatches or accesses only on command from a senior officer.

———————

"Captain," Nigel Wendham said when he lifted the cover on his bedside com unit and squinted up at the chronometer on the bulkhead across from his bed. It was 0209 hours GST.

"Sir," the image of Lt. Commander Renee Sloan said, "we have a containment problem in prison hold two. The rebels have managed to overcome their Marine guard and are in control of that deck in that frame-section. The security office has isolated them by closing the emergency corridor doors and locking all access tunnels and vents."

"Weapons?'

"As far as we know, their weaponry is limited to the stun pistols and batons carried by the guards. So far, they've been unable to break into the weapons locker in the corridor outside the hold. Security believes it would be wise to assume they have a few knives and clubs fashioned from materials available in the hold."

"Has Major Burrows been alerted?"

"Yes, sir. He's on his way to the security office to evaluate the situation."

"I'll be on the bridge in five minutes."

"Yes, sir."

"Captain, out."

"Watch Commander, out."

───────────────

Sydnee came awake instantly as a message received by her CT began to play in her head.

"Attention. The Captain has declared a Stage-One Emergency in Deck 22, Frame-section 224. Rebel prisoners have effected an escape from basic confinement. All Marine personnel are ordered to immediately get into their personal armor and stand by. All interdiction pilots from the *Perry* are also ordered to immediately don their personal armor and stand by. The *Babbage's* pilots are ordered to stand by in their quarters. All other personnel are ordered to stand down and remain in their quarters. That is all."

Sydnee leapt from her bed and pulled on the bodysuit worn under the armor, then began dressing in the lightweight Dakinium armor that would protect her from most danger. Once dressed, she checked her weapons to make sure the laser pistol and rifle were fully charged. She strapped one knife to her left thigh and one to her right calf.

As fully prepared as possible to respond to any emergency, Sydnee sat down to wait.

───────────────

"They've managed to isolate us in this part of the ship," the rebel lieutenant said to Klieppaso. "The corridor doors are closed and we can't open them. The lift doors won't open, and even the tube accesses to other decks seem to be sealed somehow."

"Keep trying. We didn't break free of a small prison only to remain trapped in a slightly larger one." Klieppaso smashed his closed fist down into his open hand as he turned to survey the situation in the hold. He'd known there were vid units in the hold, but he couldn't disable them in advance without tipping his hand. The Spaccs had responded far faster than he'd expected. They must have begun locking down the deck accesses even before his men completed overpowering the small Marine guard detail.

Klieppaso's job as a cargo foreman had earned him a senior place in the rebel military hierarchy because his civilian job had required he successfully maintain discipline among rough men in difficult and sometimes dangerous situations. But he had no formal military training and so couldn't predict how senior military people would prepare for different scenarios and respond to changing conditions. What he'd seen as 'rigid and predictable' behavior was viewed as 'disciplined and dependable' in the eyes of the military.

───────────

Sydnee sat up straighter as a faint chime in her left ear indicated that she was about to receive a CT message.

"All Marine enlisted personnel on standby report to 18-223-21-Q in full personal body armor on the double. All Marine officers and all Space Command interdiction pilots on standby report to 18-223-23-Q in full personal body armor on the double."

Sydnee jumped up from her bed, strapped on her pistol belt, clipped her rifle to her chest armor and grabbed her helmet before heading for the door. As the doors slid open, she paused to avoid running into the other pilots from the *Perry*, all of whom had been billeted in the same visitor quarters area.

Jerry Weems noticed Sydnee's doors opening, slowed, and then stopped to allow her to enter the corridor ahead of him. She smiled and stepped out, then turned to her left and double-timed it with the others toward a transport car station.

The nearest transport car station was two frame-sections away, and upon arriving Sydnee and Weems got into line to await an available car. As they waited, Weems asked, "What do you think?"

"About what?"

"This emergency."

"Um. It's not a drill."

"Is that all?"

Before Syd could answer, an empty transport car arrived and she was able to squeeze in with Weems and the other pilots. The car would whisk them swiftly towards the stern of the gargantuan ship, delivering them to frame-section 220.

"What more do you expect?" Sydnee asked. "I've never participated in a drill like this. We're guests on a strange ship, and I have no idea how we can help resolve this problem. We'll probably just sit on our hands while the regular crew handles this, and then we can go back to our quarters."

"Want to have dinner with me?"

"Thinking of your stomach again?" she said with a smile.

"What else is there to do? As you said, we'll probably just sit around with nothing to do until the problem is resolved."

"Okay, let's have *breakfast* when it's over."

When the transport car stopped at frame-section 220, the pilots stepped out. This frame-section didn't have a lift, so they used the lift in 222 to reach deck 18.

After double-timing it to frame-section 223, they followed the corridor signs to reach room 23-Q.

Marine First Lieutenant Kelly MacDonald was the only one in the small conference room when the group of pilots arrived.

"Hi, Kel," Sydnee said, as she entered the room and took a seat next to her friend. Weems took a seat on her other side.

"Hi, Syd."

"How bad is it?"

"I haven't heard any more than you. I was asleep until I received the message to put on my body armor and report here."

"Same here."

"Attention on deck," someone said as Captain Wendham and his Exec Officer, Commander Phoste, Captain Lidden of the *Perry*, and Major Burrows, the senior Marine on board, entered.

"As you were," Captain Wendham said while everyone was in the process of rising, and the Marine officers and pilots dropped back into their chairs.

"As you've heard," Captain Wendham said, "some of the rebel prisoners have broken out of confinement. They've overcome their Marine guard and spread out from the hold into the frame-section corridor. Major Burrows will now brief you."

"The rebels we rescued from Diabolisto have broken out of their initial containment," Burrows began, "and are holding their Marine guards and three of the *Babbage's* medical people as hostages. Of the two hundred three rebels rescued from the planet, twenty-six have apparently chosen not to participate in this escape attempt. They have remained separate and apart in the prison hold and have been observed conversing with Currulla, the original leader of the band. The active group seems to be following the orders of a Clidepp insurgent named Klieppaso.

"During the escape effort, thirty-six rebels were stunned, but the remaining one hundred forty-one are currently trying to force open the corridor doors to gain access to the next frame-sections and the hatches on the access tunnels to reach other decks. Thus far, their efforts have been unsuccessful, but the doors and hatches won't hold forever. We're going to ignore the lifts and access hatches for now, because even if they manage to break *in* to one, they'll have to spend just as much time breaking *out* of it on a different deck.

"They have also, so far, been unable to pry open the weapons locker, which contains two laser pistols. They have the stun weapons of the guards, but if they gain access to the laser weapons, the danger inherent in this situation rises to a whole new level. While the laser weapons assigned to each of you can only be fired by you because they're keyed to your DNA, the weapons in the prison locker are un-keyed. That's because any of the guards must be able to fire them should a situation arise that requires their use. We must regain control of this situation before the rebels get access to those weapons.

"As to their ultimate objective, we can only speculate. There's little chance they could ever commandeer this ship, so we're focusing elsewhere. They might be attempting to access one of the ships in the *Babbage's* transport hold, hoping they can use it to escape, but the only ship even close to usable condition is the freighter. And we can't imagine how the rebels might know of its existence, or even that there are *any* ships in the transport hold since the surviving crew of the freighter and the *Glassama* have been housed in another large hold further towards the stern. The two groups have had no contact with one another, and all Marine guards have been ordered not to give the rebels of either group any information. So we're discounting their having any knowledge of the ships we're transporting. If they've somehow learned of the other group, they might be trying to reach them so they can be freed in an effort to bolster their forces, but again, they shouldn't even know of the other group's presence in the *Babbage*. As we see it, that leaves just one possibility— their only objective is to escape confinement, and they haven't developed a real plan beyond that. Perhaps they believed they'd figure out what they should do next if their attempt was successful.

"All eight of our people, plus the rebels stunned during the breakout, are sleeping off the effects. If the rebels can hold out until the guards and medical personnel awaken, they might be able to secure information regarding the ship or security arrangements from them either through threats or torture, so it's imperative we overcome the rebels before that can happen.

"We have to defend against the more likely possibilities, so I've devised a plan. Computer, display Burrows 01, this date, on the screen behind me." A layout of Deck 22, showing five frame-sections with Section 224 in the center, appeared on the large wall-mounted monitor. Pointing to a part of the image using a laser pointer, Burrows said, "Here's the hold in

Section 224 where the rebels were being held. They now control the corridor outside that hold but are contained by the bulkhead doors at these two points. The corridor door that leads towards the stern is closest to the hold door, and that's where they're concentrating most of their efforts. Lieutenant MacDonald, you'll take your platoon to the other side of this door and set up a defensible position. Should the rebels break through, you'll explain to them that they should return to their prison hold. Initially you'll use stun rifles, but you'll also carry laser pistols for use as needed. If the rebels repeat the tactic of carrying stunned rebels in front of them, use the laser weapons to cut their legs out from under them or whatever other actions are required to stop their advance."

"Yes, sir," MacDonald said.

"Directly across from the prison hold is an EVA preparation room. So far, the rebels have ignored it, but if they gain access, they'll find a dozen EVA suits and an airlock that leads directly to the ship transport hold. If they manage to reach that hold, they'll have access to any of the ships secured there. What we fear most is that they might attempt to detonate one or more torpedoes. The firing mechanisms were all removed before the ships were brought into the transport hold, but we don't know what skills the rebels possess, so they might be able to find a way to jury rig something. We can't allow them to have that chance. Lieutenant Aguilo, you and the interdiction pilots will move to several of the other airlocks in that area and wait for instructions. If the rebels make it into the transport hold, you'll confront them there and take whatever action is necessary to take them back into custody. At most, you'll be facing a dozen, and all will be in bulky, unfamiliar EVA suits, while you and the pilots will be in body armor. The rebreather units in the armor will give you all the oxygen you need, and the environment in the hold will not tax the limits of your armor."

"Yes, sir," Aguilo said.

"Lastly, we must defend the door at the bow end of the corridor. Lieutenant Marcola, you'll take your platoon and secure that location. The rebels haven't made a concerted effort to open that door, and we don't expect them to, but that could change. As with Lt. MacDonald's platoon, you'll carry both stun rifles and laser pistols. Use the stun rifles first and the laser pistols as a last resort."

At the mention of her name, Sydnee sat up a little straighter. Until then she had expected to operate with the other interdiction pilots. "Um. *My* platoon, sir?"

"MacDonald and Aguilo already have assignments, and I need an experienced combat officer to take command of Lt. Kennedy's platoon and defend that corridor access position."

"But, sir, I'm SC."

"In debriefing interviews, every member of Kennedy's platoon commended your leadership of the platoon. That makes you the logical candidate for this job. I had just three Marine officers aboard the *Perry* before Lieutenant Kennedy was killed in action on Diabolisto. Now I have just two. Captain Lidden has approved this assignment."

Sydnee looked quickly towards Lidden who nodded. "Very well, sir. I accept the assignment."

"Time is short, people, so let's get moving. Lt. Aguilo, Captain Wendham's chief engineer is waiting outside this room. He'll brief you as to which airlocks should be used for your team. MacDonald and Marcola, your platoons are assembled in the large conference room across the corridor. Brief them on the assignments and get to your posts as quickly as possible."

Chapter Four
~ June 10th, 2285 ~

"Duttomon," Klieppaso yelled into the corridor while standing in the doorway of the hold. "It's time to shove a sharp stick into the eyes of the Spaccs. Take your people and rip the vid units down off the walls."

Most of the people involved in this escape attempt had been milling around in the corridor since the Marine guard detail had been overcome. Duttomon motioned to his men and they sprang to the task of ripping the four vid cameras off the walls in the hold.

Klieppaso watched as they accomplished their task. He was enjoying the rush he was feeling from having people immediately obey his every command.

─────────────

"They're finally tearing down those vid cameras," Lt.(jg) Angelo Ruscetti, the ship's chief of security, said to Major Burrows as they sat in the security center watching the activity in the hold.

"Wonder why they waited so long," Burrows said. "I would have torn them down right after their people accomplished the takeover."

"They aren't the brightest bulbs in the lamp, that's for sure."

"How many cameras and mics do we have left?"

"The same number we've had all along. Our engineers salvaged those old vid units from the *Glassama* and rigged them so they'd appear to be operational. The rebels will never spot the real cameras in a million years. We have eight in the hold and six in the corridor, plus additional units in other areas of that frame-section."

"We only had vid units in key areas aboard the *Perry.*"

"Yeah, a lot of things have changed since that old bucket came off the production line. That incident aboard the *Song—* when Admiral Carver was in command and a Raider officer snuck aboard in an attempt to assassinate her— was responsible for a lot of changes in security measures. Now, except for private quarters and heads, we have cameras everywhere. The *Babbage* has roughly ten thousand units scattered around the ship, and we can call up the image and audio from any of them in a second. The camera lenses are so tiny, it takes an engineer with a special sensor to locate a camera if the unit has to be checked out or replaced. Those bulky old vid units in the hold were only put there because the prisoners would be expecting to be watched, and we gave them what they normally see aboard their own ships."

After arriving in Frame-section 223 of Deck 22, Sydnee checked out the rooms on either side of the corridor. Their armor provided complete protection from laser and stun weapons, so the Marines had no need for cover or concealment. Sydnee was only looking for things like seating that would make the people assigned to her somewhat more comfortable through what might turn out to be a long impasse as the situation with the rebels played out. For now, the entire platoon remained in the corridor.

"Well?" Klieppaso said to the Yolongi engineer who was in charge of opening the corridor doors.

"Well, what? The doors aren't open yet."

"I can see that. When will they be open? We can't give the Spaccs any more time to get organized. We have to move out."

"Their electronic systems are nothing like ours. Their systems are so advanced that I'm just guessing, and I have no tools here. There's only so much I can do with just a sturdy piece of molding and some string."

"If you can't handle it, tell me. I'll put someone else in charge."

The engineer stopped what he was doing and calmly turned to face Klieppaso. "If that's a threat, do it. Put someone else in charge of opening the doors. How about Duttomon? He's an engineer."

"Duttomon doesn't know his right arm from his left."

"That's true. And yet, he's the second best engineer here."

Klieppaso wanted to say that the best engineer didn't seem to be much better, but he held his tongue. "Just give me an idea of how much longer it'll be."

"I'd have to say about a thousand annuals."

"You're saying you can't do it?"

"Without the proper equipment, it appears to be imposs-ible. Get me the right tools and a good test meter, and I *might* be able to get the doors open. Without them, I don't think I have a chance. Better put Duttomon in charge."

"Why didn't you tell me that before I had Duttomon rip down the vid units?" he said angrily. "Now how am I sup-posed to get the attention of the Spaccs so I can demand they open the doors?"

The Yolongi engineer grinned and said sardonically, "Well, I'm not in charge. But if it were up to me, I'd use that," the engineer said, pointing to the intercom handset on the bulk-head entry next to the hold.

Klieppaso scowled at the engineer, then reached for the handset.

Looking at Major Burrows after picking up the handset, Lt.(jg) Ruscetti said, "Klieppaso says he's prepared to state his terms to the person in charge."

"Is he now?" Burrows said. "Well, that's real nice of him." Taking the handset, he said, "This is Major Burrows."

"Just a Major? I want to speak to the captain of this ship."

"You'll talk to me if you have anything to say. Or I could pass you back to the Lieutenant and you can tell him."

Klieppaso was silent for some ten seconds, then said, "Very well. I shall relate my terms to you and you shall immediately relay them to the Captain."

"State your business."

"First, we want to make contact with our leadership."

"No problem. All prisoners of Space Command are entitled to establish contact with family, friends, and associates in order to prepare their case in court."

"What? Why weren't we informed of that?"

"You haven't been formally charged yet. That will happen when we reach Earth. At that time, all your rights will be explained to you, as well as the potential sentence for your crimes, and you'll have communications access."

"We won't wait three or four annuals to contact our people."

"Three or four annuals? You won't have to wait that long. We'll arrive at Earth in seventeen solars."

"You lie."

"I have no reason to lie."

"We only left Diabolisto seven solars ago. The travel time to Earth is several light-annuals."

"That was true, many annuals ago. But at Light-9790 it's only about twenty-four solars."

"Light-9790 is impossible."

"At one time scientists said we'd never be able to travel faster than sound. And at one time, scientists said no one would ever be able to travel faster than light. Records and limits were meant to be broken."

"Our scientists have declared that no one will ever be able to travel faster than Light-800."

"That's an example of what I just said. Everything is always considered impossible until someone finds a way to do it. Our fastest ships travel at Light-9790. It's been that way for many annuals."

"You lie. We would have heard."

"Heard from whom? The government you're rebelling against? The government who won't permit construction of any ships that can travel faster than Light-75? The government that always lies to you?"

"We have our own resources. Now let me communicate with my leadership or you'll suffer the consequences."

"What consequences? You're still contained in the immediate area of the hold."

Klieppaso, unaware that his every move was being watched, turned to Duttomon, now standing in the doorway to the hold, and whispered something.

Duttomon turned and raced to where the medical people were still sleeping off the effects of being stunned. With the help of another rebel, Duttomon picked up one of the medical people and carried him to the corridor, where they held him up so Klieppaso could look at him.

"That's Doctor Velazquez," Ruscetti said.

"Great," Burrows said in disgust. "He's going to threaten to kill the doc if he doesn't get what he wants. Well, let the games begin."

"Are you still on the line, Major?"

"I'm here."

"I have one of your medical people with me. In sixty seconds I'm going to slit his throat. Then in another sixty seconds I'm going to kill another of your people. Then every sixty seconds thereafter I'm going to kill another."

"And what are you going to do when you run out of Marines and medics?"

"What?" Klieppaso asked in apparent confusion.

"I said, what are you going to do when you run out of hostages to murder? You only have enough to last eight minutes. Or perhaps I should ask— how long do you think you and your people will live once you kill the first Terran?"

Klieppaso obviously hadn't thought through all the ramifications of his threat. Increasing his bluster, he said, "We'll get out of here and kill every Terran on this ship."

"That's it," Burrows said after disconnecting from the line. Activating a direct connection to Sydnee, he said, "Lt. Marcola?"

"Marcola here, sir." She had been receiving a feed from the security office and had heard everything said by Klieppaso and Burrows.

"As you heard, the leader of the escape attempt is threatening to kill the doctor and the rest of the hostages. MacDonald is just on the other side of the corridor door where the rebels are congregated. If I open that door, they might panic and kill the doc, so I'm going to open the door by your end. I want you to try to talk this jerk down. Stay tough. Make him believe we've already written the hostages off and that you're just waiting until he starts killing to begin a little killing of our own. If you get a shot that will save the doc, you're authorized to use lethal force. If they lose their leader, the others might lose heart and return to the hold peacefully."

"Aye, sir, we're ready," Sydnee said, as she placed her stun rifle against the corridor wall and unsnapped the flap on her holster. To her platoon, she said, "Let's put on our game faces."

Immediately, the outer front Simage on the helmet of Sydnee and every Marine with her displayed the four-four-three's battle icon. In the animated 3D icon, steam rose from the top of the skull, and the eye sockets glowed brightly with a luminescent green color. Every couple of seconds, small flames emanated from the rhinal openings to simulate exhaling. During battle, or any other extreme physical exertion, the image would automatically change slightly to show the skull laughing maniacally.

"I'm opening the door," Burrows said as he nodded to Ruscetti, who relayed the command to the chief engineer.

As the corridor doors began to open, the noise drew the attention of Klieppaso, who hadn't known what to do after the officer hung up. He smiled for a second, thinking he'd won, until he saw Sydnee and the platoon of Marines, their stun rifles at the ready, standing in the next frame-section just fifteen meters from where *he* stood. The smile disappeared from his face. He was directly behind the doctor, his body almost completely hidden, so there was no clear shot for Sydnee. "Hold it right there," he shouted. "Come any closer and I'll kill this Terran."

With the wink of her right eye, Sydnee activated the speaker on her breastplate. It had already been adjusted to speak in Yolon. "I know," she said. "We're here to take you and your people down after you do that."

"I *will* do it," Klieppaso said brusquely.

"And I can't stop you. I'm not here to save the medic. I'm only here to see you never kill anyone else."

"I've already given orders to my people. If anything happens to me, they'll kill the rest."

"Their orders are not my concern. My orders are to kill you and all of them if you kill the medic. He's the *only* thing in this galaxy keeping you all alive right now. When you kill him, there's *nothing* keeping you and the others with you alive. You crossed the line when you threatened to kill the hostages. I'm not carrying a stun weapon. My pistol is laser. When I shoot, my target doesn't take a nap. It dies."

Klieppaso didn't have a response for that, and he hadn't fully realized how precarious his position was. He'd believed the Spaccs would cave when he threatened to kill the hostages. Now here was one who seemed to be saying she didn't care what happened to the hostages. But that had to be false. Klieppaso had heard that the Spaccs would do anything to save one of their own. "All I want is to contact my leadership and be released from this ship. I don't want to kill anyone. I'll only do that if you force my hand."

"I'm not forcing you to do anything. If you kill, it's because you choose to kill. I'm simply going to wait right here until you do it, and then I'm going to kill you and *everyone* who stands with you." Sydnee felt that her statements were adequately forceful to meet the Major's orders that she appear tough, but she was having trouble figuring out where this was leading. She didn't want to back Klieppaso into a corner where he believed the only action was the final one, but her words *were* having an effect on the other rebels. They were slowly inching their way away from Klieppaso and towards the door of the hold. Already, one had disappeared into the hold.

Switching her com to connect with the Major, Sydnee said, "Sir, I've lost sight of one of the rebels who was in the corridor. Can you see him?"

"Affirmative, Lieutenant. It appears we have our first deserter. You're doing great. Keep it up. Stay tough. It's having an effect on the others, if not Klieppaso. His bluster will diminish as he finds his support disappearing."

"Aye, sir," she said as she switched back to the external speaker.

Over the next several minutes, no one spoke and no one died, but seven more of the rebels disappeared back into the hold. Klieppaso had realized it but said nothing. Finally, to stem the tide of desertions, he said loudly to his people, "Hold your positions. She's just trying to frighten you. She isn't going to shoot anyone."

Sydnee didn't want to make a move and panic Klieppaso, so she remained perfectly still, but used her eye movements to adjust her com to channel One so she could address the platoon. "I don't want anyone to use their laser pistols except as a last resort. When things start to happen, use your stun rifles. Fire on any rebel still standing or moving in the corridor. Once the corridor is clear, fire team Alpha will remain in the corridor while Bravo through Golf moves into the hold. They will stun anyone who still wants to resist and drive the rest toward the rear of the area and away from the hostages. Everyone clear on that?"

A chorus of "Oo-rahs" was the reply.

Switching to the private link to the Major, she said, "Sir, I see a fire-suppressant nozzle in the overhead about a meter from Klieppaso. Can that be activated independently? I mean, without activating the entire system and without there actually being a fire?"

"Standby," Burrows said.

About thirty seconds later, she heard, "The chief engineer says any nozzle can be activated in test mode. He's identifying the address of that nozzle in the computer and will be ready in a few seconds. Good idea, Lieutenant. Stand by."

Sydnee shifted to Com-One and explained her plan to the platoon. Then it was simply a matter of waiting for Engineering.

"The chief engineer is ready and waiting, Lieutenant," she heard on her direct line with Burrows.

"I've briefed my platoon, sir. We're ready when you are. I think it's time to build some snowmen."

The nozzle in the overhead suddenly came to life and began directing a blizzard of white foam fire-suppressant directly towards Klieppaso, Doctor Velazquez, and the two rebels still holding the sleeping medical officer upright. The foam had the thick consistency of whipped cream, and the sight dazed the other rebels in the corridor. Klieppaso was instantly blinded as foam covered his entire head.

The corridor's width allowed no more than three armored Marines to walk side by side with full mobility. With Sydnee in the center of the front line, the platoon moved in swiftly, stunning rebels as they proceeded. The Yolongi in the corridor fell like raindrops on Diabolisto as the Marines fired with abandon into their ranks. In seconds, the corridor was littered with sleeping rebel bodies. The rebels near the hold disappeared quickly inside. Klieppaso, already buried under a meter of thick, heavy foam and unable to see what was going on, was coughing and sputtering while trying to scream orders and obscenities.

As Sydnee reached the quartet near the corridor door, she stepped without hesitation into the foam, her arms extended.

When she felt a body, she grabbed an arm and yanked with all her strength. As it came towards her without resistance, she stepped back and emerged from the foam mountain. The body belonged to one of the rebels, but it wasn't Klieppaso. This one was coughing from having inhaled some of the non-toxic foam and surrendered meekly as she pushed him into the arms of a Marine by her side.

Stepping into the foam again, the next body Sydnee found was drooping and felt like dead weight. She immediately knew it had to be Doctor Velazquez. She managed to get a good hold on the sleeping officer's uniform and yanked. He came free from the grip of the second rebel who was coughing and trying to get a breath while still supporting the weight of the sleeping medical officer. Sydnee suddenly found herself trying to carry the doctor's entire weight and had to settle for half dragging his body to safety.

When Sydnee again emerged from the mountain of white, a waiting Marine took one of the doctor's arms. Together, they managed to get Doctor Velazquez to a safe area in the corridor behind the platoon. With the doctor removed from danger, some of the Marines began laughing at the screams of Klieppaso and his lieutenant, neither of whom could find their way out of the thick foam. When the nozzle stopped spraying, fire team Alpha began discharging their stun weapons into the white substance until all noise and movement stopped.

As Sydnee had ordered, six of the fire teams had advanced into the hold and driven the rebels back to the far side, securing the area around the sleeping guards and two medical people.

An engineering team had been standing by with vacuum hoses since the plan had been put into action. As the corridor and hold were secured, they entered the corridor and connected the hoses to available wall sockets. Within minutes, the engineers had removed enough foam that the two encapsulated bodies were visible. When Klieppaso and his lieutenant, Duttomon, awoke, they would each be in a six by eight cell in the ship's brig.

As the last of the foam was being vacuumed up, the wide doors at the stern-most end of the corridor rolled back into their frame-section housings and MacDonald's platoon joined Sydnee's.

"Hey, Syd," MacDonald said, as she approached her friend, "have any trouble?"

Sydnee, still covered with globs of foam, said, "No trouble. Just a dumb rebel who bit off far more than he could chew. He'll be sleeping for a few hours."

"Anything we can do?"

"My platoon is in the hold, mopping up. Your people could give them a hand. We need to make sure we account for all the stun weapons and then pat down the rebels for makeshift weapons. I guess we should separate Klieppaso's chief conspirators and move them to the brig."

"Too bad the brig isn't large enough to hold the entire lot."

"Yeah, but I think we'll have less trouble now. The ones who wind up in cells are going to miss the relative freedom they had in this enormous hold."

"Can I vacuum you off, Lieutenant?" one of the engineers with a hose asked.

"Yes, Chief."

In seconds, Sydnee's armor again looked pristine.

"Thanks, Chief."

"My pleasure, Lieutenant."

"Well done, Lieutenant," Major Burrows said to Sydnee when he arrived to personally inspect the area with captains Wendham and Lidden as the last of the hostages were being removed to the sickbay.

The rebels lining the corridor had been searched, then dragged into the hold where they would sleep off the effects of the stunning. The rebels who hadn't been stunned had all been checked for weapons and a small collection of sharp objects confiscated. Klieppaso and his lieutenants had been separated for transport to the brig, fitted with transport chains for that short journey even though asleep, and then loaded aboard oh-gee sleds. They would awaken in their cells.

"Thank you, sir," Sydnee said.

"I knew you were the right officer to lead this platoon. Using the flame-suppressing foam to end the standoff without anyone being hurt was inspired."

"I don't think Klieppaso really wanted to harm our people, sir."

"Perhaps not, but when he's tried the court will judge him on his actions, not his possible intentions. Merely placing them in danger and threatening their lives will add additional time to his sentence."

"Well done, Lieutenant," Captain Lidden said, adding his congratulations to those of the Major.

"I agree," Captain Wendham said. "Very well done."

"Thank you, sirs."

"Okay, Lieutenant, " Burrows said. "Let's wrap this up. Two fire teams will be adequate to transport the rebel leaders. You can dismiss the rest of your people."

"Aye, sir."

As the three senior officers left the deck, Sydnee passed on the Major's orders to the platoon, then retrieved the stun rifle she had earlier left in the other frame-section.

A new Marine guard detail took up their posts as the door to the hold was closed and resealed for the first time since the escape attempt had begun. Sydnee and Kelly MacDonald followed along behind the small group headed for the lifts and ultimately the brig.

Chapter Five
~ June 29th, 2285 ~

The *Babbage* reached Mars at 0348 hours, exactly on schedule. Auxiliary Command and Control access was limited to *Babbage* officers, so guest officers and enlisted personnel hoping to catch a first glimpse of Mars or Earth after a long absence had crowded into the lounges reserved for their use. Despite the early morning hour, seating was limited.

As the first real-time images of Mars and Earth appeared on monitors throughout the ship, they were greeted with oohs, ahhs, and assorted comments. A few people even clapped or cheered. While one monitor exhibited a bleak planet the color of rust, another showed a beautiful blue planet with patches of beige and green adorned with swirls of white. As seen from Mars by the naked human eye, Earth appeared as a small ball of light in the sky. But the visual blandness created by the seventy-eight million kilometers mean distance was negated by the superb optical capability of the *Babbage's* cameras.

Her first sight of Earth caused Sydnee to reflect on her recent life. She found it difficult to accept it had been less than a year since her August 2284 graduation from the Warship Command Institute in Australia. So much had happened that it seemed it must surely have been longer, but the timeline was accurate.

In the year Sydnee had been gone, the Mars shipyard had expanded considerably. When she'd left to report to the GSC Light Destroyer *Perry*, the GA was at war with the THUGs, so the yard was operating on a 24/7 schedule. And there was still activity everywhere she looked. With Admiral Carver now working to establish law and order in vast new territories, the demand for new ships, repairs, and retrofits had never ceased.

"No matter how far we travel, I always feel a bit nostalgic when I see Earth after an absence," Jerry Weems said as he plopped down into the chair next to Sydnee's.

"Hi, Jer," Sydnee said as she glanced over. "I thought you might have decided to sleep in."

"I told the computer to wake me when we were within ten minutes' arrival time of Mars. I got here just in time to see the first images."

"I came down early. I wanted to make sure I got a good seat."

"I was surprised to find this chair vacant," he said, looking around the crowded lounge.

"Kelly MacDonald was sitting there. She got called away about a minute before you arrived."

"What's up?"

"Dunno. She got a message, said she had to go, and flew out of here."

"I hope it's not the rebels again."

"They've been pretty quiet since the escape attempt. The leaders are all still locked in the brig."

"What about the other two groups?"

"You mean the ones from the *Glassama* and the *Furmmara*?"

"Yeah."

"All quiet— as far as I know."

After a minute of silence, Weems said, "You seem distracted. Are you that worried about the Board of Inquiry?"

"Of course I am. It's been on my mind ever since we boarded the *Babbage* and I had time to reflect on how other people who weren't out here with us were going to view my actions. Each passing day brings us one day closer to the start of the investigation."

"You did great, Syd. Everyone knows that. You've got nothing to worry about."

"Um, did I ever tell you that the Captain warned me I would probably find myself sitting dirt-side on some obscure moon for the rest of my time in Space Command?"

"Lidden said that?"

"Yeah."

"No, you never told me. Was that after we came to the rescue of the *Perry*?"

"No. Way earlier. It was after I shot those two security people aboard the *Darrapralis*. And then there was the time he chewed me out for taking command of the platoon on Diabolisto after Kennedy was killed."

Weems chuckled, then said, "That one I heard about. The story I got is that he was afraid you were getting a little too far outside your job description when you led a platoon of Marines in a battlefield charge against an enemy force of vastly superior numbers. He just wanted to rein you in a little. Remember, he's still responsible for all your actions, even when you're on a planet and he's in space a million kilometers away."

"Where did you hear about it?"

"Just scuttlebutt. You know how it works. The Captain mentions something to Commander Bryant, Bryant mentions it to Lieutenant Milton, and Milty tells another officer or two that have his confidence."

"And before you know it, it's all over the ship."

"Yeah, but it's not the bad kind of scuttlebutt. Everyone gets reamed by the Captain at one time or another. I think it's part of his job description."

"I guess."

As the excitement of 'first look' diminished, the lounge began to clear as officers returned to their quarters and beds. Lt. Kelly MacDonald returned just as the queue of officers trying to leave the room ended. The seat on the other side of Sydnee was now vacant, so she plopped down there. "Hi, Jer," she said to Weems.

"Hi, Kel. What's up?"

"Just an incident in the sickbay. The security officer noticed that I was up so he called me instead of waking the Major."

"What happened?" Sydnee asked.

"One of the female slaves rescued from the *Darrapralis* wasn't feeling well, so she was taken to the sickbay. The only medic on duty was busy working on another patient, so she was placed on an examination table to wait for him to be free. As soon as the medic finished with his patient, he pulled back the privacy screen around the table. The woman, seeing that the other patient was one of the rebels, screamed, grabbed a pair of shears from a side table, and buried them in the Yolongi's chest."

"Wow!" Weems exclaimed. "Did she kill him?"

"No, but not for lack of trying. The medic said that if he was human, the wound might very well have been fatal. But since he's a Yolongi, all she did was puncture his womb sack. The medic stitched him up and he'll be fine in a few weeks."

"Oh, that's right. I forgot that the Yolongi heart is in his pelvis."

"What about the woman?" Sydnee asked.

"Her problem was minor. She's been treated and released already."

"No, I mean what happens to her now for stabbing the Yolongi?"

"Nothing."

"Nothing?" Weems echoed.

"She was held as a slave by the Clidepp Ambassador, a Yolongi, for almost three decades. I'm not going to fault her for going a little nuts when she saw that Yolongi on the other examination table. If he'd been killed, or even seriously wounded, I might have been forced to prefer charges at some level, but since he wasn't seriously harmed, I'm looking the other way."

"I, for one, support your decision," Sydnee said.

"I sort of believed you would."

"I support you also," Weems said. "Those poor women suffered at the hands of that Yolongi bastard. I think it'll take quite a bit of time for them to recover. It's understandable that they hate all the Yolongi. Too bad we haven't had a counselor on board, but neither the *Perry* nor the *Babbage* crew sizes are large enough to justify the position."

"They'll get the help they need once they arrive on Earth."

"Yes, not much longer now," MacDonald said. "And they all look much better. Their general physical health has improved tremendously."

"Not being zapped by guards for every small transgression probably helps," Sydnee said.

"Well, I'm heading back to my nice comfortable bed, ladies," Weems said. "I'll see you at breakfast, or at the scheduled 1000 meeting."

"What's the meeting about?" Sydnee asked.

"All I know for sure is that every officer from the *Perry* has orders to attend. I suspect it might be to discuss leave time and required appearances at the Inquiry Hearing. Now, I bid you both a goodnight, or perhaps a good morning."

When Weems was gone, Sydnee said, "It's so different out here now. The new stations look amazing."

"They're definitely impressive."

Work on two new Earth orbital stations had moved along briskly during the year Sydnee had been gone. One had been completed and the other was reported to be more than eighty percent complete. The first was now handling all freighter traffic and was surrounded by several shipping container farms. One farm held containers waiting to go down to the planet's surface, while another was reserved for containers that had just come up from the surface and were scheduled for departure with an outbound freighter. The third farm was for containers in transit that had been dropped off and were awaiting pickup by another freighter. The first two farms were kept separate because every container had to be irradiated to kill any organism before entering or leaving Earth orbit unless the container had a special exemption.

The station still under construction would eventually handle all passenger traffic. Each of the two new stations was over twenty times larger than any of the three large stations previously in Earth orbit and were clearly visible by the naked eye from the planet. Some Terrans were screaming that they were so large they were affecting the tides, and scientists were tiring of explaining that the new stations just didn't have sufficient mass to cause a noticeable effect.

"I'm feeling a bit of anxiety about the future," Sydnee said.

"I figured that was it."

"Figured what was it?"

"The way you've been acting for the past few weeks. After the rebels caused that brief bit of excitement, I noticed a change. I knew it didn't have anything to do with the escape attempts since you didn't have to hurt anyone."

"Yes, that worked out well."

"It should also help you out at the Inquiry Board."

"How?"

"You can't be painted as a violence-prone madwoman when they know you did your best to avoid hurting anyone after having been authorized to use whatever lethal force was necessary to rescue our people."

"Do you think I would have been portrayed as a violence-prone madwoman otherwise?"

"No, not really. But this shows them that you only use what force is necessary in each situation. I never would have thought to use the fire suppression equipment to end the standoff."

"You're not a violence-prone madwoman either. If not the foam, you'd have thought of something else."

"I'm not so sure. I'm a Marine. We've been trained to deal with situations in a more— direct way, using the weapons we've been issued and the people under our command. I would probably have been trying to position myself for a clear shot at Klieppaso, where you were definitely thinking outside the cube. But you do have a Marine's instinct for knowing when further talk won't get you anywhere and the situation calls for immediate action. We all know you certainly don't hesitate when you reach that point."

"I hope the Inquiry Board looks upon my actions as favorably as you do."

"They will. They're all professional military men and women with decades of experience."

The entire officer complement of the *Perry* easily fit into the large conference room selected for the meeting. It probably could have handled the entire officer complement of an *Ares* class battleship as well.

When Captain Lidden and Commander Bryant arrived and strode to the front off the room, everyone jumped to their feet. Lidden loudly said, "As you were," and the officers settled back into their seats.

"As you most certainly know by now, the *Babbage* has arrived at Mars. Over the next twenty-four hours, the vessels in the transport hold will be removed so the ship can depart to its next assignment. During that same period all of you will receive orders to report to one of the shuttles for immediate transport to the Space Command base in Nebraska, USNA, where temporary quarters have been arranged for us.

"The Board of Inquiry hearings will begin tomorrow. I know that sounds rather sudden, but during the weeks we've been underway, they've had plenty of time to prepare. Each of you will receive notice of where and when you'll be required to appear to give testimony. Some will have little participation in the proceedings, while others of us will be required to be there on a daily basis. If you are not scheduled to appear on a given day, you are free to spend the day as you wish and even travel to visit family and friends. However, if you *are* scheduled to appear and fail to show on time, you will be considered AWOL. Make sure you plan your away time accordingly. Those who can't make time to visit family now will receive time after the Inquiry is complete. Any questions?"

Sydnee raised her hand.

"Marcola."

"Um, sir, is there any indication of which issues they'll be investigating?"

"I imagine they'll take a look at anything and everything that pertained to our established mission and the actions of the *Perry*'s crew in response to the Clidepp rebel incursion into GA space."

"Um, including the, er, situation aboard the diplomatic ship?"

"I wouldn't be surprised," Lidden said, then added with a slight grin, "but I wouldn't worry too much if I were you. The Admiralty Board has ruled on that matter already, and I seriously doubt the Inquiry Board would disagree with their determination. They may investigate the event simply to make it part of the official record and show that slavery of Terrans has been occurring in the Clidepp Empire for decades, despite the denials of the government there. And this time we have the recovered slaves to prove our claim. I'm confident there will be a separate investigation on that issue, but once our sworn testimonies are on the record, our further presence will probably not be required at the other investigative hearings."

"Yes, sir."

"Any other questions?"

Lidden waited through fifteen seconds of silence before continuing. "That's all for now. Carry on." He and Commander Bryant then strode out of the room as the officers jumped to their feet.

"It's too early for lunch," Weems said to Sydnee, "and I don't have anything else to do. Want to grab some coffee?"

"Sure. Might as well. We'll just have to sit around anyway until we get assigned a time to report to a shuttle."

Sydnee and Weems weren't the only ones who opted to grab some coffee while waiting and the guest officers' mess was crowded. Kelly MacDonald had a table all to herself, so the pair took seats there after getting their coffee. Lt. Pete Caruthers, the other officer who had joined Sydnee, MacDonald, and Weems on Diabolisto when they went to recover the MAT, came over and joined the trio after getting his coffee.

"Hi, guys," Caruthers said as he filled the fourth and final seat at the table.

"Hi, Pete," Sydnee said. "Where have you been? We've hardly seen you on the trip to Mars."

"Mostly I've been enjoying the comfort of my bunk and catching up on my reading. I'm really going to miss the great quarters I was assigned here. I'm not looking forward to returning to my closet-sized room aboard the *Perry*."

"I don't think you'll have to," Sydnee said. "I don't think any of us will be returning to the *Perry*."

"No? And why is that?"

"The first time I returned to the *Perry* after being on Diabolisto, I performed a slow flyby around the ship. The damage was unbelievable."

"Yeah, we had to walk the hull to assess the damage."

"Well, I believe it would cost far more to repair the *Perry* than build a new ship. If the war in Region Two was still being waged, they might have tried to repair the *Perry* because a repair would probably be quicker than a new build. Everything may not have worked aboard the *Perry*, or at least not worked properly, but it would have gotten a ship back out on patrol sooner. But now that we're at peace again, I'm betting he'll be sold for scrap rather than trying to get all his old systems up to par."

"And what about us?"

"They'll probably find some other bucket to send to our sub-sector," Weems said. "That ship's crew will get a new ship, and we'll get the clunker. Perhaps we'll get something like the *Portland* or even the *Tokyo*. I think they must be the oldest warships in service with the *Perry* gone."

"Great," Caruthers said. "We're trading one old clunker for another."

"Whatever ship we get," Sydnee said, "has to be in better shape than the *Perry*. The *Portland* and the *Tokyo* are both thirty years newer. And I'm sure the quarters are much closer in size to current standards."

"I hope you're right," MacDonald said. "And I hope we Marines can be assigned an area large enough to create a new practice range. Our range was the best thing about the *Perry*."

"I'll certainly second that," Sydnee said. "I've really missed being able to pop down there to spend a few hours working out. It was a lot more interesting and fun than jogging around a hold or working out in the weight room." A chime sounded in her left ear, causing her to hold up her hand momentarily before touching her Space Command ring and stating, "Marcola," then, after several seconds, "Acknowledged. Marcola out." To her friends, she said, "Have to go, guys. I'm to report immediately to the shuttle bay for my trip dirt-side. See you in Nebraska."

Sydnee had already packed her spacechest and two smaller cases and set them by the door of her quarters where they could be picked up for transport down to the base, but before heading for the shuttle bay she returned to her quarters to grab the duffel that contained her personal armor and weapons. It was unlikely in the extreme that the equipment would go astray during transport, but while in her personal possession, there was no likelihood at all. Besides, she had signed for everything in the duffel and would have to spend a week doing paperwork if any of it was ever lost. Then too, the clothes and personal items in the cases could be replaced easily, but she wasn't so sure about the difficulty of replacing the specialized items in the duffel.

When Sydnee reached the shuttle bay, a logistics officer checked her name on his passenger manifest and told her to go aboard and take a seat. Sydnee stowed her duffel in the cargo locker just behind the flight deck door after entering the ship and then found a seat. The ship was only half loaded, so it would be a while before they departed. At least passengers weren't required to wait outside until everyone was assembled, as was required of Marines prior to an interdiction operation.

As the shuttle filled up, Sydnee buckled her seat belt and prepared for departure. She hadn't seen anyone enter the flight deck since her arrival, so the pilot must have been on board the entire time. She was normally at the controls whenever she was in a shuttle, so it felt strange to be in the rear cabin as the pilot released the skid locks and the shuttle began to move towards the temporary airlock. She wasn't concerned for her safety because military pilots were the best trained of anyone in the flying profession, but it *felt* strange.

The flight was a non-stop to Nebraska, so they avoided having to dock at Earth Station 3 and transfer to another shuttle for the flight down to the planet. Twenty minutes after entering Earth orbit, the shuttle touched lightly down at the Nebraska Space Command Base. Most of the *Perry's* company would be housed there until their testimony at the BOI was complete and decisions were made regarding new assignments. Sydnee, her duffel slung over her shoulder, was given her room assignment by a housing officer at the shuttle pad, and she trudged off in search of the named building.

It was easy to tell they were dirt-side when she entered the quarters assigned her in the forty-story building. The suite was easily twice as large as her quarters aboard the *Babbage*, and eight times larger than her quarters aboard the *Perry*.

Rather than going out to walk about the base, she opted to relax in her large bed and think about the coming days. She had never attended a BOI, but she'd heard about them. They were reportedly quite formal, but the rules were not as rigid as that of a General Court Martial, since the goal was to learn all the facts rather than trying to determine guilt. The guilt-determination part and General Court Martials would come later, after all statements had been taken.

Following her rest, she decided to send some messages. During the past two months, she had fallen back into her regular messaging routine, so everyone was up to date with her news— at least as much as she wanted them to know. Since she was dirt-side, she could have merely called home, but she didn't want to be grilled about the upcoming BOI, so she opted to send vidMails through the military system with its imposed time limits. The first mail was to her Mom.

"Message to Kathee Deleone, Park Central Towers, New York City, USNA, Earth. Begin message.

"Hi, Momma. I just wanted to let you know I've arrived on Earth and I'm at the base in Nebraska. I'm well, and everything is fine with me. Board of Inquiry hearings begin tomorrow and my presence is required, so I won't be able to come home for a visit right away. I have no idea when the hearings will end, but I expect them to last for weeks as they piece together the story surrounding the damage to the *Perry*. I'll let you know as soon as I learn anything new. Love to you and Curtis.

"Sydnee Marcola, Lieutenant(jg), BOQ-1835, Space Command Headquarters Base, Nebraska, USNA. Message complete."

The next three messages went to her sister Sheree, her brother Sterling, and her best friend, Katarina. The message was basically the same to each of the three and merely updated her status, as had the message to her mom.

She still didn't feel either hungry or sleepy when she was done, so she pulled up her personal folder on the computer and reviewed all her notes about the *Perry*, the incident aboard the diplomatic ship, and everything concerning Diabolisto and the battle that followed her return to the *Perry* with the *Abissto*.

Chapter Six
~ July 2nd, 2285 ~

The chamber where the Board of Inquiry would convene was empty when Sydnee arrived the following morning a full half hour early. When she'd awakened that morning, she'd been so nervous that she couldn't fall back to sleep, so she bathed and dressed, then skipped breakfast to walk around the Judicial building complex before going inside and entering the hearing room.

A long table with five high-backed chairs sat on a meter-high raised platform at the front of an austere room devoid of any decoration, while a small table with just one normal office chair occupied an area off to the right side of the room. A table long enough to accommodate ten office-style chairs sat facing the front of the room. Each of the sixteen places had a microphone on the table in front of the chair.

"You're not supposed to be in here, Lieutenant," she heard from behind. Sydnee turned and saw a Lieutenant entering the chamber. She wore a JAG insignia on her collar.

"I was told to report here by 0800."

"Witnesses to be deposed should wait in the appropriate witness waiting area until called. Go back out into the antechamber, turn left, and the witness waiting room for officers is the next door. The waiting room on the other side is for enlisted personnel. Both entrances are marked."

"Oh, I see. I'll be in the witness waiting room then."

As she exited the chamber, Captain Lidden and Commander Bryant were just arriving. Sydnee came to a halt and saluted.

"Good morning, Lieutenant," Lidden said as he returned her salute.

"Good morning, sir."

"Have the sessions begun early?"

"Um, no sir. The only one in the hearing chamber is a lieutenant from JAG. She told me to wait in the witness waiting room until called." Sydnee pointed to the door.

"Then I guess we should all wait there," he said as he moved towards the door.

The waiting room was enormous and had a couple of dozen chairs in small clusters about the room, in addition to a long table with about a dozen chairs where witnesses could work as they waited. Against a side wall there was a large coffee urn and another with brewed tea, plus a large rack of cups. There was also a refrigeration unit with soft drinks.

Captain Lidden selected a chair in one of the informal clusters, sat down, then pulled out a viewpad and began scanning through documents. Commander Bryant sat down next to him. Sydnee, unsure if she should sit close to the Captain or not, selected a chair in the same cluster but across from the Captain and the Commander.

As they sat there in silence, waiting for the proceedings to begin, Sydnee wanted desperately to pump her captain for answers about the future. But she supposed that, at this point at least, he didn't know much more than she did. He was probably just as concerned for his future as she was for hers. A ship's captain couldn't control every crewmember's actions, but in the military they were almost expected to do exactly that, or have a well-documented explanation— usually referred to as 'a damn good reason'— for why they didn't or couldn't.

"Sydnee?" Lidden said a few minutes before 0800.

"Yes, sir?"

Holding out a viewpad to her he said, "Here's a summary of the issues the Board will be investigating."

Sydnee accepted the viewpad and read the displayed text.

1) That Lieutenant(jg) Sydnee Marie Marcola, a member of a security complement from the *Perry* who boarded the *Darrapralis*, a diplomatic ship, with the stated purpose of verifying diplomatic credentials, did, without orders or permission, perpetrate an aggressive act against citizens of a neutral nation while aboard said ship,

2) That the *Perry*, while trying to commandeer a destroyer, the *Glassama*, stolen from a neighboring nation by rebel forces, did collide with said ship,

3) That a Marine officer, First Lieutenant Everett William Kennedy, posted to the *Perry*, against orders, led a raid against rebel forces from a neighboring nation who had established a base on the planet Diabolisto, which is clearly situated in Galactic Alliance territory. Said raid was responsible for the deaths of several rebels while the Marine force attempted to destroy armament stolen from the Clidepp Empire,

4) That Lt. Marcola did assume command of the Marine platoon after the platoon's commanding officer, First Lt. Kennedy, was killed in battle by rebels on Diabolisto. Lt.(jg) Marcola then led the Marine platoon into close combat against said forces, killing some sixty-three rebel fighters and losing two Marines,

5) That Lt.(jg) Marcola did then lead an assault against the rebel encampment and commandeer a stolen Clidepp Empire tug after killing the senior rebel military officer present,

6) That the *Perry*, under the command of Captain Anthony Frederick Lidden, did attack the Clidepp destroyer with which it had collided and was almost destroyed itself in the process,

7) That Lt.(jg) Marcola, assisted by several other officers from the *Perry* and the Marine platoon she had been commanding, did commandeer a stolen Clidepp destroyer, the *Abissto*, and engage the rebels trying to destroy the *Perry*,

8) That during the battle with the *Glassama*, the *Abissto*, under the command of Lt.(jg) Marcola, did fire upon and destroy a freighter, the *Furmmara*, after said freighter fired upon the *Abissto*,

9) That Lt.(jg) Marcola did finally ram the *Abissto* into the *Glassama*, destroying both ships, and

10) While returning to Earth aboard the *Babbage*, Lt.(jg) Marcola, commanding the platoon she had commanded on Diabolisto and in the *Abissto*, did suppress an insurrection by rebel prisoners who had taken a Marine squad and several medical personnel prisoner.

"They make everything sound terrible, sir," Sydnee said when she had finished and handed the viewpad back.

"Oh, it's not so bad. It's just legalese. We'll get a better picture when we see how the JAG officer addresses us."

At precisely 0800, the JAG lieutenant emerged from a side door into the hearing chamber and bid Captain Lidden to enter. Lidden stood up, straightened his uniform, turned his head slightly so the JAG officer couldn't see his action, and winked at Sydnee. Sydnee, just as clandestinely, smiled slightly.

When the doors closed behind Lidden, Sydnee and Commander Bryant were left alone in the antechamber. Bryant didn't seem predisposed towards conversation. His career was riding on this almost as much as Lidden's, although Lidden would take the brunt of it if the Board decided to come down heavy on them.

Over the next few hours, Sydnee's mind began to manufacture all kinds of consequences for her decisions and actions while assigned to the *Perry*, ranging from simple reprimands to severe censure, reduction in rank, and loss of pay and privileges. Since she was already assigned to the *Perry*, the dumping ground for misfits and screw-ups, there was little they could do to her assignment-wise except post her to a ground position at a base no one had ever heard of and permanently revoke her pilot credentials. To keep from dwelling on possible punishments, she began to review in her mind all of the events she believed the BOI would be investigating. She wanted to have her answers ready so she could respond without hesitation, but at the same time, she knew that no matter how well she prepared, there were bound to be questions for which she was not prepared.

At 1138, the door to the hearing chamber opened and Captain Lidden emerged. As the door closed, Sydnee rushed to him and asked, "How did it go, sir?"

"I'm not permitted to discuss the hearing with you or anyone not connected to the JAG office. You'll have your opportunity to address the Board after lunch. Be back here at 1300."

"Yes, sir," Sydnee said to his back as he walked to towards the exit.

Sydnee was surprised that none of the *Perry*'s officers were in the officers' mess when she arrived, but when she thought about it, she realized it was logical. If they didn't have to appear at the BOI hearing, they had probably either gone home or anywhere where they could enjoy their day dirt-side.

After eating alone, she strolled around the base, heading back to the Judicial Center at 1250. The waiting room was empty when she arrived, so she took her seat and waited.

When the doors to the hearing chamber opened at 1300 and the JAG lieutenant gestured to her, Sydnee rose, straightened her uniform, and followed the lieutenant into the hearing room.

Three SC officers and two Marine officers occupied the chairs on the raised platform. Two of the officers were Rear Admirals (Lower), one was a Marine Brigadier General, and the other two held the rank of SC Captain and Marine Colonel. The three general officers occupied the center seats, with the captain and the colonel sitting on opposing ends. When the JAG lieutenant gestured towards the chairs at the long table facing the hearing officers, Sydnee sat down, then immediately had to rise again to identify herself for the record and take the oath.

Admiral Holden, according to the nameplate on the table in front of him, took a minute to explain that the subject for this day's hearing would be the events that occurred aboard the diplomatic ship, *Darrapralis*.

"Lieutenant," the JAG officer said, picking up a viewpad from the table near the right wall, "I'll be posing the questions from a prepared list, but you'll address your answers to the Board. They can interrupt at any time and directly ask you questions which might be required to clarify your previous statement or to ask you something which might be unrelated to your answer. Do you understand?"

"Yes, ma'am."

"Do you have a prepared statement to read to the board regarding the subject which will be covered today or any questions about the procedures?"

"No, ma'am."

"Very well. Let's begin."

Over the next four hours, the board listened to Sydnee's version of what had happened aboard the *Darrapralis*, viewed the video from her helmet cam, and queried her extensively about her motivations.

"That will be all for today, Lieutenant," The JAG officer said after the Board chairman had declared the proceedings in recess for the day. "Be back here tomorrow at 0800."

"Yes, ma'am," Sydnee said as she rose and braced to attention, facing the admirals and captains. She then turned and left the hearing chamber.

Sydnee sat in the waiting room throughout the next two days while the Board began their investigation into what had happened after the *Perry* located the *Abissto* in orbit around Diabolisto. Since she hadn't been aboard the *Perry* when the collision with the *Glassama* occurred, she wasn't called to testify. The Board recessed for the weekend, with plans to resume on Monday morning.

Sydnee debated whether to go home over the weekend but decided against it. It would be a major distraction and she wanted to keep her head clear for Monday in case she was called.

Over the next month, Sydnee spent her weekdays either sitting in the witness waiting room or testifying to the events on Diabolisto or the events in space after she located the damaged *Perry*.

The Board of Inquiry finally recessed to consider the testimonies and deliver their findings. Sydnee was required to remain available during all weekdays until further notice in case the Board needed additional testimony. She was too keyed up to go home anyway. The Board hadn't been easy on her. They had pressed her for specifics and motivations for practically every minute of her time on the planet and in space until the *Glassama* was out of action.

The Board had apparently been so thorough that no one was recalled to give additional testimony, but it was twenty-three more days before they issued their preliminary report and recommendations. The Admiralty Board took just one day to review the findings and approve all recommendations.

"Lieutenant(jg) Sydnee Marcola reporting to the Captain as ordered," she said as she entered the office being used by Lidden and braced to attention. Lidden's XO, Commander Bryant, was present and sitting in a side chair.

"At ease, Sydnee," Lidden said. "Have a seat."

Sydnee was a little surprised by the informality. Lidden had used her given name before but only when they were alone in his office. He had once said that when she was told to have a seat, it meant she wasn't in trouble. But on a later occasion he'd told her to forget that because she was in trouble up to her ears. Because of the mixed messages, she was unsure of what was to come.

"Sydnee, the BOI report has not been officially released yet, but they've concluded their investigations and made their recommendations to the Admiralty Board, which then voted to approve all recommendations. Following the AB vote, certain information was relayed to me with the stipulation that it have limited distribution until the official report is released. At this time, only you and Commander Bryant will be briefed.

"First, the Board has confirmed that your actions aboard the *Darrapralis* were right and proper for the situation. That was almost a given since the Admiralty Board had already reviewed the incident and ruled. But now the official record will state that even key government members in the Clidepp Empire have been privately buying and selling Terran slaves while publicly denying all allegations. The recovered victims were deposed in the hospital as they were being treated and their testimony has become part of the BOI official report. The Empire will never again be able to deny any involvement in perpetuating the slavery problems."

"Um, does that give us the right to free them if we encounter any ships holding slaves?"

"Ships in GA space do not have immunity from slavery laws, except diplomatic ships."

"So the situation has not improved, sir?"

"On the contrary. The GA is pushing the Empire to officially renounce slavery and free all slaves. Unfortunately, they're presently involved in a civil war and we can't expect any legal remedy until the issue of who will control the Empire is settled. Eventually it will be settled, and if the new governing body doesn't adopt the proposed ban and free all slaves, they will find the GA unresponsive to their needs and calls for assistance as they try to rebuild their nation after what we expect will be a horrible, protracted war."

"Um, that's something I suppose."

"It's a great deal more than just something. It's not going to happen right away, but it's going to happen, and we'll be out there to help keep an eye on it.

"Second, the Board, on recommendation from the Mars shipyard engineers, has decided not to repair the *Perry*. It will be stripped of its weapons and armament, then scrapped and recycled. The crew will be reassigned to another ship with orders to return to the sectors we've been patrolling."

"Um, the *entire* crew, sir?"

"Most, as far as I know at this time. Those details are still being decided. A couple of the Marines have reached the end of their enlistment and haven't re-upped yet. There will be one SC officer leaving the ship. Lieutenant Bronson, for failing to react properly during the envelope merge, will be reduced in rank to ensign and reassigned to a post dirt-side."

Being posted dirt-side was about the worst thing that could happen to a bridge officer. It was even worse than the loss of rank.

"That's too bad," Sydnee said.

"He was mainly responsible for the damage to the *Perry*. He only lost his concentration for an instant, but it was the precise instant when his concentration was of paramount importance. If he had dissolved the envelope when he was supposed to, the damage to both ships would have been considerably mitigated and perhaps even non-existent."

"Um, and the rest of the crew, sir?"

"I have been absolved of any responsibility for the initial damage to the *Perry*. The Board ruled that I was performing correctly in accordance with established procedures. My last orders to Lt. Kennedy was that he should perform recon activities only until support arrived, so I'm not being held responsible for the deaths on Diabolisto. I will be given command of the ship assigned to patrol the sectors along the Clidepp border, with Commander Bryant as my XO.

"A number of Purple Hearts will be awarded for injuries sustained during battle, and you'll be receiving a Purple Heart for the injury to your arm. All members of the *Abissto* crew, who performed so valiantly under your command, will receive a GA Star for coming to the rescue of the *Perry* in a severely undermanned and partially disabled ship. Depending on their branch of service, that will either be the SC Star or the Marine Star.

"For your actions and bravery on Diabolisto and throughout the entire period, including preparing the *Abissto* for our use and captaining the ship during the battle, you'll be receiving, in addition to your SC Star, the Bronze Comet. A number of the *Perry's* crew will also receive commendations for acts of selfless bravery during the attacks. And lastly, a commendation has been added to your file for your actions and fast thinking that prevented injures to the captured medical staff during the recent prisoner insurrection aboard the *Babbage*."

"Um, thank you, sir."

"All I did was make the recommendation. The Board agreed that you deserve it and approved the recommendation."

"Um, thank you for the recommendation, sir. Do we know what ship we'll be getting, sir? I hope it isn't the *Tokyo*."

Lidden and Bryant both chuckled.

"No, it's not the *Tokyo*," Lidden said. "We'll be sailing on the *Denver*, GSC-DS2026."

"DS2026?" she said, her eyes lighting up. "A Dakinium-sheathed Destroyer?"

"Yep," Lidden said with a grin, "a brand new *Lyon*-class DS Destroyer that's being christened in several weeks."

"Wow!"

"Wow, indeed. Captain Bersmeister is mad as hell; he was supposed to get the next DS Destroyer. But the Admiralty Board decided that with things worsening in the Clidepp border area, our crew has to get back out there as quickly as possible. And they acknowledge that we'll need the newest ship available to handle the influx of refugees and control potential border skirmishes between the Empire and the rebels. Bersmeister will get the next destroyer off the line and everyone else in the queue will slip down by one position. The situation isn't so bad, though. I understand the Mars shipyard is currently turning out a new, full-sized warship every few weeks and at least one new Scout-Destroyer every single week.

"The Scout-Destroyers have proven to be invaluable in fighting most of the threats facing the GA, but they can hardly fit every need. Admiral Carver used them effectively as her primary weapon in the war against the THUG-pact members because they're highly maneuverable, completely resistant to laser weapons, and almost indestructible against torpedoes. As a result, Light Destroyers, Light Cruisers, and Frigates have been completely phased out, and the Destroyers have been increased almost to the size of the former Frigates. The *Lyon*-class Destroyer is 580 meters in length and 280 thousand tons with 18 decks. The crew complement is 958, and the ship has a top speed of Light-9793.48. I've also learned that our ship designers have come up with some interesting variations on other ship classes."

"Really? Like what, sir."

"We'll save that for later. The only reason I brought it up is because the design-modification training is going to cut into your leave time. I'm sorry to inform you that there won't be time for an extended visit home for any of us. Today is Friday, and I need everyone to begin training on the *Denver* next week so we're ready for our space trials in two weeks. You should be starting on Monday, but I've excused you for that day. However, you'll have to be aboard the *Denver* on Tuesday at 0800, alert and ready for training classes. That means just three and a half days leave."

"Um, I understand, sir. Three and a half days is enough time. I usually start getting antsy after two days with my mother. I love her, but she drives me crazy sometimes because she's always after me to resign my commission."

"Really? You still have about five years left for your educational requirements."

"My stepfather has a lot of pull with politicians, and he says he can get me a job in a Space Command support role that will allow me a special exemption so I can leave the service immediately. I've told him I don't want to leave the service, but my mother keeps nagging him, so he keeps offering to *help* me resign."

"I hope he never succeeds, unless you really want it. You're a fine officer, and I'm confident you'll eventually be a superior warship captain."

"Um, thank you, sir."

"I just wish you would stop 'umming' me all the time."

Sydnee looked at his face closely before speaking. She believed he was only half-serious. "I'm trying to break myself of that annoying habit, sir, but it slips out when I'm nervous."

"You're nervous now?"

"U—, yes sir."

"Don't be. You're a valued member of my crew, and you've done nothing wrong. The only time you should be nervous around me is when I'm screaming in your face like a Marine DI, or perhaps just scowling at you."

Sydnee allowed herself a small grin. "Yes, sir."

"Okay, Sydnee, that's all. Remember not to discuss anything that's been said here today until the BOI officially releases its report, and don't say anything to anybody about the new ship designs. That's still classified information, although I'm sure the secret was leaked some time ago when construction actually began and workers realized the changes."

"Yes, sir. I'll keep it confidential."

"Good. Now go pack your things and go home for a visit, but be aboard the *Denver* for first watch Tuesday."

"Aye, sir," Sydnee said as she stood. She then braced to attention, turned on her left heel, and left the office.

Riding the tube from Nebraska to New York City didn't take much longer than taking an airborne shuttle, owing to the extreme, never-ending traffic congestion over the NYC area. The Express train trip through the vacuum tube to Chicago took twenty minutes. Then it was just another thirty minutes to the recently completed uptown station in NYC. The enormous new station occupied a substantial part of the land where Harlem had stood until the big earthquake in the mid twenty-third century. A wide split centered on the 125th Street earthquake fault line created a new water connection between the Hudson River and the East River when a three-hundred-foot-wide swath of Manhattan sank below sea level. The result was six boroughs instead of just five.

The final leg of the twenty-four-hundred kilometer trip was completed via oh-gee cab. The ride to Park Central Towers added just five minutes to the trip once Sydnee was able to find an available taxi in the train station. A landing pad on the ninety-fourth floor of the towering building left only a short walk from the cab to the front door of the family's co-op.

Sydnee had left almost all of her personal possessions at home when she entered NHSA, so she didn't have her master key with her, and the door wasn't accepting her handprint. After five minutes of waiting for someone to open the door, she slumped down against the wall. She had no sooner reached the floor when the door opened and her sister Sheree peered out.

"What are you doing on the floor?"

"Waiting for someone to open the door."

"Sorry. I'm the only one home and I was in the shower. Where's your key?"

"I left it here when I went to the Academy. This is my first time home, and my palm print wouldn't open the door."

"The control unit burned out last year. We had a new one installed and had to reload our prints and voices."

"Voices?"

"Yeah, it's also voice activated now. Curtis wanted to set it up so it would only respond to an eye scan because he said it's the most secure, but Mom and I put our foot down. We told him we weren't going to stick our faces up against some sensor in the hallway when we got home. There's no telling who could have touched it while we were out, and God only knows what kind of germs they might have left on it."

"How do I set it up for my voice and handprint?"

"Come on inside. We can do it from in here. I'm half naked and I'm not coming out into the hallway dressed like this."

From her position, Sydnee had only been able to see Sheree's head. She stood up and entered the apartment, only then realizing Sheree was naked except for the large towel wrapped around her and knotted above her bosom. "You mean *undressed* like this. But what's the big deal? That's ten times more cloth than you wear when you go to the beach."

"It's a towel, not a swim suit."

"The last bikini I saw you wear had less cloth than it takes to cover my palm."

"On the beach everyone is almost naked, so I don't feel out of place. Standing next to you in your uniform and boots I feel naked even with this towel. Do you always have to wear so much clothing? I can see why your love life is so dismal."

"How do you know my love life is dismal?"

"It must be. Look at yourself in a mirror."

"I see myself like this every day."

"That's another thing. You not only dress like the boys, you're starting to look more like them every day. No wonder you can't find a guy."

"Who says I can't find a guy?" Sydnee said with feigned indignation.

"You've found somebody?"

"Maybe," she said coyly.

"Who is it?"

"Um, he's a shipmate."

"Why the 'um?' You only do that when you're nervous."

"I'm not nervous. It's just that— well— nothing is settled yet. We're still learning about one another."

"Have you had sex?"

"That's one of the things that's not settled yet."

"Don't you know?"

"Of course I know. The answer is no. And I don't know if we should. We have to work together— a lot. It could get awkward."

"Doesn't he want to?"

"He's sort of made a few minor overtures."

"Overtures? Are you talking about having sex or listening to Beethoven?"

"Having sex."

"The way you talk about it, listening to Beethoven sounds more exciting."

"Funny." Pointing to the control panel for the security system, Sydnee said, "Show me how to use this thing to record my voice and palm print."

"I wasn't kidding about germs before. If you can, use the voice activation only. Use the palm print in the hall as a *last* resort."

"What's going on? You never used to be worried like this, and you never mentioned anything in your vidMails."

"We don't know. There have been a number of unexplained deaths in the building recently. Everyone is nervous. I've been showering four or five times every day, and Curtis just installed a new internal environmental system after sealing off the building's air-purification vents inside the co-op. He had air samples taken and they were negative for any harmful airborne bacteria, but he decided to separate us from the rest of the building as a precaution until they discover why so many people are dying."

"How many?"

"I've lost count. Somewhere around twenty-six I think."

"Oh my God! Twenty-six co-op residents in one of the most exclusive buildings in the city? I can tell I'm going to sleep well tonight."

"Sorry, sis, but I thought you should know. Here, just place your right hand against the palm plate and enter AJ8-2Emc2. After it accepts your print, tell it your name. Then leave your hand on the glass and talk about anything until the machine tells you it has an adequate sample. The instructions suggest you assist the unit by saying something like, "Open the door, Jeeves."

"Jeeves?" Sydnee said with a giggle.

"Curtis named it."

"Nuff said," Sydnee said with a grin.

Chapter Seven
~ September 7th, 2285 ~

"Sweetheart, why didn't you tell me you were coming today?" Kathee Deleone said as she arrived home and saw her two daughters sitting on the living room sofa."I would have stayed home so I was here to greet you."

Sydnee rose as her mother hurried over with outstretched arms to embrace her. After their hug and cheek kiss, Kathee stepped back to give her daughter the once-over. "You look thin. Are they feeding you enough?'

"Momma, I'm four pounds heavier now than when I entered the Academy."

"Well— you *look* thin."

"Perhaps it's because I'm in better physical condition than I was back then. You know, more muscle, less fat. I run every day and work out."

"Men prefer their women with a little fat, sweetheart. They want a few curves. You should put on a few pounds— in the right places of course. I know a great surgeon who can change your whole life in just a two-hour visit."

"Big boobs and hips are what *some* men want. Others want a sharp mind and a healthy body."

"None that I've ever met."

"You were never in the military."

"No, I wasn't. And I wish you weren't either."

"Momma, don't start. I love my job. I love being in the military. I can't imagine a life of simply living for the next party or social event. If that's what you want for yourself, that's fine. But I want more."

"You're going to get yourself killed out in space, and I won't even know you're gone for several months. We never did get your father's body back. They told me the area of the ship where he was fighting at the Battle for Higgins was totally destroyed and open to space. They never found anything they could identify as coming from him."

"That was true of many good people, Momma. According to the logs, the last contact they had with dad indicated he was doing his job and making a difference. That's all I want people to be able to say about me— that I did my job and my efforts made a difference."

"Well, I'm just glad they sent you out where you'd be safe instead of shipping you off to Region Two to die in that terrible war."

"Um— Momma, I have a confession."

Kathee Deleone's face instantly reflected shock. "You're not going to tell me you've been in Region Two all this time, are you?"

"Um— no."

"That's a relief. I was afraid you were going to tell me you've been in extreme danger during that time when we couldn't contact you."

"Um— that's sort of what I have to tell you. I haven't been entirely truthful in my vidMails because I knew you'd worry. But everything will come out now, as soon as the Board of Inquiry findings are released to the press."

"What do Board of Inquiry findings have to do with you? You said you weren't even on the *Perry* when it suffered the damage."

"The BOI is why I haven't been able to come home since we arrived back on Earth. I had to be available for the hearings."

"Hearings for what? Did you do something illegal?"

"Um— no. But it's complicated. Come into the living room and sit down. I'll tell you everything."

Seventy-two minutes later, Sydnee wrapped up her story. Her mother had listened attentively to every word and somehow refrained from asking any questions until she was done.

"So, you shot two men aboard a diplomatic ship that had been attacked by rebels and disabled. Then you landed on a planet where rebels were living and attacked them in order to destroy their weapons. Then you fought them in a ground battle when they came after you, but in doing that, they killed the Marine in charge. Then you had to take command, and two more Marines were killed. Then you killed a rebel officer who was trying to kill you with a missile, you stole a Clidepp tug, and two fighters pursued you and tried to kill you. Then after reporting to your ship, you returned to the planet and were attacked by a giant sea monster. After that, you took command of a rebel destroyer and attacked another rebel destroyer that was attacking the *Perry*. Then aboard the *Babbage*, you put down an insurrection by rebels that broke out of their prison hold. Is that about it?"

"Pretty much. Except— I, um, injured my arm when we collided with the rebel ship."

"How bad?" her mother asked anxiously.

"Nothing to worry about. It's all healed now. It was just a dislocation at the shoulder joint. But they're going to give me a Purple Heart because it happened during battle. And, um, they're also going to give me an SC Star and a Bronze Comet medal for the other stuff I did."

Kathee Deleone sighed and shook her head sadly. "And here I thought you'd been safe and sound during the past year. You told me all you were doing was checking passports and inspecting cargo."

"That's the way it began. It all changed when a rebellion broke out in the Clidepp Empire. Until then I thought I'd die of boredom."

"You can't die of boredom, sweetheart, but you can die if someone shoots you or blows you up." Her mother sighed loudly before adding, "I'm almost sorry I begged Curtis to make sure you didn't go to Region Two. You were probably in more danger in that backwater sector."

"What? You begged Curtis to change my posting? Momma, how could you?"

"I'm sorry, honey. I was so fearful you might be killed in Admiral Carver's war that I couldn't stop myself."

"It wasn't Admiral Carver's war, Momma. She didn't want it any more than you."

"You can say that, but she's always *right* in the middle of any fight."

"That's because she's the best military strategist and commander we have. Smart political and military leaders have always put their best people in charge when war is forced upon us. I can't believe you begged Curtis to change my assignment."

"I did it for you, honey."

"Well, please don't do it for me again, Momma. I'm not a child anymore."

"I'm sorry, dear. I won't do it again. Are you going back out to that same border area, or are you going to try to get posted to Admiral Carver's command?"

"I can be more useful at the Clidepp border than in Region Two. I believe we're about to get overrun with war refugees. The GA Senate has ordered us to turn them back if they haven't been issued visas."

"That's inhumane. They're only trying to escape the war."

"We don't make the rules. I understand their plight and sympathize, but I can also see the plight of the planetary leaders who fear they won't be able to assimilate millions and millions of new immigrants. Immigrants need jobs, which in turn establishes incredible competition for available positions and lowers the wages of the entire workforce. A flood of immigrants *always* brings a flood of new or previously eradicated diseases that the planet is unprepared to fight, and most of the immigrants will have to be cared for by the taxpayers of the planets for decades at a time when wages are falling due to the influx of too many new job seekers. It's a complex situation. Try to act humane, and you place an incredible burden on yourself, your family, your neighbors, and your nation. The GA Senate has made the very tough decision that only people with official visas will be allowed in. Our difficulty will be in stemming the tide of illegals and turning them back to their home nation."

"So you'll be right back in a dangerous situation?"

"Yes, we're going back to our patrol sector very soon, but it's doubtful we'll run into any more Clidepp destroyers out there. The most recent patrol was extremely unusual. From now on all we'll face will be illegal aliens and smugglers."

———————————————

The shuttle flight to the *Denver*, which was docked at an open framework in the enormous shipyard that orbited Mars, was uneventful. As on the trip down to Earth from the *Babbage*, Sydnee was just a passenger. For safety reasons, shuttles only had windows on the flight deck, and the large monitor at the front of the main cabin hadn't been activated, so Sydnee was unable to see an outside view of the *Denver*. It didn't really make much difference. Once she'd seen the outside of one SC destroyer, she'd pretty much seen them all.

All SC warships had a similar exterior appearance, with length and beam being the main difference. They were long, and essentially cylindrical, with concealed openings from which laser arrays and torpedoes could emerge on a moment's notice. All had side-mounted engines in rotating nacelles that retracted into recessed areas when not in use. The stern engines provided all the thrust for normal sub-light travel, with the side-mounted engines only used to assist in fast maneuvering. For FTL travel, a DATFA generator would extend from a protected repository in the sail area to build the envelope.

Warships in centuries past had been sheathed with titanium, and then later with Tritanium, but all new warships were currently being sheathed with Dakinium. The Tritanium outer surface of the *Perry* had been scarred, pitted, and dented even before the collision with the *Glassama*. Decades of contact with space junk and micrometeorites had taken its toll. The outer surface of the *Denver* would never exhibit such damage because it was nearly impregnable. Since being discovered on Dakistee, where it had been used to cover the outer surface of an underground facility created by an ancient civilization, the alloy known as Dakinium had been the focus of the largest scientific program in the history of Space Command. They had sought to replicate the material, but had never quite been able to match it exactly. As it turned out, that failure had been fortuitous because the new alloy produced the DATFA double-envelope that made Light-9790 possible. The original material discovered on Dakistee, while slightly more resistant to damage than SC's Dakinium, was unable to produce the resonance required for the amazing speed improvement. The scientists had continued to work on the alloy, and had even managed to improve their version slightly while still producing an alloy that could establish the necessary double-envelope resonance.

When viewed from outside, Tritanium-sheathed ships appeared bright bronze in color, while Dakinium-sheathed ships were jet-black. The color was naturally occurring but almost seemed like an intentional statement of increased lethality.

Sydnee spent her short time aboard the shuttle reflecting on her recent visit home. Her mother never seemed to stop dropping hints that Sydnee's life would be so much better if she wasn't in the military. After the first day, Sydnee hadn't even responded. She simply tuned the messages out whenever her mother started. She'd really enjoyed the time spent with her sister Sheree, even if Sheree was becoming just like Momma. But at least Sheree never once tried to convince Sydnee to resign her commission as soon as possible.

Sydnee wished Sterling had been able to come home while she was there, but he was involved in a very complex business deal for Curtis in South Africa and couldn't get away for a few weeks. By then, Sydnee would be aboard her new ship and might even be out of the solar system as space trials in the *Denver* began. She'd have to be satisfied with vidMails. Now that they'd reconnected, she and Sterling exchanged vidMails at least once every two weeks.

Since the shuttle would be immediately returning to Earth, it didn't enter a shuttle bay. Rather, it simply docked with a larboard airlock. As soon as the connection was made and verified air-tight, the eight occupants of the shuttle rose, collected their personal items, and moved into the *Denver*. Sydnee, as the only officer aboard, was allowed to exit the small ship before the other passengers.

"Welcome aboard the *Denver*, Syd," Lt. Carstairs said as she stepped over the threshold and into the ship. Security protocol required that at least one SC officer and one Marine be posted at any open access point in the ship. Lieutenant(jg) Elton Carstairs had been the OD on the day she had first reported aboard the *Perry*.

"Thank you, El. What do you think of him?"

"He's first rate. What a difference from our old *Perry*. So far almost everything has worked to perfection. I've only had to call Engineering once when there was no hot water in my head the first day. They fixed it in seconds. They said a 'tee' valve inside the bulkhead was still closed from a system test. Since then everything's been perfect."

"Great. I'm looking forward to seeing my quarters."

"Do you have your assigned quarter's info?"

"Not yet."

"Hold on." Carstairs used his CT to acquire the frame-section, deck and compartment number, then gave the information to Sydnee.

"Thanks, El. I'll see you later."

"After you settle in, take a tour of the ship, Syd."

"I will." Turning towards the Marine on the other side of the door, Sydnee said, "Hello, Rogers. How are you doing?"

"Hi, Lieutenant, I'm doing great. Welcome aboard."

"Thanks."

Using the ship layout charts available on monitors mounted on corridor bulkheads throughout the ship, Sydnee was able to find lift locations and the access points for transport cars. It was a lot easier to navigate her way through the *Denver* than it had been through the *Perry*. The door to her quarters opened immediately as she stopped in front of it, and as she stepped inside, the lights came up to half intensity. Her new quarters, like those of everyone else on board, were incredibly spacious when compared to those on the *Perry*. Her space chest and smaller cases had already been delivered, so after a few minutes spent exploring the three rooms, she unpacked and stowed her gear, then stacked the empty cases one inside the other and placed the large space chest on the deck in her wardrobe locker.

Sydnee was reading though her schedule for the next day when the visitor announcement system said, "Lt. Kelly MacDonald is at the door."

"Open," Sydnee said. As the door slid into its pocket, Sydnee said, "Hi, Kel. Come on in. Welcome to my new quarters. Where are yours located?"

"Hi, Syd," MacDonald said as she entered. "I'm one deck down and three frame-sections back. Corporal Rogers reported that he'd seen you come aboard earlier, so I decided to come up and say hi. It's about time·you showed up. When you didn't show up yesterday, we began to wonder if you'd been transferred."

"I didn't get any leave until the BOI finished its investigation, issued its reports, and they were voted on by the AB, so Captain Lidden gave me an extra day of weekend leave."

"No other leave at all?"

"Nope. Captain Lidden, Commander Bryant, and I had to be available for questioning every single day until the investigation was completed and filed."

"So you only got a few days at home?"

"Yeah, but that was enough. I've told you how my mom is about my being in the military. I love her, and I know she wants the best for me, but sometimes she drives me *crazy*."

"I think a lot of moms are like that. They have trouble letting go and remembering you're all grown up and need to make your own decisions."

"I guess. So how was your leave?"

"Great. I got to see my two brothers and three sisters, as well as all the spouses and nieces and nephews, plus my folks, aunts, and uncles."

"I've always wondered what it must be like to have a big family. My dad's folks never approved of his marriage to my mom and cut off all contact before they were even married, so I've never met anyone from his side of the family. My mom was orphaned when she was nine and raised by an aunt who passed a few years ago, and there's no other family on her side."

"You got to see your sister and brother, didn't you?"

"I spent almost the entire three days with my sister. My brother was away on business, so he couldn't get home over the weekend. Curtis has him involved is some big deal in South Africa."

"A big deal? With dolls?"

"No, his company is trying to expand into sports equipment now."

"Sounds exciting," Kelly said, with a bored expression.

"Yeah, it's lay-awake-at-night-dreaming-about-big-orders-for-footballs kind of stuff," Sydnee said with a matching expression.

"Well, I've got something exciting to tell you. The Marine complement aboard ship has been doubled in size to a full company. After our little foray on Diabolisto, I guess they figured we have to be equally ready to handle both refugees and rebels."

"Have you seen their files and evaluated them yet?"

"No, not yet. Why?"

"I'm just wondering if Space Command and the Corps will continue past practices. The *Perry* was always the dumping ground where everyone in the military sent screw-up's, malcontents, and undesirables that they didn't have justification for booting from the service or even posting dirt-side. Speaking of which, poor Bronson will probably never have a post aboard ship again. So, the question now is— will the *Denver* become the new dumping ground?"

"You've spent quite a bit of time with our Marines, and you've even commanded a platoon on two occasions. Do you feel that any of them are screw-ups?"

"Not that I experienced. I've found every one of them to be dedicated, hard working, and hard fighting members of the Corps. I've been proud to serve alongside them and to lead them."

"So maybe the people sent to the *Perry* for being screw-ups weren't really screw-ups at all. Maybe the people who sent them were the screw-ups. Rhett was allegedly sent to the *Perry* because he bumped into a general and the general was splashed with coffee. Who's to say the general wasn't at fault? Maybe he wasn't watching where he was walking and bumped into Rhett. But nobody could ever suggest such a thing openly because he was a general. And what about Carstairs? All he did was pass on a joke about his captain to someone he trusted. I'll concede that he shouldn't have done it, but it had nothing to do with his competence in performing his duties or his dedication to SC. The trusted friend who ratted him out was more a screw-up, if you ask me, and I won't even comment on the captain if it happened the way Carstairs said it did."

"I guess you have a point."

"Damn straight. But if we do occasionally get saddled with a genuine screw-up, it's our job as officers to get that individual toeing the mark. And if we need help— well, that's why we have noncoms. Sergeants and petty officers have been keeping the enlisted men and women under them in line and properly trained for hundreds of years."

"You're right. I guess I was just wondering if what we accomplished against the Clidepp rebels was going to show others we're not just a ship of misfits."

"Is this post-leave blues I'm hearing?"

"No, it's a genuine concern. I think we've proved that we deserve a second chance to be viewed as something other than a dumping ground. Will we get it?"

"I don't know. But I have news that will excite you. Drum roll please— an area twice the size of the one we had on the *Perry* has been set aside for the Marine Practice Range. We can begin setting it up as soon as the space trials are over and we leave for our posting sector."

"*That* is great news. I can hardly wait until it's ready for use."

"Martin Aguilo is already working up a new design. He says it'll blow our minds when we see it and test our skills like never before. In addition to the city combat range and the jungle combat range, we're going to have a shipboard combat range in a reconfigurable alien vessel."

"Wow, that's great. Everything has been so wonderful lately. First the news from the BOI, then learning that we were getting this incredible new ship, and now this."

"What did the BOI tell you?"

"Nothing directly. Captain Lidden briefed me with some highlights, such as the medals awards and our getting the *Denver* to replace the *Perry*."

"That's all?"

"All?"

"I mean, nothing about what they intend to do with the rebels? They killed three of our people."

"I don't think the BOI gets involved with that end of things. They were just charged with determining if *our* actions were just and proper. The GA Senate will probably have to decide what justice the rebels will face."

"Yeah, you're probably right. Hold on." Touching her Space Marine ring, she said, "MacDonald." After listening for a few seconds, she said, "Yes, sir. MacDonald out." To Sydnee she said, "Gotta go. The Major wants to see me."

"Coming back?"

"I don't know how long I'll be. I'll see you tomorrow."

"At breakfast?"

"Sure. The usual time? See you then."

"Bye."

Sydnee finished her preparations for the next day and decided to forego a tour of the ship. She was tired and expected to be on the ship for a long time, so she began preparing for bed. After setting the controls of the gel-comfort bed she smiled and slipped between the sheets for the first time. It was just as wonderful as she'd expected it to be. The lights dimmed on her vocal command and she began to sink into a deep sleep.

Chapter Eight
~ September 11th, 2285 ~

"Good morning," the Space Command officer standing before the large monitor at the front of the bridge said to the others arrayed around the *Denver's* control consoles. "I'm Commander Nassat. This gentleman standing on my left is Dr. Edward Galton. He's the chief design engineer for the new bridge consoles, so pay careful attention because you're going to learn how to operate this equipment from the very best authority." Turning towards the civilian, he said, "Dr. Galton?"

"Thank you, Commander," Galton said as the Commander moved aside and he moved to Nassat's former position. "Good morning, everyone. As you can plainly see, the consoles on the bridge of this new ship are unlike anything you had on the *Perry*. Their appearance is not all that dissimilar from the previous Lyon-class destroyers, but the function is radically different. The envelope merge failure of the *Perry* and near loss of the entire crews of both ships finally convinced the SHQ decision-makers to allow for slightly more automation than had previously been acceptable.

"For two centuries, fear that rogue computers would one day take control of mankind if draconian restrictions were not in place to prevent computers from making unsupervised decisions in command and control situations has prevented scientists from offering many of the capabilities and advancements we knew were possible. Personally, I find the idea that a computer or cyborg could *ever* dominate mankind to be totally absurd. We will always be the controlling force, not the other way around. But we're not here to debate philosophical views, so let's begin the orientation.

"The bridge consoles provide full control of the ship, just as they always have in the past. The differences are the interfaces and the advanced level of control possible with the help of computers. I've referenced the failed envelope merge already, so let's use that as an example. The merge failed because the helmsman aboard the *Glassama* altered the flight of the lead ship at a critical moment, ostensibly to prevent the merge procedure from being successful. When the *Glassama* performed a slight roll and yaw, the helmsman aboard the *Perry* lost his concentration for just an instant. He didn't cancel the envelope at the precise moment intended and thus allowed the two ships to collide. This was confirmed through a review of the bridge logs and all sensor information. A computer would not have lost its concentration and would have cancelled the envelope in time to either minimize damage or avoid it altogether if the computers had been allowed to control the ship. From this time forward, they will be.

"Once the helmsman initiates the envelope-merge procedure, the computer will monitor the flight of both ships. In less time than it takes you to blink an eye, the computer will take control of the ship, fire the lasers at the designated target, and cancel the envelope, thus saving the ship from harm. With the computer in command of the ship's flight, there will be almost no chance of deadly accidents resulting from an envelope merge.

"But the biggest improvement this new system offers is that officers will no longer have to press buttons or push levers at the consoles. The buttons and levers are still there because we realize it will take time to adjust, but there's no need to use them. Each bridge officer will wear a lightweight sensor interface over his or her left ear. Your CT will authorize your command of the console through the interface device, and all you'll need to do is look at the function on the console and think the command. The computer will then carry it out. For those of you who are interdiction pilots, it will seem similar to the procedure used for com channel and private conversation selection when wearing the helmet of your personal body armor."

Dr. Galton stopped and pointed to Bryant, who had raised his hand. "Yes, Commander?"

"Dr. Galton, will there be a conflict when the individual manning a console asks a question of myself or someone else? And can the computer distinguish with absolute certainty between a command and mere bridge chatter."

"When someone needs to address another person, they simply say, 'Deactivate link.' When they're done, they say 'Reactivate link.'"

"I see. And when the link is deactivated, does the computer ignore all sensors?"

"No, and that's the best part. When the operator is out of the loop, the computer takes full control of the ship's functions handled by that console."

"I see. If someone forgets to deactivate the link and responds to a question, is there a chance the computer can interpret that as a command change?"

Dr. Galton was silent for a second before answering. "Well—it's possible, depending upon the eye movement of the console operator, that the computer could perceive it as a command change."

"I see. And is it possible to lock the computer out altogether and perform all operations manually as we've done in the past?"

"That would have the effect of invalidating all the new safety protocols. The computer would not be able to correct for operator error."

"Then it is possible?"

"Uh, yes, it's possible. Space Command stipulated that such an option be available. But then the console operator and the watch commander become equally responsible for any accidents."

"I see. And how would the console operator, or in fact anyone on the bridge, know that the link was either active or inactive for that console."

"There are two tiny LED lamps on the console to signal the status. Green means the link is active and red means the link is inactive."

"So, red means the computer has control?"

"Yes, Commander."

"And if the computer has been locked out entirely?"

"Then both LEDs would be dark."

"What if one or the other burn out?"

"That's hardly likely. But all console functions and displays are under constant monitoring by the Engineering computer, and any problems, such as a burned-out LED or display, would be immediately reported to the Engineering Maintenance section."

"I see. Thank you, Doctor."

"You're welcome, Commander Bryant. Are there any other questions? Anyone?" When no one spoke, Dr. Galton said, "Then I ask that all third watch personnel go to the Auxiliary Command and Control bridge. Yard engineers are waiting there to instruct you in the use of the new systems. The first and second watches will be instructed here on the much larger bridge. All consoles on both bridges have been locked into demonstration mode."

As Sydnee and Jerry Weems walked through the corridor, they passed the yard engineers who were the instructors on the main bridge. Once beyond the hearing range of the yard personnel, Sydnee said, "I don't like it already."

"Why?" Weems asked. "You haven't even given it a chance."

"I don't want any computer being able to override my instructions. I don't mind suggestions, but not outright control."

"Galton said that the computer would only take over in extreme situations and that you could block it if you chose."

"Yeah, that's what he said. But the computer systems aboard our ships have always been designed to make sure they *couldn't* take control away from an operator. Now they apparently can. And we're to be the first test. What if the computer code isn't as bug-free as they like to think it is?"

"Then we just shut the computer out, as Galton told Bryant."

"Yeah, if it allows us to shut it out."

"Allows us? Are you becoming paranoid?"

"Maybe. But being a little paranoid isn't always a bad thing. It keeps you on your toes and watchful for possible danger. Instead of thinking of it as being paranoid, think of it as being very security conscious."

"I guess it's all in how you look at it and which side of the issue you're on."

"Yeah. Mark me down on the skeptical-until-proven-foolproof side of any new computer system that can take total control without the consent of the operator."

By the end of the first day, the bridge crews affirmed they fully understood the operation of the new systems. They already knew their jobs and how to do them, so they only had to learn how to interact with the computer.

On day two, all pilots were ordered to report to one of the *Denver's* shuttle bays. Upon arriving there, they learned that the bay contained a newly designed tug and a new Marine Armored Transport, designated respectively as the CPS-14 and the MAT-14. The tug was the largest Sydnee had ever seen or even imagined. At double the size of regular tugs in all dimensions, it was unbelievable that it had managed to squeeze into the bay using the temporary airlock. Then Sydnee glanced over at the temporary airlock on this new ship and realized it was twice the size of the one on the *Perry*. It made sense, because if they had to depressurize the entire bay and then open an outside hatch fully without using the temporary airlock, it was going to dramatically reduce the effectiveness of the new tug. But most importantly, the new tug and the new MAT were both pitch-black in color. Sydnee wondered if that meant what she thought it might mean.

Three Space Command Flight Instructors were standing by to begin the day's session as the pilots took their seats in the chairs provided. Speculations about the new ships and their intended uses began immediately among the assembled officers.

"I'm Commander Belinda Halworth," the senior officer said at exactly 0800. Everyone stopped talking at once and gave her their full attention. "The ships you see behind me are the newest designs in the Space Command and Marine Corps fleets. Although the new Marine aviators haven't reported aboard yet, you will have a full complement of ship and flight personnel when you deploy.

"As you can see, both designs are radical departures from previous ships. First, the ships are sheathed in Dakinium. That gives them the ability to travel at Light-9790. However, the MATs, by themselves, are still only capable of limited sub-light travel speeds in space and oh-gee flight in atmo. And I'll admit right now that the MATs are almost as ungainly in atmosphere as previous models. This new model has stubby wings housed between the passenger deck and the equipment hold. In atmo they swing out to provide greater stability, but the ship still requires a very steady hand and excellent piloting skills. They're even boxier than the MAT-12 when the wings are withdrawn because they're designed to be joined together and/or joined to the tug. Our tugs have always had both sub-light and FTL speeds, in addition to oh-gee flight, so the marriage of these two ships gives us an immense new capability.

"The tug, now renamed as a Central Propulsion Ship, or CPS, can have up to four MATs attached, two on either side. The engine nacelles on this new ship have been moved upward and back, almost to the stern, to allow the MATs to link almost seamlessly with the CPS frame. As on most ships other than warships, the side-mounted engines provide all of the thrust in sub-light speed. When extended and parallel to the fuselage of the ship, they can rotate three hundred sixty degrees vertical. When not parallel, they can also rotate up to ninety degrees forward or aft.

"Finally, although we don't have one in here for this session, the *Denver* will be receiving twenty-four habitat units, each being a self-contained unit with air and water recycling capability, food preparation and dining space, and full sleeping accommodations for up to one hundred six individuals. The habitats are each ten meters deep by twenty meters in length by twenty meters tall with four interior levels for living space, plus an Engineering level. They can comfortably accommodate the largest sentient species in the GA, the Nordakians. I'm sure the significance of the habitat size isn't lost on you. They are exactly one-half the length of full-sized shipping containers. That's for good reason. It's to allow them, when two are joined together, to be transported by normal freighters in a Lewiston Link. However, they also have special couplings that allow them to be joined with a CPS. And— they're Dakinium-sheathed. So when attached to a CPS, they can be enclosed in the double-envelope and be transported at Light-9790 like the CPS-14 and MAT-14s. A fully configured unit will include the CPS, up to four MATs, and up to eight habitats."

By this time, the mouths of half the pilots were slightly ajar as their brains processed the implications of this moon-shattering information.

"Where the battleships have a docking collar beneath them for a Scout-Destroyer, the *Lyon*-class Destroyers have docking clamps for up to twenty-four habitat units. That's only possible because the habitats are Dakinium-sheathed."

"Wish we'd had one on Diabolisto," Sydnee said under her breath to Weems.

"Woulda been nice."

"The new flight simulators can realistically represent any configuration of the CPS-14s, MAT-14s, and habitats. I'm sure they'll get a considerable workout in the months ahead as you complete your space trials and return to your patrol sector. In the past, pilots were required to return to Earth for flight training and certification on new craft. That limited the certified aviator availability on ships in remote areas. The new simulators are so accurate that it's no longer necessary. One of the pilots from the crew will be named as a certified flight instructor before you leave for your posting. Your certification can be earned without ever leaving the ship.

"I have a holographic image of a habitat where you'll get a basic understanding of its functionality. When that presentation is concluded, we can take a break, during which any of you who might be interested can take a look at the CPS-14 or MAT-14. Any questions before we continue?"

Sydnee held up her hand.

"Lieutenant Marcola, isn't it?" Halworth said, as she pointed to Sydnee.

"Yes, ma'am," Sydnee said as she stood up. "I'm assuming the CPS, habitat, and MAT configuration was created to add another dimension to the fighting effectiveness of our destroyers with remote positioning. What about Marine fighters? A few of those would have helped us immensely on Diabolisto."

"The Marine fighters are not sheathed in Dakinium, so they would prevent the creation of a Light-9790 envelope if they were secured to the configured ship."

"The FA-SF4 Marine fighter has folding wings to conserve space when parked. Couldn't we just use a half-sized shipping container sheathed in Dakinium as a fighter bay in place of one of the habitats? It could probably hold a dozen fighters and maintenance parts, or possibly just four fighters and a few tons of extra supplies."

Halworth looked over at the other two flight instructors for a few seconds, and then back at Sydnee. "I know for a fact that that has been discussed, but no decision has yet been reached."

"How about sheathing the Marine fighters in Dakinium? Then they could be attached to the outside of the CPS configuration and also provide the ultimate in protection for the pilots."

"That is also under consideration. It's been a matter of priorities. The demand for Dakinium is incredible. The Mars shipyard fights to get every ounce they can, and we've just recently completed outfitting every Marine and interdiction pilot in the service with personal body armor made from Dakinium. We have urgent requests for more Dakinium from weapons manufacturers and numerous other approved military suppliers. The fact is, we just can't produce all that's needed right now. Supreme HQ is working on plans to step up manufacture, but security is so tight around Dakinium facilities that it's difficult. We can't allow any to fall into the hands of unauthorized people. Every single ounce of produced Dakinium must be accounted for. The material gives us a considerable edge over every other nation and every criminal organization, and we're striving to maintain that. Eventually, someone will develop a similar product, but we're not going to do anything that will hasten that day. We'd love to see fighters sheathed in Dakinium, as well as *all* Space Command vessels, but it's just not possible right now. Most support ships, where Light-9790 isn't a priority, are still being sheathed in Tritanium."

"I see. Thank you," Sydnee said as she sat back down.

"Anyone else?" When no one spoke up, Halworth said, "Okay, let's proceed with the holographic presentation of the habitat modules."

"I can't wait to schedule some simulator time," Sydnee said excitedly to Jerry Weems as they walked to the officers' mess at lunchtime. "I haven't been at the flight controls of a small ship since we left Diabolisto in the *Babbage*. Even some simulator time would be great."

"Yeah, it's been about three months for me also."

"So, um, what do you think of the new CPS system?"

"It's amazing. A modular spaceship where the configuration can be changed in minutes to suit multiple purposes and which can be disassembled easily to fit inside, or attach to, a destroyer. It's only weakness seems to be a total lack of weapons, unless there's more to it than they're telling us at this point."

"Weapons would be easy to add."

"Really? How?"

"Remember the torpedoes the rebel freighter fired at us while we were attacking the _Glassama_?"

"Yeah," he said matter-of-factly, then realized what she was driving at. "Oh, yeah, a habitat unit could be outfitted with weapons and ordnance. If you're going into a hostile situation, you simply take a weapons unit in place of a habitat unit. They could even look the same so no one would know until and unless the weapons were needed."

"Yeah. And I hope they decide to use a disguised container to transport some Marine fighters as well. If we're going into a hostile situation like the one on Diabolisto, they'd be worth their weight in gold. Can you imagine if we'd landed there with a full CPS and habitat unit instead of just a MAT? We wouldn't have had to trudge through kilometers of swamp, and we could have wrapped up the whole operation in one day. We could have used a couple of the habitat units to hold the rebels in a lockdown and then gone looking for the _Perry_ in the CPS."

"Assuming the entire habitat unit didn't disappear into a sink hole."

"Well, yeah, there's that."

"It seems that no matter how well prepared you are, there's always something you didn't count on or prepare for."

"I guess something unexpected is always a possibility. I sure never expected to be attacked by a man-eating Lampaxa Vorheridine."

"It did make for an exciting five-minute fight."

"Five minutes? Is that all it was?" With a sigh of exasperation, she added, "It seemed like an hour."

The two weeks of intense training was grueling, but it was finally over and the ship was ready to deploy for its space trials on time. The crew of Light Destroyers like the *Perry* had been officially established at five hundred, but because of the war in Region Two, the *Perry* had been limping along at a mere four hundred two. A full crew complement for *Lyon*-class Destroyers was established at nine hundred eighty-eight, but when the *Denver* deployed on its space trials, it was manned by only eight-hundred ninety-five. Space Command promised that the ship would have its full complement of SC and Marine staff when it left on patrol.

There were so many new faces aboard ship that Sydnee almost felt like she was on the wrong vessel. It was only when she reported for her watch on the bridge that the ship really began to feel like home because the bridge was fully staffed by the same old watch teams. Lt. Bronson was gone now, of course, and Milty was no longer the second officer. Milty had owed his third watch commander position to the officer shortage. A new SC Lt. Commander, Melissa Avery, would now be the second officer and Lt. Mark Milton became third officer until another new Lt. Commander reported aboard. As temporary third officer, Milton moved to first watch and would be the watch commander whenever Captain Lidden wasn't on the bridge.

At one time, a new ship, or one that had previously undergone considerable refurbishing or upgrades, would deploy for space trials for as long as six months. This was reduced to ninety days when the shortage of ships on patrol necessitated the cut. Now the space trials had been further cut to only sixty days unless severe problems or exposed potential problems demanded an extension. But rigorous pre-launch testing standards at the Mars shipyard had been implemented since the first Scout-Destroyer, the *Colorado*, had been built, and most new ships experienced few of the serious problems that occurred aboard that small ship in its early days. And none had ever experienced the massive electrical failure that left the *Colorado* adrift in deep space without power or communications.

In addition to the new crewmembers, a horde of test engineers and instructors were aboard the *Denver* when he deployed. The instructors were there to evaluate the crew's response to new technology and provide training if requested. A half dozen simulators were available for pilot testing and certification, although none of the new CPS-14s or new MAT-14s had been brought aboard. Nor was a single habitat unit attached to the *Denver's* keel.

"So, what do you think of our new home?" Captain Lidden asked his XO, Commander Bryant, during their daily status meeting.

"I've fallen in love. We tolerated the *Perry*, mostly because we had no choice, but the *Denver* is another matter entirely. He's everything I could have wished for. Even during these space trials, we haven't had one percent of the problems we'd see on a daily basis with the *Perry*. And the engineers can replace parts without constant worry that they're going to burn out during the first thirty seconds because they weren't designed for an ancient ship that should have been melted for scrap half a century ago."

"It's wonderful when things work the way they're supposed to. How about the crew?"

"Not a single complaint that I've heard, other than the fact that it takes too long to get anywhere because the ship is so much larger. And in reality, the time factor isn't even true— it just seems that way because we have to travel so much further. Yes, the ship is longer, but the transport cars can whisk you the entire length of the ship in under a minute. On the *Perry* it took four minutes for that trip in non-stop mode, and the ship was two hundred thirty-five meters shorter.

"I guess people will always look for *something* to complain about."

"I suppose. Even the yard personnel have only had minimum complaints."

"The yard personnel have been complaining about the *Denver*? This is supposed to be their show horse, their first opportunity to show the military that computers are better able to take care of their ship than people can."

"They're not complaining about the ship. Their complaint is with us. Most of the console operators on the bridge deactivate the computer control when they man their station at the beginning of their watch, if it's even active when their watch starts. The yard personnel are upset that no one trusts the computers and are running on manual, as allowed by Space Command."

Lidden laughed. "I've been so busy with other matters that I hadn't noticed."

"I haven't said anything to anyone, but I've noticed the console lights that indicate the link is activate are *always* dark. Everyone is running on manual."

"It will probably take awhile for the people trained to operate the ship to begin trusting a computer to do it. I imagine future generations will be less hesitant to trust them."

"I guess only time will tell."

"Tell me, Bry, were you in their place, would you trust the computer?"

"I trust it to gather and interpret the information flowing from sensors and to report that information to me, but putting my life and the lives of every member of the crew into the electronic 'hands' of a computer? I don't think so. Even so, I believe that under certain conditions, such as an envelope merge, the computer is far more capable of responding quickly and without emotion. I would definitely activate it in that situation."

"Let's hope we never have to perform a merge again. We got lucky the last time."

"We have a Dakinium hull now."

"We have a hull sheathed in Dakinium that's impervious to laser weapons and almost impervious to torpedoes. I'm not so sure how we'd fare if the ship impacted another ship. Would the Dakinium keep the steel bulkheads from collapsing? I asked a yard manager while we were at Mars and he sort of sidestepped the issue by saying that someday we'd have enough Dakinium available so that the entire framework would be constructed of it. I don't know if they've ever tested the current designs from the perspective of having the ship crushed."

"Then we'll just have to avoid using the envelope merge until we know."

"Yeah, that would be best. Anyway, there's one thing we know for sure— no one can get away from us now that we have Light-9790 speed."

"That's for sure."

Chapter Nine
~ November 23rd, 2285 ~

The *Denver* returned to the Mars shipyard on schedule after completing its space trials. Everything had gone exceedingly well. Problems were far less than the ship's engineers were used to handling on any average day. There were complaints about temperatures in quarters exceeding the high or low settings, slight electrical problems with equipment failing to function, gel-comfort beds failing to maintain their settings, and lights not illuminating on command, but all were resolved quickly. The more serious problems were reports of leaking pipes and a lift with three crewmembers aboard who got stuck in the tube. The most serious problem was a defective sensor on the hull that required a team of engineers to suit up in EVA equipment and walk the hull to replace the defective unit. The necessary parts to fix all problems were available in the parts lockers, and the issues were always resolved quickly.

Most of the new crewmembers who hadn't been able to reach Mars before the space trials began were waiting to board the ship when it returned. They quickly settled in as final preparations for deployment were completed. The only personnel issue that affected the bridge crews was that Lt. Milton lost his temporary third officer command position when the new Lt. Commander reported aboard.

Three fresh-off-the-line CPS-14s arrived and were housed in a hangar bay. Sydnee was there to watch as they came aboard, and all three used the temporary air locks. Another bay accepted seven MAT-14s, while a third got a full squadron of twelve FA-SF4 Marine Fighters. Meanwhile, habitat units were being attached to the keel with special docking clamps. As with freight containers, each unit could be entered for inspection via a hatch in the roof of the habitat without having to suit up in EVA gear when it was locked into a link section. When placed on a planet, crew would enter or leave via an airlock located on the lowest level. Once victualing of the ship was complete and spare parts from the ship's lockers used during the space trials were replaced, the ship was ready to depart.

The *Denver* left the Mars shipyard late on the second day following its return. Its destination was the sector along the Clidepp border where the *Perry* had patrolled for the past six years.

"Underway at last," Kelly MacDonald said as she sat down to breakfast the next day.

"You're not kidding," Sydnee said. "I'm beat."

"Me too," Jerry Weems said. "The space trials were grueling. How many bridge simulations did we run anyway?"

"I think it was about ten thousand," Sydnee said.

"I think that might be a *slight* exaggeration, but it certainly feels accurate. I hope we get some sack time over the next few days. I'm headed to my rack as soon as I have breakfast." Looking towards MacDonald, he said, "You Marines had it easy."

"Easy?" she said. "While you guys were running battle simulations on the bridge twenty-four hours a day, we were learning everything about the new MAT-14, breaking in two new platoons just out of Basic, and repeatedly practicing assault tactics in an empty hangar bay. In our free time, we worked on the new practice range. There wasn't a single day I didn't have to drag my bones to the sack each night."

"I thought you couldn't start work on the new range until the space trials were over," Sydnee said.

"That's what I'd been told originally, but the Major gave the go ahead for us to start during the trials. In our spare time, of course. Martin is right. The new range is gonna be kick-ass."

"I can't wait to try it out. As tired as I am right now, I'd go down and run through one round if it was available. I suppose it's best that it's not available today. I really need to get some sleep. At least watches will be easier now that we're away from the congested space lanes around Earth."

―――――――――――――――

A week into their deployment, Sydnee was on final approach in a MAT-14. She had a full platoon of Marines on board and was fighting a severe crosswind gusting to 50 mph. The stubby wings on the MAT-14 did make for a slightly more stable approach than would have been likely in a MAT-12, but it was taking all her flying skills to keep the new ship from being buffeted off her approach as she neared the hot LZ. When she heard a soft chime in her left ear, Sydnee immediately suspended the simulator program and reached for her Space Command ring. Before she even touched it, a message began to play in her head.

"Attention, this is the Captain. I've just received a disturbing communication from SHQ. Two days ago, on the opening day of the First Annual Galactic Alliance Trade Show on the space station known as Freight-One, several violent explosions destroyed large sections of the station. The Trade Show was being attended by GA Senators from all over Region One and by thousands of exhibitors and attendees. It's estimated that as many as three thousand men, women, and children may have perished in the explosions or through exposure to open space. SHQ states there's no question that this was the work of terrorists. One person is already in custody and more are being sought. That's all we have for now. Any new reports will be broadcast as we receive them. Please keep your vid-Mails to a minimum. You'll be notified immediately if any members of your immediate family were injured or worse, and a complete list of the casualties will be accessible in the computer as such information becomes available. Lidden out."

Sydnee was briefly numbed by the news, but that gave way to anger. It seemed as though terrorism would never disappear completely. Most terrorist activity had ended on Earth during the twenty-first century when the nightmare everyone feared had come true. A nuclear arms race had begun in the Middle East after the country of Iran managed to develop nuclear weapons. Fearing their neighbor's often erratic and unpredictable behavior, other nations in the region immediately sought weapons of mass destruction as a nuclear deterrent. The end finally came when a radical Islam jihadist group managed to steal a nuclear weapon from a weapons depot and, in a fit of blind rage, use it against another radical Islam jihadist group with whom they had been fighting for decades over control of various Middle Eastern territories. In retaliation, their opponent fired their own stolen nuclear weapons. Within minutes, without even knowing who had started it, every country in the region, fearing they were about to be attacked, was sending their own weapons of mass destruction speeding towards longtime foes. In just a few hours, every country from the Mediterranean to Bangladesh was basking in the glow of radioactive fallout.

The tens of millions killed in blasts were the lucky ones. Many tens of millions more would die slowly over weeks and months in pain and agony, either from direct exposure or later from contamination of soil and water as radioactive clouds were swept eastward across Asia by prevailing winds. Few were left to mourn the loss of the radical Islamists who perpetrated the initial detonations, but their act of destruction was responsible for the deaths of a hundred million peaceful Muslims who weren't trying to force the rest of the world to convert to a particular radical religious ideology. Also among the dead and dying were Christians, Jews, Hindus, Buddhists, and followers of many other religions who lived in the affected areas.

It was amazing that the rest of the world hadn't gotten caught up in the insanity, but leaders outside the Middle East managed to keep their heads. Everyone expected North Korea to flex its tiny nuclear muscles, but it turned out they were smart enough to know that Pyongyang, and indeed their entire small country, would disappear almost instantly in a blinding flash of light if they ever targeted anyone with a nuclear weapon. When a weapon of mass destruction was used, the gloves came off, and the populace better head for shelters because their lives were about to change in ways they couldn't even imagine.

Sydnee sighed quietly and wondered who was responsible this time, and what cause could possibly justify the mass murder of innocents at a trade show. *Well, we'll find out eventually*, she thought. *We always do.* Managing to put all thought of the incident behind her for the moment, she reactivated the simulation program and completed her approach.

"What's the latest on the terrorist attack?" Jerry Weems asked as he joined Sydnee and Kelly MacDonald at the breakfast table the following morning.

"I just got off third watch when you did," Sydnee replied. "I haven't heard anything new."

"I saw a news broadcast just after I rolled out of my rack," Kelly said. "They showed vid images of the station. It was really bad. The terrorists planted explosives in the main exhibit hall and detonated them just before lunch when the hall was most crowded. They weren't just trying to make a statement, they were going for maximum body count. The announcer said that over four hundred of the dead were Terran school children under the age of sixteen."

"Good Lord," Weems said. "Why were so many kids there?"

"It was a special class outing. It was the very first trade show in what the promoters hoped would be an annual event, eventually drawing exhibitors from all over Regions One, Two, and Three. The exhibition committee offered a free ride up to the station for one thousand school children. The schools felt it would be the most memorable event in the lives of many of the kids, so they all wanted to send a child.

"Video imaging of the exhibit hall has allowed them to identify everyone killed there, but there are many more still missing. The missing are believed to have been at exterior viewing lounges around the perimeter of the station when explosions opened it to space. The investigators are combing through all the vids from security feeds in an effort to identify everyone in the images. It could take a few more days, but they promise they will know who was lost. Space junk sweepers are out looking for bodies, or body parts."

"Do they know who's responsible yet?" Sydnee asked.

"They've identified one individual for sure, and they're looking for others who were observed in places they weren't authorized to be. When they find someone suspicious, they have the computer perform facial recognition and body-movement searches of recorded images from all thirty-seven thousand cameras in the station. They piece together a second-by-second history of that person's movements, with emphasis on contact with any other individual. There's no doubt they'll get them. All flights leaving the station are limited to wounded and emergency services personnel with impeccable credentials. However many perps were involved, they're still on the station."

"It's days like this that I wish the GA hadn't outlawed corporal punishment," Weems said.

"I'd like to take them to Diabolisto and toss them into a swamp with a Lampaxa Vorheridine," Sydnee said. "I'd give them a sporting chance though. Each would have a knife."

"As I recall, you had two knives and personal body armor," Weems said.

"I said I'd make it sporting. I didn't say I'd give them an edge."

"Brrrr. Remind me never to make you angry with me," Weems said.

"Jerry, *never* make me angry with you," Sydnee reminded him with a grin.

Three weeks later, the *Denver* was nearing the Simmons Space Command Base. They had been charged with delivering a container of parts and supplies to the base. Since they were coming this way anyway, it made sense to have them deliver it instead of having a quartermaster ship make the run.

"Attention all crew, this is the Captain," Sydnee heard when she responded to the chime in her left ear. "Tomorrow we will dock at Simmons SCB. We've all worked hard the past couple of months, so all crew who are not scheduled for duty can enjoy liberty until we leave in two days. That is all. Lidden out."

Two days of liberty wasn't much time when stopping at an SCB, but most of the crew had enjoyed an extended time ashore during the BOI hearing. Sydnee would have to work third watch on the bridge, but she hoped to spend some time on the base and get some shopping done. She immediately called Kelly MacDonald to arrange a time convenient to both of them.

The brief layover at Simmons SCB had been enjoyable for everyone. The merchant stores on the civilian concourse were well stocked with everything the well-groomed Space Command officer or enlisted person could ask for. With so much time in space, it was great having a place where they could spend some of their back salaries, and the merchants were only too glad to serve them.

"That was great," Sydnee said at breakfast the first day out, "I suppose it'll be a year before we get back here."

"I wouldn't be so sure," Kelly said.

"Why? What did you hear?" Sydnee asked in a conspiratorial whisper.

"Hear? Nothing," Kelly said sotto voce.

"Then why do you think it won't be a year before we come back to Simmons?"

"A group of Marines came aboard just before we left Mars. You had gone to get some sleep before your watch, so you didn't see them."

"A group of Marines? Not ours?"

"I've never seen any of them before. What was most strange was their ranks. There was one captain, one first sergeant, and the rest were staff sergeants."

"How many noncoms?" Sydnee asked.

"Eleven."

"Eleven? And all E-6 through E-8?"

"Yep."

"That is strange."

"Yeah."

"Ever seen anything like that before?"

"Just once on a summer cruise during my third year at the Academy. They were a Special Ops team. I never got a chance to talk with any of them. They stayed in a hold the entire time they were aboard. They slept there and cooked their own food there. Then they transferred to another ship."

"How did you know they were Special Ops?"

"My commanding officer told me. In fact, that's all he would tell me. He said the rest was 'need to know,' and I didn't need to know."

"So what do you think they're doing here?"

"I don't have a clue. Perhaps SHQ expects the Clidepp Empire to try something along the border and wants to be prepared."

"I suppose it could be that— or a dozen other things."

"Maybe we'll find out eventually, or maybe we're just delivering them to some other destination."

When Sydnee awoke in the afternoon, she had a message informing her she was excused from third watch and should instead report to Major Burrows at first watch the next day. She felt like a run, so she headed to the track in the exercise hold and ran around the track for an hour. When she stopped, she was exhausted and felt great. A quick shower and then an hour in the simulators practicing control exercises in CPS-14 and the MAT-14 ships helped pass some more time. To wrap up her day, and purely for fun, she spent an hour flying an FA-SF4 Marine Fighter at treetop level through the canyons and valleys of Earth and at wave-top level across a great expanse of blue water.

Another message was waiting for Sydnee the next morning when she awoke. It instructed her to meet Major Burrows in the conference room on Deck 12, Frame-section 78. She had plenty of time, but she hurried to shower and dress so she could enjoy a leisurely breakfast. She was surprised to see Kelly MacDonald already there. MacDonald usually ate at 0815, just after Sydnee finished her watch.

"You're early," MacDonald said. "I didn't expect to see you this morning."

"I was excused from my watch. I have to report to the Major at 0800."

"On Deck 12?"

"Yeah. You too?"

"Yep. There's something in the air."

Sydnee sniffed. "I don't smell anything unusual."

Kelly grinned. "It's an old expression. It means that something is going on."

"Oh. Yeah. Any ideas?"

"Not a one. I guess we'll find out at 0800."

"Come in, ladies," Major Burrows said as Sydnee and Kelly entered the designated conference room. A Marine captain was already seated at the table with Burrows. "Take seats at this end of the table. Only the four of us are meeting at this time. This is Captain Blade. Captain, this is First

Lieutenant Kelly MacDonald and Lieutenant(jg) Sydnee Marcola."

Blade nodded without saying anything but never took his eyes off the women as he appraised the way they moved.

"MacDonald is my senior platoon commander, and Marcola is a bridge officer and interdiction pilot."

"Don't you have any Marine pilots?" Blade asked.

"Before the *Denver*'s space trials began, I was informed that we would be getting four. Then, during the trials, they informed me that we would only be getting two. Last week I was informed that maybe they'll be able to send us one Marine pilot in six months. Something big must be going on somewhere if all available pilots are being forwarded to that area."

"Probably another hot-button issue along this border. I suspect this area is really going to heat up over the next five years. But, getting back to the staffing for this operation, don't you have a Lt. Commander available— or at least a Lieutenant? This mission is too critical for a wet-behind-the-ears jg, even if she can handle a shuttle fairly well."

Burrows chuckled. "Lt. Marcola was just awarded the SC Comet, the SC Star, *and* a Purple Heart," he said. "You won't find a better pilot, faster quick draw, or more experienced jungle fighter in all of Space Command."

With raised eyebrows, Blade looked at Sydnee again. "Jungle fighter?"

"Our platoon on Diabolisto was pinned down and taking heavy RPG and mortar fire. When the platoon commander was killed, Lt. Marcola took command, ordered a breakout, and attacked an enemy of vastly superior size, killing some sixty-three while losing only two of our Marines. I've been told by Marines present that day that Lt. Marcola was never less than two meters out in front of the line as they charged the enemy positions."

"Diabolisto, eh? I heard a little about that charge, but I didn't know a Space Command officer was leading it. I take back what I said. Lt. Marcola is perfectly acceptable for this mission."

"Um, what mission, sir?"

"We're going to Yolongus. We're going to get the damned bastard responsible for the GA Trade Show bombing."

Chapter Ten

~ December 27th, 2285 ~

"Yolongus?" Sydnee said in surprise. "The home world of the Clidepp government?"

"The very same," Blade said.

"And you *know* who is responsible?" MacDonald asked.

"We do."

"Um. And we have the permission of the Clidepp Empire to enter their space for this operation?" Sydnee asked.

"No, they refused to assist us in this matter."

"Do they know the individual responsible?" MacDonald asked.

"Our ambassador never even had a chance to tell them who it is. They immediately said they're too busy with the uprising to help us look for a petty criminal and then had him escorted out of the building. They might still be upset with us for exposing their lies about condoning slavery in their nation."

"So we're going to violate their sovereign space and kidnap one of their citizens— if we can locate him?"

"Exactly. And we're not coming back without him, dead or alive."

"Um. And exactly how do we know who was behind it?"

"We caught three of the bombers. A fourth one committed suicide as our people closed in."

"And this operation is sanctioned by the GA Senate?" MacDonald asked.

"We couldn't afford a leak. They'll be informed after it's over."

Sydnee took a deep breath. "Then it's sanctioned by the Admiralty Board?"

"They haven't made a decision yet, but SHQ and the Marine High Command is confident they will. If the Admiralty Board decides we shouldn't do it, we'll simply return. In the meantime, we're going in. It'll take about a month to get there at Light-9790 once we cross the border, so we want to be poised and ready to move in when the Admiralty Board approves the mission."

"Participation is strictly voluntary," Major Burrows said. "If you don't want in, we'll move on to another candidate."

Sydnee took a deep breath and said, "Um. I'm in, sir."

"I'm in also, sir," MacDonald said.

Burrows smiled. "I was sure I could count on both of you. I wish I could go as well. We need to show these people they won't get away with committing terrorist acts in GA space."

"Um. What's the plan, sir?" Sydney asked.

"We go in with my people," Blade said, "plus six fire teams from the *Denver*. We land the CPS in a very remote area and separate from the MAT. The CPS then enters a lake and settles to the bottom to wait until they hear from us. Its black coloration will conceal it completely in the spot we've chosen because the bottom is black sand from ancient volcanic activity. The MAT then travels to a selected location four klicks from the package's home and four of my people make their way to the vicinity of the package's home where they set up two observation posts. When we know the subject is at the house, the entire team moves in under cover of darkness. We take him into custody and link up with the CPS, then return to Simmons where the terrorist is turned over to SC Intelligence."

"It sounds so simple," MacDonald said. "I'm sure it won't be."

"That was just a broad overview. It's not really a complex plan, but there are numerous fine details. A number of questions still exist, but they can only be answered by someone on the scene as we acquire intel from the observation posts, such as how many people are in the house, how many are armed bodyguards, how many are non-combatants, and how many sentries patrol outside the house. The plan is designed to be fluid until we have all the answers."

"Um. And just how do we evade the Clidepp Planetary Defense?"

"Clidepp technology is far behind that of the GA. They still use radar and lidar to track ships in their space. SC Intelligence has told me that a Dakinium-hulled ship is impossible to detect by any means used by the Yolongi because the alloy literally absorbs electronic signals. Since no radar or lidar signals are bounced back, nothing appears on scopes. In GA space, our ships always use a transponder, unless they're operating in stealth mode and traveling at Light-9790. If the ship isn't using a transponder beacon, no one knows it's there. So, we sail in at Light-9790 right up to their atmosphere, then drop softly onto the planet at the remote location. The Dakinium-sheathed MAT will also not show up on any ground radar screens. It will hug the ground as it flies to the designated location at treetop level using its noiseless oh-gee engines, where it drops off the observation teams."

"Um. May I make a couple of suggestions?" Sydnee asked.

"Of course. I want your input."

"First. I'd bring two MATs."

"Why two?"

"Um. We had two MATs loaded with Marines ready to land on Diabolisto when one developed mechanical problems and had to turn back. If we're going to be a month inside Clidepp space, we should have a backup craft with us."

"Okay. What else?"

"Um. Since I can't pilot two different ships at the same time, I assume your plan calls for another pilot. If your plan only calls for two pilots, I'd recommend a third."

"We're not going to use a second MAT unless the first one is down."

"Um. I understand that. But what happens if one of the two pilots is sick or injured and unable to do their job? Do any of your people know how to fly a CPS or a MAT? We're going to be many light-years inside Clidepp space. I hope we don't need a backup pilot, but he or she could be vital."

"And do you have any suggestions as to who might be willing to go on this mission?"

"Yes, sir. The same two pilots who supported me on Diabolisto— Lieutenants Weems and Caruthers. I recommend Caruthers as CPS pilot and Weems as MAT pilot and backup commander. Both have spent considerable time in the simulators for the CPS-14 and the MAT-14."

"Neither has any actual experience in the two ships?"

"Um, none of us do, sir. Those two models are brand new, and we haven't even been granted access to the craft yet. I've only been able to walk around the exterior. But the simulators are reported to be an almost totally realistic flight experience. And all of us are experienced with earlier models, such as with the MAT-12."

"Anything else?" Blade asked.

"Um, that's all I can think of at the moment, sir."

"The purpose of this meeting today," Burrows said, "was only to ascertain your willingness to participate, since this mission is voluntary, and to lay out the general plan if you would be participating. Support personnel rosters will be determined later. Captain Blade and his Special Ops people are the lead unit in this plan, while you and MacDonald were tentatively designated as the *Denver's* SC and Marine team leaders. As always, inside the spacecraft, whether on the ground, aloft, or in space, Lt. Marcola will be the ultimate authority. Outside the craft, the Marine officers take on that role."

"Yes, sir," both Sydnee and MacDonald said.

"If you want to examine the interior of the new ships, I'll arrange that as soon as we're done here. Within ten minutes of making the call, you'll have full access."

"Thank you, sir. I *would* like the opportunity to check it out."

"Captain Lidden has consented to excuse you from all watch duties until this mission is over, Marcola," Burrows said. "Report here again tomorrow at 0800."

As the two women walked around a CPS-14 ship parked in one of the *Denver's* shuttle bays, Sydnee looked up at the hull and said, "When we received our initial orientation, the engine nacelles were extended to their normal sub-light positions, so I never realized they retract completely inside the ship when not in use. These are like the envelope generator on a warship that disappears into a repository topside. The engines on most tugs simply retract close to the ship or perhaps into a recessed area. But these completely disappear behind sealed hatches."

"Is that significant?"

"I believe so. Perhaps it's just to minimize possible damage when docking with the MATs, but there would be no need for a cover that seals so effectively. They appear to be air-tight."

"What do you think the reason is?"

"It has to be to protect them from immersion in water. Blade did say that the CPS is supposed to enter a lake and settle onto the sand at the bottom. Let's go inside."

"Oh my God!" Sydnee said as she stepped onto the flight deck of the CPS-14.

"What's the matter?" Kelly MacDonald asked as she entered right behind Sydnee.

"The flight deck is *enormous*."

"Well, we knew the ship was twice as wide, twice as high, and twice as long as a normal tug from the outside dimensions."

"Yeah, but I guess I thought the extra space was all devoted to engineering needs. I wasn't expecting the *flight deck* to be so much larger. This is *nothing* like the simulator. And I do mean *nothing*."

"What's wrong with it?" MacDonald asked as she looked around. "It looks fine to me."

"The simulator made it appear like a standard tug config-uration with pilot and copilot seats facing forward and two jump seats facing rearward. This— this— is like a regular bridge in a— scout ship." As she walked around, she elabor-ated. "This chair on a raised platform in the center of the deck is obviously a command chair since there's no associated console. And it has small monitors attached to the arms, just like the command chairs on any warship. Then we have a chair and console that appear to be the helm," she said as she moved to view the console, "positioned directly in front of the command chair. The configuration on this console is exactly what you see in the simulator. Then, to the left of the helm we have what appears to be a navigation station, with an engin-eering console to the far starboard side of the deck. Immedi-ately to the right of the command chair is a com station, and this," she said as she walked to the larboard side of the com-mand chair, "appears to be a— tactical station? There's no way one person could pilot this ship properly. You can handle all ship movements from the helm console, but there's no com within reach, and the navigation console is too far away to be accessed by the helmsman unless they leave the helm un-attended. And *why* would you need a tactical station on a tug?"

"It would appear there's a lot more to this small ship than we've been told. Perhaps that's why you weren't allowed inside before."

"You know, Kel, the flight deck looks very similar to a scout-destroyer bridge, but— more compact."

"Maybe that's it, Syd. Maybe this was intended to be a modular mini-scout-destroyer. You can put together whatever configuration you need to meet the current situation, and all the components fit inside a *Lyon*-class destroyer until needed, or they're Dakinium-sheathed and can be attached outside."

"Do you suppose some of those habitat units attached to the hull contain weapons?"

"That would explain the tactical station. Maybe that's the main reason no one was allowed inside. Any bridge officer or pilot would immediately recognize a tactical station."

"My team for this mission is going to be more than double the size I envisioned. I'd say six to properly handle this ship, plus one pilot for the MAT and a backup pilot."

"You think eight is enough?"

"Unless this ship has more requirements than we see here. Maybe we should check out the engineering section."

"Let's go."

A minute later they were standing in the engineering space.

"Add one more engineer to the one on the bridge," Sydnee said. "That makes a crew of nine if the plan only requires one MAT."

"I guess when you think about it, it makes sense," MacDonald said.

"Sense? How does any of this make sense?"

"A tug is principally designed to lift one ten by twenty by forty meter fully loaded cargo container from a planetary sur- face into space. This ship is designed to lift eight loaded, half sized containers, *plus* four Marine armored transports. The size of the load is ten times as great as that of a normal tug. It reasons that the ship has to be bigger and more powerful, and will require a larger crew."

"That's true, but this ship is so much more than that. When you consider all of the configurations possible, it seems that rather than starting with a normal tug design and adding features, they started with a scout-destroyer and figured out how to modularize it. Operating this ship will be a more complex task than I anticipated. I hope this is the end of the surprises."

Sydnee and Kelly MacDonald returned to the same conference room the next morning. Again, only Burrows and Blade were in the room.

"Did you get a good look at the CPS-14?" Burrows asked of Sydnee as she took her seat.

"Yes, sir."

"It was an eye opener, wasn't it?"

"Um. Yes, sir. You've been inside?"

"Of course. Have you reevaluated the size of the crew you'll require for this mission?"

"Um. Yes, sir. Most definitely. I estimate the minimum number of staff required to properly handle that ship will include one bridge officer for helm, one bridge officer for navigation, one tac officer, one com chief, two engineers, and a commanding officer. Plus you'll need one pilot for each MAT and a backup."

"We only intend to use one MAT-14, so that would add two more to the crew, for a total of nine. That agrees with what the SCI recommended. Have you created a list of the individuals you'd like to have?"

"Um. Yes, sir," Sydnee said and slid a viewpad gently across the table towards him.

Burrows looked at the list and then up at Sydnee. "All good people. I notice you still want Weems and Caruthers if they agree to participate. "

"Yes, sir. Both are excellent pilots, and I would trust my life to either one."

"That's exactly what you'll be doing," Blade said. "This mission isn't going to be the cakewalk you had on Diabolisto. There's a chance none of us will be coming back. The Clidepp Empire isn't going to be happy about us invading their space and taking one of their citizens. If they learn we're there, I'm sure they'll pull out all the stops to capture or kill us. And we all have to understand that getting the package is the most important part of this operation. If necessary, everyone is expendable. Do you understand?"

"Um, yes, sir. And I'm prepared for that eventuality."

"Good," Burrows said. "Okay, you have my permission to recruit all these people for the mission. The *Denver* will reach the jump-off point in three days. You must be ready to go as soon as we arrive there. You may use this room to interview potential team members. As soon as you provide the names of any volunteers, I'll see they're relieved of all shipboard duties aboard the *Denver* for the duration."

"Yes, sir. I'll begin contacting them immediately."

━━━━━━━━━━━━━━━━━━━

"So let me get this straight," Caruthers said after Sydnee had told him that she was recruiting for an extremely dangerous and strictly voluntary mission. "You expect me to join you and a bunch of Marines on another crazy dirt-side mission. This wouldn't happen to involve Diabolisto, would it?"

Weems chuckled. "If it does, I'm out before we even start."

"No, it's not Diabolisto, but I can't give you any specifics unless you sign on."

"You want us to risk our lives on a highly dangerous mission, and you can't tell us about it?"

"I can't brief you on mission specifics unless you've volunteered to go, but I can tell you the mission objective. We're going to retrieve the person responsible for the bombing of the GA Trade Show on Earth's Freight-One orbital station."

Neither Weems nor Caruthers said anything initially. They just stared at Sydnee's face.

"You're serious," Weems finally said. "You wouldn't be able to hold that somber look this long if you weren't."

"Darned right, I'm serious. We're going to get that bastard— or die trying."

"Now see, you had me until you said 'die trying,'" Caruthers said.

"This isn't a joke," Sydnee said.

"Who's joking?"

"Okay, you're out. Jerry, what about you?"

"I'm in, babe. Just tell me what we have to do."

"Okay, welcome aboard. Caruthers, you'll have to leave."

"How come you call him Jerry and me Caruthers?"

"Because his name is Jerry and yours is Caruthers. Do you want me to call you Jerry also?"

"Yes, call me Jerry also."

"Okay, Jerry Also. You'll have to leave since you aren't part of this operation and can't hear the specifics until it's over."

"Come on, Syd, I was only joking."

"So you don't want to be called Jerry Also anymore?"

"Now *you're* joking. I didn't mean *that*. I mean about going. I'm in also. I want to get the bastard responsible for the deaths of those three thousand innocents just as much as you do."

"Okay, Jerry Also, you're in. I believed you'd want to be a part of this, but you had to say it."

"Come on, Syd. Just call me Pete, or Caruthers."

"Okay Pete— and Jerry, here's the plan. We're going to ferry a group of Special Ops people into Clidepp space. They know the location of the person who planned and financed the terrorist attack. We're just providing their ride. We never leave the ships. And the ships are Dakinium-sheathed, so the danger to us should be minimal."

"This sounds like my kind of operation," Caruthers said.

"I knew you'd like it. None of us enjoyed our time on Diabolisto."

"So, where is this person we have to retrieve?" Weems asked.

"On Yolongus."

"I— uh— take it back," Caruthers said. "This isn't my kind of operation after all. You want us to fly to the capital of the Clidepp Empire and kidnap a Clidepp citizen? Seriously?"

"Yes, seriously. One of the terrorists on Freight-One talked and named the person responsible."

"I bet he didn't talk willingly," Weems said.

"I didn't ask. Marine Captain Blade is heading up the retrieval mission. We take them in, drop off two observation teams, and fall back to wait until they ascertain the situation. Then we bring in the remainder of the Special Ops folks and half a dozen fire teams from the *Denver* and pull back to wait until they're ready to be picked up. When they call for their ride, we pick them up and head for home."

"Home?" Caruthers said.

"GA space."

"It can't be that easy," Weems said.

"Easy?" Caruthers said in a shocked voice. "We have to fly for weeks through a foreign nation without permission, then somehow sneak down to their heavily fortified home planet, then wait around to be discovered while the Marines are planning their raid, then pick everyone up and try to get away unnoticed. That's *not* going to be easy."

"Whether it's going to be easy or not, we're going," Sydnee said.

"Say, Syd," Caruthers said, "how come you're in command again? I'm senior in grade."

"Don't start that again, Pete," Weems said.

"I'm curious. Did I do something to piss somebody off or something?"

"Well, I'm not supposed to say anything, but..." Sydnee said and then let her voice trail off.

"What? What is it? Tell me. What did you hear?"

"Well, I heard there was time a few years ago when you made a joke about Admiral Carver. It got back to her and..."

"And what? Tell me."

"She insisted that you *never, ever* be put in charge of any Special Ops mission to Yolongus where we have to kidnap a Clidepp citizen. So, as you can see, Captain Blade and the Major had no choice."

"You're a laugh a minute today, Syd," Caruthers said with a grin.

Weems got the joke and laughed so hard he started coughing. Caruthers slapped him on the back a couple of times and that seemed to cure it.

"Okay, the truth is that I was picked because the mission on Diabolisto was so successful. That I was in charge down there was just the luck of the draw. If my MAT had suffered engineering problems instead of Jerry's, he might have wound up in command of the Marines and gotten all the attention."

"I never would have been able to pull it off," Weems said. "For one thing, that rebel Colonel would have killed me before I could draw my pistol. Only Quick Draw Marcola could have won that matchup."

"I was lucky. If the Colonel had fired a few inches lower and slightly to his right, I would have had an RPG round in my chest."

"Like the man said, if I had to choose between being lucky or handsome, I'd pick lucky," Weems said stoically.

"You got your wish," Caruthers said with a grin.

Weems just grimaced and then grinned. "So what now, Syd?"

"Spend as much time in the simulators as you can. Concentrate mostly on the CPS. The MAT-14 handles very much like the MAT-12."

"I never flew the MAT-12," Caruthers said.

"Then this is a good time to learn. The simulators are incredibly accurate and realistic."

"I'll probably crash every time," Caruthers lamented.

"Not every time," Weems said. "Probably just the first two or maybe three— hundred times."

"Just keep at it until you have a dozen successful flights in a row. If any of our people are going to die, we don't want it to be because we weren't prepared. We reach the jump-off point in two days."

Chapter Eleven
~ December 29th, 2285 ~

Sydnee completed her recruiting interviews quickly once she had the pilot positions filled. Everyone interviewed had been part of the *Perry* crew and felt they owed their life to her, but that wasn't the reason they immediately signed on to a man— or woman. They were just as adamant as Caruthers that the person or persons responsible for the bombing be caught and prosecuted to the fullest extent of the law. Where she didn't know the individual personally, she knew their reputation. She needed people who could handle the job and who would not crack and fall apart under pressure, because replacements wouldn't be available where they were going. Caruthers might appear to be flippant most of the time, but he was all business when the situation was serious, and he would stand by his crewmates to the end. Weems had a good sense of humor and a kindly nature, and, most importantly, he was as dependable as they come. Sydnee knew she could trust her life to everyone she selected, and she would protect them with her own.

Captain Lidden ordered the DATFA temporal envelope to be cancelled when the *Denver* reached the jump-off point a hundred billion kilometers from the Clidepp border on January 1st. Since maximum DeTect range was four billion kilometers, no one in Clidepp space could have any idea the *Denver* was this close to the border. Within minutes, with Caruthers at the helm, the selected CPS-14 in the shuttle bay rose up on a cushion of oh-gee waves, turned, and moved to the temporary airlock area in front of the outer hatch. The fit was so tight that he had to nudge the craft to a new position twice before it was properly placed within the alignment markers. When the bay's alignment-verification system confirmed the ship was completely within the airlock's allowable boundaries, all lights across the alignment-warning display on the helm console went to green. Caruthers then sent the command to lock the ship to the deck so it wouldn't move while the air was evacuated. Since Dakinium wasn't magnetic, the new ship's airlock had a clamping system where steel half-circular clamps rolled up over the skids, then recessed slightly to lock the ship in place. The temporary airlock walls began to swing down from the overhead area and close around the ship almost immediately.

Once the CPS-14 had deployed from the *Denver* and was sitting a few hundred meters away, two MAT-14s left another of the *Denver's* bays and linked with the CPS. Piloted by Sydnee and Weems, one MAT was linked on either side of the CPS in the top link location. It took a few minutes to get them properly aligned, but once locked to the CPS, automatic systems took over and pulled both small ships tight against the CPS, forming an airtight seal around the access hatches as the final step.

As Sydnee and Weems were shutting down the systems aboard the MATs, small, remote-controlled tugs were bringing two enormous storage tanks to the ship. One tank was attached to each side of the CPS in the lower MAT linking location. Meanwhile, other remote-control tugs were detaching three habitat containers from the keel of the *Denver* and ferrying them over for connection to the keel of the CPS. Each container was already fitted to a modified version of the Lewiston container link.

The Lewiston, as it was known, was a linkage section that allowed up to four full-sized cargo containers to be locked together. Abutted end to end, they extended one hundred sixty meters in length when complete. The entire section would then be added to a freighter's cargo load and increase the length of the ship by ten meters, plus two meters for each link section. The modified link for the CPS was only one-eighth as long and only held one container, but it created the same type of airtight tunnel above the containers that allowed access to each of them.

Although containers were attached to the rear of a freighter, the habitat containers were attached below the CPS-14 to the keel. When the three containers were connected to one another, the assembly beneath the small ship was twenty meters high and twenty meters wide. Like the full-sized Lewiston links, the modified links were twelve meters deep, so the habitat group would extend thirty-six meters from bow to stern.

As the habitat units were locked into position against the keel, the electrical and electronic connections made the containers part of the ship. Marines who had traveled over in the two MATs walked through the ship and climbed down into the center habitat container as soon as the airlock seals were tested and certified.

All in all, it took just twenty-eight minutes to fully prepare the CPS for deployment from the second it left the shuttle bay. Anyone seeing the completed ship configuration would never guess it came from the *Denver*.

"Captain," the com chief said to Sydnee, who had entered the bridge and taken her place in the command chair, "the *Denver* is asking if we're ready to depart."

"Engineering, are we a go?" Sydnee said to Lt. Barron at the console on the starboard side of the ship.

"Everything is secure and Engineering is a go, Captain."

"Navigation, is the course laid in?"

"Course laid in and we're a go, Captain," Lt. Olivetti said.

"Tac?"

"We're a go, Captain," Lt. Templeton said.

"Helm?"

"We're ready to build our envelope on your command, Captain," Caruthers said.

"Com, inform the *Denver* we're ready to build our envelope and depart."

Seconds later, CPO Lemela, the com chief said, "The *Denver* wishes us good luck and a safe journey."

"Helm, build our envelope."

"The envelope is built, Captain," Caruthers said two minutes later.

"Engage the drive to Light-9790."

The image on the front monitor shifted from real-time vid to a simulated view created from sensor feeds as the ship instantly achieved the maximum speed. Since travel was inside a temporal envelope, there was no sensation of acceleration.

"We're away, Captain."

Lt. Olivetti at the navigation station said, "We'll cross into Clidepp space in roughly thirty-four seconds, Captain, and reach Yolongus in twenty-nine days, eighteen hours, sixteen minutes, and forty-one seconds."

Sydnee swiveled her command chair to face where Marine Captain Blade was standing. "Captain, you'll have full bridge privileges while you're aboard, but since there can only be one captain aboard a ship, you'll be referred to as Major from this point forward."

"I understand, Captain. I'm going to check on my people now."

Sydnee nodded and turned her chair forward as Blade left the bridge. There were no ships in evidence at the border as the *Denver* passed into Clidepp space seconds later.

"May I have your attention, please?" Sydnee said as they began to settle into a routine. "It occurs to me that we should have a name for this ship. It's certainly more than just a tug. Does everyone agree?"

It seemed that everyone nodded their heads.

"Okay. Any suggestions?"

"How about Revenge?" Lt. Barron, the engineering officer said. "We're getting revenge for all the people they butchered."

"It's certainly a dynamic name," Sydnee said. "What does everyone else think?"

"I think it's a little too dynamic," Caruthers said. "We're looking for justice, and Revenge sort of implies vigilantism."

"Okay," Sydnee said. "Anybody else have an option?"

"How about Justice?" the com chief said.

"Yes, that's a good alternative, Chief. Anybody else?"

"I like Justice," Navigator Olivetti said. "It's like revenge, but with the rule of law behind it."

"Okay, anyone else?" Sydnee asked.

"I'm fine with Justice," Caruthers said.

"Any other suggestions?" When no one spoke up, Sydnee said, "All in favor of Justice?"

Everyone raised their hands, including Lt. Barron.

"Any other suggestions before it becomes final?" As Sydnee looked around, everyone simply shook their heads. Turning to the com chief, she said, "Have the computer submit a request to Space Command that this ship be officially named 'Justice.'"

"Aye, Captain," he said with a smile.

"Captain," the tac officer said, "If you have a minute, I'd like to show you something."

Sydnee stood up and moved to the tac station. "What is it?"

"I've been thinking of this as a security station like those found on freighters rather than a tactical station because we have no weapons. I expected to be scanning space looking for possible danger."

"Yes, I agree."

"But look at this," he said as he touched a few points on his console. A weapons list immediately popped up on one of his monitors.

"What is that?" Sydnee said. "A simulation?"

"That's what I thought at first. I thought it was simply part of the tactical station self-test software. But I've been seeing it ever since the connections with the habitat units went live, and every time I've cleared the screen there's a weapons status icon on the bottom left corner. Touching it brings up this list showing the available weapons remaining. According to this, we have forty-eight missiles in the bow of the ship and forty-eight missiles in the stern. Additionally the list says I have eight laser arrays that give us three hundred twenty degrees coverage horizontally and three hundred twenty degrees vertical. Our only weapons-blind area is directly above the ship."

"Do you believe that information to be accurate?"

"Well, the computer believes it's accurate. I've studied all the specs for this ship and never seen any provision for weapons, so I'd like to fire one of the missiles and see if anything actually leaves the ship."

"No, let's not fire any missiles. But perhaps we can fire a laser."

"Yes, ma'am. Do I have your permission to try?"

"Not yet. Since there're no weapons showing on the hull, they would have to be recessed. Any attempt to use one would probably cause an interruption in the continuity of our envelope, which would result in it being cancelled. But we'll try it as soon as it's practicable."

The limited size of the crew meant that everyone would work twice as many hours as normal, and not every station could be manned during all hours. The helm was the most important station, so it was imperative that an experienced helmsman always be available.

Lt. Olivetti, the designated navigator, was an experienced pilot who also piloted shuttles for interdiction activities and had occasionally been assigned to fill in at the helm aboard the *Perry*. Having been part of the second watch while Sydnee was third watch meant the women had had little work or personal contact in the past, but Olivetti had a fine reputa- tion for precision in all her work and was reported to be an excellent navigator and pilot. She had performed with distinction during the attack between the *Perry* and the *Glassama*. Having spent a considerable amount of time in the flight simulators over the past few months, she was perfectly able to take the helm of the *Justice* when Caruthers was off watch or on a break.

Since there were two engineers, Lt. Barron and Chief Petty Officer Luscome, they would alternate duties at the Engineering console and performing maintenance activities.

The Communications station had to be manned constantly, so one of the Marines would alternate with Chief Petty Officer Lemela.

The Tactical station would alert the bridge crew if the ship's sensors detected another ship or a dangerous situation, so the tac officer could fill in at other stations as the need arose.

Until the ship reached Yolongus, there would be no need to have all stations manned around the clock.

Unlike the *Denver*, or any other warship, there was little to do aboard the *Justice* other than stare at a console or at the stars on the front monitor. Sydnee finally turned the bridge over to Caruthers, whose place at the helm was immediately filled by Olivetti, and went her office/cabin.

Tugs normally had just a dozen square feet of space behind the pilot seating. It served as both a galley and an area where an off-duty pilot could lay down after unrolling a piece of oh-gee cloth. The *Justice* was a different breed entirely. It had clearly been designed to provide comfort, albeit limited, to the crew during long periods of separation from the host ship. The captain had the only private space in the form of a tiny office with an attached sleeping compartment. The office part was barely large enough to accommodate the captain plus three seated adults, but it gave a small amount of privacy for conversations. The sleeping compartment was even smaller than her cramped quarters on the *Perry*, but it did give Sydnee a bit of privacy.

Across the corridor from the captain's quarters was a small galley with several tables for eating. Fresh coffee and tea were always available, and there were food synthesizer machines for preparing meals.

Aft of these areas was a corridor that ran the width of the ship. At the end of each corridor was an airlock to an attached MAT, if needed. A stairway led down to the engineering level, where airlocks for two additional MATs were available, and a ladder led down to the linkage tunnel used to access the habitats.

Sleeping accommodations are important. The crew couldn't perform properly if they weren't rested, so a crew sleeping area, designed to provide maximum comfort and sleeping privacy, was on the top level just aft of the stairway down to Engineering. The area was first divided into six small but completely separate rooms with two stacked beds on each side of each room. Up to twenty-four crew members would have their own bed, and each bed was like a small bit of heaven. As a crewmember slipped into their bed and enjoyed the sensation of the gel-comfort mattress, they could either converse with other crewmembers or seal their bed for privacy. Overhead, a curved transparent panel would rotate down and block all outside noise or seal in the sounds of a noisy sleeper. When the panel was lowered, the bed became a fully self-contained environment with heating and cooling adjustments and fresh air ventilation.

But the curved panel was more than just a clear panel. It was actually a Simage panel. The bed's occupant could leave it clear, adjust it from transparent to translucent to fully opaque, or any degree between. When opaque, the bed's occupant could select from any of a dozen colors and shades, or display any of the hundreds of scenery images stored in the CPS main computer. The flat panel at the back of the bed had the same capability in order to provide a surrounding image, and there was even a sound generator to provide the sounds associated with the selected image.

Sydnee had sent vidMails to her family and Katarina that they were entering a blackout period and that it might be several months before they heard from her again, so she wouldn't have any vidMails to brighten her day for months.

After tossing and turning on the captain's bunk, which was identical to the bunks in the crew quarters, Sydnee decided to do a bit of exploring. She had looked over every inch of the *Justice*, but she hadn't been inside any of the habitat containers. She'd seen holo-layouts of the five-deck living units, but that wasn't the same as seeing it in person.

Aware that the Marines had immediately moved into the center habitat unit, Sydnee didn't know that the two outside units were sealed until she descended down into the linkage tunnel and walked to one of the closed access hatches. A keypad mounted in the top of the hatch controlled the locking mechanism. Her CT provided her identity data, but she still had to enter the captain's password given to her when she accepted responsibility for the ship and crew. The hatch made several clacking noises before the light on top turned from red to green, then began to rise up on its hinges. At the same time, the interior of the container below was flooded with bright light.

Halfway down the access ladder on the first level, she paused and looked around. A short tunnel extended toward one side of the container, then branched into a corridor that ran in each direction. She finished her descent and, upon walking to the corridor, discovered that it ran the entire length of the container. Doors, similar to what would be found on a ship's hold, lined one side. Taking a deep breath, she depressed the control to open the nearest one.

As the two doors parted and the enclosed area illuminated, Sydnee saw two gleaming, eight-meter-long rockets mounted in ejection housings. An ejection housing manually launched its load out of an enclosed space where it would not be safe to ignite an engine. Achieving a safe distance, normally about ten meters, the rocket's engine ignited and it would head towards whatever its memory had recorded as the target. The container's designers had done such an effective job at concealing the outer doors that Sydnee had never noticed them from the outside.

On each of the four levels in the container, Sydnee found the same layout, accounting for forty-eight rockets in total. She also found doors that led to holds containing laser arrays on gimbal platforms. When the outer doors were opened, the arrays could be rolled out far enough to provide maximum coverage around the lower half of the ship.

As she climbed back up the access ladder to the linkage tunnel and resealed the hatch, Sydnee was glad the mystery of the ninety-six rockets and eight laser arrays had been resolved. Knowing they could fight back if challenged might help her rest more peacefully, but she felt it would have been nice if the designers had mounted a couple of laser arrays in the sail area of the ship.

As she lay back down on her bunk, she thought about the way Commander Belinda Halworth, the instructor at the Mars shipyard, had reacted when Sydnee suggested using a Dakinium-sheathed container to house weapons. Surely it couldn't be a secret that would last very long once the first container with weapons was deployed. And she hadn't been told by Captain Lidden to suppress information about the container. So why the secrecy when introducing pilots to the CPS-14? Sydnee sighed. Perhaps it was just shortsightedness on the part of Halworth in thinking she could keep it a secret aboard ship. Very few secrets remained secret aboard ship.

While the CPS-14 and its attached habitat unit was a world apart from the space available aboard a regular tug, it began to feel extremely confining after a few days to people used to running around an exercise area, or even a hold, aboard a destroyer. There were four corridors in the Marine habitat, one on each level, but only one person at a time could run in each, and all they could do was run to the end, stop, then run back the other way. Some of the Marines found unique ways to exercise by using furniture and other objects for weight-lifting and bodybuilding. Heavy furniture was normally bolted to the deck to keep it from shifting during sub-light speeds, but a few pieces had been freed for special use. Everyone was beginning to feel effects similar to cabin fever by the time the *Justice* neared Yolongus.

Space Command personnel usually only visited the Marine habitat during mealtime, mainly because they were otherwise preoccupied with bridge duties, and they always slept in the bunks in the CPS to be near the bridge in case there was an emergency. Only Sydnee was a frequent visitor in Marine Country, as the habitat was being called, because of Kelly MacDonald. On other occasions Kelly visited Syd in her captain's cabin. It was there that Kelly confided a secret.

"These Special Ops people are a strange breed," MacDonald had said.

"They've seemed normal enough to me," Syd replied.

"You're not living in close proximity. My people and I have all reached out to them, but they want nothing to do us on a personal level."

"Do you think it's because we're the crew of the *Perry*? Do you think they feel superior and don't want to mingle with Marines they feel are inferior?"

"I just don't know. As soon they've finished their meals, in total silence, they immediately return to their quarters."

"Their quarters? They're in a room with twelve bunks just like the crew quarters but with three up."

"They immediately commandeered the room at the very end of the sleeping level and then hung blankets to cordon off their area. We can hear them laughing and joking, but it stops if one of my people sticks his or her head in."

"And you have no idea why?"

"There's only one thing I can think of."

"And?"

"It's possible they believe this is a one-way mission for many of us, and it's always harder when someone you know has their ticket punched."

"I promise I'll do everything in my power to ensure that doesn't happen."

"I know, Syd. We're talking about them. I'm sure they've been on many life-and-death missions."

The day before they made planetfall, the Major asked Sydnee to attend a mission briefing in the habitat and bring her two chief pilots. When they arrived, they found that the dining room had been cleared of tables. All available chairs had been placed facing the large monitor that was usually used for entertainment, but most of the Marines would have to stand during the briefing.

The Major wasted no time getting down to business. "Here's the home of our package," he said as an aerial view flashed onto the monitor. "As you can see, it's quite remote. There are no first-floor windows, and the upper floor widows appear to be sealed. I imagine they're probably bulletproof and bombproof as well. The roof is flat and the package only enters the house from the roof.

"The plan calls for us to drop two observation teams into mildly rugged terrain four klicks from the house as soon as we reach the planet. They will then make their way to observation points we've selected, disguise their presence by using a holo-projector to erect a camouflage bubble over their positions, and monitor all movement into and out of the house. They'll use thermal detectors to observe movement in the house and determine the optimal time for our attack. When we're sure the package is home and settled down for the night, we'll move in. That may take a day, a week, or even a month. We've been told the package has two homes and alternates between them.

"After dropping off the observation teams, the MAT will return to the *Justice* to await further orders. The *Justice* will then sink into the lake and wait, hidden on the bottom.

"When we're ready to attack, the MAT will separate from the CPS, float to the top of the lake, and bring us to the house, where my team will lower down on ropes from the hovering

MAT in as stealthy a manner as possible. Lieutenant Mac-Donald's people will then be dropped off in the field next to the house in preparation for surrounding the house at the perimeter wall.

"My people will attempt to penetrate the house without disturbing the household, locate the package, stun him, and carry him to the roof, where the MAT will pick us up, then pick up the Marines on the perimeter and the observer teams.

"We'll return to the *Justice* and immediately leave the planet, heading for the border.

"That would be the ideal mission, but things don't always go as planned.

"If my team is unable to open the door on the roof easily, we'll attempt to cut our way in, being as silent as possible, but we may be unable to gain access that way and have to use explosives. Or, we may trigger an alarm. In either case, we'll then have to move swiftly to accomplish our objective.

"On word from me, Lt. MacDonald and her platoon will scale the wall and attack the house to create a diversion. They will use explosives to gain entry to the house and put down any security people they encounter. One of our teams will be successful. At that point we get into the MAT as quickly as possible and leave the area because armed forces will no doubt be on their way.

"Questions?" he said, looking at Sydnee.

"Is that an aerial view of the actual house or a computer representation?"

"An aerial view of the actual house."

"Then we have someone local?"

"No. When a GA representative visits any planet, the diplomatic ship automatically begins mapping the surface. Given enough time, we collect high resolution images of the entire surface. My information is that this image was recorded two years ago when our ambassador was delivered to the planet. As soon as the ship arrived it began mapping Yolon-gus."

"I see. Then the roof may possibly appear different now?"

"Possible, but doubtful."

"Why doubtful?"

"Our envoy flew over the house a month ago and recorded an image. It doesn't have the clarity of this shot, so I opted to use this one."

"I see."

"Anything else, Captain?"

"Not at this time, Major."

"Then we'll rely on you to tell us exactly when we'll arrive down on the planet so my observation teams can be ready to deploy."

"Tomorrow, 0330, give or take five minutes. I can give you an exact time once we reach the planet and see what kind of space activity we'll have to avoid."

"Excellent. We'll plan on having my observers on the ground by 0400."

Chapter Twelve
~ January 30th, 2286 ~

The *Justice* had passed within DeTect range of numerous ships during their journey to Yolongus, but from all appearances he seemed to have been invisible to all. Even if he hadn't, no one would have had time to react before it was just a memory, nor could they do anything to the ship while it was enclosed in a double envelope.

As the small ship approached the planet, the tac officer, Lt. Templeton, was extra vigilant. There were no formations of military ships in orbit or even any small groups. Traffic around the planet was about as expected as Caruthers cancelled the envelope and they suddenly appeared near the center of the thermosphere.

From that point the oh-gee engine would be called upon to take the ship on a gentle descent to the planet. Since the *Justice* was in a planetary umbra caused by the planet's position with its sun, its black color would render it virtually invisible, except when it momentarily passed between stars and any celestial observers. Anyone on the planet using a telescope would probably assume a satellite had momentarily passed in front of their view. Chief Lemela was monitoring all known military channels for any word of an alert, but their arrival and presence seemed to have gone undetected.

Lt. Weems was standing by at the controls of the MAT, waiting for the unlink command as the *Justice* passed through the planet's troposphere, the level of atmosphere closest to the surface. The Special Ops observer teams were in the rear compartment, strapped in and ready for whatever came, and the oh-gee engine was humming almost silently, ready to be engaged at any instant.

The *Justice* descended quickly to the planet and headed for the separation coordinates. Yolongus had two tiny moons, but neither offered much illumination at night. It was dark even when both moons were full and visible in the night sky.

When Weems received his order to detach, the *Justice* was just five kilometers from the home of the package. As he flipped a switch on his control console, the small ship separated from the CPS. At that same instant, the oh-gee engine ramped up and held the craft almost in the same position until Weems began directing the energy flow. Within minutes the MAT was settling to the ground in the chosen clearing four kilometers from the package's home.

The observation teams were up out of their seats and out the hatch with all their gear in less than two minutes. Weems applied power after they had closed and locked the hatch and were clear of the ship. He took the ship up to treetop level and headed for the rendezvous point with the CPS, twelve minutes' flight time away.

"Tactical, release the two observation spheres," Sydnee said as the *Justice* hovered above a clearing near the remote mountain lake where it would remain until the operation was nearly over.

"Observation spheres released, Captain," the tac officer said. As his console began to receive telemetry data from the spheres, he added, "Both have reached their assigned positions one-quarter kilometer from our planned position in the lake.

The observation spheres were very similar to the oh-gee cameras used by the Marines for surveillance of enemy operations. They floated inconspicuously at low altitudes, using the same camouflage technology as the Marine personal battle armor. By projecting the image seen from the opposite side on the side facing the observer, they became nearly invisible. Unless someone performed an electronic sweep, no one would ever know they were there.

The *Justice* was still hovering over the clearing near the lake when the MAT piloted by Weems arrived at the rendezvous point. It took just minutes for the MAT to re-link with the ship. As the airtight connection was established, Caruthers lifted the *Justice* above the tree line and moved it out over the lake until they reached the intended coordinates. He set the CPS down gently on the lake, allowing it to settle slowly onto the water. On an order from Sydnee, the bridge engineer touched two spots on his console and the enormous tanks mounted against the hull beneath where the MATs were linked began filling with water. The only sounds to break the night's stillness were bubbling and gurgling as air bubbles rose to the lake's surface and burst. The sub-light engines were already fully retracted into their airtight repositories, and the descent to the bottom was controlled by the oh-gee engines.

In five more minutes, the *Justice* was settling gently into the coarse black sand on the bottom of the lake. It would remain there until the night of the attack, unless it began taking on water. The engineer checked the ship's sensors and determined that all compartments in the ship, the MATs, and the habitat units were, so far, perfectly dry. And no one had reported any leaks. Satisfied that there was no need to move the ship, Lt. Barron touched a spot on his console that would release a small antenna for communications with the observation teams. Only the very tip would extend above the water line. Being black, it was unlikely anyone would see it.

If Sydnee expected the mission to continue at a brisk pace, she was mistaken. Four days later, everyone was anxious to get on with it, but the observers were still reporting no activity in the house. Only one image had been seen on the thermal recorders, and that had been at a small cottage near the rear of the property. During the day, a gardener was observed tending to the grounds inside the perimeter wall, so the determination was that he represented the lone thermal image at night.

The observation spheres were reporting increasing activity on the shoreline of the lake. Apparently the lake was a favorite vacation location, even though there were no structures anywhere within five kilometers. The crew spent hours watching vacationers enjoy water activities. At one point the communications antenna was retracted because fishermen were trolling in the area.

———————

"Captain, you should see this," Templeton said on the seventh day.

"What is it?"

"A news broadcast about this lake. And us."

"Put it on the front monitor."

As the broadcast began to play, the computer provided a translation in writing across the bottom. A Yolongi, speaking into a mic, appeared in front of a spot along the shoreline.

"'This is Erillwa Quissropp reporting from Lake Ranbuzzo. Once again rumors of giant monsters in Ranbuzzo are being circulated at this popular vacation spot. Several campers have sworn they were awakened in the middle of the night by popping and hissing noises out on the lake a week ago. One camper reports awakening in time to see a giant black beast sink into the water. Although no one has ever been attacked up here at the lake and no images have ever been captured of the mythological beasts reputed to live in the water, stories continue to abound. This has been Erillwa Quissropp report-ing from Lake Ranbuzzo. Good day."

"So now we're a mythological black underwater monster," Sydnee said with a smile. "I wonder what they'll call us when we depart the area."

"A mythological black *flying* monster, probably" Caruthers said from the helm console.

Finally, ten days into their vigil, the SO observers reported the arrival of an oh-gee vehicle. After landing on the roof, three individuals exited the craft and entered the house.

Everyone aboard the *Justice* began making preparations for the assault. It was tentatively scheduled for early morning two days hence.

———————————

On the morning of the operation, Sydnee was on the flight deck of MAT-One. She had decided to take this part of the mission herself. At 0312 she released the last remaining link with the *Justice* and let the small ship float to the surface of the lake. On board was the entire Marine contingent of the *Justice*. It was so crowded in the rear cabin that the Major had joined her on the flight deck and was sitting in the copilot seat.

As the small ship broke the surface, it was difficult to tell which was blacker— the dark, cloud-filled sky, or the color of the Dakinium that sheathed the MAT. As the ship began bobbing slightly from the disturbance caused by breaking the serene surface, Sydnee applied power to the oh-gee engine and lifted clear of the lake. The course to the package's home had been entered into the navigation computer, and as she engaged the oh-gee engines, the ship headed directly to that location.

The flight time to the house, located some seventy-eight kilometers from the lake, was twelve minutes at sea level. At 0328 the MAT was hovering just meters above the roof and the Special Ops team began silently rappeling down ropes from an open hatch. As SO people moved towards the roof access door that led to the house below, Sydnee lifted the MAT up and away.

When the ship settled onto the field just outside the perimeter wall, the remainder of the Marines deployed and raced towards the house. Sydnee remained where she was, ready to pick up the SO team and the package when they called for her. She was monitoring all three radio frequencies in use for this operation: the general Com-One channel used by all Marines; Com-Two, reserved for officer use; and Com-Three, the channel reserved for the Special Ops people. Additionally, she could have a private conversation with any officer or noncom.

Roughly ten minutes of silence on the Com-One channel followed as the Marines at the wall hunkered down with taut nerves. There was seldom any admonishment from commanding officers about the use of Com-One since the voices couldn't be heard outside the helmets. Noncoms and officers only interceded if conversations became too boisterous or when arguments broke out. And that wasn't because there was any danger of giving away positions, but simply because proper battlefield behavior was being breached. Boisterous conversations and arguments meant that people probably weren't concentrating on the job at hand.

Com-Three, on the other hand, was in use almost constantly as the SO Marines prepared to assault the house. Much of the early conversation would have been confusing to the uninformed because it was a form of shorthand unique to Special Operations personnel, but it became more recognizable as the operation progressed.

⸻

As the SO Marines reached the roof and unwrapped themselves from the rappeling ropes, most spread out slowly to hunt for trip wires and alarm sensors. One by one they reported that their section of the roof was clear. Meanwhile, the team at the access to the house was examining the entrance door the way a safecracker would examine a vault.

"No keylock or keypad," a nameless voice on Com-Three said. "Must be a wireless entry."

"Burn it."

"Back. Igniting."

Suddenly, red lights began flashing on the roof and sirens began blaring. An alarm had been tripped, and the SO team hadn't yet gained access to the house.

"Damn, second door inside."

"Blow it," a voice that sounded like Blade's said.

"Back."

An explosion on the roof disturbed what little was left of the nighttime silence a few seconds later as the SO team blew open the second, more heavily armored door. At the same time, the Major gave the order for the Marines on the ground to assault the house. From Sydnee's vantage point, she could see Marines scaling the three-meter wall and dropping into the gardens. She lost sight of them at that point. Expecting that she would be needed soon, she lifted the MAT a couple of meters off the ground, ready to zoom to the roof. There was a lot of chatter on the com channels now.

"Clear," a nameless voice said loudly on Com-Three.

"Move," another said.

"Watch that door."

"Nothing. Clear."

"Next level."

"Female cowering in closet. No weapons."

"Stun her."

"Clear.

"Empty bed in here," another voice said. "Residual heat. Must have been occupied."

"Find them," Blade said.

The SO Marines continued to move from room to room in the mansion, calling 'clear' as they checked each room for occupants.

"Safe room," someone finally shouted on Com-Three.

"Blow it."

"Damn," another voice said. "This looks solid."

"This is taking too damn long. Speed it up."

Suddenly, a Marine screamed over the Com-One channel, "Ahhh! Something's grabbed me. It's wrapping itself around my legs."

Then another yelled, "Something's got me too. It's coiling itself around me like a boa."

The two calls for help were immediately followed by a chorus of voices all reporting generally the same thing, and the situation worsened as some voices said they had been pulled down to the ground and were now totally helpless.

"I managed to get to my knife," someone screamed. "I cut the thing in half. It's still holding me down."

"Damn, I shot it with my pistol. It made no difference."

Others were also reporting that they had either stabbed the monster or shot it but that their defensive acts had had no effect.

"Kelly, this is Syd," Sydnee said quickly on the officer frequency, "What's happening?"

After an interminable period of silence on Com-Two that lasted a full three seconds, Sydnee heard, "All my people are down. Something's wrapped itself around us. It's like a hundred Lampaxa Vorheridines. But when you shoot them with a laser or cut them with a knife, they split apart at that point and become two separate snakes, or whatever they are. We need help Syd. We can't get out of this on our own."

The threat console on the MAT suddenly came alive with flashing lights and messages of vehicles approaching at high speed. The display indicated that as many as twenty were on their way towards the home of the package. They were still at maximum distance, but the threat board had picked them up because they were headed directly towards the MAT's location.

"Back. I'm blowing the door," was heard over Com-Three.

"That him?"

"Yeah, that's him."

"Stun him."

"What about the woman with him?"

"Stun her and leave her. He's all we want."

"Both stunned."

"Let's get him to the roof."

"Captain, this is the Major, we have the package and we're almost ready to be picked up. Bring the MAT."

"We need to help the Marines on the ground, Major. And we have at least twenty emergency or security vehicles headed this way. They're coming from the distant city, so they're about twenty minutes out."

"Pick us up, Captain. We must vacate the area before the police or military can reach us here. We have the package and must bring him back at any cost. We don't have enough time to free the people on the ground before the enemy arrives. The fire teams are lost to us. But my observers are packed up and waiting to be recovered before we head to the *Justice*."

"You expect me to just leave our people behind?"

"We can't help them. There isn't any time. Now come pick up my team. That's an order."

Sydnee gritted her teeth and raised the ship above the height of the house before pushing the throttle forward slightly and moving towards the roof, then remembered her conversation with Kelly MacDonald when MacDonald had spoken of the detachment the SO Marines exhibited towards the *Denver*'s Marines. She wondered momentarily if this was part of Blade's plan from the beginning. Could he have foreseen this difficulty, or one similar, and instructed his people not to form attachments with MacDonald's platoon because he fully expected to desert them if trouble arose? If the forces headed this way stopped to collect the Marines, the SO teams with their prize would have no problem getting clear. If they stopped to help the Marines on the ground, the forces headed towards the house would probably arrive before they could clear the area. Sydnee leaned forward and pushed the throttle to the stops as she lifted the ship ten meters. Selecting the special frequency for the *Justice,* she reached Chief Lemela. "This is the captain. Let me speak to Lt. Weems."

Weems was on the line almost immediately. "This is Weems, Captain. We've been monitoring the com frequencies. Caruthers is next to me and listening. What are your orders?"

"Hop into MAT-Two and pick up the Major and his people on the roof, then the observation teams. I'm going to see what I can do to help *our* people. Lieutenant Caruthers, under no circumstances is the *Justice* to leave the lakebed without my explicit orders, unless I'm captured or down. Is that clearly understood?"

"Understood, Captain."

"I'm already climbing into MAT-Two," Weems said. "I should reach the house in sixteen minutes."

"Negative, Lieutenant," Blade suddenly screamed into the com line. "Remain where you are. Captain, you will return here immediately and recover my team. That's an order. If you fail to comply, I'll have you court-martialed when we return to GA space. Now get your ass in gear, lady, and pick us up."

"Lt. Weems, carry out my orders. I take full responsibility."

"Aye, Captain," Weems said.

"Captain," Blade screamed, "I'm in command here, and I order you to return immediately."

"Sir, Major Burrows said that you were in command on the ground, but I'm in command in the air. Well, sir, I'm in the air. And up here, *I'm* in command. There's a MAT coming to pick you up and will arrive in fifteen minutes. I'm going to see what I can do about those emergency vehicles headed towards the house. You should be safe until MAT-Two arrives."

The Major may have realized the futility of further discussion because the channel went silent. Sydnee concentrated on her flying and watching flight information about the approaching oh-gee vehicles.

Mat-One encountered the first of the approaching oh-gee vehicles some twenty kilometers from the house. Sydnee could see numerous other lights in the distance headed in her direction. The house was in such a remote location that all respondents had to come from the city.

The MAT was armed with a large, remotely controlled laser weapon that could raise up from a hidden gun port in the roof, but Sydnee had a better idea for clearing the oncoming traffic. There was virtually no chance that the Dakinium-sheathed MAT could be damaged by contact with an oh-gee vehicle. At most, the only evidence of a collision would be some scrapes of paint from the oh-gee cars and trucks.

Sydnee aimed the ship directly at the lead vehicle. It wasn't a heavily armored military vehicle. It looked more like a standard police or security company vehicle. She didn't really want to kill anyone— she only wanted to stop them. So at the last second she swerved and sideswiped the first car. It effectively knocked it off its path while caving in the passenger side. The damage was sufficient to send it spiraling down towards the surface, some ten meters below. Since it was a moonless night, and the MAT was black, it was doubtful the driver and any occupants of the vehicle even knew what hit them.

As the seconds and minutes ticked by, Sydnee lined up on the next vehicle and knocked it out of the sky as well. Fortunately, the vehicles were pretty well spread out, so she had enough time to target them and meet them on her terms. It became like a game of billiards at one point when, upon being sideswiped, a vehicle crashed into another, and both went down. One vehicle got past her because two came at the same time on different vectors, so after knocking the first down, she chased after the second. When she caught up, she ducked low and then hit it on the stern from underneath with enough force to actually cause it to cartwheel several times before dropping to the surface.

When all vehicles responding to the alarm had been knocked from the sky and her threat screen was clear, Sydnee headed back to the house. She had learned from listening in on the com channels that MAT-Two had arrived and recovered the SO team and the package from the rooftop. MAT-Two was presently retrieving the two observation teams.

Once at the house, Sydnee positioned the MAT high over the gardens, then set the MAT's computer to circle the house while dropping a dozen hover flares. Set to float at ten meters above ground level until used up, the flares would light up the entire property.

As the incredibly brilliant lights turned night into day, Sydnee could see the Marines writhing on the ground in the grasp of untold hundreds of snakelike creatures. The doom and gloom chatter on the general com channel was suddenly replaced with someone yelling, "I'm free. It let me go and disappeared back into the ground." Then a "me too," was heard. Then another. In minutes, everyone was free and running for the perimeter wall like the devil himself was behind them. Within another minute, they were over the wall and safely outside the compound. Whatever the creature was, it hadn't been able to penetrate the personal body armor worn by the Marines, so everyone was still perfectly healthy.

Sydnee set the ship down in the field next to the house and Marines began climbing in as soon as the hatch was open. The rear compartment was soon filled with the sounds of exuberant voices. As one of the Marines in the rear compartment closed and sealed the hatch, Kelly MacDonald entered the flight deck and dropped into the copilot chair. Sydnee depressed a contact point and all of the flares winked out.

"Thanks, Syd. You really saved our asses."

"You would have done the same for me."

"How did you know those flares would frighten those things back into their holes?"

"I didn't. Not for sure. But there had been no reports of those things during the daylight hours when the gardener was tending the grounds. I thought perhaps they were nocturnal and didn't like daylight. I admit they disappeared even quicker than I dared hope. Is everyone accounted for?"

"Yep. Everyone's aboard."

Looking at the threat console, Sydnee saw that a new group of vehicles was headed towards the house. "I've had enough excitement for tonight," she said. "But I don't want to head directly back towards the lake."

"But I thought they couldn't track this ship because of the Dakinium?"

"They can't. But as we've seen at the lake, there always seems to be eyewitnesses on the ground, even in the most remote places. And those sirens have been sounding at the house long enough to draw the attention of anyone within earshot, such as the estate gardener. Let's take a little side trip in a direction that suggests an alternate destination for anyone who might observe us from the ground."

"Why not."

As Sydnee raised the ship into the air, a new chorus of happy cheering could be heard from the rear compartment. She and Kelly shared a smile as she aimed the ship in a direction that was about ninety degrees off the course to the lake. It would take them over mostly woods and mountains, but there were a couple of housing developments on the way.

After traveling about a hundred kilometers, Sydnee said, "What say we head for the *Justice?*"

"Works for me," Kelly said. "Ya know, I'd really begun to think we weren't coming back from this one. Thanks for ignoring the Major."

"You can be a character witness at my court-martial."

"No matter what they do to you, Syd, always remember that you saved the lives of twenty-eight Marines today by disobeying the Major's orders."

"Those things probably couldn't have killed you, thanks to the body armor, but they may have held you incapacitated until the Clidepp military got here."

"We've all heard stories about the Clidepp death camps. Being taken by the Clidepp military is said to be an immediate sentence of death."

"I'm glad we didn't have to find out."

When MAT-One arrived at the lake, MAT-Two was sitting on the shore. The MATs didn't have ballast tanks that could be filled with water, so they were unable to sink down into the lake to link up with the CPS.

After Sydnee ordered Caruthers to bring the ship up, he had the engineer start the pumps and force the water from the tanks mounted on the sides of the ship. In minutes, the *Justice* was floating on the surface. Weems and Sydnee moved their ships into position and linked to the CPS.

Once Sydnee had shut down MAT-One's engines and all power systems, she left the small ship. As she emerged into the CPS corridor, she was greeted by the six fire teams of Marines who had been incapacitated in the garden. Grateful to have been rescued, they whooped and hollered and clapped as she passed them. She was moved by this spontaneous expression and smiled as they passed through the corridor, but she had to get to the bridge, so she didn't pause to address the platoon.

At the T-junction in the corridor that led to the bridge, Sydnee encountered Blade coming the other way from MAT-Two.

"I want to talk to you, Captain. NOW!"

"I'm sorry, Major," she said calmly. "I'm needed on the bridge right now. I have to get this ship up and off the planet. Once we're clear and are on our way back towards GA space, we'll have time to talk." She left Blade there in the corridor, fuming. She expected him to follow her to the bridge, but perhaps he didn't want any witnesses to what he intended to say.

"You're relieved, Lt. Caruthers," Sydnee said as she entered the bridge. "Please resume your duties at the helm. Then take us up and off this planet. Keep us in the umbra and try to avoid any military ships in orbit."

It was with relief that Sydnee sank into the comfort of the commander's chair, only to realize she was still wearing her armor and couldn't actually enjoy the comfort of the chair. But there was no time to change right now, so she sat stiffly, watching her bridge crew as they performed their duties with speed and expertise. Every muscle in her body was tense, and that sensation was exacerbated by having to sit in the armor.

She really needed a little downtime and looked forward to entering Light-9790 and a month of easy flight.

The tac officer was at his console and ready if Sydnee ordered any action. After learning that the weapon counts on his console were accurate, she had briefed him completely. He knew that if he targeted a ship with either missiles or lasers, he would indeed be inflicting damage. Sydnee certainly didn't want to start a war and would use weapons only as a last resort.

As the *Justice* lifted from the surface of the lake and rose into the night sky using just its oh-gee engines, it was possible to see clusters of lights far off in the direction of the package's home. No doubt the authorities were combing the area for any clues that identified the persons responsible for assaulting the house.

The ship climbed quickly through the atmosphere, and as it approached the thermosphere, Sydnee gave the order to build the envelope.

"Building, envelope, Captain," Caruthers said from the helm as he touched the contact spot that would build the envelope. After a second he touched that spot again. Then again a second later. "No response from the envelope generator, Captain."

Sydnee sat up a little straighter. "Engineering, confirm."

Lieutenant Barron touched several spots on his console before saying, "Confirmed, Captain. The envelope generator is offline and nonresponsive."

"Damn," Sydnee muttered under her breath. "Navigation, find us a really remote place to set down. A warm place would be preferable because our engineers will have to work outside the ship."

"Aye, Captain. Searching. There's a tiny island in the lower temperate zone that's reportedly uninhabited."

"Send the coordinates to the helm."

"Sending."

"I have them Captain," Caruthers said. "Changing course."

The ship stopped its ascent and began to drop back towards the planet. Once beyond the land mass of the continent where the package lived, they overflew water for thirty-two minutes before slowing to circle what looked like a tropical island. Caruthers set the ship down in a small clearing that was hidden from the water by rows of trees. "We're down, Captain."

"Okay, let's find out what our status is. Navigation, do the reports mention dangerous flora or fauna on this island?"

"There's nothing in the database, Captain. Literally. So there may be dangers here. The good news is that it's so remote it's unlikely any person will spot us, except from above."

"Okay. Engineering, see if you can figure out what's going on with the envelope generator. Don't venture outside without a Marine fire team in armor."

"I don't have armor, Captain."

"I realize that. Remaining on the hull at all times will minimize any risk."

"Aye, Captain."

Sydnee immediately contacted Kelly MacDonald from her chair on the bridge.

"MacDonald," Sydnee heard on her CT.

"Kel, this is Syd. Would you have four of your people in full armor take up positions outside the ship while the engineers try to correct a problem? They should be armed with laser rifles and pistols. We're not expecting trouble, but we don't know what kind of indigenous life forms we might encounter."

"I'll have a fire team outside in five minutes, Syd."

"Thanks, Kel. Marcola out."

"Five minutes before anyone ventures outside," Sydnee announced to the bridge crew.

The engineer at the console relayed the message to the other engineer, CPO Luscome, who was down in the Engineering area, also trying to identify the problem.

"Captain, may I speak to you in private now?" Blade said to her right and slightly behind her. She hadn't even known he'd come onto the bridge.

She turned slightly, looked at him for a second, then said, "In my office," as she climbed out of the command chair. "Lt. Caruthers, you have the bridge." With the ship sitting on the ground, there was nothing to be done at the helm, so Olivetti didn't move to the helm console when Caruthers went to the command chair. It was protocol to always have a clear order of command established even though Caruthers would probably not be called upon to issue any orders.

Chapter Thirteen

~ February 12th, 2286 ~

As the doors closed behind the Major, Sydnee turned to face him. She had been dreading this moment but tried to maintain as impassive an expression as possible.

Blade, his face a mottled red, spoke first, with anger and accusation in his voice. "Captain, you are solely responsible for the failure of this mission. If you had followed my orders and picked us up when ordered to do so, we wouldn't presently be in this situation."

Sydnee knew she must remain perfectly calm to keep the situation from getting worse. "Major, your retrieval from the roof was only delayed by a mere fifteen minutes, and I made arrangements to have that done before I broke off in an effort to save my Marines."

"They're not *your* Marines, Captain. Let me remind you, you're Space Command. They're *my* Marines."

"As captain of this ship, everyone on board is my responsibility. That includes you, Major. I was no more going to desert those people than I would have deserted you."

"They were lost to us. The package was the most important thing, and he was almost lost because of your recklessness. You ordered your people not to raise the *Justice* from the bottom of the lake, thereby preventing me and my team from getting to safety."

"The package was never in any danger of being lost, Major. And you were perfectly safe once Lt. Weems picked you up. No one was going to get at you while you were inside the MAT. I wasn't going to simply desert any of *our* people without making every possible effort to recover them from that situation. I don't give up quite so easily."

"Are you accusing me of cowardice in the face of the enemy?"

Sydnee's impassive expression and calm voice seemed to be making the Major even angrier.

"I haven't accused you of anything. Rather, it seems to be the other way around."

"Captain, I'm the superior officer here, and I formally notify you that I'm taking command of this vessel under the articles of seniority as established by the Galactic Alliance Uniform Code of Military Operations."

"This is my ship, Major. You have no authority to take command while you're a passenger aboard my vessel. As you *are* a member of the GA Military Forces, there might even be a case made for attempted mutiny. And do you really think any of my people are going to follow your orders when they run contrary to my own?"

"I have sufficient forces behind me to make them follow my orders."

"Do you think the twenty-eight Marines whose lives I saved today, in direct violation of your order to abandon them, are going to follow you in a mutinous action? For that matter, how do your Special Ops people feel about you so quickly abandoning six fire teams operating under your orders? Do you believe you still have the full trust and confidence of your own team? Or are they wondering how quickly you will abandon them in a similar situation?"

"How my people feel is none of your concern. Do you surrender command of this ship to me?"

"No."

"Then I'll take it by force," Blade said, pulling his laser pistol out and pointing it at Sydnee.

"And just where do you think you're taking it?" Sydnee asked. She had noticed that Blade's index finger was on the guard, not the trigger. That probably meant he had no intention of firing the weapon.

"Back to GA space."

"How? The temporal generator is broken and we can't achieve FTL or we'd already be on our way back to GA space at Light-9790. All we have are oh-gee power, thrusters, and sub-light engines. The GA border is more than seven hundred seventy light-years from here. You don't really think we're going to get there with just sub-light power, do you?"

"I don't believe you. This is another one of your tricks."

"No tricks, Major. The ship is really broken, and my people are working to find the problem and correct it so we can go home. As I see it, we have the same objective— to get back to GA space. Your mission was a success, you have what we came for, and now it's my job to get us home. So you can either fire that weapon and severely harm your chances of ever getting off this planet, or put it away and get out of my office."

Blade's face had gotten even redder as he talked, but he was still in sufficient control that he recognized the truth when he heard it. He knew Marcola's people would never follow him willingly if he shot her, and she might be the best chance for their survival. He put the pistol back into his holster, turned, and left the office.

Sydnee took a deep breath and released it. In her personal and non-professional opinion, Blade was just one short step from going over the edge. She had decided that acting emotionless was the best way to defuse him for now, so she had maintained the impassive expression and even tone to her voice the entire time. Now she hoped she could keep things under control until they managed to get off the planet.

After hours of checking electronic systems aboard the *Justice* and finding nothing amiss, the engineers decided they had to check the electronics in the repository on the top of the ship where the temporal generator was protected from damage while not in use. The Marines rechecked the area beneath the ship and the surrounding jungle for any danger before the engineers were allowed to come out and perform their tests.

When the Marines detected no signs of danger, they took up posts around the ship to maintain tight security.

Spaceship maintenance was not normally performed in a gravity environment dirt-side. In space, weightlessness was used to full advantage in concert with a simple propulsion harness. And there were any number of ways to access every part of the craft in a maintenance bay aboard ship, the usual being oh-gee carts. The carts were nothing like the small oh-gee sleds used by the Marines to ferry gear on missions. The SC carts looked like the rear area of a flatbed truck. About three meters wide and six meters in length with a flat surface that could easily support four engineers, they had small air propulsion jets for maneuvering and could rise as high as twenty meters. The Marine sleds had no propulsion and their altitude was limited to about a meter and a half. But since the *Justice* didn't have any of the oh-gee engineering carts on board, a small, remote-controlled tug used to assist with habitat docking and undocking in space was chosen as the best way to access the sail area of the ship.

MAT-One was detached from the ship so a collapsible bin stored in the MAT's hold beneath the passenger compartment could be unloaded and set up. The robotic tug then picked up the bin with the two engineers aboard and used oh-gee power to carry it up to the generator repository on top of the ship. Arriving topside at the repository, the engineers discovered the problem almost immediately.

"Captain," the engineering officer said via com, "We've solved the mystery."

"Don't keep me in suspense. What is it?"

"The repository is filled to the brim with water. No doubt some of the electronics in there have shorted out."

"Filled with water? How could that happen?"

"I'm assuming that the engineers who designed the cover mechanism were not aware the ship was intended to operate as a submersible. Since there's no water in space, there's normally no need to make it airtight."

"Can it be repaired?"

"We don't know yet. I just wanted to give you a status report. We have to bail the water out and attempt to dry the compartment, then begin disassembly of the generator and see what the situation is inside."

"Keep me apprised."

"Aye, Captain."

Sydnee took a deep breath and released it slowly. It was going to be light in a few hours. Presently, they were a black ship surrounded by blackness, but once the sun was up, they would be in a black ship surrounded by a sea of greens, yellows, reds, and beiges. They would be easily visible to any imagery satellite.

Lifting the cover to a small console in the right arm of her chair, she depressed a button that would allow her to address the entire crew, "Attention, this is the captain. The engineers have discovered that the temporal envelope repository filled with water while the ship was submerged in that mountain lake, and some of the electronics appear to have shorted out. They are attempting to repair the ship, but at this point, we don't know how long that will take. Lt. MacDonald, please report to the bridge. Carry on."

A few minutes later, MacDonald was at her right hand. "You need me, Captain?"

"It's going to be daylight in a few hours. Could you use your holo-projector technology to disguise the ship from outside observation?"

"Our holo-projectors are only intended to camouflage a fire team, not cover an area as large as this ship."

"Could we overlap the images? The area around us is heavily treed, so all we really need to do is break up the straight lines of the ship and conceal the black coloration as much as possible."

"That might work. I'll check the manifests to see how many units we have available. What we have are in the holds of the MATs. MAT-One is already detached because you needed access to the collapsible bin, but we'll also have to detach MAT-Two from the *Justice* so we can access its hold."

"Okay. Weems can unlink the second MAT and set it on the ground by the first so the holds will be accessible. The SO teams had a couple of holo-projectors. Round them up as well."

"Aye, Captain, I'm on it."

By the time sunrise broke on the horizon, the Marines had finished erecting the holo-projector screen. The Special Ops team had supplied their two units and then helped position the units in a network that would give maximum coverage. With the two MATs re-linked to the ship to minimize exposed surfaces, about ninety percent of the ship was covered, and the parts not covered did not appear as a contiguous mass. The separated holo-images made the uncovered areas appear like shadows.

"That's it, Syd," Kelly MacDonald said as they stood outside the ship, evaluating the completed work.

"Good work, Kel. I don't know how long we're going to be here and I didn't want someone coming to investigate a large, unexplained black mass."

"You really have no idea how long it will take to make repairs?"

"Not yet. I've asked the engineers to give me a briefing at 1100. Hopefully, they'll have a better idea by then. So far, they've drained the repository and used heat wands to dry the compartment. They didn't want to begin dismantling anything until there was no chance they could make it worse, but they've now disconnected the generator, unbolted it from the extension shaft, and brought it inside the ship so they can work on it."

"How could the designers not have known the ship would submerge? They designed the tanks and pumps that permit it to happen."

"Perhaps the submergence idea was an afterthought and the already designed repository cover just got overlooked. Or perhaps someone believed the repository was airtight. I don't know— but you'd better believe I'm going to make sure Space Command knows when we get back."

"Then you believe we'll get back?"

"Yes, of course. But— it may take months. The worst case scenario is that Space Command has to send another ship for us, either with the parts we need or another CPS-14 that we can link with. Their envelope can then enclose us as well. After the briefing with the engineers I'm going to send an encrypted message to the *Denver* in which I'll brief them on our condition."

"We still don't have an answer for you, Captain," Lt. Barron, the engineering officer, said. "We know what's shorted out, but we don't yet know if we can fix it. We might be able to scavenge some parts from other, unnecessary systems and devices in the ship, as we used to do on the *Perry*."

"Why don't you simply replace the entire generator?"

"Uh, we don't have a backup."

"No backup? Every military FTL ship is required to carry a backup generator, even a tug."

"Yes, ma'am. The equipment manifest lists a backup generator, and even points to the engineering storage locker where it's located. The problem is that there's no backup generator in the designated locker. There's a crated office desk where the crated generator is supposed to be."

"But I have the only office aboard this ship and I already have a desk."

"Yes, ma'am. And should you need another desk, there's one in the engineering locker where the generator should be."

"What about the other storage lockers?"

"We didn't attempt to determine if everything we should have is accounted for, but we know there's no generator anywhere in the engineering compartments."

"Then can you provide any idea at all of a timeframe for the required work? For instance, when will you give up trying to fix it?"

Barron looked briefly at Chief Luscome before replying. "As long as we're stuck here, never. But I'd say if we can't repair it in a month, we'll probably never be able to repair it."

Luscome nodded his agreement with the statement.

"Okay, men," Sydnee said, "thank you. That will be all."

"A month?" Kelly MacDonald said after they had gone.

The office was so crowded that Weems and Caruthers had to stand inside Sydnee's sleeping quarters, but they had heard everything. With the engineers gone, they came into the office.

"We can't stay here a month," Weems said. "Someone is bound to spot us. Even with the holo-projector bubbles over the ship, the view from space has to look considerably different. A mapping satellite may automatically call the changed image to the attention of someone in a geological office and then it will filter upwards until it reaches someone who might come to investigate."

"We have no choice about staying here, unless you know of a better place to conceal ourselves. It would take a lifetime to reach another marginally habitable planet outside this solar system, even a planet as awful as Diabolisto, with just our sub-light engines."

"The Major said the entire planet had been mapped by our diplomatic ship," Weems said. "The mission planners were able to identify that lake as a good hiding spot. If the Major has all the maps, we might be able to spot another good hiding place. Of course, it would have to be one that doesn't require us to submerge."

"Good idea, Jerry. Maybe you or Kelly could request that from him. I'd do it, but he isn't very happy with me right now."

"What about the envoy mentioned in the mission briefing?" Caruthers asked. "If we could contact him, he might be able to get the parts the engineers need from some shipyard. It's the power from our matter/anti-matter system that permits the envelope generation, not the generator itself, and it's the Dakinium that creates the double envelope so we can travel at Light-9790. Just because Clidepp ships don't come close to matching the speed of our non-Dakinium ships, the generator shouldn't make a difference. The Clidepp military and commercial shipbuilding companies have access to parts that let them build a temporal envelope, so maybe we just need to find out if their temporal generator parts are standard enough for us to use them."

"That's a good suggestion, Pete," Sydney said. "Perhaps we can get the parts we need from someone on this planet. But first the engineers have to identify which parts must be replaced to fix the generator. Okay, I'm going to send a message to the *Denver* and tell them of our predicament. Perhaps they'll have some other suggestions. It'll take eight days for the message to reach them and eight days to hear back after they come up with a plan, and maybe we'll come up with something on our own before then."

"I don't like people going behind my back," Blade said as Sydnee's office door closed behind him. She had rolled her eyes when the computer announced his presence outside the room but made her face expressionless before he came in.

"To what are you referring, Major?"

"You sent MacDonald to circumvent my authority. She had some of my people set up holo-projectors."

Blade's voice was calm. It was a considerable change from their last conversation.

"I'm working to keep our location secure, repair this ship, *and* get us back to GA space. I'm not playing chain-of-command power games. It's been my understanding from the beginning that this command is composed of three units— Space Command, a Marine platoon from the *Denver*, and a Special Ops teams headed by you. My orders were to get you to the home of the package and get everyone back safely. Your mission is over, it's been accomplished, and now I'm in full command. We needed holo-projectors set up to disguise our presence in this clearing. As the officer in command of her platoon, I put MacDonald in charge of that effort. I never instructed her to circumvent your authority. We're in a difficult position and I need everyone working together for our mutual benefit. I would welcome your help, if you feel you can work with us, but let's be perfectly clear on one thing. Your part of the original mission is complete and over. You were successful, and none of our people have been lost or injured. For that you are to be commended. But now, *I'm* in command. If you can't accept that, I can't involve you."

Blade looked at her intently for several seconds, then showed a hint of a smile before replying. "You're far stronger than I originally thought. That indecisive attitude and 'umming' you exhibited back at the *Denver* really had me fooled. I thought for sure you'd fall apart before the mission was over, despite Burrow's glowing recommendations, and that I'd have to take command. I admire someone who stands their ground and refuses to yield when they believe they're in the right. I apologize for testing you earlier this morning. I had to see if you could handle the stress I know is coming from being stuck in Clidepp space with a broken ship. The officer I was introduced to back in GA space hasn't been seen since we deployed."

Sydnee stared at Blade, not knowing if this was another tactic to take control of the ship or if his words were genuine. "Does that mean you'll work *with* us and not against us as we try to get this ship repaired?"

"It does. Just tell me what you need of me or my people."

"If we can't get the ship operational with what materials we have on board, we may have to run a mission to a populated area. I'm still waiting to hear from our engineers before I make a decision on that. We might be able to secure parts from a Clidepp shipyard, and if so we'll have to determine which yard has the parts and then go get them. Can you provide a contact number for the GA envoy? I checked the DB and there's nothing in there."

"With good reason. When the civil war officially began, the GA pulled our ambassador and the entire diplomatic staff out, except for the one envoy. Then when the Clidepp government refused to assist our efforts to find the person responsible for the bombing of the Trade Show, the GA pulled the last dip out. How are we going to learn who has the parts we need?"

"Our database is the standard DB used for interdiction purposes. It contains the complete ship schematics for every ship we've ever encountered in GA space. It's necessary so our people know where illegal aliens might be hiding or where contraband is likely to be hidden. Once we know what parts we need, the computer can perform a search and tell us who makes it and what ship uses it. If we can't find specific usable parts, we may have to 'acquire' an entire generator. That is if we can find a model compatible with our electronics."

"And if we can't find compatible equipment?"

"Then we sit here until Space Command sends another ship to rescue us. We'll have to hope the package is still so important that they'll risk another incursion into Clidepp space."

Blade took a deep breath and then released it. "We might have a possible contact on the planet— one who would be willing to help us find the right equipment. The intelligence file contains the name of a person who provided critical information about the location of the person we were seeking. When you determine exactly what we need, let me know. I'll try to reach the person who helped us before."

"Okay, stay ready."

"We're always ready, *Captain*."

"Thank you, Major."

———————

"There's still no word from Lt. Marcola," Commander Bryant said to Captain Lidden during their morning briefing session.

"It's only been, what? Six weeks?"

"Almost seven. They should have reached Yolongus three weeks ago and been on their way back by now."

"She has orders to send us a status report as soon as she leaves the planet. We should hear soon."

"I hope so. You don't think putting this much responsibility on her shoulders might have been a little too much too soon?"

"She's demonstrated an innate ability for command. I think she can handle it."

"But can she deal with Blade? He came across as being a hard man to work with."

"It'll be good experience for her."

———————————————

"Captain," Sydnee heard when she responded to a call on her CT, "I've found what might be a better location for us while we wait on the repair work." The call was from Lt. Olivetti, working at the navigation console on the bridge.

Sydnee, mulling over options as she sat on her bunk, stood up and said, "I'll be right there. Marcola out."

As Sydnee came to the navigation console on the bridge, Olivetti said, "It's right here," pointing to a dot on a surface map.

"What is that? It looks like an enormous hole in the planet."

"Let me zoom in."

A second later the area was clearly visible.

"Is that a volcano?"

"Yes, ma'am. It certainly is."

"Let me get this straight. You want us to hide *inside* a volcano?"

"It's dormant."

"So was Mt. Requetti on Eulosi thirty-five years ago. Twenty thousand Eulosians died in the three days following that eruption. Dormant doesn't mean extinct. It just means it's not erupting— *today*."

Chapter Fourteen
~ February 23rd, 2286 ~

"Mt. Requetti *had* been dormant," Lt. Olivetti said, "but in the weeks before the eruption, it began showing definite signs it was coming to life. There were powerful ground tremors in the vicinity on a daily basis, the wildlife was scattering away from the mountain, and the community's aquifer had become contaminated with sulfur. The people chose to ignore all of the warning signs."

"Are you a volcanologist?" Sydnee asked, surprised by Olivetti's detailed knowledge of an event older than she was.

"Only on an amateur level, Captain. But it's always been a passion of mine. I chose Space Command for a career in space over a career that would consist mostly of sitting in a lab on some planet while studying seismic readings, but I never lost my interest in volcanology."

"And you believe this location to be safe?"

"Yes. At the present, it seems like the ideal spot. The lava is black, so even without the holo-projectors, it'd be almost impossible to spot us."

"What if the volcano erupts? This ship is well protected by the Dakinium skin, but I don't know if it could tolerate the heat of molten lava."

"The maps created by the diplomatic ship are fantastic. We have normal imagery, infrared, surface contour, and thermal versions. The thermal readings for the volcano interior aren't any higher than those for the surrounding land mass. As you can see, vegetation has started to cover all of the outer slopes. It takes decades following an eruption for flora to establish a toehold as widespread as this in a lava field. And in addition to allowing us to hide in plain sight, the volcano is within an hour's flying time in a MAT to the three largest industrial and manufacturing centers on the planet. There are dozens of shipbuilding facilities at those centers."

"If we do this, what would be the best time to move the ship to the new location so we're always under cover of darkness?"

Olivetti glanced at the chronometer on the bulkhead before saying, "Six hours and thirty minutes from now."

Sydnee moved to the command chair where Weems was sitting. He started to rise, but she waved him down. Lifting the console cover on the chair's right arm, she pressed a contact point. "This is the captain. We'll be moving the ship to a new location in six and one half hours. Six hours from now we'll begin dismantling the holo-projector net. All equipment must be inside so the ship's exterior can be sealed and the ship can be made ready for flight. Carry on." Turning to Olivetti, she said, "Good job, Lieutenant." To Caruthers at the helm, she said, "Although the watch will have changed by then, I'd like you to take the helm for the move. It may be a tight fit getting into that cone, and you have an exceptionally fine touch on the oh-gee engines."

"Aye, Captain," Caruthers said with a smile.

To Weems, she said, "I'll be in my office."

"Aye, Captain."

Sydnee had barely gotten back to her office/quarters next to the bridge before Blade was at the door. "What's this about a move?"

"We're moving the ship to a better place of concealment. We're too exposed here, even if it is remote, and we're only partially hidden by the holo-projectors. Lt. Olivetti has found us a volcano where the interior surface is black and our coloration will blend perfectly."

"A volcano? Are you nuts? This ship can't sit on lava. We've learned it can't even sit in water."

"The volcano has been dormant for many years. I think it'll probably remain that way a little longer."

"Probably?"

"We can never be sure about anything, but the odds are in our favor. Also, it's much closer to potential sources of DATFA generator parts."

"I hope you know what you're doing, Captain."

"I'm doing the best I can with what I have, just as our engineers are doing the best *they* can. They've promised me they'll know the full situation with the generator by first watch tomorrow. At that time we'll formulate a plan to get off this planet. Have you been able to reach the contact you mentioned?"

"Chief Lemela sent an encrypted message to the last known contact address from the intelligence file, but we've heard nothing back yet. How about the *Denver*? Any word?"

"Not yet, but it's too soon to hear anyway. My message should reach them sometime in the next twenty-four hours, depending on their location in the sector."

"Sorry to disturb you in your quarters, sir," Commander Bryant said when Captain Lidden accepted the contact, "but we've just received a message from Lieutenant Marcola."

"Come to my quarters, XO."

"Right away, sir."

The door annunciator system at the captain's quarters sensed Bryant's presence as he stopped in front of the corridor door. After informing the captain and receiving the required response, the system opened the door.

Lidden, sitting on the sofa in his living room, lowered the report he was viewing on a viewpad as Bryant entered his quarters. "What's the situation?"

"I haven't listened to the message, sir. As soon as I saw it was Priority One, I contacted you."

"Let's view it, then," Lidden said as he used the controls on the viewpad to activate a large wall monitor and select the message in the queue. Since it was a Priority-One, it required a retinal scan. He was able to use his viewpad to complete that process.

"Wow," Lidden said as the message ended. "This is serious."

"Maybe we *should* have sent Milty as ship commander."

"This isn't Marcola's fault. If their FTL was working, they would already be halfway back."

"How do we handle it?"

"We wait."

"Then we do nothing?"

"I didn't say that. I'm going to send a message to SHQ informing them of the situation and asking for any inform-ation they might have regarding access to the necessary parts for the generator. I'm also going to suggest they notify Mars about a serious design flaw in the repository cover. Blade accomplished his mission, but the package is still in Clidepp space aboard the— what did they name the ship?"

"*Justice.*"

"Interesting," Lidden said, then paused for a moment before continuing. "We can't mount an emergency rescue mission that would have us invade Clidepp space unless we receive permission from SHQ, but we can begin making preparations. If we get a go, we should probably send another CPS-14. Let's make sure we have some pilots certified to fly it. I know they've all been using the simulators, but let's put a bit more emphasis on their training and practice."

"Aye, sir. Is that all?"

"For now, that's all we *can* do."

"Yes, sir."

―――――――――――

"The surface at the bottom of the crater is forty-six point eight-three degrees Celsius," Lt. Barron, sitting at the engin-eering console on the bridge, said, "and appears to be adequately flat enough that we should be able to get the ship perfectly level with the hydraulic adjustment legs in the habitat units."

"Then, in your opinion, it's safe to put down?"

"Yes, Captain."

"What about the toxicity of the air?"

Looking down at his console and tapping a few touch spots, he said, "There are slightly elevated levels of carbon dioxide, sulfur dioxide, and hydrochloric acid inside the cone. The levels don't suggest imminent volcanic activity, but anyone venturing outside the ship should have their personal body armor sealed or be using an auxiliary rebreather unit."

Sydnee took a deep breath, exhaled slowly, then said, "Lt. Caruthers, take us in."

The ship had been hovering just above the rim of the cone while the potential danger was assessed.

"Set us down nice and easy, Lieutenant. We don't want to disturb this sleeping giant."

"Aye, Captain."

The oh-gee engines held the ship perfectly level and stable as it descended into the volcano. When the ship was just fifty centimeters from the highest point beneath the habitat containers, leveling legs extended downwards from all three units and adjusted as the weight of the ship was gently lowered onto them. When the oh-gee engines were disengaged, the ship was perfectly level.

"We're down, Captain," Caruthers said.

"Excellent job, Lieutenant. I never felt even the slightest bump."

"Thank you, ma'am."

"Hopefully, the seismic sensors that are no doubt monitoring this volcano didn't record anything that will cause someone to come investigate. As soon as engineering places a signal repeater at the top of the cone so we can send and receive transmissions, we can stand down. But as always, the bridge must be minimally manned."

"Do we need to set up the holo-projectors, Captain?" Weems asked.

Sydnee thought for a second before responding. "Lt. Olivetti believes we'll be adequately hidden because of our coloration— but it certainly can't hurt. Yes. Let's set up the holo-projectors. Coordinate our effort with that of Lt. MacDonald and her people."

"Aye, Captain."

———

"It's just not possible, Captain," the engineer said. "We can't repair the damaged components. DATFA generators are protected against the freezing cold of space but were never intended to be submerged in water, and there was no protection against that. The generator is essentially scrap because we can't use Clidepp parts. Their shipboard electrical systems are totally incompatible with ours. It's like the difference between AC and DC current. We've reviewed all the schematics contained in the ship's database and haven't found anything made in Clidepp space that's close to useable. We can't even use an entirely new generator because of the incompatibilities. We had a lot of experience with electronic incompatibilities while aboard the *Perry*, but this is too far outside the realm of 'remotely possible.'

"What do you suggest?" Sydnee asked.

"We need Space Command to send us an entirely new generator. We've determined that all of the support mechanisms, such as the shaft that extends the generator to its proper height, are fine. And the cover opens and closes without a problem, even if it isn't airtight."

"No other solution?"

"None, unless you can find a derelict ship with a workable generator from the GA here on Yolongus."

"That's a thought. Would the generator from a freighter suffice?"

"It depends on the construction. Freighters coalesce their DATFA envelopes differently than those of military ships, but the basic technology and electronics are the same. We might be able to jury-rig a workable system."

"We aren't going to find any scrapped GA military vessels in Clidepp space, but a scrapped freighter might be possible. If we got you a working generator from a freighter, how long would it take you to make it ready for our use?"

"I couldn't say that until I saw it."

"Best and worst case scenarios."

"Best— a few days. Worst— a few months."

"Okay, Lt. Barron. Get some rest. I know how hard you and Chief Luscome have been working the past few weeks. I, and everyone aboard this ship, appreciate your efforts."

"Thank you, Captain. A bit of sack time sounds really good."

―――――――――

"That's the situation. Major," Sydnee said as she completed the short briefing. "We need another temporal field generator. We either get one on our own or sit here until Space Command comes to rescue us. I'm open to any suggestions."

"So you want me and my Special Ops people to find you a used generator?"

"According to our engineers, it's unlikely we're going to find a new one on this planet that will work. So a used, working generator would be wonderful."

"And what do we use for payment?"

"I have the standard deployment disbursement fund of ten thousand GA credits in my safe, but I doubt we'll find a useable temporal generator for that amount. Perhaps we can sweeten the deal with trade goods. Otherwise we'll have to steal it."

"I doubt that any equipment dealer is going to accept trade goods, so we'll have to *take* the generator, and all that that implies."

"If force is used, the authorities could be on us before we can get the ship FTL operational."

"We're still well hidden."

"That may not help if one of our people is captured."

"Then I'll have to make sure none of them is captured." In response to the look on Sydnee's face, Blade said, "It may not be a surgical operation. In fact, it may get pretty messy."

Sydnee breathed in deeply and then released it. "Do your best to keep it clandestine. If you can't, make sure no one can tie it to the GA."

The corners of Blade's mouth turned up just slightly for a second, and he said, "Aye, Captain. No witnesses."

———

"My people have been over every centimeter of our maps for the three nearby cities containing the planet's largest industrial centers and reviewed all of the information contained in the ship's DB," Blade said to Sydnee as they sat in her office. "We've located a couple of scrapyards that might potentially have the generator we need, but since we don't have a Yolongi front man, I can see no alternative other than to visit each location after they've closed for the day and perform a physical search through the scrap piles. We certainly can't just show up there and discuss the purchase of a used generator. Clidepp Intelligence would be informed immediately if we didn't show proper documentation of our identity and travel visas issued by the Clidepp government."

"What about the intelligence contact? Could he make the inquiries?"

"We've still had no response from him, Captain," Blade said.

"Very well. We have to do what we have to do. We're not going anywhere without a generator. When do you propose to begin your operation?"

"We're ready to leave tonight, if you can provide transportation."

"Of course. Lt. Weems and a MAT are at your disposal."

"Thank you, Captain. I'll have my people begin making preparations to deploy tonight."

"I have the landing site in view," Weems said over the intercom to the rear compartment of the MAT.

The SO Marines, including Blade, were ready. As soon as the MAT touched down, they popped the hatch and were outside in seconds. The selected landing zone next to a burned out factory in one of the sadder parts of the city was clear of any signs of sentient life. Even the tramps didn't want to come down here.

"We're deploying," Blade said to Weems on Com-Two. "Stay buttoned up until you hear from me or a member of my team."

"Roger," Weems said.

Blade then used some hand signals and his people moved out.

At the first scrapyard, the Marines stunned some unusual security animals that had the general appearance of gorillas and then began their physical search while Blade headed to the office and began hunting though the computer files for any indication that the yard might have scrap from a GA freighter. He found nothing in the files, so he joined his people in the physical search.

The SO Marines had studied images of GA generators and downloaded them into their helmet's memory cores. As they searched, everything they saw was compared by their helmet's computer system to the downloaded images. Anything with a ninety percent match on size and general appearance would result in an alert to the wearer.

After almost six hours, the SO team had finished searching the final piles of scrap at the extreme end of the yard.

"Nothing, dammit," Blade said angrily. "Not one damned GA generator in this entire scrapyard. And this seemed to offer the better chance of the two."

On Com-Three, Blade said, "Okay, people, let's wrap it up here. This was a wasted effort."

On Com-Two, Blade said, "Lieutenant, we're headed back, empty-handed."

The SO team closed and locked the gate as they left. When the yard was opened in the morning, the guard animals would have recovered, and no one should be aware that the yard had been scoured for a GA ship part overnight.

When the Marines got back to the MAT, they climbed in and tiredly dropped into their seats. Blade entered last and pulled the hatch closed behind him. As he dropped into a seat, he said to Weems, "Everyone is aboard. We can head for home."

"Aye, Major. Heading for the *Justice*."

"I call this emergency session to order," Admiral Moore said in the Admiralty Board meeting hall. The other admirals were all in attendance, including the newest member of the board, Admiral Lesbolh Yuthkotl of Nordakia, but only aides and senior clerks had been allowed to join them in the large chamber on this occasion. The gallery area was empty.

"I've just received a message from Captain Lidden of the *Denver*. He reports that the mission to Yolongus was partially successful. The Marines captured the package and got away clean, as far as they know, but the ship's FTL drive was damaged due to a design flaw in the repository hatch cover. The envelope generator is scrap, and where the replacement generator *should* be located in an engineering locker, there's a crate containing an office desk. So the ship is stuck on Yolongus. They have oh-gee and sub-light power only."

"Good Lord!" Admiral Bradlee said. "This could turn out to be a disaster if the Clidepp government captures our people and that ship."

"Yes," Admiral Moore said. "The question is whether or not we send a Space Command ship in to rescue them or try to work thorough our SCI network."

"Normally, I would resist all effort to involve our undercover people in this. It takes too long to recruit and train them just to throw them away on anything but the most important of assignments. But if it's the only way, we'll have to do it. However, my resources on Yolongus are extremely limited. I might not even be able to send someone to help them."

"We could send in another CPS-14," Admiral Plimley suggested, "rather than the *Denver*."

"How far can the ship get with its sub-light engines?" Admiral Woo asked.

"Sub-light engines in other than warships are really only intended to assist in planetary orbit maneuvers," Admiral Platt said, "but I imagine they can achieve a speed of Sub-Light-50. It's not the fault of the engines; it's the amount of hydrogen the ship can carry. Once they exhaust their fuel, they go ballistic, like a torpedo. And like a torpedo they lose all guidance ability once they exhaust their fuel, so it's imperative they don't exhaust all their fuel or they lose the ability to stop or change direction. They can collect more fuel as they travel outside of FTL, but the collectors aren't very large. It will take quite a while to top off their tanks again. No, the sub-light engines aren't the answer. They need a new generator."

"Where is the ship now, Richard?" Admiral Hillaire asked.

"Captain Lidden didn't include a specific location in his message but says they're on the planet. I assume they're well hidden in some isolated area— perhaps near one of the polar caps."

"That black ship against a white background would be too obvious," Bradlee said.

"You're right, Roger. They must be somewhere where their black coloration would better blend with the surroundings. I doubt they'd go back into the water."

"It doesn't really matter where they are," Admiral Bradlee said. "I'm sure the Captain has done everything in his or her power to conceal the presence of the ship. Uh, who is in command, by the way?"

Admiral Moore turned to his aide, who whispered something to the Admiral. When he turned back, he hesitated for a second, then said, "The captain is Lieutenant(jg) Sydnee Marie Marcola."

"That name sounds familiar," Admiral Ressler said. "Did you say Lieutenant(*jg*)?"

"Yes."

"That was rather an important mission. I'm surprised Lidden trusted it to a JG."

"The name is familiar from the recent BOI report," Admiral Ahmed said. "She's the young officer who performed so bravely on Diabolisto, commandeered the stolen Clidepp destroyer, and saved the *Perry's* crew."

"Ah, yes, I remember now," Admiral Ressler said. "And now I understand Lidden's confidence in her. It appears she's someone worth watching."

"Any suggestions on what action we take? Do we send in the *Denver*, another CPS, or see if Roger can handle it through his undercover network?"

"Are they our only choices?" Admiral Ahmed asked.

"No, Raihana. We'll consider anything else you'd care to suggest."

"I'd like a day to think about it and do a little research."

"Time could be critical."

"It's just one day, Richard."

"Let's put it to a vote. All in favor of giving Raihana her requested one-day delay, signify by raising your hand." Glancing around the table, Admiral Moore said, "You have your day, Raihana. We'll meet again tomorrow to make a decision on this most important issue."

Chapter Fifteen
~ March 6th, 2286 ~

The second scrapyard Blade felt might yield a GA generator was located on a strip of land bordering a swamp. The yard had outgrown its solid-ground property and was now filling in the swamp with scrap deemed useless even for recycling. Each year, the piles on dry land had grown higher and more difficult to locate anything of practical value.

When the SO team approached the yard, they scanned the area for guard animals but failed to spot any.

"Whaddya think, sir?" one of the team asked. "Do we accept that there are no guard animals here?"

"It's possible. This yard doesn't look very prosperous. Guard animals cost money to buy and feed. Let's go in and begin our search, but keep a wary eye out for any sign of movement."

Blade headed for the scrapyard office while the team began a physical search for a useful generator. The computer records were as sloppy and disorganized as the piles in the yard, and Blade was unable to find any useful information about GA freighter parts. He finally gave up and walked out of the office to assist in the physical search. By then, his Marines had covered about a third of the yard.

Despite the mess and their eagerness to be done, the team didn't give the search effort less than their best. They knew that to get off the planet and on their way back to GA space they needed to find a generator. If there was a GA generator there, they were going to find it.

"Sir, I think I see something," Blade heard over Com-Three. He hurried to where the noncom who made the report was standing.

"Where is it, Boyd?"

"Up there, sir," Boyd said, pointing to the top of a pile of scrap.

As Blade looked up, the imaging routine in his helmet confirmed that the object had the general appearance of a generator from a GA freighter.

"The question is," Blade said, "how do we get up there to confirm its origin? We don't have any oh-gee carts."

"I have a line in my backpack. I think I can scale this pile."

"It looks pretty unstable. Be careful."

"Yes, sir."

Boyd removed his backpack and pulled out the rope. He prepared the line and then let the three-pronged grapple hook fly. It caught on a piece of scrap right next to the generator. Yanking on the line to make sure it was secure, he then started walking up the pile. As he reached the generator, he paused and made sure of his footing before examining his discovery.

After several minutes, Blade heard, "No go, sir. It's just the outer cover. There's nothing inside."

"Okay, Staff Sergeant. Come on down."

Blade waited while Boyd descended slowly to the ground.

"Sorry, sir." Boyd said.

"No problem, son. It was worth a look. Okay, let's keep going."

The team spent two more hours at the yard and checked every pile, but nothing else was spotted that resembled the two-meter-long piece of equipment they were seeking. It was a depressing ride back to the volcano. Everyone wanted off the planet, and all they needed was one small generator— a generator that could be picked up almost anywhere in GA space.

━━━━━━━━━━━━━━━━━━

"I received a response from the Admiralty Board over-night," Lidden said to Bryant during their regular morning session.

"Did they give us a green light to send in a rescue ship?"

"Just the opposite. They reaffirmed that under no circumstances am I to enter, send anyone, or allow any GA personnel to enter Clidepp space without specific orders from SHQ."

"What? They're deserting our people?"

"I imagine they probably have some other plan regarding a rescue."

"They could have at least given us the go-ahead to move a ship to within a light-year of Yolongus. It could remain there, hidden in the black, and be ready to move in if their other idea fails."

"I agree, but the AB calls all the shots, and for now we just keep performing normal interdiction activities."

"Amazing."

"Don't write our people off yet. The AB members are all experienced Space Command officers. They're not going to simply forget about our folks."

"I have news, Captain," Blade said to Sydnee after entering her office and waiting until the door was closed. "I've received a message from the intelligence contact. He's agreed to meet me."

"Wonderful. He seems to be our last hope at this point. I still haven't heard anything back from the *Denver*. When's the meet?"

"Tomorrow night. In a Lelligassa park."

"Lelligassa?"

"It's a fairly large city about two hour's travel time from here. The park is in a bad section of town— so bad even the police fear to travel there after dark."

"Sounds ideal," Sydnee said with a grin.

"If I have your permission to go, we'll begin planning the operation today and be ready to leave by 1800 tomorrow. The sun will have set by the time we leave here."

"Of course you have my permission, Major. Lt. Weems will be ready to leave at that time."

"Great. I thought you'd approve. My people are already assembling for the planning session."

"Okay, here's the park where the meet is scheduled to take place tomorrow," Blade said, using a laser pointer to indicate a spot on the large monitor in the habitat's mess hall. A high resolution mapping image of Lelligassa was being projected on the monitor. First Sergeant Doyle Larson was handling the computer interface. By careful manipulation he could show that part of the city in almost any manner desired, from a two-dimensional overhead view to a full 3-D image of the smashed fountain in the center of the decaying park as it would be seen from ground level.

"Over on the left you'll see clusters of burned out or abandoned buildings in an old factory complex. That's where the MAT will set down. Once down, it'll be surrounded on all sides by tall structures and not visible to street traffic. We'll use alleyways to get out of the factory complex and use the city streets to reach the park. We'll wear the same style of full-body cloaks worn by locals over our armor to disguise our identities.

"We'll arrive at the park a full hour before the scheduled meet time and take up concealed positions." To Larson, he said, "Take us down to street level by the park." The image instantly dropped to show a 3-D image of the park entrance.

"There are three entrances to the park, and I have no idea which one our contact will use. So we'll set up six observation posts designated Tango-One through Tango-Six in the abandoned buildings surrounding the park. We naturally want to know if the contact is arriving alone or with companions. The RP is at this bench by what's left of a fountain. The team members in the park, designated Alpha-One through Alpha-Four, will remain concealed at all times. I'll likewise remain concealed until I hear that the contact has come alone. If he arrives alone, I'll go out to meet him. If he's not alone, I'll formulate a revised plan when we know how many others are with him.

"I want to make it clear that although this person may represent our best chance of getting a generator, we still don't know if we can trust him. SCI used him to locate the package for us, but that was their first contact with him.

"This is a dangerous area, but *we're* going to be the most dangerous force there. I expect we'll have one or more confrontations with the local denizens. When we do, put them down fast and permanent. We're not going to waste time with inner-city scum. This is especially important for Tango-One through Tango-Six. We have no way of knowing who or what you'll contact when you enter the building selected for your observation point. If anyone tries to interfere with your mission, make sure they never interfere with anyone again. The police are afraid to travel in this part of the city after dark and with good reason. Bodies won't be discovered until the following day, if they're discovered at all. I'm sure there are a lot of small, hungry carnivores hiding in those buildings that will make quick work of a free meal.

"First Sergeant Larson will remain with the MAT to help protect it. I have no doubt that some of the locals would love to capture such a prize. We'll have to show them how unwise that idea would be.

"We shove off at 1800 hours tomorrow. The First Sergeant has your individual assignments."

―――――――――――

"Tango-Two, this is Sierra-Leader. Do you have eyes on our contact?"

"Negative, Sierra-Leader. No one has entered the vicinity of the RP since we took up position."

"How about you, Tango-Six? Anything?"

"Negative, Sierra-Leader. Nothing moving on the streets outside the park."

"Continue surveillance."

Blade leaned back against the tree so that he was completely hidden in the shadows. The contact should have been there ten minutes earlier.

An hour later, and still without any sign of the contact, Blade was about ready to pull in his guys and head to where the MAT was waiting.

"Sierra-Leader, this is Tango-Three. I see movement at two o'clock from my position."

"Tango-Two, can you confirm?"

"I haven't seen anything from my position— wait, I see something now. Someone is in the shadows by the corner of the building."

"Tango-Five confirms. I see it also. There's just one figure so far."

"Tell me if the shadow moves to the RP location."

It was another ten minutes before anyone saw movement again.

"Tango-Five to Sierra-Leader. The contact is moving towards the RP location."

"Tango-Three confirms."

Two minutes later, Alpha-One said, "The contact has reached the RP and is standing in the shadows next to the tree."

"Any other movement?" Blade asked. "Has he been followed?"

"Tango-Two. No other movement observed on the streets outside the park."

"Tango-Three confirms."

"This is Sierra-leader. I'm moving in. Stay alert for anyone on the perimeter."

Blade moved to the edge of the shadow created by the tree and stopped. One more step and he'd be exposed to view. He knew his spotters would alert him to any sign of outsiders entering the vicinity, so he stepped out and walked calmly towards the believed contact some forty meters away. Wearing the traditional cloak worn by most residents in the Clidepp Empire, it was impossible to distinguish Blade from any of the three sentient species in the Empire.

"Tallaggio," Blade said as he stopped a meter from the other person. It was the contact name he'd established in their communications.

"Melorriat," the other individual, also wearing the traditional cloak with the hood pulled up, said as his recognition name.

Beneath the cloak Blade was wearing his Marine personal body armor, so when he spoke, everything he said was translated into Yolon and emanated from the speaker in his breastplate. The slightly muffled words were a clear indication that he was using electronic equipment, but it was standard practice for people meeting to discuss illegal activity to use voice-altering equipment. "Pull back your hood," Blade said. "I like to see who I'm dealing with."

The Clidepp Empire was home to three sentient species, but Yolongus was almost exclusively inhabited by Yolongis, while elsewhere in the Empire all three species could be found in great numbers. The Yolongi had an appearance not unlike the urban legend 'greys' of twentieth century Earth, but that was mere coincidence. The Olimpood had flabby bodies, which allowed them to be equally at home on land or water, while the Mydwuard had an exoskeleton like that of crustaceans and insects on Earth. Since all three were about the same height and bipedal, it was impossible to tell which species they were while they wore the heavy, full-length cloaks common on the planet.

The contact complied, pushing back his hood far enough for Blade to see he was Yolongi and get a good look at his face before pulling it back into place.

"Now you," the contact said.

As Blade pulled back his hood, the helmet of his armor was exposed, but the faceplate was clear.

"Let me see your face, Terran," the Yolongi said.

Blade made an adjustment so the outer Simage plate displayed a simulated image. It bore no resemblance to his actual features and even mimicked the muscle movements of his face as he talked. It was enough to satisfy the Yolongi. When he nodded, Blade blanked the Simage plate and pulled the cloak forward to conceal his helmet. Anyone passing by wouldn't see anything suspicious in two Yolongis having a discussion in the park.

"Were you responsible for the kidnapping?" the Yolongi asked.

"What kidnapping?"

"The Minister of Antiquities was kidnapped from his home recently. The authorities are baffled. No one has yet claimed credit for the abduction, and no demands for ransom have been received."

"Nope, not us. We just arrived on the planet."

"We?"

"Obviously I'm not here alone."

"No, that's true. How many are you?"

"More than one."

The Yolongi was quiet for a few seconds, then said, "What do you want of me?"

"I need a temporal envelope generator designed to work with GA systems."

"How did you get here without a generator?"

"Ours was damaged by a micro-meteorite while we were stopped in space in this solar system. It's beyond repair. We need a replacement to get home."

"What are you even doing in Clidepp space? I thought all GA citizens and government representatives had been pulled out."

Expecting to be asked, Blade had concocted a cover story. "We've been tracking a Raider ship with Terran slaves on board. We learned they crossed into Clidepp space an annual ago and that their destination was Yolongus, so we followed."

"The Raiders don't take Terran slaves anymore. Space Command put an end to that."

"Don't kid yourself. The Raiders stopped their ship piracy, but they still deal in slavery. They simply abduct their women from planets now. No one pays much attention when a person or two disappears if there were no witnesses to the abduction. Hundreds of thousands of people disappear every year in the GA. Usually it's nothing sinister— just people moving away without telling anyone they were going, but kidnapping, slavery, and murder are more common than the authorities like to admit. It's well known that Yolongi men like Terran women, so for a slave ship, a destination of Yolongus was understandable. They're aboard a single-hull freighter."

"And Space Command didn't stop them at the border?"

"There's so much refugee activity at the border right now that less than one ship in a hundred entering GA space is being stopped. And with ships outbound from GA space, that number is probably one in ten thousand."

"Okay. So you need a GA-compatible generator. I think I can arrange that. It's not contraband, so I won't have any trouble transporting it if I can locate one. But it's going to be expensive."

"How expensive?"

"Oh, for a working generator, I'd say about a hundred thousand GA credits."

"Too much. We don't have that kind of money with us."

"Too bad. I guess you're stuck in Clidepp space for the foreseeable future."

"I could give you ten thousand credits now, and have Space Command deposit one hundred twenty thousand GA credits into any inter-nation account you name within thirty solars once we ascertain the generator is in good working condition."

The Yolongi hesitated for a moment, then shook his head. "It could take an annual to actually have the funds available to me."

"But you'd have the safety and security of the GA to guarantee the funds would be there when you went to use them. With the civil war raging here, how safe is the monetary system?"

Blade could tell the Yolongi didn't seem too keen on the idea. When he shook his head, Blade said, "How about trade goods?"

"What do you have?"

"Food, medical supplies, and clothing."

"I don't trade in any of those items. How about weapons?"

"No weapons."

"Then I guess we're not able to do any business, unless…"

"I'm listening?"

"What are you going to do with the Raider ship when you find it?"

Blade immediately realized why the Yolongi had refused his offer of GA credits. Melorriat had been wondering how he could get his hands on the Raider ship ever since Blade first mentioned it. He knew Space Command had no use for seized freighters and usually sold them as part of the interdiction process. "We'll free the slaves and imprison the Raiders."

"But what about the ship?"

"We're too far from GA space to take it back. We'll probably just send it on a one-way trip into the nearest star."

"I'll get you what you need in exchange for the ship."

"If we get the ship, we can take their generator. Most Raider ships are made by the Uthlaro, and their systems are compatible with ours."

"But without an envelope generator, you'll never catch them. They'll have FTL, while you're limited to sub-light."

"We might not catch up to them at all."

"The GA usually gets what it goes after. I'm patient. And I trust GA officers to always stick to their word."

Blade hesitated for a second, then said, "Okay. You have a deal. Get us a good, useable generator compatible with our system, and you get the Raider freighter when we capture it. All we want are the slaves and the Raider criminals."

"Done," the Yolongi said. "I'll be in touch as soon as I've found your generator."

Blade watched as the Yolongi turned and walked away without another word, then turned and walked back to his former position. "All Alpha posts. Any other activity in the park?" Blade asked his people.

"Nothing," Alpha-One said.

"All clear," Alpha-Two said.

"Clear," both Alpha-Three and Alpha-Four said.

"Okay, let's head back to the ship. We'll meet at the entrance to the park before heading into the factory complex."

Weems had set the ship down in the designated location at the deserted factory complex roughly half a klick from the RP when they'd first arrived. The area was large enough for the MAT and surrounded by supposedly empty buildings. After the Major and his people exited the ship, First Sergeant Larson had joined Weems as he resealed the MAT, then remained on the flight deck while they used the craft's external vid units to scan the area continuously. Thermal scans had shown a number of vagabonds watching the ship cautiously from concealed locations among piles of trash, and their numbers had been growing. Perhaps they believed this was an opportunity to enrich their miserable lives.

"Lieutenant, this is the Major. We've concluded our business here and are returning to the ship."

"Major, the neighborhood here has gotten very unfriendly since you left. It might be better if I came to the park to get you."

"Negative. The fewer people who see the MAT, the better."

"Then exercise extreme care as you approach the ship. Thermal scans show at least thirty individuals hiding in the trash piles around the ship."

"Thanks for the heads-up. We'll be ready for them."

As Blade and his team assembled at the park entrance, all hell suddenly broke loose.

"This is Tango-Two. My way out is blocked by people in filthy cloaks yelling and swinging clubs."

Tango-Two's post had been on a rooftop from where he could see for blocks.

"Use your laser rifle, Tango-Two. Put them down."

"Roger, Sierra-Leader."

As Tango-Two started firing into the crowd, the screams grew in intensity. At the same time, Tango-Six reported a similar situation and that he was about to use the same solution. The teams listened as the two men reported their progress, then Tango-One reported running into the same trouble. The problem was over in a few minutes. Once the Marines began using their laser rifles, the scum melted back into their hiding places.

Several minutes later, the team was reunited at the park entrance.

"Everyone okay?" Blade asked.

A chorus of oo-rahs came back over Com-Three.

"Okay, let's move out. We can probably expect to get the same reception back at the MAT. The Lieutenant reports at least thirty individuals hiding in the piles of garbage near the ship. Be ready for anything."

As the team approached the small ship, street people emerged from everywhere. The thirty or so hiding in the trash piles were just a tiny sample of the force that had gathered inside the buildings. They had probably been assembling since the MAT landed. It was no wonder the cops feared to come down here after dark. All at once, the dirty and bedraggled charged, screaming and waving clubs or whatever weapons they had. But if the street people had known who they were dealing with, they would have stayed in their garbage heaps.

The Special Ops Marines pulled back their cloaks to reveal weapons already drawn but being held under their cloaks until needed. As they began firing into the screaming, rushing mass, bodies started to fall. At the same time, blinding and deafening explosions from flash-bang grenades landing in the midst of the attackers added additional chaos to the scene. A large, remotely controlled laser weapon suddenly appeared from a hidden gun port in the roof of the MAT and added it's firepower to that of the Marines on the ground. Within seconds, people were rolling on the ground, screaming in pain, or simply lying there, staring at the sky with unseeing eyes.

The tramps who realized they had made a serious error in judgment when they'd attempted to overcome the eleven cloaked figures turned and fled. A few foolhardy individuals, perhaps high on fermented juice or drugs, continued to attack until they met their end. The Marines never fired at anyone running away, so the attack was over in minutes.

"Lieutenant, you can open the hatch now," Blade said to Weems.

"Aye, Major."

Within two minutes the Marines were inside the MAT and strapped in. Weems lifted off and headed back to the volcano, hugging the ground as much as possible once outside the city.

Chapter Sixteen
~ April 2nd, 2286 ~

Sydnee listened quietly as Blade recounted the details of the evening. Their relationship had improved immeasurably since Blade's blowup over Sydnee's refusal to leave the Marines at the package's home.

"That's wonderful news, Major. You've done very well. My engineers are at your disposal if you want to take one of them when you go inspect the generator."

"I'll do that."

"It can't happen soon enough for me. I want to be off this planet and on our way back. How's your prisoner doing?"

"The brig the engineers of the *Denver* constructed in the habitat before we departed is great. He hasn't been out of it since he was taken. He's gone off a few times, calling us assassins and demanding that he be allowed see his ambassador, but the guards have orders not to converse with him at all lest they say something they shouldn't reveal. Not being able to get any response really sets him off. If he gets too vocal, the guard puts him to sleep with a stun weapon. Then we enter the cell and put him on his bed and the doc checks his condition. When he awakens seven or eight hours later, he appears fine."

"How many times have you had to stun him?"

"Eight, I think. Have you heard from the *Denver*?"

"Not yet."

"It seems we should have heard back by now. Perhaps we should query them?"

"Normally, I'd agree without reservation, but we're not in GA Space. And since we're so deep inside Clidepp space, we're trying to keep communications to a minimum by restricting them to vital information only. I'm sure the *Denver* can't enter Clidepp space without permission from SHQ, so they're probably waiting for that to come through."

"Surely the Clidepp military can't read our encrypted transmissions?"

"We hope not. But we don't know for sure, so it's best not to risk it. And the more often we broadcast out on Space Command frequencies, the greater the chance the Clidepp military can pinpoint our location. Everything is sent in burst mode, and the outbound signal only lasts a microsecond, but it's still better to be cautious when behind enemy lines. Any idea on when you'll hear from the contact?"

"He'll be in touch as soon as he finds something for us. He was almost salivating when I agreed to let him have the Raider ship."

"What will he do when we fail to give him a ship?"

"I told him we might never find it, but he wanted the deal anyway. Maybe we can get him some old hulk that was impounded for smuggling or something."

"But he'll have to come to the border to get it."

"Of course. I didn't promise we'd deliver it."

"Then I guess we just sit back and wait. Whether your contact comes through or the *Denver* comes to get us, we're getting out of here— eventually. What's his name, by the way?"

"The name he's using is Melorriat. He knows me as Tallaggio."

———————

Sydnee was used to activity, and sitting around wasn't to her liking. The corridors on all four levels of the Marine habitat were always busy with runners racing from one end to the other, so she began to use one of the weapons containers for that purpose. As the Marines were doing, she would run the twenty meters from one end to the other, then stop, turn around, and run back. She always felt better after an hour of running and looked forward to a hot shower. Once dressed, she'd relax by relieving the watch officer and then sit in the command chair on the bridge. She happened to be in the bridge when an alarm sounded at the engineer's console.

"Captain, the temperature outside the ship is rising rapidly," Lt. Barron said.

"How high is it?"

"Fifty-eight point one-three degrees Celsius."

"That's still well within the acceptable range. Lt. Olivetti, your opinion as a volcanologist?"

"It might simply be the release of pressure through a steam vent."

"Might?"

"I can't know for sure unless I go outside to investigate. But venting is common in dormant volcanoes, and there have been no other signs of volcanic activity."

"No one goes outside until the temperature stabilizes. If this thing is preparing to blow, I want us ready to take off immediately without having to retrieve people first."

"Aye, Captain," Olivetti said.

"Lt. Barron, monitor the temperature closely. Lt. Caruthers, be prepared to lift off at a moment's notice."

"Aye, Captain," both men said.

Then it was simply a matter of waiting and watching the gauges. In addition to the temperature, Barron was closely watching the toxicity levels outside the ship. If they jumped appreciably, it was another sign the volcano might be coming to life.

"Dormant volcanoes vent gases and heat from time to time, Captain," Olivetti said. "It doesn't mean it's going to erupt. In fact, sometimes it acts as a release to keep pressure from building up beneath the cone."

"And venting doesn't mean it's *not* going to erupt, so let's keep a close eye on things. Do you have an alternate site for us if we have to leave here?"

"I've found a couple of possible locations. One is in a deep valley high in the mountains. The images show no sign of sentient life, but there are numerous animals. There might be hunters, or the animals might even be domesticated, requiring herders to watch over them."

"And the other?"

"A desert location. It's all sand, but it's incredibly remote. However, we'll stand out like a large black bug on a bowl of oatmeal."

"The holo-projectors can cover most of us, but parts will still be exposed. Good job, Lieutenant, but keep looking. There has to be another ideal place like this one but with less danger from nature."

"Aye, Captain."

———————————

Fifteen days after making contact with Melorriat, an encrypted message arrived for Tallaggio. The com chief put the message in Blade's queue and notified him.

"I've heard from Melorriat," Blade told Sydnee a short time later. He claims to have found a generator in excellent condition. He wants to meet again at the same place."

"Is that wise? The police might be watching that area now because of all the dead bodies you left lying around last time."

"It's been weeks, and the police don't like to travel in that area anyway." With a slight smile he added, "They seem to think it's too dangerous."

"Okay, I'll defer to your judgment on that issue, Major. When's the meet?"

"I arranged it for tonight, three hours after sundown."

"Okay, I'll notify Lt. Weems to be ready. The same-sized team as before?"

"Yes, I'll take all eleven of my people. I'll leave one at the MAT to watch for trouble like before. If the scum starts gathering, they can use the topside laser weapon to convince them to leave long before we get back to the ship. The other ten will accompany me to the RP."

Sydnee nodded. "Good luck, Major."

Blade and his ten people were positioned on rooftops and in the shadows around the RP for an hour before the meet time and were getting antsy when Tango-Two reported that someone was approaching the park.

"It appears to be the same individual as last time," Tango-Two said. "At least he walks the same way."

"Is he alone?" Blade asked.

"He appears to be. No, wait. There are three individuals behind him."

"Are they with him?"

"They seem to be hanging back. It's impossible to tell if they're with him or tailing him."

"Keep an eye on them. Alpha Team, be ready. This may turn into something more than a simple meet."

"The contact has reached the RP," Alpha-One said. "The tail seems to be holding back."

"I don't like this," Blade said. "Everyone hold positions until we know what's going down."

It was about five more minutes before anything happened.

"The tail is moving towards the dog," Alpha-One reported.

"Tango team, do you have eyes on anyone other than the four near the RP?"

"Tango-One. I see no one else within a thousand meters."

"Tango-Two. Confirmed. Nothing else moving in the streets around the park."

"Tango-Three, confirming. There's no one else in the park or on the streets surrounding it."

One by one the other Tango spotters confirmed that no one else was on the streets around the park.

"The tail is still moving toward the dog," Alpha-One reported. "They looked determined."

"Alpha Team, weapons on ready. I don't like the looks of this."

"The tail has reached the dog," Alpha-One said. "They seem to be arguing. The dog is trying to pull something out of his cloak. It's a pistol. Tail-One has grabbed it. They're fighting. Tail-Two has a club. He's beating the dog. The dog is down. Now all three are beating him with clubs."

"Alpha Team, drop the tail."

Light flashes emanated from four different directions for several seconds. The three attackers stopped beating the contact and fell to the ground, unmoving.

"Alpha team, this is Sierra-Leader. Move in."

Quickly, but cautiously, the Alpha team moved towards the RP.

"Damn," Blade said as he reached the prone body of his contact. Melorriat appeared to be unconscious. "Flight Jockey, do you read?"

"Flight Jockey reads you five-by-five."

"Have you been monitoring?"

"Affirmative, Sierra-Leader."

"We need you here."

"Affirmative. Will lift off as soon as Beta-One confirms the hatch is closed and locked— confirmation received. Lifting off."

"Tango team, come to the park on the double."

Less than thirty seconds later, Weems was gently touching down in a grassy area as close to the RP as possible. As Beta-One opened the hatch, the Alpha team began carrying the four bodies into the ship. As soon as Sierra-Leader, the Alpha team, and the Tango team were aboard, the ship lifted off and disappeared into the blackness of the night sky.

"Strip the bodies of these three jokers," Blade said. "I want anything they have that might identify them. Timmons, pictures and prints. Padu, check the clothes for IDs. Collect everything they have."

"No personal effects," Padu said after going through all the clothes. "Not even any labels or money in the clothes. Each of them was carrying a small lattice weapon of the same make and model, in addition to their similar truncheons. They might be one of the Clidepp Military Secret Police goon squads."

"Lieutenant," Blade said on the com channel, "When we're halfway across the ocean, stop and hover a couple of meters above the water. We have some food for the fish, or whatever they have on this planet."

"Roger, Major." Weems said.

"I found this in the contact's pocket," Padu said, holding out a view pad, "plus some money, a wallet, and a bunch of assorted junk."

"Give me the viewpad and save everything else in a sealed pouch."

Blade looked at the viewpad and scowled. It was locked with a password. He slid it into a pocket of his cloak and removed his helmet, then sat down and tried to relax his taut muscles.

An hour later, Weems halted the ship so the three bodies could be jettisoned. As the hatch was closed and locked, he applied power and the MAT surged forward again.

Roughly fifty-two minutes later, the MAT was linking up with the CPS. As the final connection link was made and the airlock seal was certified, the hatch was opened. Two Marines with an oh-gee stretcher rushed in and picked up Melorriat, then strapped him to the stretcher. They hurried out with the unconscious Yolongi and headed for the sickbay in the habitat. The only corpsman on board was waiting and immediately began examining Melorriat.

"I understand it went badly," Sydnee said as Blade sat down in her office.

"It couldn't have gone worse. I didn't know what was going down with the contact and the three men following him. I didn't know if they were together or what, so I held my team back. When they started beating him, we were still under cover, but I ordered my people to take the three attackers down. The contact was already unconscious when we reached him."

"What about the attackers?"

"We figure they were Secret Police. We dropped them off."

"Where?"

"In the middle of the ocean. But we were humane. They were already dead."

"Well, thank goodness for that."

Blade looked at her in disbelief, until he realized she wasn't serious. Then he burst into a wide grin. "You continue to surprise me, Captain."

"Because I don't have compassion for three men who tried to beat a fourth to death?"

"Because you continue to prove how wrong I was about you in every way."

"It's happens, Major."

"Not to me. At least not very often."

The Yolongi known only as Melorriat continued to cling to life for four days following the beating. On the fifth day, his heart stopped beating. The corpsman explained that his death was most likely owed to the skull damage and especially to the brain, which had swollen considerably and on which he had worked daily to drain off excess fluid.

"Sorry, sir," the corpsman said to Blade. "I tried everything I know, but what we really needed was a neurosurgeon experienced in Yolongi physiology. I've never studied health care for this species, and I'm just a Hospital Corpsman First Class."

"I know you did your best, Doc. I wish I'd had a chance to talk with him."

"He never really regained full consciousness. He seemed to be staring at me a few times, but his eyes weren't focused and didn't move about. I put it down to sub-conscious delirium."

"Did he ever say anything?"

"Only one word, over and over. I think he might have been referring to his wife or perhaps a lover."

"Do you remember exactly what he said?"

"Uh, I entered it into the medical log." Picking up a medical viewpad, he tapped the touchscreen a few times, then handed it to Blade. 'Willownisa,' the viewpad said.

"Willownisa?" Blade repeated.

"That's what he kept repeating."

"Okay," Blade said, handing the viewpad back. "Stick the body in the freezer for now. We'll dispose of it the next time we go out on a mission."

"Sir, are we going to get off this rock?"

"Yes, son. I can't give you a date, but we're going home."

"Thank you, sir."

"My corpsman said he repeated 'Willownisa' a few times," Blade said to Sydnee. "I entered it into the Clidepp information database, but it found no direct matches. It did, however, suggest some possible near-matches. And, among other things, Willonnissa is the name of a small city on the southern continent. I checked the surface-mapping images file and learned there's a major reclamation yard there for spaceship parts."

"And you believe he was trying to tell us we have to go to Willonnissa?"

"It may be that, or perhaps it was just the last thing he was thinking about, and it kept replaying in his damaged brain. Or, it might be as our corpsman thought, that it's simply the name of a wife or lover."

"Are you suggesting a mission to Willonnissa?"

"It seems like a real longshot, but it's all I've got. If there's no useable generator there, then we'll just have to sit here until we're rescued."

"I'm already tired of sitting around. I don't want to sit here for another month, or two months, or longer. When do you want to leave?"

"Five minutes ago."

"I can't arrange that, but I'll start working on it."

"What's to work on? We just jump into the MAT and go."

"Your contact RP was only two hours away by MAT. The southern continent is about twelve hours away by MAT. And that's if Willonnissa is on the northern coast."

"It isn't. It's down near the southern coast."

"Then make that eighteen hours by MAT."

"I see your point, Captain. I'm used to being in space when we launch our missions."

"Yes, here we have to fight our way through the atmosphere the entire way."

"Couldn't the MAT climb above the atmo and then drop back down over the southern continent?"

"Yes, but the problem is potential visual identification. If the MAT is observed, the Clidepp military will be on it before it can land. The CPS, even considering it's much larger size, is far better equipped to avoid detection because of all our hull sensors and the fact that we have an entire bridge crew working to conceal our identity."

"I see."

"And— if we are discovered and challenged, we can fight. The MAT is really just a ferry. It's almost indestructible, but it wasn't designed to participate in battle."

"That laser weapon that popped up out of the roof was a pleasant surprise."

"There are actually two more. They're mounted on either side near the stern. They face rearward in case someone nasty such as a fighter is behind you. But beyond them, the ship can't do very much against an enemy."

"Unless Captain Marcola is piloting it."

"I only used its indestructibility to best advantage. That wouldn't have worked against a warship. However, the CPS *can* take on a warship— and win."

"Wait a minute. You're telling me this ship is armed?"

"I guess the scuttlebutt didn't make it to your team. I've heard they've been shunning the other Marines. Yes, this ship is armed. Armed to the teeth. Missiles and laser arrays."

"Where? I mean, I've seen no sign of any weapons."

"You don't have access to the other two habitat containers. They're, uh, not habitats. They're weapons platforms."

"I'll be damned."

"Don't feel bad. I wasn't briefed either. I learned about it after my tac officer asked why his console indicated that missiles and laser arrays were available to him. He wanted to fire one and see what happened. I told him not to and began investigating. The two weapons platforms are sealed and require the captain's ID to open the hatches."

"And here I thought that if we ran into trouble all we could do was run away."

"That would be the preferable response since we're trespassing in another nation's space, but I like having the extra option if we can't run away."

"So when do we leave?"

"I'll let you know within an hour. I have to discuss it with my bridge crew to determine the optimal time to avoid possible detection."

"Great. I look forward to your call."

"What's the best location you've found near the bottom of the southern continent where we can hide the ship?" Sydnee asked Lt. Olivetti.

"I haven't really scouted that part of the planet actively because you wanted warmer locations."

"Oh, that's right. It's winter down there, isn't it?"

"Well, it's coming into spring now, but it's still pretty cool."

"We need a good hiding place as close to Willonnissa as possible."

"I did see a dormant volcano down there."

"Another dormant volcano?"

"This one has been good for us."

"Yes, it has. How long has the new one been dormant?"

"Six GST years."

"Not very long."

"You never know with volcanoes. At one time, the one we're in right now had only been dormant for six years."

"What does its history and its current readings tell us?"

"It appears stable. The readings are similar to what we've seen here. But since they're on different tectonic plates, I wouldn't expect them to have similar histories or futures."

"Assuming that would be the best location, what would be the optimal hour for us to move to that volcano?"

Olivetti tapped a few spots on her console. "Eight hours, fifteen minutes would be optimal."

"Okay. That's when we go. Lt. Barron, is there anything to be done outside or recovered from outside before we leave?"

"No, Captain. As per your standing orders, we're ready to lift off at a moment's notice."

"Excellent. Okay everyone, we lift off in eight hours and fifteen minutes."

After relaying the information to Blade, Sydnee returned to her quarters to grab some sleep. She had been up for seventeen hours and wanted to be sharp for the trip.

"There it is, Captain," Lt. Olivetti said as the volcano's wide cone came into view on the front monitor.

The slopes around the outside of the volcano were bare of any flora, proving it hadn't been very many years since the last eruption.

"You still feel confident this volcano isn't going to erupt anytime soon?" Sydnee said to Olivetti.

"The chances are low according to the readings we're getting."

"I hope you're right. Okay, everyone, same drill as before. No one ventures outside without permission from the watch officer, no equipment is left outside after a necessary trip, and we must be ready to leave on a moment's notice."

"I can't believe you picked another volcano," Blade said from where he was standing next to the command chair.

"It worked out well once."

"Yeah, well…"

"Are you ready to go?"

"My team is standing by."

"Lt. Weems, you're up. Good luck with the search, gentlemen."

Chapter Seventeen
~ April 6th, 2286 ~

Blade was sitting in the copilot seat as they came within sight of a reclamation yard that seemed to stretch on forever. "There it is," he said to Weems.

"I'll put her down over by that water tower. It looks quiet there."

As the MAT settled onto its skids, the hatch opened and Marines poured out. In addition to Blade's people, there was Lt. MacDonald, three of her fire teams, and Lt. Barron, the engineering officer. The plan called for the three fire teams to take up positions outside the reclamation center and watch for security or unwanted intervention while Lt. Barron and the SO team went shopping for the needed generator. Before heading to the reclamation center, they had loaded an oh-gee sled with the equipment they believed they would need.

As the search party neared the front gate, two large animals reared up on their hind legs and began growling menacingly from inside the fence.

"*God*, they're big," Blade said. "They look sort of like grizzly bears, but larger." To Staff Sergeant Padu, he said, "Stun them."

Padu aimed a stun pistol at one of the beasts and pulled the trigger. The beam shot out and seemed to be responsible for quieting the beast in mid-growl. It looked surprised, as if it had never been affected by anything like the stun weapon before. As it partially collapsed to the ground, Padu shot the other animal. The beasts were down, but not even close to being out. The stun charge was usually enough to knock a human out for six to eight hours, but the two animals were only temporarily dazed. They were trying to regain their footing but having great difficulty. However, they were persistent in their attempts.

"Hit them again," Blade said.

This time the two animals went down flat on the ground, but they remained conscious. They continued to growl as they struggled to regain motor functions in their limbs.

"Hit them again," Blade said.

With the third blast, the growling stopped, but the eyes of the beasts were still open.

"Again," Blade said.

After the fourth blast, the animals finally appeared unconscious.

"That did it," Blade said. "Everyone note that if we encounter any more of these animals, hit them four times before approaching them. Padu, open the lock."

Padu opened a case on the oh-gee sled and removed a laser torch. With one quick slicing motion, the lock fell apart and dropped to the ground in two pieces.

"Okay, it's time to find our generator. We all know what to look for. We'll split up into the assigned teams and search the grounds. I'll head for the office with Lt. Barron to see if we can find anything there that talks about GA-compatible generators. Let's move out."

The reclamation center seemed to be about the size of a small city. Willonnissa had originally grown from a housing complex erected just for reclamation workers and, despite being categorized as a city, actually had less land mass than the reclamation center. When seen from the ground, there seemed to be no end to the reclamation grounds.

The Special Ops Marines spread out in pairs and were quickly lost among the mountains of spaceship parts and equipment while Lt. MacDonald and her fire teams established a secure position around the entrance to the facility.

Two-plus hours later, Blade and Barron were ready to give up in the office. Blade's helmet immediately translated everything he looked at, but he'd found no reference to GA ships being recycled.

Barron, being an engineer, didn't have personal armor, and thus a helmet that would perform translations, but he'd been scanning computer listings looking for anything that appeared to have come from the GA.

"Sierra-Leader, this is Alpha-Four," Blade heard on the Com-Two channel reserved for direct contact with team leaders and officers.

"Sierra-Leader. What do you have?"

"We've found what looks like an old generator. Most importantly, it has Amer writing on it."

"Send me a continuous signal tone, Alpha-Four."

As they left the office, Blade took a reading and determined the direction. Then it was simply a matter of getting to where Alpha-Four was waiting. As the pair raced past millions of tons of spaceship scrap, Blade continued to follow the improving signal. When the signal was at full strength, they stopped to take a final direction reading.

"Over here, sir," Staff Sergeant Stromgard said. "To your right."

Blade turned and saw his men standing between two rows of scrap that reached for the sky. He and Barron walked to them.

"There's what we found," Stromgard said, pointing to a huge metal container.

Barron immediately began to inspect the container. "It's a GA temporal envelope generator, all right. Good work, Sergeant."

"But is it in good working condition?" Blade asked.

Pulling a piece of test equipment from a holster-style case on his belt, he said, "We'll know soon enough." Looking around, he said, "It appears we're in a section devoted to GA ship parts. While I check this out, perhaps the rest of you can continue searching in this immediate vicinity to see if you can find any other generators."

"You heard the man," Blade said, "Let's check these other piles."

As the others spread out to see if they could locate other units, Barron began his examination. He lifted off part of the cover, but as he turned to put it down, one of the scrap-yard guard animals raised up on its rear legs and swiped at him with a huge paw. It's long, deadly claws sliced through his uniform and opened wide gashes in his chest. As Barron screamed in pain and fell backwards, the animal moved in. The noise seemed to enrage the animal, or perhaps it sensed fear and weakness. Whatever its motive, it fell on Barron and began ripping him apart.

The animal screamed in pain as the first laser shot passed through its body. Shots to its head and chest then came from several different directions and the animal dropped on top of Barron.

As Blade and his two men approached the animal cautiously, Blade fired once more. His shot cut off a paw, but the animal never moved.

"Help me get this monster off the Lieutenant," Blade yelled to his men as he began pulling at the beast. "I think it's dead."

When they finally managed to roll the animal's body off Barron and saw the condition of the his body, Blade uttered, "Damn."

There was no doubt that Barron was dead. His chest was torn apart, his throat was ripped open, and it also appeared that his neck was broken. The best surgeons on Earth wouldn't have been able to save him if they already had him on a table in an operating room.

"What do we do now, sir?" one of the SO Marines asked Blade. "We've lost the only person who could tell us if the generator is worth taking back. This was our last shot at getting off this planet without being rescued by Space Command."

"First things first. Get a body bag from the sled and take care of the Lieutenant."

"Aye, sir."

On the com channel reserved for direct contact to the MAT, Blade said, "Flight jockey, this is Blade."

"Here, sir."

"Patch me through to the Captain."

"Aye, sir, one second. Go ahead, sir."

"Captain?"

"Yes, Major?"

"We've lost Barron. He was killed by an animal in the scrapyard."

"Damn. Anyone else injured?"

"Negative. But we're without an engineer and no one else can determine if a generator we found is worth hauling back to the ship."

"Understood. I'll send Chief Luscome."

"Aye, Captain. Blade out."

As the call ended, Sydnee announced on the bridge, "Lieutenant Barron has been killed at the reclamation center by one of the guard animals. Chief Luscome, I need you at the scrap yard. You'll have to inspect a generator and determine if it's worth bringing back here."

"Aye, Captain. I'll be ready to go in two minutes."

"MacDonald," Blade said on the Com-Two, "are those two animals still there? Both of them?"

"Affirmative, sir. Both are still where they fell."

"Blade, out." Turning to Com-One, the general chatter channel, Blade said, "Attention. Lieutenant Barron has been killed by one of those grizzly bear sort of animals. It was *not* one of the animals from the front gate, so keep an eye out for any more. Don't mess with these things. If one comes at you, use your laser weapons and put it down permanently. Blade out."

Blade was certainly glad now that Sydnee had ordered the main ship be moved to the southern continent. If they'd had to wait almost a day for another engineer to arrive, they would have lost any chance of getting a generator here. Once the break-in was discovered, it would not be wise to come back here again.

MAT-Two landed just outside the gate fourteen minutes after Blade made his report. When the hatch opened, Chief Luscome stepped out, followed by Sydnee.

"Captain, it's not safe here," Blade said. "You should stay in the MAT."

"I have my armor on, so I'm protected pretty well. We never should have lost Lt. Barron to a damn security animal. If we ever again have a mission like this, I'm going to insist that every team member have personal armor."

"I concur. For a mission like this, personal armor should be mandatory, even if the team member isn't expected to leave the ship. Time is running short. We have to move quickly now. This way to the generator."

Five minutes later, Luscome was examining the generator. Sydnee had taken two of MacDonald's Marines and ordered them to protect Luscome at all costs. She had simply shaken her head sadly when she saw the dead animal and the pool of blood where Barron had died.

While Luscome worked with the Marines covering his back, Blade and Sydnee teamed up to scour the area for other potentially useable generators. The rest of the SO Marines had continued to search the site, but so far, no one had found a second possible unit.

"Major," Luscome finally said on Com-Two, "This generator is kaput. It's in even worse condition that the one in the CPS."

"Understood, Chief. We'll keep looking."

Hour after hour, the Marines scoured the yard. Dawn was no more than an hour away when Alpha-Six reported finding a possible GA generator. Luscome, with his two guards, Blade, and Sydnee raced to Alpha-Six's location.

The generator looked to be in excellent condition, but external appearance could mean next to nothing with electrical and electronic equipment.

"I'll be damned," Blade said, as he looked at the unit that Luscome was already examining.

"What is it, Major?" Sydnee asked.

"Look at that," Blade said, pointing to part of the unit's cover.

Sydnee looked closer. There was a tag glued to the surface. It said, 'Sold 98S28R34051 Hold for Melorriat.'

"I'll be damned," Sydnee said. "This is the unit Melorriat intended for you, Major."

"It would appear that way, Captain."

Looking around at the enormity of the reclamation center, Sydnee said, "What are the odds that we would stumble across this?"

"We had an advantage," Blade said.

"Which is?"

"Melorriat obviously made arrangements to buy this. Before that, it might have been buried under a million tons of other salvage. They pulled it out, cleaned it up, put a hold on it, marked it for easy identification, and left it where access would be easy."

"True. But I'm glad we finally stumbled across it."

"After eight hours of searching."

"This unit appears to be functional, Captain," Luscome said.

"Great, let's get the oh-gee blocks on it and move it to the MAT."

The generator was soon floating half a meter above the ground, courtesy of oh-gee freight-handling blocks. Once raised above the ground, one person could move almost any weight, but it was imperative that the movers remember that every floating object still had mass and could get out of control. Weightlessness removed the burden of gravity but didn't affect the laws of physics with relation to inertia.

Blade recalled his team with instructions to rendezvous at the front gate, while Chief Luscome, his protection detail from the gate, and the two SO Marines guided the generator from the location where it had been found. Blade and Sydnee followed along behind.

The teams converged at the gate and everyone was ready to depart as soon as the MAT was loaded. The generator was almost to the gate opening when someone yelled on Com-One, "Behind you!"

Sydnee spun in time to see one of the two previously stunned beasts towering over them with razor-sharp claws extended. She, Blade, and Luscome were trapped between the brute and the generator. Sydnee and Blade were wearing armor but Luscome had none. Without hesitation Sydnee threw herself between Luscome and the enormous animal that was about to fall on him. The weight of the beast had to be a metric ton, so as it reached Sydnee, it knocked her into Luscome, who was knocked into the generator.

Personal armor is able to absorb energy weapon fire and prevent penetration of teeth and claws, but the need for the wearer to move easily meant that it wasn't solid like the armor a medieval knight might have worn. However, the Dakinium fabric reacted in a microsecond at the subatomic level to outside force, strengthening many times over, which is how the armor prevented serious damage to the wearer from small projectiles. If Sydnee hadn't been wearing the armor, her body and Luscome's would have been utterly crushed by the weight of the beast. As it was, Luscome benefited from the characteristics of Sydnee's armor even though he wore none himself. Sydnee's arms were straddling Luscome's form as the armor strengthened, reducing the crushing effect of her body into Luscome's. Best of all, the brute's claws never penetrated Sydnee's armor. Even so, the animal's bulk couldn't help but cause some serious damage to the two Terrans as they were squashed between it and the generator.

As the weight of the animal overcame the inertia of the generator, it was sent careening into the gate, whereupon the oh-gee blocks came loose and the generator crashed to the ground. Sydnee and Luscome were injured and lying helpless as both beasts reared up to attack anew. A light show of laser fire suddenly lit up the pre-dawn darkness as dozens of bolts came from every direction and struck the two beasts.

One of the two animals fell over backward, never to move again, but the other fell forward, on top of Sydnee and Luscome. Marines immediately rushed to pull the creature off the downed officer and chief.

"Are they dead?" Sydnee asked as she was uncovered.

"Aye, Captain, they're dead," Blade said. He had only narrowly missed being run down himself.

"How's Chief Luscome?"

"We'll know in a minute," Lt. MacDonald said as she tried to make her friend more comfortable by straightening her legs, which caused Sydnee to scream in pain. "Uh-oh, I think we have a problem, Major. The Captain might have a broken leg, or perhaps two broken legs. She was crushed against Luscome and the generator. I hope she doesn't have extensive internal injuries."

"Luscome is unconscious," Blade said as he hovered over the engineering chief. "Someone bring two stretchers," he shouted.

"Major," Sydnee said, "have Weems bring MAT-One over here, then load up the generator and our people. Once the two ships are loaded, Weems should link them together. They're designed to operate as one ship, so he'll have full control over all engine functions and controls of both ships. Get us out of here before someone shows up for work. We don't want to get into a firefight with security guards."

"Aye, Captain. Rest easy. We'll get everyone back to the safety of the ship. Weems, did you hear the Captain?"

"Aye, Major, I'm listening in on all non-private Com channels. I've already lifted off and I'll be there in seconds."

MAT-One appeared in the sky over the gate area before Weems even finished his message. He set the craft down next to MAT-Two outside the gates, leaving enough room between the small ships so they could be easily loaded.

"How's the generator look, Padu?" Blade asked the Marine who was directing the effort to get it upright and loaded onto oh-gee blocks again once Sydnee and Luscome were taken away on stretchers.

"The outer case is a bit banged up, sir. I don't know if the unit itself is damaged or not. Chief Luscome will have to answer that."

"Yeah, if he lives."

"Did he look that bad, sir?"

"Impossible to tell. The Captain threw herself between him and those monsters. It's not the same as having armor, but it kept the brute's claws from harming him. If he lives, it's because of her, but she's seriously injured as well."

"We're almost ready to leave here, sir. Should we lock the gates?"

"It's not like they won't know we were here. Don't bother. Just get that generator into the MAT and we'll get out of here."

"Aye, sir."

―――――――――

As soon the MATs linked with the CPS, Sydnee and Luscome were rushed to the sickbay. The corpsman did a quick triage procedure and decided to work on Sydnee first. He administered painkillers before he started.

"How's the Chief?" Sydnee asked as the corpsman worked to remove her armor and then determine the exact damage to her legs, arms, and torso.

"He's got some serious internal injuries, but I've stabilized him for the moment. I'll work on him as soon as I take care of your legs. Now just lay back and relax, Captain, and let me concentrate on healing *you*. Both legs are broken, you know."

"Yeah, I kinda figured that was the case."

By the time the corpsman had finished with Sydnee, hundreds of thousands of surgical nanobots were coursing through her veins, searching for damaged bone and soft tissue, then collecting in those areas to work on correcting the damage. She had multiple simple fractures in both legs and one cracked rib. The corpsman had placed air splints on her legs to immobilize them as the nanobots performed their repair efforts.

Sydnee then watched from her bed as the corpsman worked on Chief Luscome with speed and efficiency. Corpsmen often worked long, hard hours without receiving all of the recognition they deserved.

When the corpsman was done and sat down to rest, Sydnee asked, "How is he, Doc?"

"He'll be fine in a few months. He has multiple broken ribs, a punctured lung, and a fractured disc in his spine. I've reinflated the lung, and the nanobots will repair the damage to it and the damage to the ribs and spine."

"How soon can he get back to work?"

The corpsman chuckled. "Work? Captain, he has to remain immobile for at least two weeks. Perhaps in six months he'll be ready to return to full duty. He can return to light duty in three."

"How soon can he direct engineering work from here if we set up a monitor above his bed?"

"Perhaps a week, but he must remain perfectly immobile. He won't even be able to manipulate a robotic arm for at least two weeks."

"Then I guess we're stuck inside this damn volcano for a while."

"We're in a volcano?"

"You didn't know?"

"No ma'am. The last I heard, we were on some tropical island, but we couldn't go outside because there might be dangerous plant or animal life."

"That was almost two months ago. I didn't feel the island was secure, so we moved to a dormant volcano, a different volcano than the one we're in now."

"I guess I should start spending more time with the guys. I've been staying in here because I've been studying to upgrade my skills and hopefully earn a promotion."

"You keep studying medicine and taking care of our health, doc, and I'll worry about the safety of the ship."

"You've got a deal, Captain," he said with a smile.

"It appears to my untrained eye that the generator wasn't seriously damaged in the fall," Blade said to Sydnee the next day.

She had been moved to her quarters since she didn't require constant medical attention. As long as she remained immobile for two weeks and then restricted her activity for four more while always wearing the inflatable casts, her legs would heal properly. Although the armor hadn't prevented the breaks, it did prevent the simple fractures from being compound fractures.

"It's going to be a couple of weeks before Chief Luscome can even be involved in determining the condition of the generator, and then only remotely from his sickbay bed. Are any of our Marines mechanically able to function as his hands in testing and then installing the generator?"

"I've reviewed the files, and there are a couple of Lt. MacDonald's people who might fill the bill. Of my people, Staff Sergeant Padu is the most mechanically talented on the team."

"Okay. The doc will tell me as soon as the Chief is well enough to work remotely from his sickbay bed. In the meantime we stay buttoned up and ready to leave at a moment's notice. Anything on the news about the break-in at the reclamation center?"

"It's all they've been talking about. Even though we burned the ground where Lt. Barron was killed, they discovered it was Terran blood, and they've begun a manhunt in the area for any Terrans. And they're all up in arms about the deaths of their three *pets* at the facility. The animal is known as a Mulasster, by the way."

"Pets? Four meters tall with half-meter claws as sharp as filleting knives?"

"That's the way they talked about them on the news. They called them their 'beloved pets.'"

Sydney shook her head. "I guess that ends our repair efforts until the Chief is a bit healthier. Anything else?"

"No, that's all I have. I guess we just stand down for a while. Thank God the Chief wasn't killed."

"Amen to that."

Sydnee hadn't reported to the *Denver* in weeks, so she prepared a very detailed report on their situation and sent it to Captain Lidden as soon as the major left.

A little more than ten days later, the message reached the *Denver*.

"Message from the *Justice*, Captain," the com chief reported as he forwarded it to the captain's message queue.

Lidden stopped what he was working on and opened the message, leaning in for a retinal scan since the message was Priority-One.

When the message ended, Lidden sat back, took a deep breath, and exhaled slowly. SHQ had still not made a decision about a mission to recover the *Justice*. Meanwhile events occurring in Clidepp space seemed to be spiraling out of control. One *Justice* officer was now dead, an informant and three attackers had been killed, two Space Command personnel had been seriously wounded while breaking into a Clidepp facility, and the Clidepp government was now looking for the Terrans responsible for the break-in. If the government put two and two together, they might assume the kidnapping was also the work of Terrans. If things didn't calm down, the Clidepp Empire might wind up declaring war on the GA. If that happened, Lidden knew whose head was going to be on the block. It didn't matter that he wasn't personally involved in the problems on Yolongus. He had selected a Lieutenant(jg) over the Lieutenants he could have named to head the SC part of the mission. And it also wouldn't matter that the reason for the problems was solely owed to a design flaw with the CPS generator repository that allowed it to fill with water and then short out when they tried to use it.

Lidden sighed. They all seemed to be caught up in problems not of their making, with the crew of the *Justice* seemingly abandoned in the Clidepp Empire. And now the ship's captain was laid up with both legs broken while the crew was taxed to the limit because it was too small for the job it was being asked to perform.

Chapter Eighteen
~ April 20th, 2286 ~

"I call this emergency meeting of the Admiralty Board to order," Admiral Moore said. "As you know all too well, during the past several months, two of our new Dakinium-sheathed Scout-Destroyers, the *Yenisei* and the *Salado*, have disappeared in Region Two. At this time, we still have not located either ship. But I'm embarrassed to say that while we've been concentrating our attention on that mystery, we've ignored another very important issue we had tabled. The CPS-14 ship sent into Clidepp space on a Special Ops mission, which suffered FTL loss as it attempted to return due to a design flaw with its generator repository, is still sitting on Yolongus. Captain Lidden forwarded a copy of a recently received message from the captain of the *Justice*. *Justice* is the name assigned to the small ship by its crew since Space Command doesn't name tugs."

To his aide, he said, "Play the message."

"Good Lord," Admiral Bradlee said when the message had ended. "The ship's captain, Lieutenant(jg) Marcola, has suffered two broken legs while trying to acquire a replacement generator because we forgot about them?"

"Plus they've lost an engineering officer, and the Chief is completely immobilized by serious injuries," Admiral Platt said.

"And they're hiding inside the cone of a dormant volcano to avoid the Clidepp military," Admiral Woo said, shaking his head. "I haven't even read a fictional story this crazy in years."

"Let's remember that this Lieutenant Marcola is the same one who saved the *Perry*." Admiral Hillaire said.

"Yes, her actions and courage under fire are the main reasons Captain Lidden named her to head this mission," Admiral Moore said. "We discussed all this months ago."

"What have we been waiting for?" Admiral Bradlee asked. "As I recall, Raihana requested a day to do some investigating, and then reported back that she was trying to locate a freighter from the GA that made regular trips into the Clidepp Empire which would hopefully agree to take a generator to Yolongus. That way the military wouldn't be involved. Isn't that why we tabled this issue?"

"Yes, that's true," Admiral Ahmed replied. "We began searching for a ship's captain we could trust to perform this mission, but most of the cargo companies have cancelled all operations to Yolongus and even into Clidepp space because of the war. I turned the matter over to one of my officers, but I'm ashamed to admit I've been so busy with other matters that I haven't followed up."

"So what do we do?" Admiral Bradlee asked. "If the Clidepp military is on high alert following the kidnapping and is now investigating the break-in at the reclamation center, which has been attributed to Terrans, do we dare send another ship to rescue the first we sent?"

"It hardly seems necessary now," Admiral Plimley said. "I deeply regret the loss of life and injuries to our people, but they now have a generator. Since the *Justice* seems to be well hidden and has plenty of food, water, and other supplies, let's just hold off until things settle down on Yolongus. Although they don't yet know if they can make it work, let's give them a little time to solve their own problems."

"You're asking us to ignore the plight of a valiant Space Command crew?" Admiral Ressler said.

"No, I'm merely suggesting we allow them some time to solve their own problems rather than risking another mission into Clidepp space."

"I hate myself for doing this," Admiral Moore said, "but let's have a show of hands for those who favor Admiral

Plimley's motion that we wait— sixty days, to allow the *Justice* to resolve its own dilemma.”

“I just heard from SHQ,” Lidden told his XO during their daily morning meeting.

“Are we going into Clidepp space, sir?”

“No, they've decided to table the issue until further notice because the *Justice* was able to acquire a generator. We're still forbidden to try a rescue.”

“Then we're just leaving the crew of the *Justice* to their own devices?”

“That's about the size of it. I've given the matter a lot of thought recently. When I received the most recent message from Marcola, I began to have new doubts about selecting her for this mission. There wasn't any doubt about her ability but rather about the *appearance* of placing a jg in command. However, the more I've thought on it, the more sure I've become that it was the right decision. I would rather have Sydnee in command of that ship under the present circumstances than any jg or lieutenant in the fleet I could name. She was my choice, and if any junior officer can bring that crew home, it's her.”

It was difficult, but Sydnee managed to remain off her feet for a full fourteen days, although she probably couldn't have done it without the help of Kelly MacDonald and Jerry Weems. They brought her meals and provided company during their off-duty time, and Kelly assisted her with bathing and dressing.

Although she didn't have anywhere near the famed recuperative power of Admiral Carver, the nanobots substantially reduced the time for healing. Where a simple break might have once taken twelve to fifteen weeks to mend naturally, the nanobots should make it happen in six to eight.

If they had been aboard the *Denver*, Sydnee would have had access to an oh-gee brace after her first two weeks. When strapped to it, it raised the patient off the floor and had small air jets to provide propulsion. Far better than crutches at keeping the weight off mending bones, the brace greatly assisted mobility during healing.

Two Marines devised a sort of substitute using two oh-gee freight blocks connected together by a wooden crosspiece. The blocks, wrapped in cloth for comfort, slipped under each armpit. Holding the remote in one hand, Sydnee could raise or lower herself. There were no air jets for propulsion, but she could usually count on there being someone around to give her a slight push, or even guide her to where she wanted to go. She was even able to visit the Marine habitat. She simply positioned herself over the access tube and lowered the freight blocks until she was at the level she wished to visit. The sickbay was in the habitat, so the device enabled her to visit the Chief.

"That's a nifty device, Captain," Luscome said the first time she visited.

"I'll loan it to you when you're ready to get up, Chief."

"I won't need it for several months, I'm afraid. The doc says I won't be able to put any pressure on my back until the broken disc is completely healed."

"There's no rush, Chief. As long as you're not in pain and the little nanobots are slaving away to fix the broken parts, everything is good."

"But I want to get back to GA space. And I'm more than a little nervous about hiding in a volcano cone, even if the volcano is dormant."

"I've lined up a couple of Marines, Staff Sergeant Padu and Lance Corporal Addams, to help us do exactly that. As soon as you're ready, we'll begin."

"Not for several months, Captain. I'm stuck here for the immediate future."

"What I was thinking is that you could supervise using a monitor mounted over your bed. The Marines would provide the hands, and you would provide the brain. They're both intelligent and have good mechanical skills, but they don't have your knowledge of the subject, so they need direction."

"It might work. When do we start?"

"As soon as you're ready. We've cleared a work area in MAT-Two, and have the old generator and the replacement generator just sitting there waiting for someone to begin work."

"I'm ready now."

"Okay, I'll get the guys to mount a monitor in here, and then we'll give it a try."

The next day, Luscome and the Marines tried out the new system. They had mounted four stationary cameras from their surveillance equipment locker and added a floating camera that Luscome could move to whatever position he chose with a simple joystick controller. Using the joystick only required using the muscles in his right arm, so it wouldn't affect the requirement that his torso remain absolutely rigid.

The disassembly of the recently acquired generator went smoothly. It didn't appear that the unit had suffered any damage, other than to the outer case when it was knocked off the oh-gee blocks at the reclamation center. And the outer case couldn't be used anyway because it wasn't made from Dakinium and wouldn't allow a double envelope to fully coalesce.

The basic disassembly of the generator was the easy part. Any decent mechanic could have performed it. The real test came when the two Marines were required to perform highly complex tests of the intricate circuitry and then make adjustments that would allow the generator to work with military spec equipment. The progress slowed considerably, but they continued to move forward.

Sydnee was reclining on her bed when the ship began shaking. It'd been six weeks since her legs had been broken, and one of the two inflatable casts had already been removed. The doc said he would probably remove the other in a week. Although all bones had knitted, he felt that one break still needed a bit of strengthening.

Sydnee jumped up and hobbled to the bridge, which fortunately was just meters away. "Is anyone outside the ship?" she asked loudly.

Weems, sitting in the command chair, said, "The Marines working with Chief Luscome are outside."

As more violent shaking occurred, Sydnee said, "I'm relieving you, Lieutenant."

Weems jumped up out of the command chair and Sydnee practically fell into it.

"Is this shaking owed to some testing with the envelope generator?" she asked.

"Negative, Captain," Lt. Olivetti said. "The tectonic plates beneath the volcano are shifting."

The doors to the bridge opened and Blade entered. "What's going on?" he demanded.

Sydnee ignored him and said to the com chief, "Tell the Marines they have twenty seconds to get back inside."

After passing on the message, the com chief said, "They say it will take at least twenty minutes to disconnect the new generator and bring it in."

"We're not staying here twenty minutes."

The com chief relayed the message and then said, "They say they can't leave it."

"Is the repository open?"

"Affirmative," Weems said. They're making connections to test some circuits."

"Chief, tell them to get inside the repository and hunker down as much as possible, then hang on to their asses and whatever else they want to save because it's going to get damn windy damn quick." To the tac officer, she said, "Sound the emergency signal and tell me when the ship is secure."

A few seconds later the tac officer said, "All access hatches are closed and sealed."

"Chief, are our Marines in the repository?"

Chief Lemela relayed the question, listened for a couple of seconds, then said, "They're inside and hanging on."

"Take us up, Lt. Caruthers. Veer away from the cone as soon as we're above the rim. Head upwind. Speed Plus-Point One."

It was a tense five minutes as the small ship rose out of the volcano and headed north. Plus-Point One speed was six kilometers each minute.

"Tac, split the bridge screen. Half back, half forward."

"Aye, Captain."

The large monitor at the front of the bridge immediately showed two images side by side. On the left was the image provided by a rearward facing camera on the hull, while the other was provided by the forward-looking camera.

A plume of black smoke was now rising from the center of the cone they had just left. Sixty seconds after leaving the cone, the small ship was six kilometers away. If not for the Marines hunkered down in the repository, they would have been traveling ten times faster, but Sydnee feared they might be sucked out if she increased the speed. As it was, the ship was traveling three hundred sixty kilometers an hour, and the Marines were probably hanging on for dear life.

As the small ship achieved a distance of almost eighteen kilometers from the cone, the entire top of the mountain blew apart. Dust, dirt, rock, and ash filled the sky. After a couple of minutes more, a flow of molten rock could be seen winding its way down three sides.

"How are the Marines in the repository?" Sydnee asked the com chief.

"They say they're okay so far but want to know if they can please come inside now," the com chief said.

"Are they okay to hang on for another five minutes?"

"They say 'aye.'"

"Tell them we'll set down as soon as we reach a safe distance."

"Aye, Captain."

Sydnee leaned back, took a deep breath, and released it. "What's going on?" she asked, belatedly repeating what Blade had said to her earlier. "Just another boring day in the life of a Space Command officer, Major."

Blade scowled, nodded, and left the bridge without comment.

As soon as the ship was a hundred kilometers away, Sydnee ordered it down so the Marines and the equipment they were testing could be brought inside. When that had been accomplished, she said, "Navigator, plot us a course to that tropical island where we spent the night a couple of months ago."

"The first volcano would give us better concealment, Captain," Lt. Olivetti said.

"Perhaps, but I've had my fill of volcanoes for a few days."

"Aye, Captain," she said with a grin as she forwarded the course to the helmsman.

During dinner with Kelly MacDonald and Jerry Weems in her compartment, Sydnee said, "Wow. I hate volcanoes. They're just too— unpredictable. Don't tell Lt. Olivetti I said that."

"I'm glad you came to the bridge when you did," Weems said to her quietly. "I probably would have given them the twenty minutes they requested, and we'd have been caught in that explosion."

"Saving the ship is always the most important consideration."

"Even if premature action meant we don't get home?"

"The ship and the people aboard first, last, and always."

"You didn't seem to feel that way the night you saved our asses at the package's home," Kelly said with a grin.

"That night I was only risking my own life. If I'd picked up the SO team as the Major ordered, it would have been a diff-erent story, and you might now be prisoners of the Clidepp military."

"Is that the way you always think?" Weems asked.

"Pretty much. I can risk my own life, if I choose, but I won't normally risk anyone else's unless we've been backed into a corner. And before you mention it, I know that as we climb higher in rank and responsibility there will be times when we must make tough decisions that favor the good of the many over the good of the few."

"How are you feeling, Chief?" Sydnee asked Chief Luscome three days after arriving at the island.

"Better every day, Captain."

"Great. Best estimate, how close are we to having FTL?"

"The test results have been very positive, Captain. We could have FTL in as soon as two days."

"Two days?" Sydnee practically shouted.

Luscome smiled. "That's the absolute soonest. Perhaps we may not have it for two weeks."

"I'd even take two weeks. I want to get us off this planet before someone spots us and the Clidepp military comes to investigate."

"The Marines you assigned to work with me have been doing a great job. They were beginning the install the day we had to get out of that volcano. That emergency exit cost us four days. Captain, give me another full day to complete the connections and perform a full system test, and we might— and I say *might*— be ready to head out."

"That's the best news I've heard since I learned the SO people had captured the package. Keep me posted, Chief."

"Aye, Captain."

"Keep your fingers crossed, everyone," Sydnee said with a smile. "Okay, Lt. Caruthers, get us off this hunk of rock."

The small ship lifted off the tropical island where they'd been parked for seven days and began climbing through the atmosphere with oh-gee engines straining. As the ship reached the stratosphere, Caruthers engaged the sub-light engines. It was predawn on the island, and he'd kept the ship in the darkness of the planet's rotation until they were well away.

"Cancel sub-light engines, build our envelope, and engage the drive, Lieutenant," Sydnee ordered as the ship reached the thermosphere.

The envelope was already beginning to coalesce as the sounds of the engines echoing inside the ship faded to silence. Some of the bridge crew held their breath and a few offered up a prayer.

The image on the screen suddenly shifted from live vid feeds to sensor imagery as the ship entered faster-than-light speed.

"FTL, Captain, but the console tells me we're only traveling at Light-75."

Sydnee sighed. Light-75 would get them home, but it would take roughly ten and a half years if they were expected to travel the entire distance on their own.

"Understood, Lieutenant. Continue on course for GA space."

"Aye, Captain."

Bridge crew members surreptitiously stole glances at Sydnee as she stared at the monitor at the front of the bridge. Her face appeared impassive, but her brain was working overtime on the best way to proceed. They didn't have nearly enough food to last ten years. All water was recycled so that would last indefinitely, and the matter/anti-matter engines had enough fuel for fifty years. So the main problem was food. She finally decided to proceed on course until they were well away from Yolongus rather than returning to the planet to try to fix the problem there.

"Lt. Caruthers, you have the bridge," Sydnee said as she rose from the command chair. Caruthers left the helm and moved to the command chair as Lt. Olivetti moved to the helm. Sydnee was able to stand on her own feet now, the second cast having been removed the previous morning.

Once off the bridge, Sydnee headed for the sickbay. This was the first time she'd had to climb down the ladder. Previously, she had simply floated down using the oh-gee harness. But it was great to have her legs back.

"I'm sorry, Captain," Chief Luscome said as she entered the sickbay and before she uttered a word.

"Don't be sorry, Chief. We've achieved Light-75. It's going to take a while to get home at that rate, but at least we'll get home. Um, do you have any ideas on how we might improve the rate of envelope generation?"

"Not at this moment. I'll have to review all the test data and view the live systems information we're getting now that we're under way. Our engines are certainly up to the task. There has to be something out of whack with the generator. Perhaps a connection isn't solid, or perhaps something is mis-aligned and needs recalibration. Studying the live feedback data might point to where we should start. How long before we can stop and work on the generator?"

"We're covering about one light-year every five days, so I'd say we should continue at this speed for three weeks. That will put us far enough from Yolongus that it should be safe to stop to make repairs without being spotted or interrupted by the Yolongus Home Guard. We'll move to an area away from the normal shipping lanes to avoid all traffic while we're stopped, and our Dakinium surface will help hide us from sensor nets. Okay, Chief. Carry on."

Sydnee returned to her quarters instead of the bridge and plopped down onto her bunk. This day had held so much promise and then been a bit of a disappointment. But, on a positive note, they were *finally* away from Yolongus.

Deciding that she had to inform the *Denver* of their status, she got up and moved to her desk to record a message to Captain Lidden.

"You wanted to see me, sir?" Commander Bryant asked as he entered the Captain's briefing room on the bridge.

"Yes, come in Bry. I just received a message from Marcola. I thought you should view it. I've watched it once already."

As Bryant slipped into one of the overstuffed chairs in front of Lidden's desk, the message began playing on the wall monitor. When it was over, Bryant smiled and shook his head. "So she has resolved her own problems and they're headed back?"

"Yes, but if they can't get their speed up over Light-75, it's going to be a long trip. I've been drafting a message for SHQ. I'm going to request permission to send in another CPS to meet the *Justice* and bring them home."

"The situation hasn't really changed. They were able to get off the planet before and meet a CPS in space."

"Yes, but now they'll be light-years from the planet when we link up rather than someplace in the Yolongus solar system. I think that makes a considerable difference."

"Perhaps, but I wouldn't bet any money on it. I admit I'm confused by the reluctance of SHQ to let us mount a rescue mission, but they seem pretty adamant they don't want us intruding further into Clidepp space. Perhaps the first mission was only approved because everyone was caught up in post tragedy hysteria."

"I hope it wasn't just that. Those are our people over there, performing a job we sent them to do. I don't believe we can just close the book and forget about them for ten years."

"Maybe SHQ has another plan— one they're not telling anyone who isn't involved."

Lidden stared at Bryant for a full minute before responding. "Why wouldn't they tell us if that was the case?"

Bryant just shook his head slightly and shrugged his shoulders.

"I don't think it's that. There must be something else."

"What?"

"I just don't know. Perhaps it has something to do with the missing ships in Region Two."

"That's a very long way from here. The *Yenisei* and *Salado* couldn't have anything to do with the bombing, could they?"

It was Lidden's turn to shake his head and shrug his shoulders.

———————————

Sydnee longed for an hour's run in the weapons container, but she was still under strict orders to take it easy. She was able to walk without assistance devices, but the doc kept reminding her that although she felt good, her legs were still not one hundred percent. So she wandered around the ship and dreamed of the day she'd be able to run until she was exhausted.

The attitude of the crew had improved considerably once they were off the planet and in FTL, as was to be expected. Even though they could only achieve Light-75, the conversations were light and happy.

Sydnee was climbing up the ladder from the Marine habitat when the feel of the ship suddenly changed. If she hadn't been in direct contact with the ship's surface, she might not have realized it right away. She finished climbing to the main deck in the CPS and hurried to the bridge.

As the doors opened, everyone turned towards her expectantly.

"What's happened?" she asked.

Caruthers, standing next to Olivetti who was seated at the helm console said, "We don't know, Captain. The envelope generator suddenly went off line."

"What do you mean by 'went off line?'"

"It just shut down. We're stopped in space."

"Is the power flow steady?"

"Yes, the matter/antimatter engine is working perfectly, and there's plenty of power. The generator just isn't producing envelopes."

"Was there any reduction in envelope generation just before it shut down?"

"No, Captain," Olivetti said. "It was working fine one second and then nothing the next."

"Wonderful," Sydnee said, without moving her lips and under her breath so no one could hear.

Chapter Nineteen

~ June 7th, 2286 ~

"I believe I've found the problem, Captain," Chief Luscome said four days later. The generator had been removed from the repository and been brought inside for disassembly after testing outside failed to detect any issues. "The main induction coil is cracked."

"How long will it take to repair it?" Sydnee asked.

"About two days, if we had the part."

"I don't like the sound of that last part. No pun intended."

"I'm not happy about it either, but without a replacement part, I can't fix the generator."

Sydney took a deep breath and released it slowly as she thought. "An induction coil simply changes electrical current, right? Is there any equipment on board that can be cannibalized for its induction coil?"

"We became experts at cannibalizing parts while we were on the *Perry*. But this is an extremely sophisticated assembly, manufactured to very tight tolerances. It's not like the simple induction coils people are generally familiar with. It doesn't even look like one from the outside. It looks more like a very thick, flat dinner plate with a hole in the center. All the circuitry is embedded within a— a— sort of a reinforced ceramic shell."

"How could this coil have cracked while the generator was mounted on the shaft?"

"It couldn't."

"Pardon me?"

"It couldn't have cracked while the generator was mounted on the shaft, unless it was struck by something. And there would be clear evidence of a strike if that had happened.

When mounted, the coil is very well protected from impact. It had to have been cracked before we mounted the generator. It likely occurred when the unit was knocked off the oh-gee blocks at the reclamation center. Or it might have even been that way earlier. Perhaps that's why the generator was at the scrapyard. It might have been failing and been replaced by the freighter that had used it originally."

"But it was functioning?"

"Yes, but the crack could very well be the reason why we were limited to Light-75. Perhaps there was a micro-fissure that didn't extend across the entire surface when we began using it, and a small amount of vibration caused the micro-fissure to expand."

"So what do we do?"

"There's nothing we *can* do. Not unless we get a replacement."

"How common are they?"

"That's the good news, if there is any good news. They are very standardized, and it's not uncommon for a freighter to have more than one in its parts inventory. I'm not saying they're a one-size-fits-all kind of part. And the units here in the Clidepp Empire are different than the same assembly in GA space. But a freighter built in GA space is very likely to have a spare on board that we can use."

"That's a small ray of sunshine, I suppose."

"Sorry, Captain. It's the best I can offer."

"Okay, Chief. How are you feeling by the way?"

"Better every day, Captain. Perhaps in another month I'll be able to get off this bed."

"That's great Chief. I gave Doc the oh-gee rig the Marines made for me. I hope it helps get you up sooner."

"Thanks, Captain. Doc told me it would help because there would be less stress on my spine."

"You've done a great job for us, Chief. I guess it's up to me to find a solution for our new problem. Keep this information just between us. If anyone asks, you're still working on the problem. Carry on."

Sydnee went to her office and plopped into her desk chair after leaving the sickbay. The news from Chief Luscome conveyed the worst possible situation she could have imagined. They had traveled more than three light-years since leaving Yolongus, were still about seven hundred seventy light-years from the GA, and all they had available was sub-light power. Sub-light power wouldn't get them to a habitable planet in her lifetime.

Sydnee touched her Space Command ring to open a carrier and said, "Lieutenant Weems." A second later she heard, "Weems here, Captain."

"Jerry, don't repeat what I'm going to tell you. Chief Luscome says the generator can't be repaired unless we get a part common only to GA ships, so we're limited to sub-light power."

"I understand, Captain."

"How's our hydrogen supply?"

"Stand by." Weems touched a spot on the small monitor by his left hand and the fuel reading flashed onto the screen. "We're close to being topped off. The amount we used to get through the atmo at Yolongus was negligible."

"Good. Open the collectors. We're not going to be traveling at FTL, so we might as well collect fuel as we go. Then engage the sub-light engines to maximum. Cut the fuel when we're down to ten percent so we'll have a bit of control if we need it, and we'll go ballistic until the tanks are topped off again."

"Our destination, Captain?"

"Same as before, the GA border. We might as well keep traveling instead of simply sitting in space. Every kilometer gets us closer to home."

"Aye, Captain."

"Carry on."

"I just received a new message from Marcola," Captain Lidden said to his XO during their daily morning meeting.

"Have they corrected their problem with the generator and gotten their FTL speed up to Light-9790?"

"No, just the opposite. Their generator has died completely. They're limited to sub-light propulsion."

"Oh, no."

"Oh, yeah."

"SHQ can't refuse to let us go in now. Before, the *Justice* at least had a chance to get home on their own, but without a working envelope generator and being stuck out in space without a chance to get parts or a replacement, they'll die of old age long before traveling even fifty light-years at Sub-Light speeds."

"That's what I'm going to tell SHQ when I send a message later today."

―――――――――――――――――

"Good morning, Chief," Sydnee said as she entered the sickbay.

Chief Luscome was laying on a bed in the sickbay. The nanobots had slaved to repair his broken body and he had responded to their efforts. He still wasn't permitted to put pressure on his spine, but even that had improved to the point where he no longer required medication for severe pain.

"Good morning, Captain."

"Chief, I was thinking last night about our problems, and a question popped into my mind. We're headed towards the GA border at Sub-Light-46, but we're traveling ballistic because we had to turn the sub-light engines off when our fuel ran low. Once the tanks are topped off again, we'll reignite the engines and improve our speed. But if we had a larger fuel capacity, we could increase our speed dramatically."

"But our tank size is fixed. There's no way to make them larger."

"No, but we can increase our capacity."

"I don't understa— Are you suggesting we use the water tanks that allowed us to submerge the CPS?"

"Exactly."

Chief Luscome didn't reply right away. He got a far-off look in his eyes and rubbed his forehead a little as he thought. When he had thought it through, he said, "It's possible. We can reroute the flow from the hydrogen collectors directly to the water tanks fairly easily. Then we can feed the larger supply through the regular hydrogen tanks to take advantage of the established flow system. Yes, it should be fairly simple. But it won't increase the rate at which we can pull hydrogen in. The collection process is limited to the collector size. And it will take fifty times longer to top off the tanks."

"That's okay. If we can increase our speed to Sub-Light-100 or higher, and then go ballistic, we'll get to wherever we're headed a lot faster. Over a few months, it will more than make up the time we spent collecting fuel."

"Okay, Captain, but I have to be a part of this effort because we're talking about something that can destroy the entire ship if everything is not done perfectly."

"Of course, Chief."

"And I can't participate until I'm out of here. The doc says he'll spring me in another month."

"That's fine, Chief. We're going to be traveling for a long time, so a month won't matter. I know you're not ready to work on this yet, but I wanted to run it past you so you could be thinking about it."

"Okay, Captain. I'll work on it in my head until my body lets me work on it with my hands."

"Do you have a few minutes, Captain?" Blade asked from the doorway of her office after the door opened to admit him on her order.

"Of course, Major. Come in."

Blade entered, followed by Staff Sergeant Padu and Lance Corporal Addams.

Once the door had closed, Blade said, "Everyone is concerned about losing our FTL, and it's all they're talking about. Padu and Addams have come up with an idea they'd like to present to you."

"I'm always open to new ideas. What have you come up with, men?"

"Captain," Staff Sergeant Padu said, "each member of the SO team was issued a special new epoxy before this mission. It's designed to seal areas that've been checked for combatants and cleared. It hardens in seconds, and it's better than a heat weld because there's no chance of igniting gas fumes or flammable liquids. Lance Corporal Addams and I have been playing around with it today, and we think it could be used to repair the broken component in the envelope generator."

"I see. You do understand the component was manufactured to very strict tolerances?"

"Yes, ma'am, we do."

"Where's this epoxy now?"

Padu produced a white tube from his pocket and held it out for Sydnee to take. She accepted it and looked it over.

"How do you say this name?" she asked as she tried to pronounce the chemical formulation. It was the only thing written on the tube.

"We don't know, Captain," Addams said. "It's a real tongue-tangler. We just call it Molly."

Sydnee unscrewed the top and squeezed the tube just enough to push out a tiny drop. She deposited it on the framework of a viewpad up near the top where it would be virtually unnoticeable, then put the top back on the tube.

"How long did you say it takes to dry? Seconds?" she said, looking at Padu, who nodded.

Sydnee waited ten seconds, then touched the spot with the viewpad stylus. The outer surface of the drop of epoxy was slightly hardened and none of the epoxy transferred to the stylus, but the dot was still slightly flexible. Looking up at Padu, she said, "It does get hard, right?"

"Like steel, in less than a minute. But in ten seconds it's already hardening, and you can't open the door where it was used unless you use a laser torch to cut through the epoxy."

"Is it flammable?"

"No, ma'am."

"I don't know if a repair to the damaged part is possible or not, but I'll discuss it with Chief Luscome and get back to you. Dismissed."

"Thank you, Captain," Blade said and followed the Marines out of the cramped office.

"That's the proposal, Chief. They think they can repair the fractured component with this." Sydnee handed him the tube of epoxy.

"I just don't know, Captain. My first reaction is that the part can't be fixed— but who knows? And it might be the only shot we've got."

"What about using the same part from the old generator? I know most of the components were fried, but was the induction coil destroyed?"

"We thought of that, but the military generator is too dissimilar from the freighter versions, even if the original could be used."

"So this might be our only hope."

"I don't think *might* applies here. I'll perform some tests on this epoxy and see if it offers a chance of working," Luscome said as he looked at the tube. "Ya know, I heard of this stuff quite a while back, but I've never been able to get my hands on any. I put in three requisitions while we were on the *Perry*, but they were always rejected with the reason marked 'Out of Stock.'"

"If this doesn't work, all we'll have is the sub-light engines. Give it your best shot, Chief."

"Will do, Captain. Do you still want me to work on the hydrogen system?"

"If this works, we won't need it. Let's put all our effort into this idea."

Over the next several days, Luscome worked with Padu and Addams on developing a plan for the attempted repair.

"It appears we'll have just seconds once we start," Luscome said. "We have to spread the epoxy quickly and evenly, then join the two pieces together under pressure. If the alignment is off even a fraction of an inch, it's all over. We only get one shot."

"We need a jig," Padu said.

"What kind of jig?"

"You know, a jig. A jig that only allows the pieces to slide together one way. That way we can't screw it up."

"Yeah," Addams said. "And to make sure they can't buckle at the fissure. Once we slide them together, their alignment can only be perfect if there's no allowance for shifting or buckling."

"How do we guarantee an even coating of epoxy on the two surfaces?" Luscome asked.

"Some kind of brush, I suppose," Padu said. "We can't just squirt it out of the tube."

"Hey, how about a toothbrush?" Addams said.

"It might work," Luscome said. "And how about we put a piece of masking tape on the top surface of the broken halves. We squirt some epoxy onto the toothbrush, then quickly brush it along one side of the break. We slide the pieces together in the jig and lock them in place to set up, then rip the masking tape off the top to remove the excess epoxy."

"Sounds like a plan," Padu said.

The two Marines, with Luscome supervising, spent the next week designing the jig and manufacturing it from wood scavenged from the pallet that had held the generator at the reclamation center. Once the jig was ready, they practiced the procedure over and over without epoxy until they felt they had the process down.

Very little happened aboard a military ship without the full knowledge of the crew. The term scuttlebutt purportedly originated aboard sailing ships many centuries ago. Fresh water was available on deck in a scuttled butt. Butt was the term for the cask, and scuttled meant that it had been damaged; i.e., the end was broken open to provide easy access to the water. This was the original office water cooler where rumors and gossip were exchanged when people paused their daily routines to get a drink. Rumors always spread like wildfire, and, as a result, secrets didn't last very long in the close confines aboard a ship.

Two weeks after the idea was first proposed, the three-man team was ready to try the epoxy procedure for real. They knew how much was riding on them and that this was a one-shot deal. They were appropriately nervous. What they didn't know, and which would have made them even more nervous, was that the entire crew was looking on. Someone had happened across the vid frequencies the trio was using for transmitting the images of the work progress from MAT-Two to the sickbay. As the trio began the final step in the repair, every pair of eyes on the ship was glued to a monitor somewhere, whether it was the large monitor in the dining room of the habitat, the monitor on the wall of Sydnee's office, or even the ultra large monitor at the front of the bridge. The outcome could dramatically affect everyone on board, and everyone was naturally and intensely interested in watching.

Luscome was watching on the monitor in the sickbay, while Padu and Addams prepared themselves in the work area. When all was set, Padu and Addams took a depth breath, then Padu brushed on the epoxy. As the toothbrush cleared the edge of the plate, Addams gently but firmly pushed the loose half, secured to a wooden plate that only allowed it to slide one way, tightly against the anchored half and clamped it down with a wood brace. Padu pulled the masking tape off both sides a second later as the excess epoxy stopped spreading out over the break. Then both men leaned back and began breathing again.

In the sickbay, Luscome realized he too had been holding his breath. He released what he had in his lungs and drew a deep breath of fresh air. Throughout the ship, everyone was doing the same.

"Good job, guys," Luscome said. "If this works, you get all the credit."

"When will we know if it worked?" Padu asked.

"I know the epoxy is supposed to dry rock-hard in less than sixty seconds, but let's give it five minutes in the jig. After that, if the bond is holding, we can move to step two."

"What's step two?" Addams asked. "We've only discussed step one until now."

"In the engineering area, there's a laser saw with an extremely fine focus. We'll mount the piece on it and carefully guide the laser across the top and bottom surface of the repaired piece to remove any excess epoxy. We got most of the epoxy on the top, but I'm sure there's going to be some dripping out under the piece. The laser saw will allow us to cut down to within a micron of the plate's surface."

"Is that necessary?" Addams asked.

"Yes, to maintain the integrity of the electrical flow in the piece."

"Then what?" Padu asked.

"Then we begin our testing. We'll perform the same tests we performed when we were looking for the original problems. The results of those tests will tell us if we were successful. If the repair allows us to achieve even Light-1, it will have been a success."

"At Light-1, it will take us almost seven hundred seventy years to get to GA space," Padu said. "I was hoping for a bit better."

"As am I," Luscome said, "but even Light-1 is faster than any of the sub-light speeds, which is where we are right now. I'm just trying to remain realistic so no one becomes too depressed if this repair doesn't work. And let's keep news of this work to ourselves until we know if we were successful."

All over the small ship people were turning off the monitors. They realized there was still more work to do and great results were still possible, but their enthusiasm was dampened slightly by Luscome's practicality.

"That's it," Padu said the next morning as he removed the piece from the laser saw and visually examined the cutting work. "You can't tell the piece was ever broken."

"The human eye can't see things smaller than five microns," Luscome said, "so you'd need a microscope to see any residual epoxy on the surface. And if there's only a micron of epoxy remaining there, it shouldn't affect the performance of the piece."

"What now, Chief?" Addams asked.

"As soon as you guys are rested, we begin the tests."

"I'm rested," Padu said.

"So am I," Addams said. "I want to get on with it."

"Okay, guys. Let the testing begin."

"The tests indicate that piece should function in the generator, Captain," Luscome said to Sydnee after she went to visit him in the sickbay. "It's mounted in the unit, and we're ready to take it topside and bolt the unit to the extension shaft."

"That's wonderful news, Chief. What kind of speed can we expect to attain?"

"I wish I could give you that information, ma'am, but I can't. All we know for sure is that the broken piece is whole, and current appears to be flowing properly. We won't know if the piece will perform properly when the envelope process begins, if it will actually coalesce an envelope, or even if it will last in the sub-freezing temperatures of space."

"You think the epoxy might fail from the cold?"

"I don't know. I couldn't find any specs or test data in the ship's DB. All we can do is mount it and give it a try."

"When do you want to mount it?"

"As soon as you can stop the ship."

"Is that necessary?"

"It's prudent. It's safer for the people who have to work outside."

Sydnee mulled the matter over in her head for a minute. While traveling ballistically, that is, at a constant speed with no chance for deviation, there was no sense of movement in space. Anything traveling with the ship at that point would likewise be traveling at the same constant speed and in the same direction. It wasn't like being atop a vehicle in atmo where you had to consider wind resistance and gravity, and where, if someone were to fall off, they would be left behind and lost.

"I see no advantage in stopping the ship, Chief. If we were traveling FTL, it would make perfect sense because the envelope wouldn't encapsulate anyone outside the ship. But I see no benefit in stopping and an enormous potential downside in doing so. If the generator fails to function, we'll have exhausted our hydrogen supply stopping the ship, and it'll be weeks before we can collect enough to proceed again. In the meantime we'll be helpless to even move the ship if an emergency arises. The oh-gee engines are useless in space, so I can't see wasting our fuel just to give someone peace of mind about a problem that doesn't exist."

"Okay, Captain. Then in answer to your question, we can be ready to mount the generator as quickly as Padu and Addams can get into EVA gear and take the generator topside."

Two hours later, Padu and Addams were bolting the generator to the shaft that raised it to the height necessary for use. When it was firmly affixed, they began making the final connections.

"Captain, I'm getting a strange reading on my screens," the tactical officer aboard the Clidepp Destroyer *Laggesttig* said. "It's an anomaly that only appears once in every seven or eight sweeps, and then only for an instant."

Captain Wurrassow rose from his command chair and walked to the tactical station. He would have been able to see the image on a monitor by his hands, but he wanted to stretch his legs. It had been a boring watch, and he'd been sitting in the chair for hours.

"Where?" was all he said to the tac officer as he reached the station.

"Give it half a juwote, Captain." Pointing to one of his screens, he said, "It will appear right here."

Wurrassow watched closely, and about twenty-three seconds later the anomaly flashed on the screen, then winked off. He was intrigued. "That's strange. What do you think it is?"

"No idea, sir. I've been watching it for about ten juwotes, trying to determine what it might be. Do you suppose a smuggler has developed some kind of cloaking method?"

"Let's go find out. Send the coordinates to the navigator. Navigator, plot a course and send it to the helm. Helm, take us there at top speed. If these *are* smugglers, we want to jump them before they know we're coming."

Chapter Twenty
~ June 28th, 2286 ~

"Captain, we may have a serious problem," the tac officer aboard the *Justice* said. "There was a distant contact on the DeTect screen. It was traveling across our course, so I dismissed it, but it's changed course and is now proceeding straight towards us."

"They've been able to see us?"

"That would appear to be the case, ma'am."

"How? Our Dakinium hull is supposed to be invisible to anyone other than Space Command ships. Could they possibly be Space Command?"

"The computer is identifying it as a Clidepp *Bernouust*-class destroyer."

"And it changed direction so it's now headed *directly* towards us?"

"Aye, Captain. Perhaps they got a radar reflection off the EVA suits our guys are wearing."

"Com, get an update from our two people topside. How much more time do they need?"

The com chief spoke into his mic, and a few seconds later said, "They report they've completed the install and are now performing tests."

"Chief, tell them to pick up their tools and get back inside immediately. Tell them trouble is headed this way."

"They want to know if they can have two more minutes to complete the present test."

"No. I want them inside now."

"They understand and are complying, Captain."

"Tac, tell me as soon as they're inside the airlock and the outer hatch is closed and sealed."

"Aye, Captain."

"How long until that Clidepp ship arrives?"

"ETA is one minute, fourteen seconds."

And it will take probably two minutes or more to get our people inside, Sydnee thought.

"Tac, what's the time to that anomaly?" Captain Wurrassow asked.

"One juwote, two kliseds, Captain."

"Is the image still only appearing every half-juwote?"

"Yes, sir."

"And other than the occasional blip, you have no other information?"

"That's correct, sir. It's as if it isn't there, and then it just— is. And then it's gone again."

"It has to be smugglers. Well, we'll show them how we deal with their kind. Ready all weapons."

"Tac, update," Sydnee said.

"Ten seconds before the Clidepp ship arrives, Captain."

"Com, where are our people?"

"Headed for the airlock, Captain."

"Tac, be prepared to roll out the laser arrays, but don't open the outer doors unless I tell you."

"Aye, Captain."

"Helm, as soon as our people are inside, use thrusters to roll the ship so our keel is towards the Clidepp destroyer."

"Aye, Captain," Caruthers said, adding, "That will expose the Marine habitat to potential fire."

"Yes," Sydnee said.

"The computer indicates the anomaly is twenty-five thousand kilometers off our bow, Captain," the tac officer said.

"Give me maximum magnification on the vids and sensors. Show me what's out there."

"We're at maximum now, sir."

"But I see nothing except blackness."

"That's all I see also, sir, but the computer says there's something there."

"Let's see if that's accurate. Fire a torpedo at the anomaly."

"Torpedo fired, sir."

"The Clidepp ship has stopped twenty-five thousand kilometers away and fired a torpedo at us, Captain," the tac officer said. "Should I attempt to shoot it down with our lasers?"

"Negative. Com, where are our people?"

"Opening the airlock, Captain. They're moving as fast as they can. They understand the urgency."

"Time until the torpedo strikes us is one minute, fifty-seven seconds," the tac officer said.

Sydnee stared at the image of the destroyer on the front monitor. Having commanded one of that same class made her aware of its capabilities and the lethality of their torpedoes. She could visualize what was happening on the bridge. They were probably confused and had fired just one torpedo to see what they could learn.

"The airlock hatch is closed," the tac officer said. "Now it's locked."

"Rolling the ship," Caruthers said.

"There was a fifteen klised period when the anomaly solidified, but then it disappeared completely, Captain. It was like a door opened and then closed. The torpedo will reach the former position in— three seconds."

For a few seconds, the monitor at the front of the destroyer's bridge white'd out as the explosion temporarily blinded the sensors.

"Target struck, sir," the tac officer said.

"What target? I still see nothing."

"And the anomaly isn't showing anymore."

"Is there something there or not?"

"There has to be something there. The torpedo struck *something*."

"But is it a natural phenomena or manufactured?"

"Unknown, sir. The evidence of my eyes says there's nothing there."

"Let's see if we can put a dent in it— whatever it is. Prepare to fire a full spread of torpedoes."

"Aimed at what, sir?"

"The same place you put the last one."

"No damage reported from the first torpedo, Captain. What's our response going to be if they fire again? Can I roll out the mobile laser platforms?"

"No, not yet. Helm, build an envelope and engage at maximum speed."

"An envelope, Captain?"

"It can't hurt to try. Our Marines said they had completed the installation and were testing the unit. I can't think of a better test than this one."

"Aye, Captain. Building envelope." Caruthers suddenly said excitedly, "Captain, the generator is on line! It's building an envelope!"

"Get us out of here as soon as possible, Lieutenant Caruthers."

"We're ready to fire a full spread of torpedoes, Captain." The tac officer said.

"Fire," Wurrassow said.

Everyone on the bridge watched the front monitor as ten torpedoes raced away from the destroyer. When just a few seconds remained, the tac officer performed a countdown— "Five, four, three, two, one, zero."

"What happened?" Wurrassow asked incredulously.

"Nothing, Captain. The torpedoes are still running hot, straight, and normal. There's nothing there now."

"Was there *ever* anything there?"

"The first torpedo had to have hit something."

"It could have struck a rogue micro-asteroid too small for our sensors to get a proper lock, right?"

"Uh, yes, sir. It might have. And the asteroid could possibly have been obliterated by the explosion."

"Helm, return us to our former course," Wurrassow said.

"Yes, sir."

"Tac, detonate those torpedoes so they don't become a hazard to innocent shipping."

"Aye, sir, detonating. How should I log the use of eleven torpedoes, Captain?"

"Target practice. I'm not going to be the laughing stock of the fleet for firing at natural phenomena. And I'd better not hear any crazy stories about this incident. That goes for everyone on the bridge. Forget it ever happened."

"Wow, the one on this end of the spread must have missed our stern by millimeters, Captain," the tac officer said.

"Dakinium is supposed to be impervious to laser fire and torpedoes, but I wonder if anyone ever tested it against a full spread like the one they fired. We can thank Chief Luscome, Staff Sergeant Padu, and Lance Corporal Addams for getting our generator working so we weren't a test case for damage by enemy torpedoes. Lieutenant Caruthers, what's our speed? Have we exceeded Light-75?"

"Unknown, Captain. There something wrong with the readouts. The console is reporting Light-2241.63."

"Wonderful. That's a great deal better than Light-75."

"But I thought Light-9793.48 was the only speed constant for double-envelope travel."

"I believe that was the constant established by Space Command engineers to avoid having a variable speed above Light-800 cause problems. The *Colorado* experienced a massive power overload that left them stranded almost a hundred parsecs from the *Prometheus* when they tried to accelerate to maximum speed and the double envelope tried to form from a single envelope. The helm consoles are always rigged to prevent anyone from using anything except Light-9790 with a double envelope."

"Then how can we be traveling at Light-2241.63?"

"All I can surmise is that the problems with our generator are responsible. But I'm not complaining if we really are traveling at Light-2241.63. I'm anxious to get home and this speed is a tremendous improvement over anything we've had since arriving at Yolongus. And nobody better cancel our envelope because we might not be able to reestablish it again. If it's going to break down on us, let's get as much mileage as possible out of it first. But I would like to know if the speed readout is accurate. Lieutenant Olivetti, take some position readings over the next hour and compute an approximate speed so we know where we stand. Lieutenant Weems, you have the bridge."

After Sydnee stepped down from the command chair, she headed directly to the sickbay. Chief Luscome had already heard that the *Justice* had been able to generate an envelope and he was grinning from ear to ear. Padu and Addams were with him.

"Gentlemen, everyone on this ship is indebted to you. We are once again traveling FTL and it appears to be almost thirty times faster than when we left Yolongus."

Luscome stopped smiling. "Thirty times faster than Light-75? That's impossible."

"We just had that discussion on the bridge. The helm console shows Light-2241.63."

"But the systems are set for only Light-9793.48 when using the double-envelope speed. We have to cancel the envelope right away, or we could experience a massive power loss. Everything could get fried, including us, and we don't have the staff necessary to work through the problems like the *Colorado* did."

"Yes, but everything seems stable."

"It might be the calm before the storm, Captain. We have to stop and check the generator."

Sydnee took a deep breath, turned around, then walked to the end of the room and returned as she thought. "I realize there's a danger. I also know that sometimes fortuitous conditions occur that, if cancelled, cannot be replicated at a later time. I'm going to maintain this speed either until the generator breaks down again, we cross the GA border, or we suffer a calamitous event. At this time, we're not even sure the console readings are accurate. For all we know, we might be traveling at Light-5 or Light-50. All we know for sure is that we left the Clidepp destroyer in the dust, so to speak, and the hull sensors have shifted from optical to digital. We're assuming those two things mean we're traveling FTL.

"I've asked our navigator to take position readings over the next hour. When I have that information, I can make more informed decisions. I just came down here because I wanted to thank all three of you for your hard work and a job well done. Getting the generator online when we did allowed us to escape that Clidepp destroyer. Even if they couldn't harm us with their torpedoes, just having them learn who we were would have sent political ripples back to the GA that could have resulted in our going to war with the Empire. I don't believe the people aboard the destroyer ever got a good look at us. Carry on, men."

No one said anything until the door closed behind Sydnee.

"I don't know guys," Luscome said. "I guess I just get nervous when people do things that go against what I've been taught by people far smarter than I am."

"Her reasons seem sound to me," Padu said. "In the Corps, we're trained to improvise and adapt."

"I have to go along with the Lieutenant," Addams said. "She's one smart cookie. I was on Diabolisto with her. She may be SC, but she thinks and fights like a Marine. I'd follow her anywhere."

"I never told you," Luscome said, "but I asked the Lieutenant to stop the forward motion of the ship while you worked on the generator outside. That's what we were taught when I was in engineering school. She refused. She has the rank, so I couldn't argue with her. Afterward I thought about her response. It made a lot of sense. Since then, I've revised my thinking about stopping the ship to work outside. So maybe the Lieutenant's right about this also."

Instead of returning to the bridge, Sydnee went to her office to think. So many things had happened since leaving GA space that it seemed like she was in a simulation back at the GSC Warship Command Institute in Australia and the testers were throwing every catastrophic problem and disaster at her they could dream up. She was tired of all the life-and-death decisions she'd been making lately and simply wanted to get home to the GA and enjoy some down time.

When the annunciator system said Kelly MacDonald was at the door, she said "Come." The door disappeared into the pocket until MacDonald was inside the room.

"Hey, Kel, what's up?"

"When the Clidepp Destroyer was attacking, did you order the ship turned so that the Marine habitat was directly exposed to their fire?"

"Not you too?"

"Not me too what?"

"It seems like whatever action I take, or whatever I say, it's being questioned."

"That's what happens with decision-makers. Other people may have differing opinions."

"I know, but it's beginning to seem like no one has confidence in me anymore."

"Maybe sometimes they just want to understand why you do what you do for their own peace of mind. You still have their confidence."

"You want to know why I turned the ship so the Marine habitat was fully exposed? Okay, here's why. I knew the ship and the habitat could both withstand a laser or torpedo strike from the Clidepp destroyer because both are sheathed with Dakinium. However, the repository for the envelope generator on the topside was open and the generator was extended and fully exposed. Although both the generator cover and the extension shaft are sheathed with Dakinium, it's only to allow the creation of an envelope, and I don't know how thick their Dakinium sheathing is or how thick it must be to protect them from torpedo damage. When a warship goes into a fight, the generator is retracted and the repository is covered. I didn't want to risk the slightest bit of damage to either generator or shaft because it might mean an end to our chances of attaining FTL. So, when the well-protected habitat was facing the destroyer, the less protected generator was facing directly away."

MacDonald smiled and nodded. "Makes perfect sense. I knew you had to have a good reason."

"Did someone put you up to this?"

"Don't get paranoid on me, Syd. I just overheard some scuttlebutt. Now I'm going back down to permanently destroy any rumors about you endangering the habitat for no reason."

Sydnee smiled. "Okay, Kel."

"And Syd, I'm sorry if I came off a little harsh. You saved our asses on Yolongus by risking your own. We haven't forgotten. That's why it seemed so foolish for anyone to question your actions, but I needed to know the reason so I could squash any doubts about your leadership before they start. When they hear the reason for rotating the ship, they'll feel so foolish for questioning your actions that they'll be even less likely to question them next time."

"Thanks, Kel."

After MacDonald left, Syd thought about the times she had questioned the actions of superiors. She'd never done it openly, but she'd wondered from time to time why they'd chosen one action over another. Then she thought about Captain Lidden and the burden he bore. On the *Justice*, Syd had just fifty lives in her hands. On the *Denver*, Lidden had almost a thousand. She wondered if she'd ever be up to the task of being a warship captain. She had once wondered how Admiral Carver dealt with being responsible for the hundreds of billions of lives in Region Two. She wondered if it got easier after a certain point or if it continued to get significantly harder.

Syd was brought up out of her reverie when her CT chimed. She touched her ring and said, "Marcola."

"Captain, this is Olivetti. Do you have a few minutes?"

"Of course, I'll be right there."

"I'd rather we meet in your office, Captain."

"Very well. Come whenever you can."

"I'm on my way."

Seconds later the annunciator said that Lt. Olivetti was at the door.

"Come," Sydnee said.

Olivetti barely waited until the door was closed before she began talking. "Captain, I knew you'd want to see this right away." She held out a viewpad to Sydnee. On the face were plot points and calculations. The number that jumped out at Sydnee was 12,241.63.

"What is this?"

"As you ordered, I began taking position readings as we traveled. After an hour, I compiled them and then calculated our speed. The answer was so crazy that I started all over again. The information you see on the viewpad is the second set of calculations. The speed reading was identical to the first. If you press the back arrow, you can see the previous calculations. There's no doubt about it. We're traveling at Light-12241.63."

"But the helm console only read 2241.63."

"I think perhaps the console is only capable of showing four significant digits and two decimal positions because the fastest speed possible was believed to be Light-9793.48."

Chapter Twenty-One
~ July 7th, 2286 ~

"Come in, Bry," Captain Lidden said. "I just received a message from Marcola. You're going to love this one." Lidden started the message playing on the large wall monitor as soon as Commander Bryant was seated.

When the message ended, Bryant looked at Lidden with his mouth slightly ajar. "Is she serious? Light-12241.63? No, that's impossible."

"Impossible? When Admiral Carver set the speed record, all the scientists in GA space had been in agreement for years that the highest FTL speed we could ever attain was Light-842. She knocked them all on their ear. From what I hear, scientists still don't fully understand double-envelope theory, but we couldn't ignore the benefits of using it while they study it. So who knows what's possible? Perhaps we're only at the threshold of the speed scale. Perhaps we might one day achieve Light-1000000. We could go galaxy hopping the way we currently go planet hopping."

"I don't even want to think about numbers that high. So what now?"

"Well, now I compose a message to SHQ." With a chuckle he added, "I wish I could be there to see their reaction. I bet they're going to be as shocked as we were when we heard Light-12241.63. You know, at that speed, if they don't burn out their generator, the *Justice* will be back to GA space in just under two weeks."

"I know most of you had other plans for today, but this news couldn't wait. The *Justice* has resolved its problems with its envelope generator and is on its way back to GA space."

"That's wonderful news, Richard, but it hardly justifies calling an emergency session on a weekend," Admiral Platt said. "I have tickets to an opera in Milan tonight."

"Then how about this, Evelyn," Admiral Moore said with an amused smile. "The *Justice* is on its way back at Light-12241.63."

"What?" Admiral Woo, the Director of Scientific & Expeditionary Forces said as he jumped to his feet.

"Has this been verified?" Admiral Bradlee asked.

"Roger, it's just happened. Of course it hasn't been verified yet. Here, let's play the message sent by Lieutenant(jg) Marcola to Captain Lidden."

"As you can see," Admiral Moore said when the message had ended, "the *Justice* has managed to resolve its problem without any assistance from us and possibly set a new speed record while doing so."

"I can't see how modifying an induction coil could possibly be responsible for a twenty-five percent increase in envelope-generation speed," Admiral Woo said.

"I agree," Admiral Plimley, the Director of Weapons R&D, said. She was also the individual responsible for ship production at the Mars shipyard. "Altering an induction coil can't possibly make such a difference."

"And yet, they claim that's all they altered and were astounded when their speed registered as Light-12241," Admiral Hillaire said. "Of course, their Light-75 speed was only because the induction coil was fractured. And as I recall, Loretta, you were highly skeptical when Admiral Carver reported her speed record."

"Our scientists have been studying double-envelope theory for years now, and they all agree that Light-9793.48 is the absolute fastest speed possible," Admiral Plimley said.

"Are these the same scientists who all agreed that Light-842 was the highest speed we could ever attain?" Admiral Platt asked.

"How do you then account for Lieutenant Marcola's reported speed, Loretta?" Admiral Hillaire asked.

"Obviously, her measurement equipment is faulty."

"Perhaps," Admiral Moore said, "but I'm not so willing to dismiss this young officer's claims. We've seen many amazing scientific advances during our lifetimes, some by people who were unaware that what they were attempting to do had been declared impossible by scientists and experts. I've learned to keep an open mind. The *Justice* still has the package on board. After he's been dropped off to the Intelligence people waiting at Simmons SCB, let's have Marcola bring her ship directly to Mars."

"There's another matter to discuss as a result of this news," Admiral Bradlee said. "If merely redesigning the induction coil in the generator *can* improve envelope generation speed by twenty-five percent, every ship in the fleet can see an almost instant speed upgrade. And— perhaps even greater speed increases can be achieved once we learn what might have caused this anomaly. And most importantly, do we share this information with commercial shippers and passenger liners? They've all been screaming because we won't share the secrets of Dakinium. This might get them off our backs a bit. A passenger liner that can currently travel at Light-300 will be able to simply swap out its induction coil and achieve a sustained travel speed of Light-375 or greater."

"If this report is accurate," Admiral Woo said, "I don't see how we can prevent the information from getting out." He had retaken his seat as the discussion progressed. "We'll have to share it with commercial users."

"I think Roger is right," Admiral Moore said. "Sharing this information with commercial vessels should get them off our backs a bit with the speed issues, but— let's hold off making this public until we know for sure exactly what's responsible for the speed increase. We don't want the newsies hounding us day and night until we're ready to release the data."

"I'd finally found a freighter who would take a generator into Clidepp space and pass it to the *Justice* while in orbit around Yolongus," Admiral Plimley said, "and now we don't need them. But they've already departed, so we'll have to pay the transport fee."

"An insignificant matter, Loretta," Admiral Bradlee said. "I can arrange to have someone pick up the generator and bring it to our embassy there so we'll have one on hand if we ever need it again."

"Is our embassy there still open?" Admiral Burke asked. "I was under the impression the embassy staff had all been recalled."

"Not for business, but there's a caretaker staff of Yolongi employees there. They maintain the grounds and buildings, keep squatters from moving in, and prevent vandals from damaging the property."

As the *Justice* drew closer to the GA border every day, the mood aboard the ship became noticeably lighter. This illustrated a diminishment of the stress and strain everyone had been feeling. Chief Luscome was using the oh-gee harness made by the Marines for Sydnee and was elated to be able to get out of the sickbay during the day. He still slept there because the corpsman wanted to monitor his continually improving condition until he felt it was prudent to release the Chief.

"Almost home," Kelly MacDonald said to her best friend as they sat drinking coffee in Sydnee's office.

"Well, almost to GA space anyway," Sydnee said.

"That's what I meant. How far is it to the border from here?"

"Oh, roughly about eight light-years."

"That sounds *so* far away."

"It is, but at Light-12241 it's less than six hours. At Light-9790 it's about seven and a half hours. And at Light-1, the speed of light, it's eight years."

"I'll take Light-12241, thank you."

"As will I. I wonder what will happen now."

"To who?"

"To the *Justice,*" Sydnee said.

"What do you mean?"

"When Admiral Carver broke the speed record, the *Colorado* was taken away from the *Prometheus* for study. The Admiral didn't get it back until, as commander of Stewart SCB, she was facing the Milori invaders."

"Well, it's not the same thing, is it? I mean, the *Colorado* is a ship. Even though it's not classified as a warship, people still live aboard it on an extended basis. This mission was supposed to be short, lasting only as long as it took to get to Yolongus, snatch the bombing perp, and return. Nobody suspected we would still be trying to get home more than six months later."

"I guess you're right, Kel, and we do have a new home. I wonder if the shooting range is finished yet?"

"Wow. I can't believe I'd forgotten all about that."

"It's understandable. We've all been under a lot of stress. But in a few more hours, we can relax. What was that, Kel?"

"What was what?"

"You didn't feel it?"

"Feel what?"

Sydnee leaned back in her chair and put her hand against the bulkhead. "Something's wrong. The ship doesn't feel right." In seconds, Sydnee was up out of her chair and headed for the bridge. "Sit rep," she said as she entered the bridge.

From the command chair, Weems said, "The envelope generator seems to have shut down, Captain. We're trying to determine the reason. "

"Did the ACS sense an obstruction ahead?"

"Negative, Captain," the tac officer said. "The area ahead is clear."

"How about behind us?"

"Uh, clear, Captain. We haven't changed course."

"When the *Colorado* first traveled at Light-9790, the ACS shut down the drive. They later learned that a ship passes through solid objects while in double-envelope travel. The ACS is supposed to disengage when the ship is traveling at Light-9790. But we were traveling at Light-12241."

"The ACS was disengaged, Captain," Caruthers said.

"Helm, rebuild the envelope."

"I've tried, Captain. The generator is off line."

"And just six hours from GA Space," Sydnee mumbled under her breath. "Why now?" Then raising her voice she said, "Okay, let's crank up the sub-light engines. Full power, Lieutenant."

"Aye, Captain," Caruthers said.

"Cancel the engines when we have just ten percent of our fuel left," she said to Weems.

"Aye, Captain."

There was a noticeable lurch as the sub-light engines engaged, but once the gravitative inertial compensators kicked in, everything settled down.

"Anyone seen Chief Luscome?" Sydnee asked.

"He hasn't been on the bridge this morning," Weems said.

"Okay, I'll find him."

Luscome wasn't in the sickbay, but Sydnee found him sitting at the console in the engineering section of the ship.

"Before you ask, Captain, I don't know yet. But I'm working on it. I'm checking all the readings for the past several days. There has been a slight but constant increase in internal heat in the generator housing since the generator was activated. I was surprised by that because of the freezing temperature of space. I guess that without the cold, the unit may have overheated much sooner. It was probably related to the rate at which new envelopes were being created since heat is generated by the flow of electrons. That generator was only designed for a maximum of Light-150, not Light-12241."

"You're saying it's burned out?"

"For now I'm only saying the temperature far exceeded the safe operating temperature."

"Why didn't someone notice?"

"Lt. Barron is dead, and I've been laid up in the sickbay. In fact, if the doc finds out I've been sitting in here, he'll have a fit. I'm not supposed to be putting any stress on my back yet. I'm not even supposed to be upright except when I'm in the oh-gee support unit you gave me. And there was no one else to monitor the ship's operating condition."

"How do you feel, Chief? How's the back?"

"I feel great, but the doc says I'm at a delicate point. My back is healing and I feel good, but if I try to push it a little too fast, I can undo everything and wind up bed-ridden again."

"He's right. Better get back in your floating support."

"What are you going to do now, Captain? We haven't reached GA space yet, right?"

"That's right, Chief. So I guess it's time for another hull walk with you monitoring— from the sickbay. I'll tell Padu and Addams to suit up."

"Aye, Captain. I'm headed for sickbay."

The *Justice* had exhausted ninety percent of its small fuel supply and gone ballistic before the two Marines left the airlock. As soon as they were topside, they set up a vid unit and went to work. As before, Luscome watched on the monitor from the sickbay and directed their efforts. When the results were in, the two Marines packed up and returned to the airlock.

"Not a chance, Captain," Luscome said. "It's fried. That generator will never work again. It's as kaput as the one that had been submerged in water when we tried to use it."

"Recommendations?"

"I have none. Without a spare generator, we're going nowhere fast."

"Okay, Chief. Thanks. I guess I'll have to try to pull a rabbit out of my hat."

———

"We just got a message from Marcola," Lidden said to Bryant when the XO arrived at Lidden's office in response to a summons.

"Is she back in GA space?"

"No, and she not going to get here on her own. She's about eight light-years inside Clidepp space and her envelope generator has burned out. She believes it's owed to the rapid generation of envelopes in a generator only designed for Light-150."

"Like you predicted."

"I wasn't serious. I didn't really expect their generator to burn out."

"Perhaps you weren't serious, but the more you think about it, it was a good call. So what do we do now?"

"I'm considering a rescue mission."

"Have you received permission from SHQ to enter Clidepp space if it was absolutely necessary?"

"No. Every time I've asked, they've refused."

"If you send in a rescue team, you could lose your ship."

"Yes, if SHQ learns about it."

"You'd withhold information from SHQ?"

"I've always played it by the book, but I'm not going to desert our people. I sent them into Clidepp space, and I'm damn sure going to make every effort to bring them out. I love my job, and I love this new ship, but I couldn't look at myself in the mirror each morning if I just turned away now."

"So are you asking me to volunteer?"

"No, I've already selected someone." Looking up at the chronometer on the wall, he said, "He should be here any minute."

"Lieutenant Mark Milton is at the door," the annunciator system said.

"Right on time. Come."

The door opened and Lt. Milton entered.

"Come in, Milty. Have a seat." When Milton was seated, Lidden said, "We have a little problem, and I'm hoping you can solve it."

"I'll do whatever I can, Captain."

"I know. I want you to illegally enter Clidepp space and rescue our stranded shipmates."

"Shipmates?"

"The *Justice* is stalled between seven and eight light-years over the border. I need someone to go get it."

"The *Justice*?"

"The CPS-14 that Lt. Marcola took into Clidepp space. Their generator is fried and they're stuck."

"Took inside Clidepp space? With permission from SHQ?"

"Yes."

"Can't they simply replace their generator?"

"They could if they had one. It seems the Quartermaster Corps decided to give them an extra office desk instead of a spare generator."

Milton looked first at Bryant, then back at Lidden to see if they were joking. There were no smiles. "You're serious?"

"Perfectly. You haven't been included in the briefings until now, so it's understandable you're confused by what I've said. Only myself and Commander Bryant have been on the inside track since Marcola's mission began. Here're the basic facts. She took a Marine Special Ops team and a platoon of our

Marines inside Clidepp space in an effort to catch the person responsible for the bombing of the GA Trade Show."

Milty's mouth dropped slightly in surprise. He recovered quickly. "So that's where they went. There's been a lot of speculation, but no one suggested they might have been in Clidepp space all these months."

"You can't imagine what they've been through. Their envelope generator broke, and instead of a spare generator in the engineering storage locker, there was an office desk. We're lucky that so far there's only been one casualty— Lt. Barron."

"Bill Barron is dead?"

Lidden nodded. "Yes. He was killed by a guard animal while they were trying to get a replacement generator from a scrap yard on Yolongus. Sydnee was also injured by one of the beasts and had both legs broken. Chief Luscome received a serious back injury, broken ribs, and a punctured lung. Both Sydnee and Luscome are recovering. But now the used generator has broken down and they're stuck seven light-years on the other side of the border."

"How soon do I leave, sir?"

"Before you decide, I have to tell you that SHQ has forbidden us to rescue the *Justice*."

"Forbidden a rescue mission? Why?"

"They haven't been forthcoming with that information, and we can't imagine a reason."

"So you want me to go against the dictates of SHQ?"

Lidden looked him in the eyes and said, "Yes. And I'll be just as culpable for asking you to go. And if you're successful without getting us into a shooting war with the Empire, no one will ever know except me, Commander Bryant, you, and whomever you select for your team. Plus the people you rescue, of course."

Milton was silent for about ten seconds. "Sydnee risked her life to save the lives of everyone aboard the *Perry*. I couldn't live with myself if I didn't make every effort to save hers."

"Think you can put together a bridge crew that can keep their tongues in check?"

"In a heartbeat, sir."

"Everyone has to understand the potential risks to their career and understand they can never talk about it afterward."

"Not a problem, Captain. When do we shove off?"

"As soon as you're ready."

"How many people can I bring?"

"How many can you get?"

"Far more than I'll need."

"You should have a crew of seven, including yourself."

"No problem, sir. How will I find the *Justice*?"

"Marcola sent us her position. We'll load it into the navigation computer aboard the CPS. She's currently traveling ballistic at Sub-Light-45. The navigation computer will continue computing her approximate location. When you're near, contact her and home in on her signal."

"Aye, sir. Is that all?"

"Yes."

Milton stood and started to leave, then stopped and didn't move for several seconds. When he turned back to face the Captain, he had a strange look on his face. "Sir, on second thought, I really don't think I should get involved in something not sanctioned by SHQ."

"What?" Bryant said incredulously.

"I don't think this is a good idea, sir. I don't want to be part of anything not approved by SHQ. And I don't think you or Commander Bryant should be involved in anything like this either. It could mean the end of your careers. I think it best that we all completely forget the idea, no matter how well-intentioned it was. SHQ is the final authority in matters involving travel in the territory of a foreign nation without prior approval, and we cannot take that responsibility upon ourselves. However, if you permit me, I'd like to use a CPS for twenty-four hours. The simulators are great, but the real thing is always better. I'll put together a team and we'll cruise around this part of the border area running battle simulations and trying to get a real feel for the ship."

Lidden smiled. "You're right, Milty. It was an absolutely crazy idea, and I'm glad you're not going to do what I suggested. Let's forget I ever said anything. And of course you can use a CPS for twenty-four hours to get some hands-on experience. Take anyone you wish along."

"Thank you, sir."

"Have a good trip, Milty," Bryant said.

"Thank you, sir." Milton braced to attention, then turned and left. As the doors of the captain's office closed behind him, he immediately began contacting shipmates and asking them to join him in his quarters.

"He really had me going for a minute," Bryant said after the door had closed.

Looking at Bryant, Lidden said, "He was right, Bry. It *was* a foolish idea. If SHQ ever learned we sanctioned a trip into Clidepp space against their orders, both our careers would be over. But it would sure be nice if he happens to run across our missing CPS while he's conducting his training mission. Make sure his navigation computer has the latest maps and information so he doesn't accidently stray into Clidepp space."

Commander Bryant smiled knowingly. "I'll take care of it immediately, Captain."

Chapter Twenty-Two
~ July 20th, 2286 ~

"That's all I can tell you unless you agree to go," Milty said to the four officers in his sitting room. As the third officer on the *Perry*, he'd been assigned the quarters normally reserved for a Lt. Commander. Aboard the *Denver* his quarters were the standard size for a lieutenant, and they were still triple the size of his former quarters.

"You want us to agree to something without telling us what it is?" Lieutenant(jg) Balarro said. During the discussion he had sort of assumed the role of spokesman for the group.

"I've told you what it is. It's a rescue mission. But you can *never* talk about it because it's not sanctioned."

"Not sanctioned by whom?"

"By anyone above our level. So nobody, outside of the people involved, may *ever* know about this. You can *never* talk about it after it's over. If anyone learns of this, it could end all our careers. But I promise one thing— if we pull this off and no learns of our involvement, you'll never regret doing it."

"And just who would we be rescuing?"

Milty drew in a deep breath, and released it. "Okay. But this is *all* I'll say unless you agree to go. We're going to rescue our shipmates. The ones who left here on January 1st."

"You mean the ones who left in the CPS?"

"Yes."

"I'm in," Lieutenant Redding said.

"I'm in also," Balarro said.

The others immediately agreed as well.

"Okay, so tell us, now that we've all agreed to go," Balarro said. "What's the mission?"

"I told you. It's to rescue our shipmates."

"Why do our shipmates need to be rescued?"

"Because they're stuck in Clidepp space. Their envelope generator broke down eight light-years inside the border, and they don't have a spare."

"And the captain approved our entering Clidepp space?"

"No. Absolutely not. I knew he couldn't grant that permiss-ion, so I asked him if I could use a CPS for a training mission. I told him that even though the simulators are great, the real thing is always a little different. He's agreed to let us have a ship for twenty-four hours. We're going to find our shipmates, link up, and bring them back here. It's twelve hours from here to where they are, and then twelve hours back— a quick, one-day operation. If we find them and bring them back, the story is that we were training and came across the other CPS on *this* side of the border. Are you still with me?"

"More than ever," Balarro said. "When do we shove off?"

"We five are command, tac, navigation, helm, and engin-eering. We still need a com chief and an engineering chief. Will, if you can find us a good engineering chief who can keep his mouth shut, I think I know who can handle our communications."

"I'll take care of it, Milty."

"And in case I forget, we need to ensure there's a spare envelope generator in the engineering storage locker and not a damn office desk."

While the CPS-14 moved to the temporary airlock aboard the *Denver*, a ground crew chief was attaching oh-gee blocks to a crate that contained a brand new office desk. The storage locker in the CPS where the desk had been residing now contained a brand new envelope generator.

As the CPS cleared the *Denver*, the bridge crew prepared to begin their training mission.

"Navigator, do you have a recently added training mission chart?" Milty asked.

"Aye, Captain."

"Pass the suggested course to the helm. Helm, build the envelope and take us out at maximum speed if the AutoTect board is green."

"Aye, Captain, building our envelope." Two minutes later, the helmsman said, "Engaging FTL at maximum speed."

Milty sat back in the command chair and relaxed as the image on the front monitor shifted from an optical view to an electronic composite created from sensor data. There would be little to do over the next twelve hours except watch the digital representations of stars.

─────────────

"Captain," the tac officer said, "there's a ship coming this way. I didn't see it at first. It was apparently traveling dark. I spotted it when it began broadcasting an AutoTect signal."

"Did it alter course to intercept, or was it coming this way from the time it first appeared on the AutoTect screen?"

"From the time it first appeared."

"Is it coming directly at us?"

"No, ma'am. It should pass us on our larboard side with about a two-million-kilometer separation."

"Then it's probably an unintentional encounter. But why was it traveling dark?"

"Should I prepare weapons just in case?"

"Negative. Let's stay buttoned up and they might not even see us. I don't want to start a shooting war out here unless we have no choice, and if we open a weapons platform we lose the Dakinium's ability to absorb radar waves."

The seconds crawled by as the bridge crew waited to see what the other ship would do, if anything. As demonstrated with the Clidepp destroyer, the *Justice* was practically invisible if it didn't have a sun or star cluster behind it. So the best thing to do was let their Dakinium coloration work for them. They were flying ballistically, so there was no telltale ion trail behind them, and the generator was fully retracted into the repository.

"Captain," the com chief said, "I'm receiving what I think is a hail from a ship calling itself *Lifeguard*."

"*Lifeguard*? For us?"

"Yes, ma'am. They seem to be hailing the *Justice*."

"Let's hear it, chief."

The com chief pressed a couple of spots on his console and a message replayed through the overhead speakers on the bridge. "This is *Lifeguard,* seeking a little *Justice*."

"That's all they keep saying. Captain. I might be wrong, but it sounds like Chief Tanzetti's voice. There's a peculiar sort of drawl with the word 'lifeguard.'"

"Respond to the message, Chief. Tell them *Justice* is a dish best served cold."

The chief sent the message and then listened before saying, "They say any dish will get cold if you don't keep a lidden on it."

Sydnee smiled.

"The ship has changed direction slightly, Captain," the tac officer said. "It's coming directly at us now. They must be tracking our outbound signal."

"Tac, are there any other ships on the DeTect screen?"

"Negative. All I see is the one ship."

"Helm, turn on our running lights. We don't want them running into us."

"Aye, Captain," Caruthers said. All around the outside perimeter of the ship, small Dakinium covers rolled back and lights protruded from small pockets before illuminating.

"I have a firm fix on them, Captain," the tac officer aboard the CPS calling itself *Lifeguard* said. "And it appears they've just turned on running lights."

"Tac, are there any other ships on the DeTect grid?"

"Negative, Captain. Except for the *Justice*, we're all alone out here."

"That's the way I like it. Helm, turn on our running lights as well."

"Aye, Captain."

When the *Lifeguard* reached the *Justice*, it used a laser signal to communicate so no one else could possibly pick up the broadcast. The *Justice* did the same.

"Hello, *Justice*," Milty said. "I heard you folks need a little help. The *Lifeguard* is here to provide it."

"Hello *Lifeguard*," Sydnee said, "Did you bring us a generator?"

"We have a spare generator on board, but I sort of figured it's more important we get out of this neighborhood as quickly as possible. We'll link up and create an envelope, then travel home."

"You won't get any argument from me."

"Is your generator retracted?"

"That's affirmative. We have a nice flat surface topside."

"Roger. Better retract your sub-light engines before we attempt to link up, just to be safe. I'll contact you when we're ready to head home."

"Roger," Sydnee said.

"Helm, link us to the *Justice*."

"Aye, Captain," Lieutenant(jg) Balarro said.

In minutes, the *Lifeguard* was positioned directly over the *Justice*. The *Justice's* sub-light engines had been retracted into their storage positions inside the ship. They weren't being used anyway and wouldn't be needed any time soon. And the

Justice had also closed her hydrogen collector to prevent possible damage.

As the helmsman lowered the *Lifeguard* slowly towards its sister ship, he realized the alignment was off. He was trying to match speed, course, and attitude to a ship traveling at forty-five thousand kilometers per second, so it was a bit more difficult than it sounded at first.

On the second try, the alignment was even further off than the first time, so the helmsman lifted up, repositioned, and tried again.

Milty gave the helmsman five tries before interceding.

"Lieutenant, I think you need a bit more practice in the simulator. When we return to the *Denver*, try to spend some time on the Linkup routines."

"Sorry, sir."

"Lieutenant Redding," Milty said to the navigator, who was also an experienced pilot and helmsman, "would you care to give it a go?"

"Aye, sir," Redding said as she changed places with the helmsman.

It took Redding four tries, but the two ships were finally linked.

"Good job, Lieutenant. But I think you also need a bit more time with the Linkup routines in the simulators."

"Aye, sir. I'll concentrate on that after we get home."

"Com, connect me with the *Justice*."

"You're connected, sir."

"*Justice*, this is *Lifeguard*. We're linked up and ready to go. Shut down your running lights and anything else that might attract unwanted attention. We should clear this space in a bit over seven hours. During that time I ask that you purge any reference to this encounter from your bridge logs and communication logs. We were never here."

"Understood, *Lifeguard*. You were never here."

To Lieutenant Redding, he said, "Helm, build our envelope and take us home at top speed."

"Aye, Captain."

"What does he mean, 'We were never here?'" Caruthers asked Sydnee. Since the *Justice* was now just along for the ride, they had shut down most of the bridge functions and begun to relax in a less formal environment.

"This entire mission has been dark," she said, "but because of all the difficulties we've had, we may not be able to deny that a GA ship entered Clidepp space to arrest a terrorist without the permission of the Clidepp government after they refused to take action. Perhaps SHQ doesn't want any record of a *second* ship violating Clidepp space. Let's do as he asks and erase any record of contact with a ship calling itself *Lifeguard*. I really doubt that's a registered name anyway."

Eight hours later, the two linked CPS-14 ships were almost half a light-year inside GA space.

"Captain, we're being hailed by Lt. Milton on wideband," the com chief said.

"I guess this is for public consumption. Put him on the overhead, Chief."

"Lt. Milton, this is Lt. Marcola."

"Hello, Lieutenant. We're on a training mission. We were passing by and noticed that you're traveling at sub-light speeds. Do you require assistance?"

"Affirmative, Lieutenant. We've developed a problem with our envelope generator. Do you have a spare generator aboard?"

"Yes, we do. But we could just link up and take you back to the ship."

"We haven't completed our mission yet, Lieutenant. It would save time if we could simply borrow your spare generator. I have a couple of people aboard who have gotten very adept at swapping them in and out."

"Okay, Lieutenant Marcola. We'll dig it out of the engineering locker and hand it over as we come alongside. Give us fifteen minutes."

"That's perfect, Lieutenant. I'll have my people suited up and outside to accept it."

"Milton, out."

"Marcola, out."

"Chief, notify Padu and Addams that I want them to suit up and be ready to swap the generator."

"Aye, Captain."

Over the next ten minutes, the *Lifeguard* unlinked from the *Justice* and positioned itself for the generator transfer. When Padu and Addams were topside and ready, a small automated tug delivered the generator from the second CPS. After securing it to the Justice so it didn't drift away, the two Marines began removal of the burned-out unit. Chief Luscome was closely watching every move from the sickbay.

The work progressed swiftly, owing to the number of times the pair had worked on the generator, including several removals and installations.

"All done, Captain," the com chief said. "They're coming in."

"Tac. Let me know when the ship is closed and sealed."

"Aye, Captain."

"Chief, put me in touch with Lt. Milton."

"Go ahead, Captain."

"Milty?"

"Yes, Syd."

"Thanks."

"We were happy to do it. What now?"

"Once our people are back inside, we're heading to Simmons to deliver a package."

"Great. I guess I'll see you back at the ship."

"You bet. Thanks again, Milty. Marcola out."

"Milton, out."

Ten minutes later, the *Justice* built an envelope and disappeared from view in an instant. The second CPS waited until it was gone, then built its own envelope and disappeared.

As the second CPS came to rest inside the *Denver's* maintenance bay and all power systems and recording devices were shut down, Lt. Milton addressed his team.

"Guys and gals, thank you. I think we've made a small down payment on the debt we all owe Lt. Marcola. I know she wouldn't have hesitated to do what we did today, were the positions reversed. Watching each other's back is what keeps us so strong that no one can ever break the bonds between us.

"Remember, ours was just a routine training mission. We encountered the *Justice* in GA space and assisted her repairs. We never entered Clidepp space, even for an instant. Dismissed."

As Milton left the ship and walked towards the exit, he received a CT message. "Lt. Milton, report to the captain's quarters."

Milton touched his ring and said, "Understood. Milton, out."

According to the chronometer in the corridor as he walked towards the captain's quarters, the time was 0438. The Marine guard at the Captain's quarters stepped away from the doors, which opened to admit Milton. The Captain was standing there in a robe and slippers, holding two drinks. Lidden extended one towards Milton.

"How was your training session, Lieutenant?"

"Very productive, sir," Milton said as he accepted the drink. "I've recommended that two of my officers spend a bit more time in the simulators. They performed very well, but I think there's a little bit of room for improvement."

"So, all in all, it was just another dull flight?"

"Actually, we had a little bit of— diversion. We came across the *Justice*, commanded by Lt. Marcola. It seems her envelope generator failed about a light-year this side of the Clidepp border."

"Yet you returned alone?"

"Yes, sir. Lt. Marcola reported that she hadn't yet completed her mission. We gave her our spare generator, which her people swapped out with the broken unit while we watched. When they were done and the *Justice* had left for Simmons SCB, we completed our training mission and then returned here."

"Excellent, Milty. Thank you for lending an assist to the *Justice*."

"It was our honor and privilege, sir."

"Well, I think I can sleep now."

Milton tossed the drink down and winced slightly at the strength of the Scotch. He rarely drank and never took it straight up when he did. "Good night, Captain," Milton said as he turned towards the door.

"Good night, Milty."

As the door closed behind Milton, Lidden sipped from his glass and moved to the sofa. He was glad he had violated SHQ's orders and helped save Marcola and her people but sad for the loss of a crewmember and wondered how SHQ was going to explain the death of Lt. Barron. They'd probably attribute it to a training accident or perhaps an engineering mishap. Perhaps one day he'd be able to tell the Barron family the truth, that Lt. Barron had died bravely on a distant planet while working to bring justice for the people who had died in the Trade Show bombing.

———————————

The SO Marines would not be returning to the *Denver*, so Sydnee took some time to go down to Marine Country before they arrived at Simmons to congratulate them on a successful mission and thank them for their service and support during a difficult time.

After addressing the team as a whole, she addressed Padu personally. "The extra work you performed with the generator, Staff Sergeant, made it possible for all of us to be back in GA space today. Lance Corporal Addams credits you solely with the idea for using the epoxy. Without the repair you and Addams performed on the induction coil, we'd probably still be stuck near Yolongus."

Taking a step back, she said, "It's been an honor and a privilege to work with all of you. I wish you the very best in the years ahead as you continue to serve the GA with the same dedication and effort I've seen over the past months. Good luck."

The SO team clapped as she turned and left the quarters area. As she opened the door to her office, she realized Major Blade was behind her.

"May I come in for a minute, Captain?"

"Of course, Major," she said as she entered the office.

As the door closed, he said, "It's time for me to thank *you*. I know I was pretty rough on you early on. In the past, I've always believed I had to be that way with SC officers— especially junior officers. The day we completed the snatch on Yolongus, I learned what you were really made of. It's been a long time since I've been impressed by a Space Command officer, but I've been impressed by you. Thank you for taking on the responsibility for getting us to Yolongus, and thank you for getting us back safely. No one could have performed their duties in a more exemplary manner."

"It's been an honor to work with you, Major. I wish you continued success with all your missions."

As the door closed behind the Major, Sydnee smiled. Thinking back to the day Blade had pulled his pistol and aimed it at her, it was hard to believe he had uttered the words she just heard.

There was no end of stares from people standing at the viewing ports when the *Justice* docked at Simmons SCB. They had never seen a ship configuration like that of the

Justice before and might not see one again for some time. The military people, and probably most of the civilians, immediately knew the outer surface must be Dakinium, and what that meant— the ship was faster than most ships in outer space and almost indestructible.

As the airlock seal between MAT-Two and the station was tested and certified, the SO Marines began filing out. Their prisoner had been loaded onto an oh-gee stretcher and strapped down after being stunned for about the twentieth time. There was an opaque cover over him so no one could see who was on the stretcher, and the stun was necessary so he couldn't cause any commotion as they passed through the crowds trying to get a look at the ship.

Sydnee was anxious to return to the *Denver* so she intended to depart as soon as her passengers were offloaded, but as the last Marine passed through the airlock ramp, a Space Command officer entered the ship. He waved off the other Space Command personnel with him so he could speak to the captain alone. Sydnee immediately braced to attention.

"Lieutenant(jg) Marcola, I presume," the officer said. "I'm Rear Admiral Ramos."

"Yes, sir. I'm Lieutenant Marcola."

"I imagine you're in a hurry to return to your ship, but I have a different destination for you. You're to proceed directly to the Mars shipyard, where you will turn over the generator you were using when you achieved the claimed Light-12241speed. Additionally, all bridge logs and records will likewise be turned over, as well as any and all supporting documents and/or materials related to the generator work. Is that clear, Lieutenant?"

"Yes, sir, Admiral."

"Good. Then you're cleared to depart as soon as you can seal the ship, unless you have other business on the station."

"No, sir. I have no other business on the station."

"Very well. Safe trip, Lieutenant."

"Thank you, sir."

Sydnee raised her hand in salute and held it until the Admiral returned it. As he left the ship, someone on the airlock ramp closed the MAT's hatch. When the lock had cycled, Sydnee turned and passed through the hatch on the opposite side to enter the *Justice*.

Chapter Twenty-Three
~ July 25th, 2286 ~

"I just received new orders from Admiral Ramos," Sydnee said as she stepped onto the bridge. "We're to proceed directly to the Mars shipyard where we're to turn over the damaged generator for study, along with all bridge logs, records, and all supporting documentation and materials. So I guess we'll be spending another six weeks aboard the *Justice*. I'd better inform the Marines. Com, the admiral said we're cleared— but let's do it by the book and get permission from departure control anyway."

"Aye, Captain," Caruthers said.

Sydnee lifted the small cover by her right hand and pressed a couple of buttons, then said, "Attention all hands. I've just received new orders from the commanding officer of Simmons SCB. We're to proceed directly to the Mars shipyard. It appears they're hot to begin investigating how we established a new galactic speed record. So, our return to the *Denver* will be delayed by at least six more weeks. Carry on."

"Departure control says we're cleared to depart, Captain," the com chief said.

"Tac, are we clear on AutoTect and Detect?"

"The board is green, Captain."

"Okay, helm, take us out."

Kelly MacDonald was on the bridge within two minutes from the time the announcement ended. "Can't you swing by the *Denver* and drop me and my people off? We're going stir crazy after almost seven months cooped up on this small ship."

"I'd like to, but the Admiral's orders are to proceed *directly* to the Mars shipyard. There's no ambiguity there to exploit." Lowering her voice, she added, "I understand. Believe me.

I've been dying to run until I drop ever since my legs fully healed. It won't be much longer, Kel. And we're in GA space now so the danger is all behind us."

"Okay, Syd. I know you're just following orders."

"It should be an easy time now. The SO team has moved on, and our mission was successfully completed. Let's just relax and look forward to the day we can try out the new Marine range aboard the *Denver*."

"Okay," MacDonald said with a smile. "I'll see you at dinner, Syd."

"Right."

The three-week trip to Mars at Light-9790, while a bit dull, was actually a welcome time after the stress of the mission. Still, Sydnee wished they could have made the run at Light-12241 so they could already be on their way back to the *Denver*, but it might be a long time before anyone traveled that fast again. However, simply knowing that such a speed was possible meant it should one day be available. When scientists accepted that seemingly unscalable barriers existed, most stopped trying to scale them— until someone came along to show them that, except for the one in their mind, there had been no real barrier to begin with.

As the *Justice* was given clearance to enter the Mars shipyard, it was immediately routed to an area of enclosed docks only large enough to accommodate ships of Scout-Destroyer size or smaller. When two yard tugs approached the *Justice* and began to hook up, Sydnee had the com chief contact the yard office to report that the *Justice* was only there to deliver a broken envelope generator. The dispatcher replied that there was no mistake, and that they had been ordered to bring the ship into a slip. While the small yard tugs continued their task, Sydnee began her efforts to learn what was going on, but by the time she reached someone who had some responsibility for yard operations, the *Justice* had already been brought inside and was being secured in place as the doors began to close.

"I don't understand," Sydnee said to an assistant yard manager. "Admiral Ramos at Simmons SCB ordered us here to drop off an envelope generator. That's all."

"I'm sorry, Lieutenant. We've only done what we were told to do. SHQ arranged for this enclosed slip and ordered us to put the CPS-14 inside and secure it in place as soon as you arrived. Beyond that, I'm as much in the dark as you are. We haven't even received the work order yet. Everything has been verbal."

"Who should I speak to about this?"

"I suggest you contact the First Fleet Administration office at SHQ. They're the ones who ordered a slip be made ready to take your ship when you arrived and to bring you inside."

"Very well. Thank you."

"Good luck, Lieutenant. Welcome back to Mars."

With the ship secured inside the dock, there was nothing to do on the bridge except monitor communications. Space Command protocol required that the bridge of any active-duty warship always be fully manned 24/7. But the *Justice* wasn't really a warship, at least not in the usual sense because no one had been assigned to her, and there was no regulation stating that tugs or shuttles be manned 24/7. And then there was the fact that they were sealed inside a pressurized shipyard dock. That seemed to further diminish any requirement that the bridge be manned, but Sydnee decided to play it safe and required that at least one of the four command officers be on duty at all times. The com chief would rotate his watch with the Marine who had been sharing the duty since the beginning.

Sydnee spent an hour trying to find someone at the First Fleet Administration office who could tell her what was going on, but she kept being passed from office to office until she found herself back where she started. Frustrated that she could get no answers, she went to get a cup of coffee and a snack.

"The dock is fully pressurized, Lieutenant," the work foreman told Sydnee the next day, "so we're going to begin work on the ship."

"What work— exactly— are you going to start?"

"We have orders to replace the repository hatch cover and install sensors that detect the presence of water in the repository. All new ships are receiving the redesigned hatch cover as part of their construction, and all completed CPS-14's are being recalled and retrofitted. The first ship to get the new hatch was tested to a depth of two hundred meters and passed with flying colors."

"That's good to hear. How long will this take?"

"Seven work days. The hatch is an integral component in the construction of the ship, so we literally have to cut away a large section of the hull, and Dakinium is difficult to work with."

"Do we have to vacate the ship?"

"That's not necessary since the dock is pressurized, but if you wish to do so, I can arrange quarters at the Mars-Three housing complex."

"If our remaining aboard doesn't slow the work in any way, we'd prefer to remain aboard."

"Not a problem. Technicians must have access to the bridge and engineering areas though to modify systems software for the new sensors."

"Your people may have access to the ship any time, at any hour."

"Thank you, Lieutenant."

"We have the original generator that was damaged by water in our engineering section, and we have no spare. Can you swap a new generator for the one that was shorted out?"

"Of course, Lieutenant."

"Thank you."

At least Sydnee understood the reason for being pushed into the dock in such an expedited manner. The yard had to perform the retrofit whenever it could get any of the CPS-14s back to the yard. There were still two more ships in the *Denver*, but it was unlikely either would need to submerge in water in the near term, so their retrofit would wait until it was more convenient.

The yard workmen were already hard at work the next day when an SC officer and a work team of two arrived at the *Justice*.

"Good morning, Lieutenant, I'm Commander Cardona from Weapons R&D. I've come to collect your broken envelope generator and whatever materials, logs, and statements are available."

"Good morning, Commander. I have everything prepared. The generator is in the starboard MAT. It can be taken out through the airlock there."

"Do you have any theories as to how you were able to achieve a record-breaking speed?"

"None. I'm neither a physicist nor an engineer. All I know is that we were only able to achieve Light-75 when we installed the used generator and then traveled just three light-years with it before it stopped working. My engineering chief and two Marines discovered that the induction coil was broken. They epoxied the two halves back together, very precisely, and we were all delighted that it worked and then astounded by the speed we achieved. It seems that the generator burned out because it was from a commercial freighter and wasn't able to handle the heat created as a result of generating new envelopes so rapidly. The induction coil appears to still be intact and might still work if the rest of the generator components are replaced. We have image logs of all the work that was done because the chief was laid up in sick bay and had to give instructions to the Marines remotely."

"Excellent, Lieutenant. If you'll have someone show these workmen where the generator is, we'll get out of your hair."

"Yes, sir."

In late afternoon, the dock manager contacted Sydnee. "Lieutenant, there's an SC Commander here to see you. I sent him over."

"Thank you, Mr. Vogel. I'll meet him at the airlock."

A few minutes later, the airlock cycled and the SC officer stepped into the *Justice*. Sydnee saluted as he entered the ship.

"Welcome, Commander. I'm Lieutenant(jg) Sydnee Marcola."

"I'm Commander Bockman from Weapons R&D. I've come to get your broken generator."

"I don't understand, sir. The generator was picked up this morning."

"Picked up? By whom?"

"A Commander Cardona from Weapons R&D and a work party of two men."

"I know of no Commander Cardona associated with Weapons R&D. What did he or she look like?"

"Commander Cardona is male. I'd put his height at about six feet. He has brown hair, brown eyes, and a medium complexion. I'm sure we captured his image on one or more security logs."

"Did you verify his identity with the security office here in the yard?"

"Um— no, sir."

"Did he present any credentials?"

"Um— no, sir, other than he was wearing a Space Command uniform on a Space Command base, and he was already in a high security area."

Bockman scowled and said, "Send that vid log of the perpetrator to the security office here in the yard as quickly as possible, Lieutenant. I'll be back after I notify SCI and check on a few things."

Bockman then turned and reentered the airlock without another word.

Sydnee stood there staring at the airlock hatch for a few seconds. She had turned over the generator to the first person to ask for it because he was wearing a Space Command uniform.

"I messed up, Kel," Sydnee said to MacDonald later that day in the privacy of her office. "I gave the generator to someone using a false identity."

"How could you know, Syd? Nobody gets into this base unless their identity is confirmed and reconfirmed. Just the fact that he got into this dock proves that a lot of people were fooled before he even got to this ship."

"It may not matter. I was the one who actually let him take what could have been one of the greatest advances in the speed of our ships since Admiral Carver's double-envelope voyage. And it wouldn't just be for DS ships. Even the old *Perry* could have realized a twenty-five percent increase by just swapping out it's old induction coil for a newly designed one."

"That assumes the R&D scientists could have figured out what made it possible."

"They would have. And might have even improved on it. What if it's possible to double the speed? Can you imagine being able to travel to the furthest points in the GA in half the time? And I gave it all away."

"Now that they know it's possible, they'll keep working it until they figure it out, and nobody is going to hold you responsible for giving the generator to a phony Commander from R&D. If he was able to get past all the security check-points, his credentials had to be impeccable. And if they were impeccable, you wouldn't have been able to see anything that everyone else missed."

"I wouldn't be so sure about the assignment of blame. Look at Captain Lidden's history. He was sent to the *Perry* because members of an interdiction team aboard a freighter were killed, and he wasn't even aboard the freighter at the time. Milty once told me his motto is, 'Don't Never Do No Wrong.'

"Was this the same Milty who just violated Clidepp space to rescue us?"

"Um, yeah."

———————

"I was notified just before the regular meeting began that the generator which allowed the CPS-14 to attain a record-breaking speed of Light-12241 has been stolen from the Mars shipyard," Admiral Moore said to the other admirals seated around the enormous horseshoe-shaped table in the Admiralty Hall. When all regular business had been concluded, the hall had been cleared of everyone except the admirals and their aides for a special session.

"What?" Admiral Platt said. "How?

"Roger?" Admiral Moore said, looking towards Admiral Bradlee, the director of SCI.

"A man dressed in an SC uniform, claiming to be Commander Cardona from Weapons R&D, showed up at the *Justice* with two yard workmen and asked for it. Lieutenant Marcola gave it to them."

"She just turned it over?" Admiral Platt said.

"Yes."

"Without requiring any credentials?" Admiral Woo asked.

"The *Justice* is inside a pressurized dock at the Mars shipyard while workmen replace the repository hatch cover. She assumed the officer was legitimate. He had to have excellent credentials to even get near that area."

"I don't recall having a Commander Cardona on my staff," Admiral Plimley said.

"You don't," Admiral Bradlee said. "The only Commander named Cardona is on Admiral Carver's staff. And he's aboard the *Pholus* out in Region Two."

"So that's it?" Admiral Yuthkotl said. "We've lost the chance to increase the speed of all ships by twenty-five percent?"

"Not necessarily," Admiral Bradlee said. "It's true we've lost the generator, and it was very important for research purposes, but the *Justice's* logs are still intact and Lieutenant Marcola has provided new copies to replace those given to the phony commander. The logs contain images of the work being performed on the induction coil, so I'm sure our scientists will attempt to duplicate that effort and hopefully can learn exactly why the used generator was able to produce the envelopes so much faster. It's up to Loretta's people now."

"We're assembling the teams that will begin the work," Admiral Plimley said. "It would have been wonderful to have the actual induction coil for testing, but I think we'll be able to duplicate the process. After the *Justice* left Simmons, we contacted them and requested the image logs of the work showing the induction coil repair. Upon receiving those we contacted the manufacturer of the freighter generator, a small firm on Eulosi, requesting all manufacturing specifications for induction coils from twenty years before the date on the generator to twenty years after."

"Wait a minute," Admiral Burke said. "I thought the gener-ator was stolen. How can we know when it was manufactur-ed?"

"The image logs showed high-resolution, close-up images of the induction coil as it was being repaired," Admiral Plimley said. "The part number of the unit was clearly visible, and the images of the induction coil are so detailed that we've even been able to identify the manufacturing run of that part."

"I thought the increased security measures put into place after the Raiders stole the two battleships in 2266 guaranteed nothing like this could ever happen again," Admiral Hillaire said.

"The security measures *have* prevented the theft of ships," Admiral Bradlee said, "and we've caught numerous petty criminals trying to gain access to the yard in order to steal parts and supplies, but— someone was able to beat all of our security procedures. We haven't determined exactly how he secured his credentials yet, but we will. It's simply a matter of following the trail backward, just as we did with the Freight-One bombers."

"I'd say we have an extremely serious problem if someone was able to get past security so easily," Admiral Moore said. "And how did anyone even know about the generator or that the CPS was coming to Mars to deliver it?"

"This has to be the most serious security issue we've faced in years," Admiral Bradlee said. "I shouldn't be surprised to learn that the same people responsible for this were also responsible for the security breach on Freight-One that allow-ed four terrorists to gain access to the station *with* their explo-sive devices."

"Then Lieutenant Marcola wasn't derelict?" Admiral Hillaire asked.

"The masquerade of the person posing as a Space Command officer was perfect. He could never have gotten into the yard and into the dock if it hadn't been. I'll refrain from pointing any fingers or giving exemption from prosecution until we know the entire story."

———

"Where's my money, Zenno?"

"Relax, Garcia, you'll get it," the man on the other end of the phone said.

"You promised I'd have it as soon as I returned from Mars."

"I'm waiting for it to be delivered by my banker."

"I risked my freedom to get that generator. Impersonating a Space Command officer in a high-security area means a life sentence without chance for parole on Saquer Major. I need to get away from this planet before the Spaccs track me down. You can fool them a little at first, but once they turn their attention towards you, your only chance is to get somewhere they can't find you."

"And where is that?"

"You don't need to know. All you need to do is get me my money. I'm broke, so if you don't pay me now, I'll still be here when the Spaccs find me. And how long do you think it will be before I give up the man who didn't pay me as promised? If I'm going to be stuck on that prison colony for the rest of my days, I'll have the satisfaction of knowing you're in a nearby cell."

"I told you, the money is coming."

"If it doesn't come real soon I may not need it, and then neither will you."

Garcia heard a click that indicated the connection had been broken and then a computer message that the encryption routine was terminating.

It had been three days since Garcia had infiltrated the Mars shipyard and absconded with the generator he'd been sent to grab. Zenno had provided the officer's uniform and all of the identification that got him onto the base, plus a shuttle for his trip to Mars and return. Garcia was familiar with military protocols because he'd been a Marine until being dishonorably discharged for having sex with another Marine while on sentry duty. Now he had to get off the planet with the promised one million GA credits before SCI matched the security camera vid images with images in his Marine discharge file. He estimated that he had less than another day at most before that happened, and then perhaps a few more days before they caught up with him. But once they identified him, it would become impossible to get off the planet. The freighter was in orbit and would leave on schedule whether he was aboard or not. Zenno had already paid the Captain two thousand GA credits. Garcia had confirmed that before he left for the Mars shipyard. But there had been a promise of ten thousand more when he came on board. Without the million credits owed him, Garcia couldn't begin to pay the outstanding balance.

He tossed the phone bud on the table and plopped onto the couch. He was afraid to even leave the apartment Zenno had arranged for him lest one of the millions of vid cameras located along the streets of the city or inside public buildings and private businesses report his likeness to SCI.

Chapter Twenty-Four
~ Aug 18th, 2286 ~

Garcia spent the next morning pacing back and forth like a caged animal, then almost jumped out of his skin when he heard a knock at the door. He grabbed his pistol and hurried to check the vid monitor. The hallway cameras showed that his visitor was Zenno. He was alone and carrying a small case. Garcia took a deep breath and put his pistol down on the kitchen counter before moving towards the door. He stepped up to the security device and said, "Open code 54, Juan." The door clicked and slid open. "About time," Garcia said. "I'm about to go out of my mind. I have to get to the freighter by nine p.m. or I'm stuck here."

"Relax, you have plenty of time," Zenno said as he stepped inside and the door closed behind him. "Here's your money."

Garcia took the case and stood staring at Zenno.

"What?" Zenno said.

"I'm waiting for you to leave."

"I want you to count the money before I go."

"I trust you."

"Good. Now count the money. I don't want you coming back at me a year from now saying I cheated you. I'll leave when you state that every credit is in there."

Garcia scowled and groaned slightly, then turned and put the case on the kitchen counter. He was watching Zenno in the mirror for any sign of treachery, but when he opened the case and saw the stacks of thousand- and five-thousand-credit notes, his eyes dropped to the case and lingered there. Picking up one of the bundles, he riffled the edges. Only then did he realize that just the top bill was real. As he raised his eye, he saw Zenno smile. But before he had a chance to turn around, Zenno shot him in the back. Garcia was dead before he hit the floor.

Zenno smiled widely as he stepped over Garcia's body to retrieve the case and check the hall security monitor to determine the corridor was empty before playing the recording he'd made on a previous visit when Garcia had opened the door. When the door slid open, he stepped out.

───────────

"I just received a message from SHQ," Captain Lidden said to Commander Bryant when Bryant entered Lidden's bridge office.

"New assignment?"

"No, it's about the *Justice*. Sydnee turned over the generator that gave them the twenty-five percent speed improvement, but— she gave it to an impostor wearing the uniform of a Space Command Lt. Commander."

"Oh, no."

"Oh, yeah."

"Are they charging her?"

"It doesn't appear so. The imposter had impeccable ID and credentials. The transfer took place in the Mars shipyard inside a space dock. He had to have been cleared at three different points to get in there. There was no way Sydnee could have known he wasn't legitimate."

"How could an impostor even get to the Mars shipyard, and how did he transport the generator?"

"He used a private shuttle service. Perfectly legal, as long as you have proper ID. When he got to the yard, he even got an assistant yard manager to assign two workmen to move the generator to the shuttle. The yard manager checked first and verified that the generator was to be picked up that day. The impostor had timed it perfectly. He was in and gone by the time the real Commander from Weapons R&D showed up to collect the unit."

"So what about Sydnee and the *Justice*?"

"The *Justice* is having her repository hatch replaced and sensors installed to warn if water ever seeps in again. Then they'll return here."

"Tell me you have news," Commander Severson said to the SCI undercover operative who had just entered his office.

Nyers looked at him, then flopped into the chair facing Severson's desk. "I have news."

"Give."

"The local cops in Chicago got a call about a dead body. It was a Terran in his mid-fifties. They investigated and matched up his image with the image we've been circulating of our impostor. They called us, and I went to investigate. It's him."

"But he's dead?"

"As a stone statue in a cemetery."

"Any idea who killed him?"

"It was probably whoever hired him to do the deed. Clearing the back trail and all that. The perp was shot in the back, so it had to be someone he knew and trusted. We found a Space Command officer's uniform in the bedroom closet. The body and the uniform matched the images on the logs from Mars."

"Who found the body?"

"Landlord. The perp was supposed to have vacated the apartment, and the landlord went to check on the condition of the place so he could re-rent it. He used his override code to open the door and found the body just inside the living room."

"Any leads on the generator?"

"Not yet."

"So we're at a dead end?"

"Not yet. The perp didn't rent the place himself, and we're trying to track down the person who did. The security cameras recorded someone in the elevator around the time of death, and the landlord positively ID'd him as the Terran who'd rented the place. He doesn't rent any other apartments in the building, so we're pretty sure he did the deed."

"That all?"

"That's all so far."

"Then get out of here and find that bastard. SHQ is pounding on my head to produce results."

"Yes, sir," Nyers said as he stood up and turned to leave without bracing to attention first. Undercover SCI operatives were trained to forget the military deportment taught at the Academy lest it give them away, so Severson didn't complain that Nyers always acted like a irreverent civilian.

"The sensor work is complete," the yard manager said, "and the new hatch is installed. We discovered that water had leaked into other areas, so we had to cut our way through a bulkhead and remove some water that was trapped there, then dry it out and replace everything. All we have left to do is finish the exterior sheathing work and you can leave, Lieutenant. I estimate two more days."

"Thank you, Mr. Rosen. I'm looking forward to getting back to my ship."

"How do you like the *Denver*?"

"He's great. And compared to the *Perry*, it's like we've died and gone to heaven."

"I can understand that. That old bucket was so old and so beat that people couldn't even think of it nostalgically anymore."

"Has it been cut up yet?"

"Oh, yeah. Months ago. Some of the scrap was melted down and used to make new bulkheads and decking for our new ships. Very little goes to waste when we recycle a ship."

"He saw a lot of history. It's good that his ending serves a useful purpose."

"Yes. Well, good luck, Lieutenant."

"Thank you, Mr. Rosen."

———

"Severson," the commander said after touching his SC ring and waiting for the connection to be made between his CT and his office com system. He looked up at the chronometer on his bedroom wall and saw that it was 0418.

"Commander? Nyers. More news on the generator case."

"Tell me you found it."

"Not yet, but we're getting closer. We just found the perp who hired the imposter, supplied him with everything he needed to pull off the theft, and then killed him. He went by the name of Zenno. He was trying to act like a big fish, but he was just a minnow."

"Was? Did you kill him?"

"Didn't have to. He took care of that himself as we closed in. Guess he didn't want to spend the rest of his life on Saquer Major. Anyway, we found a receipt in his apartment from a package-delivery company that picked up a crate containing 'machine parts' from the shuttle service the impostor used for his trip to Mars. It was to be brought to Trans-Galaxy Freight Systems for shipment out that same day. The size and weight matches the information we got from the Mars shipyard."

"Which freighter and where is it headed?"

"We, uh, haven't been able to learn that yet. Trans-Galaxy says that without a bill of lading receipt number, they'll have to have someone manually search through the thousands of waybills created that day to see if they can match the description, and even then they can't promise success. The staff doesn't come to work until eight o'clock. I've requested a list of all Trans-Galaxy freighters that left Earth orbit since the time of the theft, and I should have that in a few minutes. I just wanted to update you."

"Let me know as soon as you learn which freighter."

"Yes, sir."

Severson heard the chime indicating the call had ended. He said, "Severson, out," to cancel his CT carrier and then relaxed on his bed. If the generator was off Earth, it could be good or bad. It would be a lot more difficult to find one small generator on an entire planet than finding it inside a freighter, but if they couldn't discover which freighter was transporting it, they'd have to stop and search every one of them until they located it. Depending on the number of departures from Earth's busy freight hub, that could prove to be a difficult task.

Severson settled back into his pillow and tried to fall asleep again, but he couldn't clear his mind of the most recent news. Since he always rose at 0500 anyway, he decided to start his day a little early. He rolled over slightly, kissed his sleeping wife on the check, and then got out of bed and headed for the shower.

———

As the huge doors of the enclosed dock opened fully, two small yard tugs arrived to push the *Justice* out of the slip. The work was complete and the small ship was headed home to the *Denver*.

It took half an hour to slowly work their way out of the yard to open space. The speed limits inside the yard were the lowest of anywhere in GA space, and the *Justice* wasn't permitted to use its sub-light engines at all. Everything was accomplished with thrusters until they were clear of the yard boundaries.

"Com, do we have final clearance?" Sydnee asked.

"Aye, Captain."

"Lieutenant, is the way clear?"

"The AutoTect grid is green, Captain. The board is clear."

"And the DeTect?"

"Also in the green, Captain."

"Very good. Let's build our envelope and head for home."

As the DATFA temporal envelope finished coalescing, Caruthers applied full power and the *Justice* disappeared in an instant. All repairs had been completed and there was a brand new spare generator in the engineering locker where a spare was supposed to be stored. The yard had been happy to take back the desk that was mistakenly put aboard the ship when it was launched.

"Captain, we've just received a Priority-One message," the com chief said.

"Put it in my queue. I'll take it in my office. Lt. Caruthers, you have the bridge."

"Aye, Captain," Caruthers said as he moved to the command chair and Lt. Olivetti moved to the helm.

Sydnee took a deep breath as she sat down in her office. *What now*, she thought. *Why am I receiving a Priority-One message? Only one way to find out.*

She had to lean in so the computer could verify her identity through a retinal scan, but when it was satisfied of her identity, it opened the file.

"Lieutenant Marcola, I'm Captain Wherton of SHQ. Our SCI people have been trying to track down the missing envelope generator since it was stolen from the Mars shipyard, and they believe they might have discovered its whereabouts. They can't be sure at this point, but all evidence points to the generator being part of the cargo with the Trans-Galaxy Freight Systems ship *Gatherer IV*. The ship left Earth orbit the evening the generator was stolen, with its first planned stop being the freight hub around Centrasia. Your ship's course to the sub-sectors patrolled by the *Denver* takes you close to Centrasia, so that makes you the logical ship to perform the interdiction stop. According to our files, you have two MATs, pilots to fly your MATs, and two dozen Marines on board.

"Since Centrasia is roughly one hundred light-years from Earth, and the *Gatherer's* top speed is only Light-225, it will take them about six months to reach their destination. At your maximum speed you should overtake them in a day. Trans-Galaxy Freight has always complied with directives from Space Command, and we anticipate no trouble from them now, but be careful. We don't know if anyone associated with the organization that planned and executed the robbery is aboard the freighter.

"Since the company cannot tell us in which container the generator might be located or even guarantee the generator is on board, you'll have to carefully search every container. The problem is compounded by the fact that the ship is maxed out with ten kilometers of containers. We instructed the company not to contact the *Gatherer* and warn them of the search to be conducted. We're monitoring all communications to ensure they don't. We also don't want you to tell anyone aboard the freighter what we're searching for, since someone connected to the robbery might try to scatter pieces of the generator, making it more difficult or even impossible to identify as being part of the generator.

"You understand the importance of that generator and its value. Be alert for any possible deception, but keep searching until you find it or you're ordered to end your search. Good luck.

"Arthur Wherton, Captain, SHQ Earth. Message complete."

Sydnee, still sitting close to the monitor from having leaned in for the retinal scan, sat back in her chair and sighed. The task ahead was onerous. Thoroughly searching every container in a ten-kilometer-long cargo section would be like searching a five-story warehouse on Earth that was ten kilometers long and one-hundred-sixty meters wide with steel bulkheads every ten meters and where many of the areas had no aisles.

If Sydnee tried to hold the freighter in place for an extended period, the company would be screaming at SHQ the entire time, and her chances of ever being promoted would lessen with each day that passed. It didn't matter that she was only doing what she had been ordered to do. She was expected to follow orders and yet find a way of doing the impossible in such a way that kept pressure off SHQ. The only solution seemed to be a search of the ship while it was still underway. That violated SOP but seemed to be the only solution in this instance.

If they got lucky, they might find the generator in the first month. If their luck was bad, they could still be looking for it when the freighter reached Centrasia, at which point they would have to impound the ship to ensure no cargo was offloaded until their search was over. No matter how she looked at it, it was going to be a nightmare.

"So that's the story," Sydnee said, wrapping up the task ahead of them to Kelly MacDonald, Jerry Weems, and Pete Caruthers as they sat in her office. Lt. Olivetti was manning the helm and would be briefed later.

"So you want us to find this freighter," MacDonald said, "and then begin a container-by-container search until we find the generator? That could take years."

"We only have six months. After that we'll have to impound the ship and the freight company will be screaming to the GA Senate on a daily basis."

"Let them scream," Caruthers said. "We've never been concerned before when ship captains screamed."

"We've never before spent six months aboard a ship, searching, nor impounded a vessel without finding a violation that justified the impoundment."

"We can always find a few violations if we want."

"Can you find smuggled goods where there are none?"

"I can if we make a side trip to Costio first. I know a little place that always has contraband available at the right price."

"I'm going to pretend I didn't hear that, Pete."

"I was only kidding, Syd."

"I know. That's why I'm pretending I didn't hear it."

"So you're saying that we find the Trans-Galaxy ship *Gatherer IV*, have them drop their envelope so we can board them, then allow them to rebuild their envelope and continue their voyage while we search for the generator?" Weems asked.

"Exactly."

"And we rely on them for food and beds and stuff?"

"No. I want no fraternization with the freighter crew. Our people will operate in shifts, with half sleeping in the MAT when off duty. The seats in the MAT fold down to make a bed, and the area above the seats folds down to make another bed. For food, we'll use emergency rations."

"My people are going to love that," MacDonald said.

"It's better than sleeping in a cave on Diabolisto and fighting Lampaxa Vorheridines."

"For the first week, maybe. By the second week they'll be wishing they were on Diabolisto."

"Yeah, especially since they're required to wear their armor with their helmets sealed whenever they're outside the MAT."

"That's excessive," MacDonald said. "Can't they remove their helmets when they're down in the containers?"

"No, and it's not my rule. It comes straight from Captain Lidden. I'm just the captain on this small ship, which is also under his command. We will follow every rule he has in place, just as if the *Denver* was a few hundred meters away rather than a few hundred light-years away."

"How about if we move the habitat container to the freighter for the duration?"

"I doubt their link sections could accommodate a single habitat. The specs say that two linked habitats can fit into a standard Lewiston link. We only have one normal habitat and two weapons platforms. I'm not going to allow a weapons platform to be linked to the freighter."

"How about if we move the habitat unit into their maintenance section amidship?" Weems suggested. "Those maintenance sections are always large enough to accommo-date at least two of the hundred-sixty-meter-long link sections complete with twenty-meter-high containers. They have to be able to take them in to repair them if they have a serious problem."

"That's a possibility," Sydnee said.

"Are we going to get any help from any other SC ships?" MacDonald asked.

"As far as I've been told, we're the only ship involved in this operation. After we actually board the *Gatherer* and begin the mission, I'll see if I should request additional assistance from SHQ. However, I feel confident that if a warship performing interdiction activities were available, they would have been assigned this job."

"Perhaps they're just giving you an opportunity to make up for your mistake," Weems said.

With a smile Sydnee said, "Go ahead. Put more pressure on me."

"I didn't mean it like that."

"I know. I'm just kidding. I've already considered the possibility that they're giving me an opportunity to *atone* for my past mistake, but I discarded it. I felt that if they blamed me for surrendering the generator to someone whose credentials and timing had been so impeccable as to satisfy three security checkpoints before reaching the *Justice*, they wouldn't now be trusting me with this mission. They would have found another ship somewhere that could handle the job. In any event, we've been tasked with doing this, so let's do it.

"Kel, brief your people. It's too bad Staff Sergeant Padu isn't here, but Lance Corporal Addams will be able to function as the individual who can provide the first level of certification that the object is what we're looking for, if and when it's found. When Lance Corporal Addams is off-duty, Chief Luscome will handle that role, although he'll have to do it remotely from the *Justice* because he's still not fully healthy and because he doesn't have any armor.

"Pete, work with tac to find the *Gatherer*.

"Jerry, you'll pilot the MAT over to the freighter when we find them.

"Any questions?"

"How do we perform this search?" MacDonald asked.

"When we reach the freighter, I'll ask them to transmit the manifests. As you secure the area over there, our systems will be searching for anything which indicates a container might hold the generator. Those we'll search first, thoroughly. If it's definitely not in there, we seal that container and move on. If we don't find the generator in any of the most likely containers, we start at the stern and check every single previously unchecked container as we move forward to the connection point with the freighter. We'll also search all maintenance bays as we reach them and the storage lockers in the main ship. Let's assume SCI is correct and we merely have to locate the unit."

"Merely?" Caruthers echoed.

"And remember, the generator may have been disassembled to help disguise its presence."

"This is going to be one *giant* headache," Weems said.

"Yes, it is," Sydnee agreed, "so let's wrap it up as soon as possible so we can go home to the *Denver*."

Chapter Twenty-Five
~ Aug 24th, 2286 ~

"I've found the *Gatherer's* AutoTect signal, Captain," the tac officer said.

"Helm, cancel all forward speed. Leave the envelop intact," Sydnee said.

"Where are they, Tac?"

"They should reach this point in roughly two days."

The *Justice* had been crisscrossing space ahead of the *Gatherer's* estimated position for hours before finally detecting her AutoTect signal. Every ship broadcasted an AutoTect signal ahead of their ship to avoid collisions with other ships either in their path or which would be crossing their path. The signals repeated continually, broadcasting current position, speed, and course. When the Raiders were capturing freighters and passenger ships, the signals were stopped because of the information it provided. But when the pirating was ended, the AutoTect signal system was reintroduced and, in fact, mandated anew by the GA Senate for all vessels traveling in GA Space. Other nations had adopted the system, and it had become required almost universally throughout the known galaxy.

"There's no sense waiting here for them," Sydnee said. "Give Navigation the proper coordinates from their signal and let's go meet them."

"Aye, Captain," the tac officer said.

"Helm, when we get near them, cancel the double envelope and match their speed with a single envelope. Maintain a twenty-five-thousand-kilometer distance between us."

"Aye, Captain."

"Trans-Galaxy *Gatherer IV*," Sydnee said on the primary ship-to-ship frequency, "this is the Space Command ship *Justice*. Cancel your envelope and prepare to be boarded for inspection."

The image of a distinguished-looking Eurasian in a freight captain's uniform appeared on the large bridge monitor. "This is the *Gatherer*. Captain Taka Choi speaking. What's the purpose of this inspection? We've never been inspected this close to the center of Region-One."

"The purpose of this inspection is the same as for all inspections. It's to inspect your ship for illegal cargo."

"We're carrying nothing illegal. Our company has never been fined or even charged for carrying illegal goods."

"A stellar past is not an excuse to disobey an official order to heave to."

"We're on a schedule. We can't afford to stop while Space Command looks for something that doesn't exist."

"We won't know it doesn't exist until we search."

Raising his voice slightly, Choi said, "I'm telling you it doesn't exist."

"And I'm telling you to heave to."

"You don't have the authority to stop me. You're wearing the uniform of a Lieutenant Junior Grade."

"I'm wearing the uniform of a Space Command officer. I'm the captain of the *Justice*, and I've given you a legal order to halt your ship for inspection. If you fail to comply, I'll be forced to stop you and impound your ship."

With a disparaging look, Choi said, "If you're the captain of a ship, it must be a reclamation vessel. We don't stop on orders from junk-haulers."

"The *Justice* is not a reclamation vessel. We're fully armed with missiles and laser arrays. If you force me to take action, I will."

Raising his voice again, Choi said, "If you fire on me, I will file a formal protest with Space Command and our GA Senator."

"You're assuming you'll be alive after your ship is blown apart."

Choi screamed, "You wouldn't dare fire on me."

"This is getting us nowhere. I've given you a legal order, and you've refused to obey. We will now stop you forcefully. I hope you survive to stand trial. Helm, prepare to execute an envelope merge. Tactical, prepare to fire the laser arrays. Target the main ship only. We don't want to damage the cargo."

Before locating the *Gatherer*, Sydnee had instructed both men to ignore commands to do anything of the sort unless she included the word Zulu in the order but both were to pretend they were preparing to follow her orders. She had been pretty sure the freighter captain would refuse to obey orders to heave to by a Lieutenant(jg).

"Tactical is ready to fire, Captain," the tac officer said loudly, for the benefit of Choi, who was still on the communication link.

"We'll be in position for the envelope merge in eighteen seconds," Caruthers said loudly, also for the benefit of Choi.

"Captain, wait," Choi suddenly said. "We'll heave to for inspection."

"Tactical and Helm, cancel the envelope merge order. A wise decision, Captain Choi. When you've cancelled your envelope, open the larboard hatch of your maintenance bay so our interdiction team can enter your ship. My Marines will be coming over in a Marine Armored Transport. We'll also bring over a full-sized habitat container You can then close the bay and resume your voyage. Our people will conduct their search while you maintain your schedule."

"We can continue traveling while you search? Is that a new policy? We've never been permitted to do that before."

"Terrans are creatures of habit. We're taught to halt ships when conducting searches because that's the way it's always been done before. In the past, there was more reason to do it that way. But our ships are faster and more efficient now, and the people conducting the searches are better protected from harm. I have a certain amount of latitude as a ship's captain. I've checked the regs and there's nothing that *requires* an interdiction vessel to keep merchant vessels from continuing their travel while we perform our duties. It's not our goal to delay your trip. When the ship's captain cooperates with me, I'm happy to cooperate with him or her."

"Thank you, Captain. I'm sorry for giving you a hard time earlier. I promise I'll be more cordial in the future if this new policy becomes a standard."

"That's good to hear, Captain. I'd like you to transmit a manifest of your cargo. It will save time."

"Of course, Captain. I'll see to it immediately."

"Thank you, Captain Choi. Contact me if you have any questions or difficulties."

"I will, Captain. And thank you."

"*Justice*, out."

"*Gatherer IV*, out."

Sydnee took a deep breath and relaxed in the command chair. It had been tense, but she'd known all along the *Gatherer* would yield. They were unarmed and had little choice. They couldn't win in a fight against a DS ship, even if they had torpedoes hidden in phony cargo containers.

"Maintain twenty-five thousand kilometers distance, helm," Sydnee said. Caruthers knew the regulations and would have done that anyway, so the order was just for the bridge logs. If Choi decided to file a protest of her threatening to destroy his ship, she wanted the log to show she was doing everything by the book.

"Aye, Captain," Caruthers said.

When the *Gatherer* suddenly canceled their envelope, the *Justice* disappeared ahead of them. Caruthers had to turn the ship around and return to where the *Gatherer* had stopped.

Normally, Space Command officers oversaw all aspects of an interdiction inspection, but the *Justice* was short on Space Command officers, so Kelly MacDonald and her noncoms would take responsibility for conducting the search. Since they were only searching for one thing, a great deal of expertise in uncovering smuggling deceptions wasn't as important as it usually was.

As the *Justice* came to a halt, MAT-One unlinked from the ship and headed towards the *Gatherer*. The Marines had boarded in anticipation of traveling to the freighter after loading everything they would need for the search. Within ten minutes, the MAT entered a maintenance bay five kilometers behind the main ship.

Unlinking the habitat took a little longer than expected. Lt. Barron had trained in the process, but now it fell to the tac officer to perform the duty. When the habitat unit was at last free, Lt. Olivetti guided the remote-controlled tug to the link coupling and locked on. She then expertly guided the habitat into the *Gatherer*'s maintenance bay. The cavernous bay was empty except for the MAT, a shuttle, and two tugs, so it wasn't difficult to maneuver the habitat inside the ship. If the freight haulers wanted the habitat unit in a different position, they could use oh-gee freight blocks to move it after the bay was pressurized.

With both units inside, the freighter was permitted to close the maintenance bay. Once sealed, the *Gatherer* requested permission to rebuild its envelope. Sydnee nodded to the com chief and he relayed the approval. Two minutes later the envelope was complete and the freighter resumed its course towards Centrasia.

Weems had to wait until the maintenance bay was pressurized before allowing the MAT's occupants to deploy. As per standard operating procedure, the Marines piled out of the MAT as soon as the hatch opened and took up positions around the ship as bored maintenance workers returned to their jobs and looked on with non-threatening poses. An interdiction search was an old story to any who weren't on their first cruise.

MacDonald contacted the *Justice* and got a short list of the first containers to search based on an examination of the manifest listing. She divided her people into four teams and all headed for their assigned containers.

When the first team arrived at their assigned container, the staff sergeant opened the hatch and climbed down. Halfway down the ladder he stopped and looked around. Lights had come on as soon as the hatch had been opened so the contents of the first level were visible. He groaned silently as he looked at the task ahead and multiplied that by thirty-three hundred, which was the approximate number of containers being transported by the freighter. He wondered aloud if they'd have the entire job done by the time he was due to collect his pension.

Since the first containers to be checked were the most likely to contain the generator, the Marines did an extra thorough job. Crates had to be opened and then resealed after being assured by Lance Corporal Addams or Chief Luscome, who was still aboard the *Justice*, that the 'machine parts' inside weren't part of the missing generator.

The Marines didn't quit when they were scheduled to go off-duty. Instead, they remained at their task until they were done with the container. As they wearily climbed back out of the container and it was closed, the staff sergeant sealed it with special wire seals that contained a tamper switch. The small device would send a pulse if anyone tried to cut the wire or bypass the switch. When the interdiction was over, they would return and retrieve all the devices.

The idea of bringing over the habitat proved to have been a brilliant inspiration. Instead of trying to sleep in the MAT, each Marine would sleep in his usual bed after getting a hot meal in the mess area.

"Captain," Captain Choi said to Sydnee on the day following the first efforts to locate the generator, "your people won't tell us what they're searching for. We know this isn't an ordinary interdiction effort. Perhaps we can help."

"We know Trans-Galaxy is a solid company with an excellent reputation for never knowingly transporting contraband. I would gladly welcome your assistance, Captain, but we're under orders not to discuss the matter with you or your crew."

"I understand, Captain. I simply thought we might speed your effort if we knew what you were looking for."

"Perhaps it would, and I appreciate your generous offer, but I can't accept."

"A shame."

"Yes. To make our presence on your ship as unobtrusive as possible, I've ordered my people not to interfere with your daily operations or interact with your crew in any way that would take them away from their duties."

"I want to apologize again for my arrogance and rudeness during our first conversation. Naturally, we will support your search in any way we can. You need only ask."

"Thank you. Captain. I appreciate it. Good day."

"Good day, Captain."

By the end of the seventh day, the Marines aboard the *Gatherer* were dragging. They had been working day and night and had only completed checking the containers that the *Justice*'s computer speculated were *most* likely to contain the generator. They were now beginning to check containers at the stern end of the cargo section with the intention of working their way forward to the bow. Sydnee had decided to progress in this direction on the possibility that the generator was in a container added near the end of the loading. But in reality, containers could be attached in almost any order, and entire cargo sections could be separated to make space for other sections prior to departure.

Sydnee had spent her days watching images from the helmet cams of the Marines performing the search operations. She wanted to request assistance from other ships with larger interdiction staffs, but it was still early in the effort. Perhaps if they didn't find the generator in three more weeks, she could justify requesting help. But by then her Marines would be worn out if they maintained the pace they had followed so far, or they might begin to be less thorough in their searching. She would have to come up with a solution before it reached that point.

When she heard a chime in her left ear, she touched her ring and said, "Marcola."

"Syd, it's Kel."

"Hi, Kel. How are you doing?"

"I'm beat. It's been a long day, but we completed another seven containers."

"You and your guys have been doing a great job. We've been watching the images from the helmet cams. All searches have been thorough and by the book."

"Yeah, but at this rate we won't even have completed a third of the containers by the time we get to Centrasia. We need help if we're going to get this job done."

"We don't have to search all of the containers. We only have to search until we find the generator."

"But what if the generator's in the last of the thirty-three hundred containers?"

"Well, that would be against the odds. We have a fifty-fifty chance of finding it in the first fifteen hundred containers we search."

"So far we've only searched sixty-three in seven days. And we're not going to be able to keep up this pace for much longer."

"I've been giving that a lot of thought, Kel. I agree that we need help, but I haven't wanted to cry for help too soon. If we don't find the generator in three more weeks, I'll request help from SHQ. In the meantime, let's take tomorrow off. Your folks can sleep in or whatever. The tunnel in the cargo section is ten kilometers long. That's a great place to run. It sure beats the twenty meters in the habitat."

"Good idea."

"How's the food holding up? Still got plenty?"

"We have enough for five years, so I hope we're not still here when it runs out."

"I'm going to send a message to SHQ to update them on the list of containers we've searched. Perhaps they've gotten more information about which container the generator might be in."

"Put a gentle plug in for more help."

"Okay, Kel, I will. Anything else?"

"No, that's all for now."

"Okay. Keep up the great work. Marcola, out."

"MacDonald, out."

Sydnee sat and thought about the message she would send to SHQ for the next ten minutes, then walked to her office to actually record it.

"Message to Arthur Wherton, Captain, SHQ, Earth."

"Sir, as per your orders, we have spent the past seven days searching containers in the cargo section of the Trans-Galaxy Freight Systems ship *Gatherer IV* en route to Centrasia. In my experience as part of interdiction teams, the usual complaint from senior officers aboard ships stopped for searches is the time lost from their schedules. When stopping ships crossing into GA space, there's always the possibility that we'll have to turn them around, so we naturally delay further travel into our nation. That situation doesn't apply here, so, expecting this search to take considerable time and in the interest of peaceful cooperation, I've allowed the *Gatherer IV* to continue its journey towards its destination while the *Justice* travels alongside. Captain Choi has been most appreciative and given his full cooperation. He has even offered to assist our search, but since I'm forbidden to brief him, I've had to decline his offer.

"My Marines have been very thorough as they've performed their searches. I've been observing via helmet cam images as they work, and I'm proud of their diligence and the consideration they've shown for the property being searched. As each container is cleared, we seal it with the tamper-sensitive seals provided for that purpose; however, we were unprepared for an operation of this magnitude and will soon exhaust our small supply of seals.

"I'm appending a list of the containers that have been searched to date. If you had any new information regarding which container might hold the generator, I'm sure you would have forwarded that to me. We shall continue searching each and every container until we locate it; however, it appears that when the *Gatherer IV* reaches Centrasia in six month's time we will have only searched a small part of the cargo section. If the generator is not found in that time, I will be forced to impound the ship to keep the Captain from offloading containers and adding new containers. I'm sure you understand the implication of that action. It will take my six Marine fire teams well over a year to search every container in the cargo section should that be necessary. Naturally, we hope to find the generator long before then, but we must be prepared for the worst-case scenario.

"Sydnee Marcola, Lieutenant(jg) aboard the GSC Destroyer *Denver's* CPS-14 *Justice.* Message complete."

Sydnee replayed the message before sending it. She had touched on all the important topics, including the lack of manpower, the potential time needed to complete the mission, and the shortage of tamper seals. Satisfied with the report, she tapped the transmit button.

Chapter Twenty-Six
~ Sept. 2nd, 2286 ~

"Personnel from an SC interdiction ship are presently searching the freighter which my people believe is transporting the generator," Admiral Bradlee reported during the regular meeting of the Admiralty Board. "We don't believe there's any collusion between the vessel's owner, Trans-Galaxy Freight Systems, and the people responsible for the theft. It was probably just the most innocuous way to transport the device. And once something gets swallowed up among the tens of millions of items shipped every day, it can be almost impossible to find if you don't have a waybill number for tracking."

"How large is the ship, Roger?" Admiral Plimley asked.

"It's a standard bi-section freighter with a full ten kilometers of cargo containers."

"Ten kilometers? How many ships have been assigned to search the cargo section?"

"Just one."

"It will take the crew of an interdiction destroyer a year to search that ship. There has to be over three thousand containers attached to that freighter."

"There wasn't a destroyer available for the interdiction. We have a CPS-14 crew performing the search."

"A CPS-14?" Admiral Moore said in surprise. "With a crew of just seven to ten?"

"No, the CPS-14 we recruited presently has a flight crew of eight and a small Marine platoon of twenty-seven."

"I take back what I said about the task taking a year," Admiral Plimley said. "It will take five years."

"Were you aware of this, Evelyn?" Admiral Moore asked.

"No request for an interdiction stop was brought to my *personal* attention," Admiral Platt said, "but that's not unusual. I'm sure a member of my staff handled it and made the closest ship we had in the area available to SCI."

"But a CPS-14 with a crew of just thirty-five?"

"For security reasons, SCI doesn't always take my people into their confidence. It's possible the officer handling the request wasn't aware of the enormity of the task. Perhaps he or she believed it was a standard interdiction stop to inspect for smuggling where only a dozen containers might actually be searched, and then only a cursory check unless something is found."

"That's very possible," Admiral Bradlee said. "Our work necessitates that we operate on a need-to-know basis."

"It seems that, in this case, the officer assigning the assets had a need to know," Admiral Plimley said. "Why was a CPS-14 even available. Where's its destroyer?"

"The ship had just left Mars where its repository cover was replaced with the newly redesigned airtight hatch cover."

"The only active duty CPS-14 to enter the yard for a hatch cover retrofit to date is the *Justice*," Admiral Plimley said.

"That's right. The ship assigned to the interdiction stop is the *Justice*. It was headed back to the *Denver* near the Clidepp border, and the freighter was on its way to Centrasia. Their courses almost overlapped."

"So Lt. Marcola is once again involved in this issue?" Admiral Hillaire asked.

"Yes, she's still in command of the *Justice*."

"Do you have a problem with that, Arnold?" Admiral Woo asked.

"Not at all. I believe her to be extremely competent. She's done an incredible job to date. But I don't believe her small staff is up to the task being asked of them. Evelyn, are additional resources available to assist the *Justice* crew?"

"I'll check on it as soon as the meeting's over, Arnold. We're talking about the heart of Region One, so there must be at least one other ship available."

"Is there anything else to be discussed on this topic Roger?" Admiral Moore asked.

"No, I've covered everything we've learned to date. My people continue to search for other leads and information, but we've put most of our chips on the generator being somewhere among the cargo in the *Gatherer IV*."

"Okay, let's move on to the subject of naming a new commanding officer for Ethridge SCB, and then we'll review the proposed plans for the new GA Senate complex on Quesann."

"Captain, we've just received a Priority-One message from SCI," the com chief said to Sydnee.

"I'll take it in my office. Lt. Caruthers, you have the bridge."

"Aye, Captain," Caruthers said. As he rose from the helm console station and moved to the command chair, Lt. Olivetti moved to take his place.

Sydnee plopped into her office chair and pulled herself close to the monitor so she could perform the requisite retinal scan. When the computer was satisfied of her identity, the message opened. It was Captain Wherton again.

"Lieutenant Marcola, additional resources are being sent to aid your search of the *Gatherer's* cargo. Within the next two weeks you'll be joined by the Destroyer *Seoul*, commanded by Captain William Carver. The *Seoul* has adequate personnel and equipment, such as the tamper-sensitive seals that are in short supply aboard the *Justice*. It's possible another ship may become available as well, although at this time no ship has been named. I assure you that neither SCI nor SHQ has failed to appreciate the enormity of the task you face.

"Arthur Wherton, Captain, SHQ Earth. Message complete."

Sydnee, sat back in her chair and breathed deeply. It appeared the update she'd sent had had some effect. Of course, they might have been aware of the problem before and been working on a solution. She would probably never know. And it didn't really matter. All that mattered is that the *Justice* would soon have help in performing the search.

"We're getting some help, Kel," Sydnee said to Mac-Donald a short time later.

"Great. It can't come soon enough. When and how much?"

"The Destroyer *Seoul* has been assigned to assist our effort and should arrive sometime in the next two weeks. That's all I was told. Since we know they're not a DS ship, their max speed is probably about Light-375. When they arrive, the Captain will probably assume command of the effort because he'll be the senior officer present. The *Seoul* should have a full company of Marines, with at least four full platoons plus a number of SC interdiction-trained officers."

"An additional two hundred pairs of hands and eyes will make quite a difference. We might actually be able to wrap this up by the time we make Centrasia."

"I keep hoping every morning that today will be the day we find the generator."

"You're an optimist."

"Maybe. But SCI is pretty sure it's over there somewhere, and I know we'll find it if it is."

―――――――――――

"Captain," the com chief said, "I just received a request to provide our current position to the GSC Destroyer *Seoul*."

"Navigator, send a position report to the com. Chief, forward it to the *Seoul*."

"Aye, Captain," both said.

"Communication from the *Seoul*, Captain," the com chief said. "It's directed to you. There's a three-second delay."

A three-second delay meant the *Seoul* was fairly close.

"Put it on my right-hand monitor, Chief."

The image of Captain William David Carver immediately appeared on the monitor. The voice communication would be conducted via her CT.

"Good morning, Captain," Sydnee said.

"Good morning. I see you're underway. Have you completed the interdiction effort?"

"No, sir, we're still at it. I anticipated a lengthy effort so I allowed the *Gatherer* to continue its travel. If we need access, the freighter drops its envelope, we take care of the issue, and then allow them to rebuild their envelope and resume travel."

"An unusual arrangement."

"The captain has been most appreciative. If I had held them where we first made contact, I would have had him chewing on my ear every day, if not more often."

"I can appreciate that, and I think your solution is a wise one. I believe I'll try it myself in the future where circumstances permit. Since the freighter is underway, we won't be able to join you for at least four hours."

"I understand, sir. We look forward to welcoming the *Seoul* to this massive effort."

"And I look forward to getting a tour of your ship. I've seen the specs but haven't seen the new CPS-14 in person. I doubt we'll be receiving any. I don't believe our bays are large enough to accommodate the new ship. I'm sure they'll all go to the new DS destroyers."

"Probably so, sir, but in time all of the ships will be DS."

"That's true. Well, we'll see you in about four hours, Captain."

"I look forward to it, sir."

"*Seoul*, out."

"*Justice*, out."

"The *Seoul* is coming alongside, Captain," the tac officer said.

"Com, extend our greetings to the *Seoul*."

"Sent, Captain, and acknowledged. Captain Carver is on the com. Shall I put it on your right monitor?"

"Yes, Chief."

"Welcome, Captain Carver," Sydnee said as Carver's image appeared on her monitor.

"Thank you, Captain. Is everything still in order?"

"Yes, sir. My Marines are still hard at work. We've been watching the helmet cam images. I'll have my com chief send you the scramble code." Sydnee nodded to Chief Lemela, who promptly sent the code to the *Seoul* so they could view the images as well.

Captain Carver spent a few minutes watching the transmissions before speaking. "They're being very thorough," he said finally.

"I impressed upon them that if we miss it, we'll have to start the search over again from the very beginning. They're well motivated to find it on the first pass."

Carver chuckled. "As would I. Okay, Captain, my teams are sitting in MATs and shuttles ready to go. If you'll have the freighter drop its envelope, we'll storm the battlements."

Sydnee knew he was kidding, so she said, "Just tell them not to scare the mechanics in the maintenance bay when they leap out of the shuttles. So far the villagers have been friendly."

"Noted. Carver, out."

"Marcola, out."

Sydnee had Chief Lemela pass on the request that the freighter drop its envelope. At the same time, Caruthers stopped generating new envelopes but didn't cancel the *Justice*'s envelope. When the *Gatherer* had come to a stop, he would make up the distance to the freighter, then cancel the envelope. The *Seoul* did the same.

Some thirty minutes later, all interdiction teams from the *Seoul* had been transferred to the Gather and the freighter was given a green light to rebuild an envelope and continue their voyage.

As the freighter disappeared from view, Captain Carver contacted the *Justice*. "I'd like to come aboard and see your ship now, if that's convenient. How does my shuttle establish a connection?"

"It would be quicker and simpler if I sent over a MAT, sir. This small ship wasn't really designed for easy access from an older style shuttle. The linkage is different, and it's a bit difficult to establish an airtight seal."

"Very well. Will your MAT enter a bay or link to an airlock?"

"An airlock link would be quickest."

"Very well. Have your pilot connect to the starboard bow airlock."

"Yes, sir. Marcola, out."

"Carver, out."

"Lieutenant Olivetti, would you like to take a short ride?"

"I'd love to, Captain."

"Okay. Why don't you pick up our guests."

"Yes, ma'am."

In less than a second, a smiling Lt. Olivetti was up out of her chair at navigation and headed for MAT-Two.

As Olivetti unlinked from the *Justice*, she banked to starboard, then raised the MAT up and over the CPS-14. The *Seoul* had come to a halt on the *Justice's* larboard side, so she only had to slide left a thousand meters to align with the *Seoul's* forward airlock.

Five minutes after making the connection with *Seoul*, MAT-Two was headed back to the *Justice*.

"Atten-tion," Chief Luscome said as Captain Carver and two of his senior officers entered the ship. The greeting party was a small one since most of the crew was on the *Gatherer* or required to remain on the flight deck. Only Sydnee, Luscome, and Doc could be spared for the greeting.

"As you were," Carver said calmly. After introductions all around, Captain Carver extended his hand towards Sydnee and said, "It's a pleasure to meet you, Lieutenant. I've heard a lot about you."

"About me, sir?"

"Don't be modest. The story of how you saved the *Perry* crew was all over the news when the BOI made their findings official."

"Oh, I hadn't heard, sir. We've been away on a mission."

"You've been somewhere where GA news broadcasts weren't available?"

"Yes, sir. But I can't discuss it."

"That must be one hell of a story. Your career so far has been a little like that of my sister."

Sydnee smiled pleasantly but never uttered a word.

"Okay, I won't bait you. I'm here to see your ship, so let the tour begin."

"This way to the bridge, sir," Sydnee said as she turned and led the way.

Once on the bridge, Sydnee just let the Captain and two Commanders look around. There wasn't anything unusual there, so they really needed no explanation until they came to the tactical station.

"This looks more like a tactical station than a security station," Carver said.

"Yes, sir. That's exactly right. I haven't been ordered to maintain secrecy about it, so I'm sure I can alert a fellow SC officer. We're carrying ninety-six missiles and eight laser arrays."

Carver looked at Sydnee for a few seconds to see if she was jesting. When she maintained her serious expression, he said, "Where are they hidden? I saw no indication of armament from outside."

"There are two habitat containers beneath the ship."

"Yes, I noticed them. That's for your Marine complement, right?"

"The center habitat has been moved to the freighter's maintenance bay for the duration of the search. We felt it would make things easier if the interdiction teams could remain in the freighter. They have enough beds for a hundred six, so your people can share the habitat if you wish. There's plenty of food, water, and amenities, such as showers."

"Thank you, Captain. I agree it would make things much easier."

"The two remaining containers are weapons platforms disguised as habitat containers. If you'd care to follow me, I'll show you the rest of the ship, and then we can visit one of the weapons platforms if you wish."

"I wish."

An hour later the tour was over, and Captain Carver and his party were headed back to their ship. Sydnee had enjoyed the time immensely and had been especially pleased when Captain Carver had compared her short career to that of his sister, Admiral Jenetta Carver. She wondered what he'd say if he knew that, like Admiral Carver, Sydnee had been captaining a small ship when it set a new speed record that left Admiral Carver's speed record in the dust.

When MAT-Two had re-linked with the *Justice* and Lt. Olivetti was once more seated at the navigation console, Sydnee gave the order to rebuild the envelope and catch up to the *Gatherer*. Despite the disproportion in their sizes, the *Justice* would be alongside the *Gatherer* for more than an hour before the *Seoul* caught up.

After that brief break from boredom, everything fell back into routine as the interdiction teams aboard the *Gatherer* put all their effort into completing the task at hand. Captain Carver had been just as firm with his people when he told them that if the generator wasn't found by the time they reached the last container at the bow, they would start over again at the stern. It provided enough incentive to ensure that no piece of equipment larger than a size ten boot was passed by without a thorough inspection.

Naturally, there were a number of false calls but all were quickly dismissed either by Addams, Luscome, or one of the engineers from the *Seoul*. Some were for refrigeration units and cooking appliances, and one was an ancient diesel motor for a farm tractor. Since no one on the interdiction team had ever seen one before, it was good for a few minutes of diversion.

As always happens, the minutes turned into hours, the hours turned into days, and the days turned into weeks, but in the fifth week following the arrival of the *Seoul*, news that an interdiction team from the *Seoul* had found an envelope generator spread like scandal gossip at a political event.

Lance Corporal Addams raced to the container where the find had been reported. Chief Luscome, aboard the *Justice* was looking on through Addams' helmet cam.

Addams climbed down into the container and then to the fourth level down. He hurried over to where all members of the interdiction team for this container had gathered around a large crate.

"Get the entire top of the crate off," Addams said. "We can only see a little of it with the probe camera. Be careful to preserve the shipping data."

One of the Marines had a pry bar, and he began forcing the tip under the lid. As he succeeded, he pressed down on the bar and the screeching sounds of embedded nails being pulled from wood filled the space. As the cover came partly free, two of the Marines standing by grabbed the edge and lifted. The cover seemed to hang on stubbornly and then surrender all at once to the futility of the effort.

When the generator was exposed, Addams excitedly yelled on the Com-Two frequency, "That's it! I'd recognize those scars on the outer case anywhere. We've found it! We've found it, Captain!"

Chapter Twenty-Seven
~ Oct. 8th, 2286 ~

Sydnee had been working on a report in her office when news of the possible find began reverberating around the *Gatherer* but when Chief Lemela aboard the *Justice* notified Sydnee, she made it to the bridge in time to see the helmet cam images of the generator and hear Addams' excited announcement that it was the one they'd been looking for. The broadcast was like a tonic. Everyone was suddenly more awake then they'd been in weeks. They'd all begun to wonder if they might search the entire cargo section and not find the generator. In total, the teams from the *Justice* and the *Seoul* had already searched one thousand, two hundred thirty-eight containers. That represented more than a third of the cargo section.

Immediately, the other interdiction teams began climbing out of the containers they'd been searching and congregated around the entrance to the one where the generator had been located.

On Com-Three, Sydnee said, "Hey Kel, are you getting this about finding the generator?"

"Yes, Syd, I'm headed over that way now."

"Okay, I'm switching to Com-Two."

On Com-Two, Sydnee said, "Lift the cover, Lance Corporal. Make sure the generator is inside."

Since Light-9790 required that all exterior surfaces be Dakinium, the ship's original generator cover had been used on the replacement generator when it was installed, but the scarred cover from the reclamation yard had been retained and then replaced over the burnt out unit after the replacement unit from the *Lifeguard* had been installed.

Sydnee watched, along with everyone else who had access to the helmet cam images as Addams worked to remove the cover. It didn't require tools when not wearing gloves, but it was difficult without tools while wearing the gloves supplied with the personal armor. Finally, with the help of the other Marines, Addams managed to unlock the clips that held the cover on. He lifted it off and set it aside.

"Yeah, the generator is there, Captain."

"Is the induction coil there? And is it the one you worked on with Padu?"

"Yes, ma'am. It's the one we repaired."

Sydnee breathed a sigh of relief before saying, "Wonderful. Okay, Lance Corporal, let's reassemble the generator and seal the crate. Good job, everyone."

Knowing she should immediately contact the freighter's captain, Sydnee had the com chief set up a call to Captain Choi. He was working in his office and took the call there.

"Captain, we've found what we've been searching for. We'll be out of your hair soon."

"Our security cameras in the link tunnel showed most of your people exiting containers and congregating around the entrance to one in particular. I suspected you might have found what you were looking for. Can you tell me now what it was?"

"Here, I'll send you the shipping data from the crate and the info you sent as part of your manifest log."

As Choi received the info, he said, "Machine parts? That's not very descriptive."

"No, it isn't. That's why we had so much difficulty finding it. The crate actually contains an envelope generator."

"Just an envelope generator? But that's not contraband."

"It is when the generator is an experimental unit stolen from Space Command."

"What's experimental about it?"

"I'm sorry, but I can't say any more. And I ask that you not report this to your company or anyone else. The main office on Earth already knows and was told not to say anything to you or anyone until its presence was ascertained. I'm sure SCI will be waiting for whomever comes to pick up the unit at its destination, so I must ask you not to report that we've taken it off your ship. Speaking of which, I'll need your cooperation in getting it out of the container. It's far too large to fit through the access hatch. Now that everything is winding down, our people will be returning to their ships. It'll probably take an hour, at least, to wrap up everything. My people will have to remove all the tamper seals and gather up all our equipment. I'll contact you when we're done, and you can drop your envelope so we can wrap this up.

"The container is one of the inside units in that link section, so we'll have to separate the cargo section at that point and free the container from the link section so the end doors can be opened to remove the crate. After you've reassembled the link section and rejoined the stern cargo section, you're free to leave. I thank you for your cooperation in helping us to recover this stolen Space Command property."

"I have to say, Captain, that this is the most pleasant interdiction experience I've ever had in my long career. Thank you for allowing us to continue our voyage while you searched. If we'd been forced to sit for weeks back where you first contacted us, the company would have been on my back every hour and probably been screaming to Space Command and every GA Senator to boot."

"I'm glad a spirit of cooperation has made both our jobs a little easier, Captain."

"We'll cancel the envelope when you tell us, and my cargo people will be prepared to separate out that container for you."

"And I'll have my people suited up in EVA gear by the time the container is accessible so we don't hold you up any longer than necessary. *Justice*, out."

"*Gatherer*, out."

Next, Sydnee contacted Captain Carver. "I'm sure you've heard the news by now, sir."

"Yes, I was summoned by my tac officer who had been watching the helmet cam images. When the commotion started, he contacted me and we put the images up on the main monitor. It seems like an awful lot of effort for just an ordinary envelope generator."

"It's a very special generator, sir."

What's so special about it?"

"I'd love to tell you, sir. I really would. But..."

"But you're under orders not to say anything?"

"Exactly."

"I understand, Captain."

"I've asked Captain Choi to give us an hour to organize ourselves and then drop his envelope so we can pick up our people and retrieve the generator. Do you want to return it to Earth, sir?"

"I think that honor should go to you. We're glad we were able to assist your effort here, especially if that generator is as important as you think. Besides, with your speed you can have that generator back on Earth in a few days instead of a few months."

"Yes, sir. Thank you for your help, sir."

"Our honor, Captain. Carver, out."

"Marcola, out."

Sydnee sat back in her chair and relaxed. She was so happy to finally, almost, have this mission finished, and she was looking forward to getting home to the *Denver*. She wondered if the Marine range had been completed, but even if it hadn't, she'd at least be able to spend some fun time in the simulators wave-hopping over the ocean in a Marine FA-SF4 fighter.

Once the freighter cancelled its envelope, MAT-One returned to the *Justice* with all the Marines on board. Meanwhile, the *Seoul* was recovering all of its teams as well. Lt. Olivetti had her hands full with the habitat container, but she finally got it into proper position using the remote-controlled tug. Working with the tac officer, she got it locked into its link section.

Lance Corporal Addams and two volunteers suited up in EVA gear and were ready to leave the ship when the freight handlers separated the container from the link. The small, remote-controlled tug used by Lt. Olivetti to assist with docking the habitat was pressed into service as a ferry to take the three volunteers to the free-floating container.

Once the three Marines managed to unlock the twenty-meter-high doors at the end of the container, they opened one of them just far enough to get the generator out. The freighter crew had attached a small power supply to the top of the container so the gravity decking inside remained at ten percent. It wasn't enough to interfere with the Marine effort of removing the generator, but it kept everything else from immediately floating out into space. Once the generator was out of the container and anchored by rope to the remote-controlled tug, the Marines closed and sealed the container doors. Two remote-controlled tugs being manipulated by freight handlers then re-secured the container in the link section and reconnected the stern cargo section to the rest of the ship.

By the time the Marines were back inside the *Justice* with the generator, the freighter was building its envelope. It disappeared in the blink of an eye, leaving the *Justice* and the *Seoul* to complete their own preparations for departure.

"Lt. Caruthers, let's build our envelope and put a little distance between us and this part of space. Lt. Olivetti, our destination is Earth."

"Aye, Captain," both officers said.

In two minutes the *Justice* was headed for Earth at Light-9793.48.

It was impossible to hear anything that was going on below in the Marine's habitat unless she had the com chief eavesdrop using the ship's security system, but she imagined there was a bit of partying taking place. She'd love to join them, but military protocol dictated a layer of separation between enlisted personnel and officers, and especially between enlisted personnel and the ship's captain.

Sydnee remained on the bridge for an hour, then turned command over to Caruthers and went to her office/quarters to relax and compose some messages. As always, Olivetti immediately moved to the helm console. With the course to Earth laid in, there was no need for a presence at the navigation console.

Weems was coming from the Marine habitat and met Sydnee in the corridor outside her office.

"It's so great to take a long, hot shower, knowing that the search for the generator is over."

"Is that where you've been the past hour?"

"Oh, yeah. And I probably could have stayed in there another hour, but I figured I'd save some of the delight for tomorrow. You know what this ship needs? A large soaking tub."

"I'd pass on your suggestion to the folks at Mars," Sydnee said with a grin, "but they'd probably say they just got rid of our soaking tub. Or they'd probably just say you should wait until we get back to the *Denver*."

"Yeah, probably. Bunch of party poopers. Are you up for a little dinner?"

"Why not? I was going to write an update report for SCI, but it can wait."

After traveling to Earth at Light-9790, it was a little frustrating to spend the better part of a day in the traffic pattern as they slowly worked their way closer and closer to the planet. The *Justice* finally reached a point where they could adopt a geosynchronous orbit and wait until the time over North America was right for a trip to the surface.

MAT-One, piloted by Sydnee with Weems and Mac-Donald aboard, set down on a shuttle pad at the Space

Command base in Nebraska just after 0800. An oh-gee truck immediately approached the small ship and parked alongside. After shutting down all systems, Sydnee and the others exited the ship. A Space Command Lt. Commander wearing an SCI collar insignia steeped forward to greet them.

"Welcome to Earth. I'm Lt. Commander Trent. I understand you had quite a bit of difficulty finding the generator."

"You could say that, sir. The entire Marine complement of two ships spent six weeks searching through cargo containers to locate it. Of course, we never would have found it if it hadn't been for SCI."

"Yes. By working together we were able to reacquire this valuable piece of equipment. Now, if you don't mind, I'll like to get it loaded aboard the truck. The R&D people are nibbling their fingernails down to the quick waiting to get their hands on it."

"Just a minute, sir," Sydnee said. Touching her Space Command ring, she said, "Captain Wherton." A second later she said, "Sir, I'm on the base at Nebraska. An officer identifying himself as Lt. Commander Trent is requesting that I turn over the generator to him. I'm just confirming that he's the proper contact."

Lt. Commander Trent touched his ring and said, "Trent." Then, "Yes, sir, I'm at the pad with Lieutenant Marcola." Then, "Yes, sir. Trent, out."

Sydnee heard via her CT, "Yes, that's Trent, Lieutenant. You can give him the generator."

"Yes, sir, Thank you, sir. Marcola, out."

"Sorry, Commander," Sydnee said to Trent. "I hope you understand."

"Of course, Lieutenant. After what you've been through because of that imposter, we all understand the extra caution."

Thirty minutes later, the generator had been transferred to the truck and was disappearing into the distance.

"Anybody have any business to conduct on Earth while we're here?" Sydnee asked her companions.

"I know a great little restaurant near here," Weems said, "but— it's too late for breakfast and too early for lunch."

"Kel?"

"I'm good, Syd. I saw all the relatives the last time we were on Earth— and I don't know a single restaurant near here."

"Okay, guys," Sydnee said with a chuckle, "Let's go home."

———————————————

"What now, X?" his chief of staff asked. "The Spaccs now believe we were responsible for the bombing after all."

"Only temporarily."

"Temporarily? By now they've learned the Minister of Antiquities was just a dupe. They'll be coming after us soon. Being in Clidepp space won't protect us. I'm more afraid of them than I am of the Triumvirate."

"Think back. Do you remember when I told you they would blame us, then blame the Clidepp government, then blame us again, then blame the Clidepp government again?"

"Uh, yes."

"This game is just beginning. Very soon they'll be blaming the Clidepp government again. I have it all planned. I expected things to move along a little quicker, but you can't always manage intrigue like this. Mark my words, the GA will soon declare war on the Clidepp Triumvirate."

His chief of staff looked at X for a few seconds before addressing a different matter. "We haven't heard from Melorriat in some time. The last message said he was helping a Space Command ship stranded in Clidepp Space and that they had promised to turn over a Raider ship they'd been chasing if they were able to capture it."

"A Space Command ship? Other than the one that kidnapped the Minister of Antiquities?"

"We don't know. Melorriat said they claimed to know nothing about the kidnapping."

"I'd hardly expect them to admit it. I wonder if they took Melorriat as well."

"He'll never say anything. He's one of the most loyal supporters of the cause."

"But they might be able to make him talk with drugs."

"That's the way the Triumvirate operates, but Space Command doesn't do that."

"Perhaps not, but I have to wonder if he was carrying anything they could use. Did he suggest they might believe he was aligned with our cause?"

"No. They were treating him as a paid informant. He was worried though. He said there were three strangers hanging around his neighborhood. He was worried they might be the Secret Police."

"Damn, I should have been told that earlier. If the Secret Police have him and they use truth drugs on him, an entire cell could be compromised."

"He disappeared long ago. If they had any information, they would have acted before now."

"Perhaps— and perhaps not. Alert everyone to be on guard even more than usual."

Chapter Twenty-Eight
~ Oct. 30th, 2286 ~

One week out from the sub-sectors where the *Denver* normally patrolled, Sydnee had the com chief send a message requesting information about their current location. When the answer came, Sydnee had Lt. Olivetti plot a course to that approximate area.

"Almost home," Sydnee said to Kelly MacDonald as they sat drinking coffee in Sydnee's office.

"Home? Do you realize we've spent ten full months aboard the *Justice* and only a third that much in the *Denver*? The *Justice* seems more like home right now than the *Denver* does."

Sydnee chuckled. "You're right, but I'm still looking forward to being back at the *Denver*. I miss my great bed and large quarters there. The tiny bed I have here is comfortable, but the full-size bed on the *Denver* allows me to stretch my arms out without banging my elbows on the walls. And my bedroom here is so tiny, it makes my old quarters aboard the *Perry* look spacious."

"I hope we get some downtime when we get back. Not a lot— just a few days to do nothing except relax and get back into shape."

"I know what you mean, Kel. I want to go down to the track every day and run until I'm ready to drop without stopping to turn around every couple of minutes to run twenty meters back the way I've just come."

"The only good part about being on the *Gatherer* was that I was able to run every morning on that ten-kilometer tunnel track. I'd run to the stern from the maintenance bay where the MAT was parked every morning before breakfast and then take a maglev sled back to the habitat. I was always too tired at night to do any running."

"It was an experience none of us want to repeat. I just hope it was worth it."

"It will be if the R&D people are able to figure out what gave us that speed improvement and reproduce it."

"I wonder if we'll get any credit for it," Sydnee said, "It *did* happen during a covert mission."

"What covert mission? I don't remember any covert mission."

Upon seeing the expression on MacDonald's face, Sydnee smiled and said, "Who said anything about a covert mission?"

Both smiled knowingly in the way that co-conspirators often do.

As the *Justice* arrived alongside the *Denver*, Commander Bryant gave orders to link to the larboard bow airlock. Sydnee had expected to see robotic tugs approach and detach the habitat containers, so the entire Marine Complement had assembled in MAT-One. When the order for the link came through, the Marines all moved to MAT-Two, which was linked on the starboard side of the *Justice*.

Once the airlock connection was complete and the seal had been tested and approved, the Marines entered the *Denver*. Sydnee and the flight crew had to shut everything down and gather their belongings before they left the small ship.

Inside the *Denver*, Lt. Milton and the crew of the *Lifeguard* were waiting to welcome the *Justice* crew home. Sydnee stepped through the airlock first.

"Hello, Syd," Milty said, "Long time no see."

Sydney suspected that from the way he worded it, he didn't want her to say anything about the *Lifeguard* coming to their rescue, so she said, "Hi, Milty. It's good to see you again. It's *always* good to see you."

"That was a hell of a long training mission you folks had. Everything work out okay?"

"I don't know if you heard, but we lost Lt. William Barron. He died while trying to fix our envelope generator."

"Yes, I heard about that. He was a great guy."

"Yes. He'll be missed."

"I heard you and Chief Luscome were both injured at that same time."

"Yes, but our injuries were minor. We're both fully healed."

"That's good. Well, welcome back. Oh, the captain wants to see you as soon as you've put your gear away. He's on the bridge."

"Okay, Milty. Thanks. Thanks for everything."

"Our pleasure, Syd."

As Sydnee passed the other officers and two noncoms, she smiled, shook hands, and exchanged greetings. She had immediately assumed they were the crew of the *Lifeguard*. None of them knew what mission had taken the *Justice* into Clidepp space, but they knew it had to be vital to the security of the GA for an SC ship to violate another nation's space without authorization.

When Sydnee entered her quarters, she had an overwhelming desire to leap onto her bed and take a quick nap. It felt so great to be back and have the burden of command lifted from her shoulders for a while. But the captain was waiting, so she just dropped her gear and tried to make herself look a bit more presentable, or at least less like someone who had just returned from a ten-month-long 'quick' mission. She pulled a brush through her hair a few times and then left her quarters.

————————

"Lieutenant(jg) Marcola reporting to the captain as ordered," she said as she braced to attention in the captain's briefing room on the bridge.

"At ease, Sydnee. Be seated."

Commander Bryant occupied one of the two chairs facing the desk, so Sydnee only had one choice. She sat stiffly at first, then relaxed slightly.

"You had quite an adventure, Syd," Captain Lidden said.

"Yes, sir."

"How are your legs?"

"All healed, sir. I can run a marathon if I wish."

"That's great. And Chief Luscome?"

"He's healed as well, although the process took considerably longer with him. And the doc told him to take it easy for a few more months because of the back injury. His lung and ribs are fully healed."

"Excellent. I'd have less regret about losing Lt. Barron if the mission hadn't turned out to be for naught."

"Excuse me, sir? For naught?"

"SCI has determined that the package had nothing to do with the bombing. It was all a red herring."

"No."

"Yes. SCI originally believed the bombing was perpetrated by the rebels in order to drag the GA into their civil war. But then they received a tip that the Clidepp Empire was behind it to keep us from supporting the rebels. Now SCI is saying the rebels knew the Clidepp government would refuse our request to turn over the package and hoped we would declare war on the Empire."

"That doesn't make sense. How could they benefit by the GA declaring war, defeating the Empire, and annexing their space?"

"There's no guarantee we would annex their space," Bryant said, "We have too much territory to patrol now."

"Until we know for sure who's responsible, the GA Senate would never declare war," Lidden said. "SCI believes that by using a small DS ship, we sidestepped any invasion issues."

"I thought we did something really great and worthwhile," Sydnee said. "Learning it was all for nothing is really depressing."

"It wasn't all for nothing," Lidden said. "If our scientists can learn how to reproduce your speed improvement, it will have been worth it."

"Worth a man's life?"

"Look at all the test pilots who were lost pushing the boundaries of flight on Earth. Look at all the astronauts we lost pushing the boundaries of space. Was it worth it? I believe so."

"Yes, sir, I suppose you're right."

"And there's also the matter of a viewpad Blade recovered from the contact. SCI was able to crack the password code and gain access to the information it contained. As I understand it, it proves that Melorriat was part of the rebel operation. He was playing us all along. He didn't name any of his fellow rebels on the viewpad, but SCI got some valuable data from it. They tell me that that alone made the trip worthwhile."

"I'm glad we got something out of it."

"By the way, while we were in Nebraska for the BOI, I asked a friend to see if he could learn why you were assigned to the *Perry*."

"You did, sir?"

"Don't get me wrong. I'm delighted it happened, but it's always nagged at me that such a superb officer as yourself would have been sent to the *Perry* with no indication of the reason in your file. On other ships, it wouldn't even come up, but on the *Perry* there has always been something in the person's past that accounted for the posting."

"While I was home, my mother confessed she asked my step-father to make sure I didn't go to Region Two."

"Perhaps she did, but that wasn't the reason."

"It wasn't?"

"Perhaps your stepfather has less pull than he thinks, or perhaps other events just beat him to it. My friend dug into the files because he knew how badly I wanted to solve the mystery, and he got back to me while you were away. He discovered that you were never posted to the *Perry*."

"I wasn't?"

"No, you were posted to the *Ares*, Captain Gavin's battleship in Region Two."

"The *Ares*? I don't understand. My orders specifically said the *Perry*."

"Yes. There was a mistake when the orders were cut. The person we were supposed to receive was a Lawrence Marco. He was ranked four hundred twelve of four hundred fourteen at the Warship Command Institute. There was some issue about his possibly being involved with an instructor's wife, which could account for him being sent to the *Perry*. But someone messed up the orders at some point, and he was sent to the *Ares* while you received his posting to the *Perry*. When the roster was sorted alphabetically, Marco's name was just above your own at WCI. My friend at SHQ tells me Marco only lasted three months on the *Ares*. He was court-martialed for 'Conduct Unbecoming' and posted to a reclamation vessel. I read the court transcript and was surprised he even managed a shipboard posting."

"But my mother believes my step-father was responsible."

"It's always possible that he was. Perhaps it wasn't a simple clerical error but an intentional act made to look like an error. We may never know. I'm surprised the division officer at WCI didn't catch the posting error. Didn't you try to bring it to his attention?"

"I tried. He immediately put me on the defensive by asking if I was refusing to accept the posting."

"That was a bit harsh. Was he aware of your class ranking?"

"Yes, sir."

"Well, all I can say is, personally, we're glad it happened. We rarely received top-ranked officers. But, on to new business. Sydnee, Marine Captain Blade wants you as the SC mission commander of a new assignment he's been given."

Sydnee, who had slumped a little during the conversation about her past, sat up straight. "What? Blade asked for me?"

"More than just *asked for you.* He told SCI that you are the only one he deemed acceptable for the mission."

"I don't understand. I didn't think he liked me or respected my abilities."

"Apparently that's not the case."

"When would this mission take place, sir?"

"Immediately."

"Immediately?"

"Well, after you've had a few day's rest."

"And what's the mission this time?"

"You'll be returning the package to his home on Yolongus."

Sydnee just stared at Lidden without saying anything.

"We have to bring him home, Syd. We owe it to him. It's just a quick trip in, drop him off at his home, and then return."

"The last trip was just a quick trip in, pick up the package, and then return. Except it didn't turn out that way."

"There was no way anyone could have predicted the problems with the repository hatch and the other problems that developed because of it. You won't have to enter the water this time."

"Is this a voluntary mission, sir?"

"Of course."

"Then I don't know, sir. I'll have to think about it."

"I can only give you three days to make up your mind."

"Yes, sir. I'll get back to you in that timeframe."

"That's all, Syd."

Sydnee stood up, braced to attention, then turned and left the briefing room.

As the door closed, Bryant said, "Think she'll take it?"

"Yes, I think so," Lidden said. "When she thinks about it, she'll realize the importance of the mission, and she'll also want to do what she can to make amends for what we put the package through."

After a few second's thought, Bryant said, "Did you notice that she never once used *um*?"

"Yes, I noticed. Ten months of command experience in an extremely difficult situation while dealing with a difficult officer like Blade can give you confidence in your abilities and remove minor self-doubts. I'm seeing a much more mature lieutenant(jg). I believe she's ready for a promotion. She doesn't yet have the mandatory three years in grade for a standard promotion, but she's eligible for early advancement. And in ten months she'll even be eligible for standard promotion."

~ finis ~

*** Sydnee's exciting adventures will continue ***

Watch for new books on Amazon and other fine booksellers,
check my website - www.deprima.com
or
sign up for my free newsletter to receive email
announcements about future book releases.

Appendix

This chart is offered to assist readers who may be unfamiliar with military rank and the reporting structure. Newly commissioned officers begin at either ensign or second lieutenant rank.

Space Command	Space Marine Corps
Admiral of the Fleet	
Admiral	General
Vice-Admiral	Lieutenant General
Rear Admiral - Upper	Major General
Rear Admiral - Lower	Brigadier General
Captain	Colonel
Commander	Lieutenant Colonel
Lieutenant Commander	Major
Lieutenant	Captain
Lieutenant(jg) "Junior Grade"	First Lieutenant
Ensign	Second Lieutenant

The commanding officer on a ship is always referred to as Captain, regardless of his or her official military rank. Even an Ensign could be a Captain of the Ship, although that would only occur as the result of an unusual situation or emergency where no senior officers survived.

On Space Command ships and bases, time is measured according to a twenty-four-hour clock, normally referred to as military time. For example, 8:42 PM would be referred to as 2042 hours. Chronometers are always set to agree with the date and time at Space Command Supreme Headquarters on Earth. This is known as GST, or Galactic System Time.

A

Admiralty Board:

Moore, Richard E.	Admiral of the Fleet
Platt, Evelyn S.	Admiral - Director of Fleet Operations
Bradlee, Roger T.	Admiral - Director of Intelligence (SCI)
Ressler, Shana E.	Admiral - Director of Budget & Accounting
Hillaire, Arnold H.	Admiral - Director of Academies
Burke, Raymond A.	Vice-Admiral - Director of GSC Base Management
Ahmed, Raihana L.	Vice-Admiral - Dir. of Quartermaster Supply
Woo, Lon C.	Vice-Admiral - Dir. of Scientific & Expeditionary Forces
Plimley, Loretta J.	Rear-Admiral (U) - Dir. of Weapons R&D
Yuthkotl, Lesbolh	Rear Admiral (U) - Dir. of Nordakian Forces Integration

Ship Speed Terminology	*Speed*
Plus-1	1 kps
Sub-Light-1	1,000 kps
Light-1 (*c*) *(speed of light in a vacuum)*	299,792.458 kps
Light-150 or **150 c**	150 times the speed of light
Light-450 or **450 c**	134,906,606.1 kps

Hyper-Space Factors	
IDS Communications Band	.0513 light years each minute (8.09 billion kps)
DeTect Range	4 billion kilometers

B

Strat Com Desig	Mission Description for Strategic Command Bases
1	Base - Location establishes it as a critical component of Space Command Operations - Serves as home-port to multiple warships that also serve in base's defense. All sections of Space Command maintain an active office at the base. Base Commander establishes all patrol routes and is authorized to override SHQ orders to ships within the sector(s) designated part of the base's operating territory. Recommended rank of Commanding Officer: **Rear Admiral (U)**
2	Base - Location establishes it as a crucial component of Space Command Operations - Serves as home-port to multiple warships that also serve in base's defense. All sections of Space Command maintain an active office at the base. Patrol routes established by SHQ. Recommended rank of Commanding Officer: **Rear Admiral (L)**
3	Base - Location establishes it as an important component of Space Command Operations - Serves as homeport to multiple warships that also serve in base's defense. Patrol routes established by SHQ. Recommended rank of Commanding Officer: **Captain**
4	Station - Location establishes it as an important terminal for Space Command personnel engaged in travel to/from postings, and for re-supply of vessels and outposts. Recommended rank of Commanding Officer: **Commander**
5	Outpost - Location makes it important for observation purposes and collection of information. Recommended rank of Commanding Officer: **Lt. Commander**

Sample Distances	
Earth to Mars (Mean)	78 million kilometers
Nearest star to our Sun	4 light-years (Proxima Centauri)
Milky Way Galaxy diameter	100,000 light-years
Thickness of M'Way at Sun	2,000 light-years
Stars in Milky Way	200 billion (est.)
Nearest galaxy (Andromeda)	2 million light-years from M'Way
A light-year (in a vacuum)	9,460,730,472,580.8 kilometers
A light-second (in a vacuum)	299,792.458 km
Grid Unit	1,000 light-years² (1,000,000 Sq. LY)
Deca-Sector	100 light-years² (10,000 Sq. LY)
Sector	10 light-years² (100 Sq. LY)
Section	94,607,304,725 km²
Sub-section	946,073,047 km²

The two-dimensional representation that follows is offered to provide the reader with a feel for the spatial relationships between bases, systems, and celestial events referenced in the novels of this series. The reader should remember that GA territory extends through the entire depth of the Milky Way galaxy when the galaxy is viewed on edge.

The millions of stars, planets, moons, and celestial phenomena in this small part of the galaxy would only confuse, and therefore have been omitted from the image.

The following map shows the position of the planet Diabolisto and Simmons SCB near the Clidepp Empire border relative to the core planets of Region One.

Should the map be unreadable, or should you desire additional imagery, .jpg and .pdf versions of all maps are available for free downloading at:

www.deprima.com/ancillary/maps.html

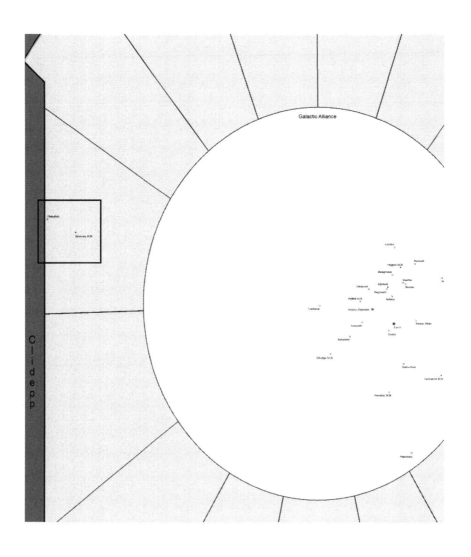

Made in the USA
Middletown, DE
10 November 2014